HEIR *to* DREAMS & DARKNESS

BOOKS BY BEN ALDERSON

Heir *to* Dreams & Darkness

BEN ALDERSON

SECOND SKY

Published by Second Sky in 2024

An imprint of Storyfire Ltd.
Carmelite House
50 Victoria Embankment
London EC4Y 0DZ

www.secondskybooks.com

ISBN: 978-1-83525-456-1
eBook ISBN: 978-1-83525-455-4

Beth, there will never be enough words to explain the impact your friendship has had on me. But I hope these 100,000+ words will help. This is for you.

Voltar

The Unknown Isle

The Thass
Ocean

ALDIAN

Avairan Crest

Saylan
Academy

Wycombe

Nests

Galloway Forest

Heart Oak

Gathrax
Kingdom

Zindina
Kingdom

Romar
Kingdom

alzmir Kingdom

PART ONE

LITTLE DEVILS

CHAPTER 1

It was hard to focus, knowing that a demon who could end the world was currently hurtling towards it.

During hours of gruelling training with Beatrice, my body coated in bruises, I would constantly look to the sky. I knew what I would find when I did, but that didn't stop me from checking if the comet was still there, a scar of red against the blue expanse.

Pain was my motivation. Training was a welcome distraction during our long voyage to the South. Whoever glorified sailing on a ship had clearly drunk far too much ale. Training was better than going over all the different outcomes of Leska and her well-being. Pain was even a distraction from the glowing comet that cut over Aldian's skies, reminding me every second of the day that Lilyth was coming.

Lilyth, an entity the elemental gods called mother, who moved from world to world, devouring souls and leaving nothing but ruin in her wake.

She filled my dreams with the promise of ruination. But only once awake would the impending doom truly haunt me.

'Simion is going to murder me,' Beatrice said, eyeing the marks on the side of my chest.

I winced, lifting my sweat-drenched tunic, inspecting the patchwork of bruises across my ribs. It stole my breath away.

'He has his focus,' I replied, lowering the top, trying my hardest not to grimace with each breath. 'I have mine.'

Beatrice eyed me, sweat glistening across her forehead. She threw a towel at me, forcing me to catch it, knowing that my hiss was proof she was right. 'You're getting better. Every day you are improving, not only in your speed but your stamina. Whatever Leska did during your training session, she really did a number on your ability as a battlemage, Max.'

Pride glowed in her eyes, lightening the brass hue to a bright gold.

Just hearing Leska's name hurt me more than my bruised ribs. 'I'm sure she would like to hear you say that, if we save her.'

'Not if,' Beatrice said quickly. '*When.*'

I dared not contemplate how many days it had been since Leska, my recently revealed half-sister, stepped through a portal and found herself in Gathrax manor of all places. Since then, we had heard little from her, only pathetic snippets our gleamers could obtain.

My teeth ground together as I forced out a smile, one Beatrice clearly did not believe. 'Find yourself a healer, and get tidied up before Simion finishes for the day.'

Perhaps Beatrice was right, but instead of seeking a gleamer to heal me, I called Inyris from her perch on the ship's hull. We were airborne within moments.

I had never seen so many dragons in one place. They filled the sky like a flock of birds. Blues, greens, oranges and browns, some so large they could devour a ship in one bite, others small enough to perch on the bow to rest their wings.

'Faster,' I urged, peering over Inyris's side. My dragon rumbled in displeasure at my command, knowing that sitting on her was causing my battered body discomfort. But we were one and the same, and Inyris knew I was as stubborn as her.

Sunlight graced over her powerful frame. Her golden scales caught the light as though she was made from metal, casting glittery light over this stretch of azure sea. I was biased, no doubt, but Inyris was the most beautiful creature ever to grace the skies. Through the taut tether that bound us mentally, I sensed her pleasure at my thoughts. Perhaps not biased then.

Beneath us the Thassalic stretched in all its cerulean glory. It was still for the first time in days, a glass-like mirror reflecting everything above it. Which, to my horror, wasn't necessarily a beautiful thing. Even in the ocean's reflection I could see the distant streak of red, as a Lilyth fell from whatever realms lingered beyond the blue sky.

Lilyth *was* coming. The star was a reminder, a ticking clock. To most people they saw it was a natural phenomenon, but to a select few, trusted with the knowledge of an impending doom headed to Aldian, it was a reminder that we were running out of time.

'Keep flying, Inyris,' I called over the winds, delighting in the rush of cold air over my face. 'I want to hide for just a little longer.'

Her armoured body rippled, wings beating harder, physically showing me her agreement.

After almost seven days of tumultuous weather, it was nice to be airborne with Inyris. Of course, the storm had not stopped Inyris from hunting food within a stretch of Galloway Forest to the west of our fleet. But it had stopped me from joining her. Dryads, if I never had to step foot on the endlessly rocking, damp-wood ship with its stench of vomit and salt, I'd be happy. But the South was still over a day away, and there was one thing that always brought me back to the fleet. The man leading the ship.

Simion Hawthorn.

I might not have been able to see him from our height, but he was always there, waiting in the back of my mind for when I called to him. My days had been full of training and planning our journey to the South. Simion had taken it upon himself to help the few phoenix-possessed survivors who joined us to understand and hone their new powers. Time had been precious between us. Even though we had been stuck on that bastard ship for close to a week, it was only in the few hours before sleep we truly got to spend time together. I craved it, just as I craved him.

Even if our moments were fleeting.

I flew for what felt like an eternity. Although it did not take long for the ice-cold kiss of Simion's presence to flood across the back of my skull. For a moment, I thought of keeping him out.

I was glad I didn't.

Maximus, we have received word from Gathrax manor.

The tone of his mind-speak, the urgency of his words, had me turning Inyris around and back towards the ship.

Coming. It was all I could manage as I felt my heart thump in my throat. This was exactly what we had waited a week to hear. News. Something to prove that Leska was okay, alongside the novice gleamers we had saved from Elder Cyder's grasp.

Inyris circled the ship thrice, before the deckhands cleared a space large enough for her to land. I was barely off her back, feet touching the warm wood of the deck, before Simion was pacing towards me.

Tension lined his face. I looked at him, truly looked at him for the first time since he had left me in bed last night. His stern nature was not exactly new, but the set of his eyes certainly suggested he was dealing with something.

He took my hands in his, and it was then I noticed the unnatural warmth of them. A result of having fire racing through his blood.

'So, what does it say?' I muttered. If he wanted quiet, it was to keep those around us from worry.

Simion forced a smile, one that didn't reach his eyes. He leaned in, placing a kiss on my cheek before whispering, 'I think we should take this conversation away from prying ears.'

I couldn't move, even if I wanted to. My heart cantered into my throat, threatening to choke me. 'Good or bad news, Simion?'

The colour drained from Simion's face. Then he replied with a final word, one with the power to drive a dagger into my chest and turn. 'Terrible.'

* * *

Out of the corner of my eye, I caught the glimpse of the *terrible news*. It waited in the middle of our bed, the first thing Simion showed me when we entered our room. It was not what was said on the rolled scroll, but the fact half of it was charred to ashes, crumbled and burned, hardly legible. It was also the same note I had penned and sent in hopes it would reach Leska. Seems like it reached Gathrax manor, but was received in the hands of fire.

'What could it mean?' I asked, my heart cantering in my chest.

'I dare begin to speculate.' There was something distracted about Simion today. If he was not pacing the cabin, he was looking at me with peaked brows.

I had been adamant not to accept the captain's offer of her cabin as our own. Although her room was lavish, with plush furnishings, portholes to let in natural light and a bed so large it could've slept the entire kitchen staff, I preferred our small little cabin. It reminded me of home. Not the North, but the small apartment in the back of Gathrax estate.

Perhaps calling it a cabin was too generous. Cabinet was

more apt. Besides the pallet I slept on, a single porthole on the starboard side of the ship and a chest of our belongings, there was nothing else. We needed nothing else. If it was cold at night, we kept each other warm. If it was warm, we stripped down, because, dryads knew, sleeping with Simion pressed against me was one of life's pleasures. Even if that was short-lived—whenever I woke, he was never next to me. He only stayed long enough for me to sleep, then would slink out of the cabin and return before I woke.

He thought I was not aware of it. But I was.

Another reason why I preferred this room was it didn't have a good view of the sky. Especially at night. Looking up and seeing the streak of red falling from the heavens was certainly not a reminder I needed.

I went to take a seat beside the charred remains of my note, but hissed as a bolt of pain radiated across my chest. Simion stopped pacing, turning his full attention on me. I practically watched the cogs turn in his mind.

Shit. I really should have seen a healer first.

'Undress,' Simion snapped, short-tempered. He had barely said more than one word at a time since I landed. Which I didn't mind because tension led to more tension led to... well, my mind was full of ideas.

'I'm fine,' I replied, a strange sense of excitement flipping in my lower stomach. 'It's just a little—'

Simion's stern expression only deepened. 'Now, Max.'

'Simion Hawthorn, the man of many words,' I replied, doing just as he commanded. I stripped the training leathers from my back whilst hissing through clenched teeth. The bruises made breathing close to impossible, the skin a multitude of blues, greens and blacks.

He shot me a look, half-displeased and half a smile, as he lifted the glass casing around the lantern. The side of his face burst with light as the flame conjured at the tip of his finger sparked to life. It engulfed the oil-slick wick before Simion returned the glass casing.

'As much as I like the brooding act, Simion,' I tried my hardest not to look at the multitude of bruises encasing my body like a corset, 'I don't like feeling as if you're angry at me.'

'No, Maximus. I am not *angry* at you. I am pissed at that.' Simion tipped his head back to the object smudged with ash, resting on our already dirtied bed sheets. Another wick burst into flame, this one taller and hotter. Simion's new powers were tied to his emotions, working off his moods like the ocean reacted to a storm. 'And the fact you have come back to me with at least...' He ran his fingers down my ribs, counting beneath his breath. 'Three broken ribs.'

Simion positioned himself behind me. His hands snaked around my waist, the tips of his smooth, warm fingers brushing my skin so carefully I was certain he was made of feathers, not flesh.

'Deep breath in for me,' Simion whispered, as the telltale rush of his healing magic spread beneath his hands. Where it was once cool, before his body was infected with a phoenix feather, his power now felt different. Inviting all the same but warmth and comfort instead of ice.

I did as he asked.

'What if we are too late?' I asked, as deft fingers carefully brushed my exposed torso. 'Whoever sent the letter back to us did it with intention.'

'Speculating isn't going to help,' Simion replied from where he stood behind me. 'Only action. A plan.'

Whilst he healed my bruises, his touch was something I enjoyed, no matter the circumstance. Since the hand fast-mark was destroyed with Camron Calzmir's death, and he could do so without the worry of causing me pain, Simion never needed an excuse to lay a hand on me.

'Then let's act!' I said. 'We should send a small group of

battlemages ahead. Scout out Gathrax manor and the surrounding areas. No one knows exactly what we are expecting to find, but that note confirms one thing.'

'Fire,' Simion said for me. 'Cyder said there was a presence of phoenix-possessed in the South. I think we can say, with confidence, that we are going to face them.'

Fire meant danger. Fire meant phoenix-possessed Southerners whose bodies and minds were controlled by a phoenix. *Until we saved them.* And if our messenger bird had reached Gathrax manor—the last known whereabouts of Leska and those Camron saved through his portal—then it also meant they were not alone.

'Lilyth. Phoenix-possessed. It is like we have enemies at every turn. Simion, we cannot afford enemies.' I grasped his hands, squeezing, as the tingling at the tips of my fingers subsided. 'We need the South, as a whole, if we are to face *her.*'

'Uniting Aldian is our focus. But right now, we are stronger as one unit,' Simion said, guiding my arm up until it was raised high, allowing him access to the tender skin above my ribs. 'If we go separating our numbers now, it will leave gaps in our armour. *As one we are great, as few we fail.*'

That sentiment had been drilled into me in the weeks after Elder Cyder's death. It reverberated across Wycombe, over people, mages and friends alike. Although there was only a select few of us who knew the seriousness behind why such a statement mattered, it still resonated with everyone who heard it.

'Then we ask that all dragon-bonded use their dragons to conjure winds strong enough to cut this journey short. We must reach Leska, Simion.'

'I know,' he said, fingers coming to a stop over the darkest smudge of bruising. 'Leska will be okay. You know she will.'

Oh, I didn't doubt it. Leska was a warrior, through and through. I knew how she fought, the resilience she mastered and used as a weapon unto itself. But I still worried. I worried because barely a week ago I had no idea she was my sister, half by blood. Which meant she was the only family I had left.

I couldn't lose her too.

Simion worked his way over my body. Even when the blue-green marks had drained from my skin and my aching bones healed, he still inspected me with the eye of an eagle. His attention to detail was impeccable.

He must have been saying something to me because I was vaguely aware of him repeating my name. Then I felt his lips. I looked down to my arm, watching Simion's mouth move from my wrist, to my elbow and up to my shoulder. By the time he was done, my skin had erupted in gooseflesh.

'All done,' he said, dropping my hand and stepping away.

I stuck my lower lip out, feigning disappointment. 'Is that it? You're going to kiss your way up to my shoulder and not finish it off?'

'Well, that would depend if you promise me not to be so reckless again. Training may be necessary, but you must be in good health for what we are to accomplish.'

He was right—of course he was.

Hand on hip, I rested my weight to the left. 'So, you would knowingly blue-ball me as punishment for having my ass beaten by your sister?'

'I would prefer my sister and your balls not to be mentioned in the same sentence.' Simion moved in a blur, closing the gap between us. The ship's sway forced our bodies together for leverage. There was something in the way Simion had to crane his neck down to look at me that set my insides ablaze. 'And as much as I would like to devour you this very minute, I have some fire-wielding warriors to attend.'

'Hmm,' I said, lifting both my hands up beside me. I pretended I was carrying something in each hand, one side weighing heavier than the other. 'Training them, or devouring my naked body, what would you pick?'

Simion narrowed his eyes. 'You are trouble.'

I began undoing his lose tunic, starting at the buttons beneath his chin, all the way down to his navel. 'Exactly why you like me.'

'That and a whole host of other reasons.'

There was no resistance as I guided his shirt over his broad shoulders. I let it fall behind him, material pooling at his feet.

'Now about your training,' I sang, nestling close into him. 'Do you think you have it in you to skip a session?'

Simion grunted his response, far too occupied with my nails as they traced over the perfectly sculpted muscles of his chest. Short curly dark hairs covered him, lingering down the middle line between his hardened abs, falling to where his trousers rested on hips.

'Fuck the training,' Simion growled, as he lowered his mouth to mine. Before our lips met, he paused, his cool breath tickling my face. There was something nervous in his expression, his mouth holding words he longed to say but feared to. I held my breath, expecting those three words to finally break the tension between us.

But before he could even utter a sound, a new voice called out.

'Mage Hawthorn?'

Our heads snapped towards the closed door. Thank the dryads ours didn't have a porthole to look through, otherwise they would've been greeted with quite the scene.

Breathless and, quite frankly, pissed that we had been interrupted at such a pivotal moment, Simion leaned his forehead against me and called out. 'If you do not step away from my cabin, novice, I will personally burn yours to cinders.'

There was heat to his words. Passion. Something that was new for Simion. A change, one of many, since he had been infected with one of Camron's feathers. It surprised me. Whoever stood beyond the door didn't reply.

Simion gazed back down to me with lust-filled eyes. 'We will pick this up again later.'

'Promise?'

There was so much I wanted to say.

Promise you will kiss me until my skin is covered in you? Promise that when you are done, you will not leave me alone?

'I promise,' Simion replied, before looking back to the door.

'Come in,' I commanded, all without taking my hungry eyes off him.

The door swung upon, revealing a young gleamer. Sun-gold blonde hair, tired russet eyes and cheeks permanently stained pink. She could barely look me in the eyes as she took in the two partially naked men before her. 'Mage Oaken, Mage Hawthorn. Captain has requested your presence.'

'For good reasons?' Simion asked, taking my hand in his, knowing something else I had yet to know.

'Yes, we have had success reaching Elder Leia and the Council.'

Simion stiffened, took a deep breath and turned to me. It was my turn to offer him the comfort of proximity and touch. There was only one thing we were waiting to hear back from Leia about.

Celia Hawthorn. Simion and Beatrice's mother. The key to discovering more about Lilyth.

CHAPTER 2

There was a heavy scent of warm ale as we entered the captain's cabin. It clung to the moist air, not helped by the lack of fresh air. But it was the tension that truly weighed us down. The anticipation. Simion had hardly said a word since we left our cabin, yet I could see his thoughts haunting him through his wide, gold-hued eyes.

Captain Trelem's cabin was the largest of all. She sat at the head of a long table, all long brown hair, serious gaze and so many scars it wasn't hard to imagine she'd been torn apart by sharks and put back together *multiple* times. Smoke lingered around her, billowing from the pipe that hung from the corner of her mouth. Whatever was in it turned the whites of her eyes red. By all accounts, Trelem was an interesting mage with a unique grasp on her battlemage abilities. Whispers on board suggested she wove her amplifier in with this ship itself, giving her power over the vessel. Which made sense, because no matter the weather, she could navigate it. Come storm or still waters, we never stopped. I could feel the humming of her magic like a constant buzz at the back of my head. A unique talent I could only thank my dryad blood for.

Seated and stood around the main table were a host of gleamers. They, like the young girl who had retrieved us, looked exhausted. A result of stretching their power for a long duration.

Simion released my hand, moving to stand beside Captain Trelem. He became like a shadow, arms crossed and serious scowl across his face, as he whispered something to her. I hoped no one used their abilities, because they'd sense my heart skip at the sight of him, not to mention the flicker of something in my groin.

Unfinished business. That was the story of our relationship since Elder Cyder—since the threat of Lilyth became a promise.

'Ah,' Trelem half shouted, voice muffled by a mouthful of pipe smoke. 'Somebody fetch our late arrivals a tankard. Wouldn't want the King to have our heads for a dry mouth.'

I cringed at the title, but kept my expression level. 'If the smell is anything to go by, Captain, I think I'll hold off on the offer.'

'More for us then.' She raised a tankard, sloshing ale down her throat and across her chin.

It was common knowledge, my ancestry. That was about all the people of Wycombe had learned. Giving them something as large as me being the legitimate son to the late Queen stopped others prying for more information.

'Thank you all for your hospitality,' Simion said, addressing the gleamers, voice thunderous. 'But if you don't mind, I would like to discuss matters with Mage Oaken and my sister privately.'

'Yes,' Trelem echoed, all high importance. 'What he said.'

Simion leaned over her chair, hand flat out on the table. 'That goes for you too, Trelem.'

There was minimal grumbling from the captain, especially after I announced that a feast had been prepared to restore some of the gleamers' spent reserves. No one stuck around long.

'Shouldn't we wait for Beatrice?' I asked, as the final person slunk from the room.

'Already here,' Beatrice replied, peeling from the shadows. Her sudden presence made me jump.

'How did you—'

'Dryads, Max,' Beatrice scoffed, amused by my reaction. 'If you weren't giving my brother the I-want-to-fuck-you-here-and-now eyes, then you might have noticed me.'

I didn't reply because, quite frankly, she wasn't wrong. After the scene we had just been interrupted from, I was practically overboiling.

'Is that true, Maximus Oaken?' Simion said, pacing around the table to me, offering me a seat.

I took it. 'Maybe,' I said, a blush creeping over my face, which only brightened when Simion leaned in and pressed a kiss to my cheek.

'Then I gather we will keep this short and sweet,' he whispered, lips so close to my ears the fine hairs across them stood on end.

'Is this a side effect of cabin fever, or does the end of the world turn people into rabid creatures?' The chair screeched across the floor as Beatrice sat, snatched Trelem's forgotten tankard and took a swig from it.

End of the world.

Hearing it aloud made my skin peel from my body. 'Yes, something like that.'

'All right, all right.' Simion ran his hand over the back of his head. 'Believe it or not, but I would rather my sister didn't gossip about my sex life.'

'That's rich,' Beatrice scoffed. Evident in the glint within her eyes, I knew she was enjoying every second of this. 'Because you lost all rights to comfort the day you stuck it in my best friend.'

'Who is to say he does the sticking?' I added, just before Simion boiled over with horror and embarrassment.

Beatrice shot me a look that had the same power as an arrow. It caught me fast and hard, knocking me back to earth. Her lips turned up into a mischievous smile, parting as she began to answer the question. 'Actually,' I said, before she could speak, 'don't answer that.'

She zipped her lips shut with her thumb and forefinger before offering me a wink. We all took a seat at the table before any more embarrassing jibes could be made. Although I could see from Simion's expression that he didn't enjoy it, I did. It was a reprieve from thinking about Beatrice's first statement—*end of the world.*

'Go on then, Bea.' Simion said. He was the only one of us who didn't take a seat. Nervous energy kept him moving.

Beatrice, however, did not seem so worried. She kicked her boots up on the table, leaning back in the chair until it balanced on the back legs. 'Nothing we did not already anticipate, brother.'

'Nothing to note about... Celia?' Simion asked. He turned his tankard around with his fingers in a subconscious twitch.

Mother. That was what he wanted to say. I saw it on the tip of his tongue.

'Leia has exhausted every means to find Celia. There is only so much the Council can do to locate someone who doesn't want to be found. And with the pressing issue of Lilyth—'

'She isn't lost,' Simion interrupted, scowling. 'She was exiled. Torn from our family.'

'And you would think she would jump at the chance to reunite with us. Exile or no, we are still her children. If I was her, the second I got the message that the exile was revoked and I was welcome back, I would be running.' Beatrice lifted her tankard and took another hearty swig. 'I say we give up on her, just as she gave up on us.'

'I can't do that, Bea.'

'Can't or won't?' she retorted.

His silence was answer enough.

I longed to reach out to him and rest a hand on the back of his. Seeing him deal with the torment of this conversation was difficult. 'It has only been a couple of weeks. Give it time. Maybe Celia has heard the calls, she just needs time to reach Wycombe. The world is big, there is no telling where she has been,' I offered, trying to conjure hope. 'And we need her, if we have any hope of understanding... Lilyth.'

I whispered the name of our impending doom as though it had the power to curse anyone who heard it.

Cyder, my mother and Celia Hawthorn were the only three people who knew enough of Lilyth to make them act. Whilst Cyder made a rebellion, my mother hid me away from my fate and Celia was punished for having a hand in it.

Two of three were known to be deceased. That left Celia with answers—answers we needed if we had any hope of facing whatever was hurtling through the sky towards us.

'We may not have weeks to spare, Max.' Beatrice tensed, unable to hide the ire from her tone.

'Then Leia and her Council need to work harder,' Simion said. 'They need to find her.'

Beatrice leaned forward, palm slapping on the table. 'She doesn't want to be found, Simion.'

Both Simion and Beatrice dealt with the memory of their mother differently. It was as if Beatrice had long ago grieved her, whereas Simion, as he held the desire to bring his sister home, had kept the same hope for his mother.

'Or maybe, just maybe,' Beatrice shouted, 'Celia has heard that there is some world-eating parasite falling from the sky, and she wants nothing to do with the doom that is coming for us?'

'Careful.' Simion slammed his tankard down, ale splashing freely over the rim. 'Anyone could be listening!'

Even I looked towards the close door, searching for a shadow in the gap beneath or the outline of a person beyond the porthole.

'When do you think they are going to start asking the right questions, Simion? What happens when this Lilyth finally touches down on Aldian?' Beatrice pointed out towards the door, gesturing more to the people beyond it. 'They deserve to know. This isn't some selective society of secret keepers. If we expect the people outside this cabin to fight for Aldian, they need to know what they are fighting against.'

I was well aware Beatrice was in the camp of telling everyone that the mother of monsters was coming to Aldian. And I somewhat agreed. But how could I explain to them what I had learned when I could barely understand it myself?

'That is not for you to decide,' Simion said, hands splayed out on the table. My nose picked up the scent of smoke before I saw the grey tendrils. They slithered from beneath his palm, where flames licked and singed the wood.

'Simion,' I snapped, before the entire room went up in flames. 'Rein it in.'

He snapped out of it, lifting his hands so we all saw the perfectly scorched handprint. 'Fuck.'

Beatrice sat up straight, genuine concern pinched across her face. 'Trelem is going to *love* you.'

I stood, snatching my untouched ale and bringing it to Simion's side. I doused the burning embers before they caught into an inferno. He continued to stare at his hands as though blood covered them.

'It's fine, you didn't mean it.' As I rested my hand on his shoulder, I felt just how warm he was to the touch. It radiated off him, fuelled by his passion, a magic that should never have belonged to him.

'Is it?' Simion asked. 'This magic doesn't fit inside of me. No matter the training, no matter the focus and techniques. I can't keep hold of it. This is why we can't tell them. Not until we are closer to being ready.'

'We need more time,' I added, before the tension rose to new heights. 'That I think we can all agree. But we also must focus. Saving Leska, uniting the North and South after years of disdain. There is much we can do whilst Leia continues searching for your mother.'

Simion's eyes widened at the use of her title, whereas Beatrice cringed away from it.

'That's all well and good, but how long do we actually have?' Beatrice practically vibrated in her chair. 'There is no knowing when Lilyth will reach us. Nor what will happen when she does.'

'She'll ruin this world.' My mind filled with the vision that had haunted me for weeks. An army of shadows; a withering, lifeless ground at my feet; a sky bathed in fire. It was destruction. It was decay. 'And if we have any hope in destroying her, we must first *understand* her.'

'Forget about Celia then.' Beatrice gestured towards me. 'She is a path where we have no idea if we will ever reach the end. We need to stop wasting resources locating her, and put it elsewhere.'

'Beatrice, you're right,' I replied.

With a wink, she replied, 'I know I am. Just about which part...'

I warmed at her expression. She recognised the pressure on my shoulders and would help ease it with the sarcasm I was most familiar with. 'All our allies deserve to know. And we will tell them. Just not yet. I need time—and I need a dryad.'

'No, not a dryad.' Simion grumbled from his chair. 'We spoke about this.'

'Spoke about what?' Beatrice looked between us, leaning forward.

'During the Claim, it showed me a... vision...'

I wasn't entirely certain what to call it. Unlike the flashes of memories that the Heart Oak showed me, the dryad gave me an insight into time. I had physically been present after Oribon split the mountain apart to free him and his kin. It was physical, and I had come away marked. Even through that was information I had yet to share with anyone but Simion, they did know that my blood ties to the gods of earth gave me a unique ability to commune with them.

'If the dryads can show me more about Lilyth, maybe we will understand her more. Then we can be better prepared to face whatever she is bringing to Aldian.'

'It is too dangerous,' Simion added.

'I think Max can think for himself, brother.'

'Both of you, stop.' Pain thrummed in my head. I found it easier to close my eyes, facing the dark rather than the tension between them. 'We may not know much, but what we do know is the four elemental creatures are her children... or they refer to her as *mother*.' I flicked through the very limited details I had gone over a multitude of times. 'Cyder believed they were important enough to her that would one day come for them. Question is, why did she leave them here in the first place?'

'And where did she fucking come from?' Beatrice added, knuckles cracking.

'Believe me,' I said, squeezing Simion's shoulder. 'I have so many questions the list is almost endless.'

Simion lifted his hand and laid it on mine. It was cooler now. Not as it once was, before Camron Calzmir's feather infected his body and changed it forever. But it was a new normal. One I was just thankful to have.

'There is more I should tell you,' Simion said.

Beatrice rolled her golden eyes. 'And here I was thinking I could call it a night. Go on, brother, add more shit to our list.'

'When the burned note returned to us earlier, I asked Trelem and the gleamers to do one more thing for me.' His pause seemed to stretch on. 'I asked the gleamers to try for Leska one more time.'

I recoiled from him, my mind whirling. Simion had told me he didn't want to speculate about Leska in our cabin, and that wasn't a lie. What he hadn't told me—or perhaps I just didn't ask the right questions—was he had a plan of his own to obtain answers.

'Go on,' Beatrice encouraged, elbows on knees, anticipation keeping her on the edge of her seat.

It was suddenly clear to me that whatever Trelem had whispered to Simion was the cause of his darkening mood.

'Promise me you will just listen.' He looked at me as he spoke.

A rush of blood flooded downwards through my body, connecting me to the floor. It was Beatrice who echoed my thoughts when she snapped, 'Fuck that, Simion. Spit it out.'

'The phoenix-possessed that Cyder was aware of in the South, they are currently surrounding Gathrax manor.'

The entire world stopped for a moment, I felt the floor shift, and it had nothing to do with the sway of the ship.

The fire. The burned message. It was the phoenix-possessed —the army Camron Calzmir promised me all those months ago.

'Leska, the gleamer novices, and those they managed to extract the phoenix feather from, have barricaded themselves into Gathrax manor alongside the innocents who were already using it as a means of hiding. Phoenix-possessed surround the building. The reason we have not been able to reach them before is because every reserve of power is being used to keep them alive long enough for us to do so.'

'No,' I said, speaking from my soul. 'They are using them as bait. The phoenix-possessed could burn through all of the South if they wanted, but they haven't. It is for a reason. They want us to come for them.'

It was Beatrice who asked the one question my brain just

couldn't form into words. 'Cyder is dead. Camron too. The rebellion controlled. If the phoenix-possessed are doing this, who is still behind them?'

Who? Who? My mind repeated the question until it no longer made sense.

My dragon, Inyris, picked up on my spike in emotion. Wherever she rested with Glamora was suddenly shattered by her roar and the flapping of wings.

Come to me. I sent out the mental command, knowing Inyris was already on her way.

'I plan to find out,' I said. I didn't know I was moving to the door until Simion grasped my wrist.

'Not like this,' Simion pleaded, eyes unblinking. 'We have to tread carefully.'

'She is my sister,' I snapped, tears of fury pricking my eyes. 'I refuse to be careful. I refuse to wait. We must act.'

'If they have held off accepting our attempts to reach them until now, what has changed?' Beatrice asked.

My emotions thickened the air, encouraging a storm to fill the sky beyond the ship. The hairs on Simion's arm stood on end as my static filled the cabin.

'Answer the question,' I demanded. There was no controlling the storm within me. It needed an escape.

'Promise me,' Simion said, 'you will not be the hero, Max?'

Beatrice was by my side, as ready as I was to leave. I knew without asking that Glamora flew beside Inyris, I felt her presence just shy of my dragon.

I snatched my arm from him, pulling free. 'Answer—the —question.'

To my surprise and Simion's horror, the answer came not from him but a knock on the cabin's door. Normally, they would wait for entry to be granted, but this time the door smashed open and Captain Trelem half ran, half stumbled in.

'Do you want the good news or the bad news first?' she

stammered over ale-slurred words, wrist dramatically waving around.

No one answered. I could barely catch a deep enough breath to form coherent words. What could possibly be worse than what Simion had just revealed?

'Well, the good news is we have finally reached the southern border of the Galloway Forest. We made it. Bad news—'

The scorch of smoke and ash reached my nose. For a moment, I thought it was Simion again, but he didn't show any signs of using his magic. No. It came from outside.

There was no need to wait for the answer, not as the orange-red fire glowed beyond Trelem in a halo. In seconds, I was running. Out the cabin door, up the stairway, until I came onto the deck. Sailors and mages stood around the side of the ship, looking out over the view of the South—my home.

The South *bathed* in flames.

CHAPTER 3

A river of ice spilled from Inyris's jaws like blue flame. She swooped down on the burning portion of Galloway Forest, extinguishing fires with her frozen winds.

It had been hours of fighting an unseen enemy, and we were no closer to winning. Dragons cut across Galloway Forest, putting out wildfire, only for more to spring up. Ash fell from thick clouds like snow, bathing the ruined canopy in a film of grey. The night had never looked so black; even the moon hung behind impenetrable clouds. I wished I could hide from the destruction too, but that was not an option. Even with the comet hidden from view, I still sensed its presence like an ever-watching eye.

There were so many dragons attempting to quench the flames that we had to fly in formation. A few at a time would dive towards the forest's crown, bathe it in icy winds and then climb back into the skies. A smudge of black scales dove at my side, the air screaming in the dragon's wake. It wasn't until the dragon expelled a torrent of her magic across the burning forest that I saw it was Glamora.

Beatrice never strayed far from me. I was thankful for it,

even if I did not sense her. My focus was entirely on saving Galloway Forest, and finding the phoenix-possessed who continued to set it alight.

Through the smog, I could see the stretch of the Thassalic ocean and the static ships left to moor far from shore. It was my call to keep them from the flames' reach. My eyes fell especially on one ship—the transport for the most precious material I brought with me on the voyage.

Heart Oak. But those plans were far off, as my entire focus was needed to stop Galloway Forest from burning.

Smaller vessels continued to transport mages to shore to help. Those without a dragon moved on foot. We would sweep the land until every last phoenix-possessed was found and healed. Except we had already been at it for hours and not a single one had been discovered.

My stomach flipped as Inyris nose-dived back towards the flames. Ice and ash stung at my cheeks, whipping my hair and slapping my cold skin. Tears streamed freely from my eyes. I dared not lift a hand to clear them for fear I would fall from Inyris's back.

Fire crackled over wood. Ice smothered flame. And on the circle went. Every second I waited for the fire to morph to black. Wytchfire. A flame no ice or wind could extinguish.

We had to stop this hell before it truly began.

Find Simion. Even my inner voice was exhausted as I sent out my command to Inyris.

I felt her reluctance as though it was my own. Just as I did with her exhaustion. Hours of this dance, and she was close to the edge. We all were.

Inyris changed course and spat her icy winds across the border of Galloway Forest, where the dense woodland met open farmers' fields. A patchwork of once-colourful flowers, wheat and produce were now mud and ash.

My attention fell on the formation of mages in the field

beneath us. They stood in three adjacent lines, all facing out towards the forest before them. The first line had their arms outstretched towards the forest. Unlike when earthen abilities were harnessed with an amplifier, I couldn't sense this new magic in the same way.

Inyris overcame my mind with hers. In a blink. I was looking through her eyes, gazing down at the world in strange, muted colours. She zeroed in on a single figure, focusing all my attention on the very man I had commanded her to take me to.

Simion. He stood alongside the other phoenix-possessed we had saved. Flames danced around his hands as he outstretched them towards the forest. He, and the rest of this new squadron, smothered the fire by absorbing it. And I could see from the ashen glow of his skin, the beads of sweat glistening over his forehead, that he, too, was struggling.

Inyris kicked me from her mind. The rush back to my body was euphoric, something I was still not used to.

My mind spinning in a vortex, I reached out, clumsily beckoning for Simion. It took a moment for the cold ice of his magic to inch over my thoughts.

We can't hold this up. I filled my mind with my voice, listening to it echo back my desperation.

It took a beat of time for Simion to respond. *They are trying to distract us. Our efforts are focused on stopping the fire, not locating the source. We must shift our focus elsewhere.*

I know. Galloway Forest would continue to burn if we don't stop it. *That is what they want. And they are succeeding—*

Simion's presence was a soft tickle of a feather. Faint and weak. *To keep us from Gathrax manor, from Leska.*

Inyris flew back to the forest, joining in with the dance of ice and flame.

Tell me what you want from me and I will do it, Max.

It was the easiest answer to give. *Survive. We haven't trav-*

elled all this way to fail the second we step foot on land. It isn't an option.

If they will not show themselves, then we have to go in and weed the phoenix-possessed out.

No. Inyris bellowed a ferocious roar across the world, echoing my own panic. *It is too dangerous. If you go into the forest, we cannot help from the sky without risking all your lives. I cannot protect you.*

Another sound from beneath Inyris. It wasn't a roar, but a song of creaking wood and shuddering earth. I could no longer hear Simion, if he responded. Not as I whipped my head around, trying to find the source of the noise.

More dragons cried out, distracted from the flames as something else took their attention.

Inyris. Show me.

Inyris snatched me back into her mind and showed the world through her eyes again. The forest seemed to shift. I thought it was my exhaustion, until blinking didn't clear the vision.

Dryads were moving through the forest.

I watched them in awe, sentient beings of bark and limb, coming in our direction. Monsters of wood. Inyris's advanced hearing picked up the creaking limbs and the cawing crack of their song as they forged towards the burning forest.

Galloway Forest had been without the dryads for a long time. History told that they turned their backs on the South after Galloway and his dryad lover were tricked by the first mages.

Hope sparked in my chest, a raging flame far brighter and hotter than wytchfire itself.

They had returned.

All around me, dragons expelled a simultaneous cry. Without a doubt, I knew that every mounted battlemage would have been shown the same thing I had. The tides had changed as the gods joined the battle.

Simion. The dryads. They are here.

He didn't respond with mind-speak, but I sensed his presence lurking. I just had to hope he had enough power left to see this through to the end.

We will force the phoenix-possessed out of the forest. I forced out the words into Simion's mind. *Be ready to accost them.*

I snuffed out the connection like blowing the flame of a candle. Fire burst to life beneath us, but this time, the dragons didn't smother it with their magic. We all turned course, focusing on the distant woodland and the dryads. We flew with renewed vigour, stopping only when the line of dryads were beneath us. As they moved towards the flames, we flew with them.

The air was alive with the magic of gods. An emerald light pulsed from the dryads, a heartbeat of power that I saw lingering around the Heart Oak. It gifted me with the energy I needed to finish this. Inyris's presence was faint in my mind too, but I knew why. She communed with the dryads below, working out their plan. As much as I longed to know what was required, I trusted them to work in tandem. Ultimately, our goal was the same.

The dryads pushed forward, the forest rippling like water, forcing the flames closer to our waiting mages. Inyris, Glamora and the riot of dragons unleashed a wall of ice at the back of the dryads' line, ensuring nothing could pass from behind.

We were so close. Simion, the rest of the phoenix-blessed and mages were ready as the final flames were pushed to the border. Anticipation tightened my throat, threatening to suffocate me. My hands tightened around Inyris's horns, her rumbling roar tickling over my palms as she, too, readied to swoop down to meet our enemy. Black light shot skywards. An earth-shattering scream split the night. Inyris banked right, missing a pillar of wytchfire as it gathered upwards in a twisting vortex of heat and force. It erupted across a dryad, covering its body within seconds, the blast so powerful it almost reached us.

Just as I believed we were close to succeeding, the tide changed once again. Fury erupted over every person, dragon and dryad. This was the desperate last attempt of the phoenix-possessed.

Dryads scattered from their kin who had perished in wytch-fire. This was a flame no one could extinguish, not without destroying the ones responsible. And out from the glow of fire and wood, figures ran into the fields beyond.

Phoenix-possessed. An army of them. Hundreds.

Inyris, fuelled by our shared ire, broke formation, folded wings into her golden scales and speared towards our enemy. Simion and the rest of the waiting mages charged forward, ready to meet the phoenix-possessed head-on.

I rose my hand skywards, calling upon my magic. Lightning cracked through the warm, heavy air. A serpent of blue light forked through the dark clouds until I grasped it. Power lit my veins, itched my skin and rattled my bones. Yet I didn't let it go. Not yet.

Before Inyris crashed into the ground, her wings burst wide as we glided over the two armies before they collided. Blinded by the desire to save the dryads from certain death, I unleashed my lightning. It crashed into the ground, scattering the phoenix-possessed apart from one another. They couldn't focus on using their magic if they were trying to save themselves from mine.

And it was enough of a distraction. Our soldiers met them head first, fire and earth rolling over one another as the battle finally came to a head.

We may not have had the numbers; but we had the magic. We had the control that came with freedom.

A powerful wave of mental force exploded over the clearing as the second line of defence joined the first. Gleamers were no longer hidden from battle, there wasn't the luxury. As one, they forced a powerful pressure across the phoenix-possessed, adding another debilitating force.

I longed to watch, but Inyris turned back and flew for the burning dryad. With a glance over my shoulder, I watched the lines finally crash into the phoenix-possessed. All I could do was hope it would be enough.

The dryad cawed out as the black fire devoured it. Its screams of agony pierced my soul. Where it withered, the other dryads made distance. But the wytchfire would continue to spread until the source was extinguished.

It didn't stop the dragons from trying. Ice formed in a circle around the wytchfire, trying to contain it. It didn't work entirely, but it slowed its spread.

Killing the phoenix-possessed was never our goal. We had come to the South to save them from possession. To remove the feather that infected them and give them a second chance. Even now our gleamers waited, ready for prisoners to be brought to them. Once the feather was located amidst the burned skin, the phoenix within would have its bond to the host severed.

I just hoped we had a chance.

As Inyris continued spitting her ice across the black flame, I contemplated if we had the time for hope. Fire clashed with fire as the battle raged across the fields below. I tried to find Simion, but everything was moving so fast. If the phoenix-possessed responsible for the wytchfire was not found the dryad would perish. Galloway Forest would not stop burning until everything was ash and ruin.

History would repeat itself.

Glamora passed over us, a blur of gargantuan obsidian against the smoke-ridden sky. I almost didn't look to my friend and her dragon, but something made me. As the large body of the dragon passed over the tops of trees, a flash of flame seemed to follow beneath. Stalking from below.

I opened my mouth to scream, but it would've been futile.

There was no warning Glamora or Beatrice.

Inyris. Move. Quickly. Intercept.

I didn't know what to expect, but the thing that exploded from the canopy of the forest was certainly more than my mind could have imagined.

A phoenix. An immense bird of gold, orange and red. Its plumage was beautiful, shimmering colours of live flames and feathers blending seamlessly into one. It was not as large as Glamora, but that didn't matter as it sank its talons into her underbelly, burying its golden beak between her scales before Glamora could so much as move. Wings of blazing flame flapped boiling winds across Glamora and Beatrice. No matter how Glamora tried to snake her long neck around enough to pry the phoenix off with her teeth, it was no use.

Panic thickened in my throat. Inyris shot through the sky towards the god of fire. Blue light built in her throat before spilling free. It crashed into the phoenix's side, forcing it to break apart from Glamora.

Dryads reached skywards, attempting to snatch the bird of flame from the sky. It released a furious screech in warning before black flame mutated from its feathers.

Keep your distance.

Inyris shivered against my command. I thought she would heed it. I was wrong. Instead of flying away from the phoenix, she flew towards it. Fire licked over my skin, the hot air suffocating. The phoenix gave chase, flying skywards as liquid flame fell from it like water. Inyris continued to follow, snapping at its flowing tail, shooting pillars of frozen winds in an attempt to extinguish it.

No matter how I tried, Inyris wouldn't listen to me. I had given up forcing commands across our mental tether. Now I was screaming, shouting so loudly that my throat hurt.

'Inyris, pull back! You'll die.' *I'll die.*

Nothing would pull my dragon from her wild fury.
Nothing.

A flash of silver caught my attention out of the corner of my
eye. Beatrice flew at my side, waving her armoured arms to get
my attention. Glamora didn't need to pound her wings as fast as
Inyris, but I could sense her struggle in the narrowing of her
eyes. The phoenix had caused her serious damage—but nothing
life-threatening.

Beatrice was shouting something at me, but I couldn't make
out the words. She pretended to undo the bindings around her
legs, then pointed at me. It took me a moment to understand.
The air was thinner, the higher we climbed. We parted through
clouds of smoke until the glistening blanket of stars could finally
be seen. I barely registered the burning comet that cut above us.

Was Lilyth watching us, delighting as her children warred
in her name?

The phoenix surprised Inyris by stopping suddenly, turning
and smashing straight into her. Fire scorched over scales. I
screamed out as the pain mirrored over my skin. My insides
were being thrown around, organs slamming into ribs as I
tumbled down and down.

I could barely open my eyes.

We were falling. Phoenix and dragon combined, talons to
scales, teeth piercing feathered flesh. Winds cried in my ears as
they battled one another.

Maximus. The familiar voice thundered through my head.
It was Simion. His panic, his anxiety so loud it was as though he
stood at my side and screamed. *Unbind yourself. Now.*

His command mimicked what Beatrice had been trying to
show me.

There was no room to think about the consequence. If I
stayed on Inyris, I would die. I had to hope Simion and Beatrice
had a plan. I reached down, the force making my arms move like
a ragdoll. The clasp at my thighs popped one at a time. When

the final one was undone, I was ripped from Inyris's back, sent spinning into the sky with a scream lodged in my throat.

Talons wrapped around my waist, catching me. The force of being caught jarred through my entire body. Every bone suffered.

I held firm onto Glamora's talons. Beneath me the world blurred. It was so close. There was no time to rejoice in being caught, not as gold fell at my side. Inyris and the phoenix fell from the sky like stones dropped into a river. Inyris was beneath the phoenix, jaws tearing into neck. Feathers and flame ripped free, falling languidly behind their descent like the red streak of Lilyth's comet.

A sob broke in my throat. I cried out for Inyris just before they both disappeared into Galloway Forest. Perhaps she finally heard me, or perhaps Inyris remembered I existed. Inyris spun her scaled body until the phoenix was forced beneath her. It happened so quickly I almost missed it. Then they both disappeared, stolen from view.

The furthest corners of Aldian would have felt the rippling force as the dragon and phoenix crashed into the ground. In a wink, the wytchfire that had ravaged below was extinguished. Gone, just like that. Everything stilled. I reached inside my mind, pulling on the tether that bound me to my dragon... but it was silent.

CHAPTER 4

Inyris lay broken and bleeding amongst a mound of feathers. Beneath her was the smattered remains of the phoenix. If it wasn't for the feathers surrounding me, covering the ground in a bed of red and yellows, I wouldn't have known what the remains had been. The force of the fall had popped the god apart like a berry between teeth. Gold blood oozed out like rivers, catching feathers that languidly floated in puddles of gore.

The air was thick with ash. It fell from the skies, caught by the trees above like snow. The sound of battle still raged on at a distance, but that didn't matter to me. I couldn't think anything of the song of a sky full of dragons, the fields full of mages and the forest full of dryads.

Not a soul could stop me. The moment Glamora returned me to the ground, I was running. Boots kicking through feather, ash and blood until the thunderous footfalls were muffled. Then I was with her, wrapping my arms around her golden-scaled neck, a keening sound cracking out of my body.

'Inyris,' I choked on her name, barely able to speak through the heartbreak and panic.

A storm-grey eye blinked up at me where I gathered her snout onto my lap. The relief that flooded through me was all consuming as her heartbeat cantered above my palm. I thought she was dead. The bond that tethered us was so silent I had run to the place she fell expecting to find death. Finding Inyris alive was almost a concept I didn't understand in my panic.

It soon became clear as to why the bond between us felt broken. As I ran my palm over her golden scales, wondering in the warmth of her flesh, Inyris opened up the connection, giving me a view into her mind.

Pain assaulted me. It was so sudden, so powerful and sharp, I took an intake in breath and screamed. Inyris quickly smothered our connection, severing me from her agony.

That is what she blocked me from. She wasn't dead, she just didn't want me to suffer as she did. And from the glance of her torment, it was a wonder why she still held onto life.

'Simion!' I screamed his name out into the dark forest. It was a futile attempt, but he was the only person who might be able to heal Inyris. 'Simion, please!' *Inyris needs you, I need you.*

I tried to reach him with our mind-speak, but it was as though he didn't hear. There was no knowing what was happening on the battlefield. Was he even alive? I started to imagine everyone I cared about, everyone I dared to love, dying. Because that is what happened. My father, my mother. Even people who were my family by blood like the Queen and Elder Cyder. Dead. All of them. Gone.

My grip on Inyris grew tighter. I dared not look at the mess of her limbs, her ripped leather wings and the way some of her scales looked like cracked glass. All I focused on was the beat of her heart against my hand and how it was gradually growing weaker and weaker.

'Don't you dare leave me, Inyris,' I hissed, staring deep into her eyes. 'I still have a promise to fulfil. I forbid you from leaving me.'

It was a miracle if she understood me through my heavy breaths and broken sobs. I lowered my forehead to hers, pressing my skin against her scales as the forest sang around me. It was faint, at first, until it seemed as though every tree had begun to sway and dance to the sound. I lifted my gaze into the dark to find an abundance of glowing eyes looking back at me.

The dryads.

They moved with grace. Everything about them was slow and methodical. Legs made from root and trunk shifted over the earth, disrupting the soil beneath them. Hair of vines and leaf were parted by crowns of branch and twigs. Some looked more human than others, with faces carved into the body of trunks. Others looked like the most ancient of trees, tall and towering with small woodland creatures watching from the hidden shadows of a thick canopy. These were the creatures whose blood ran through my veins.

In that moment, beneath the glare of the gods of earth, I felt as though I was a giant. Protectively, I hunched over Inyris's face, covering her with my body as much as I could.

I knew the old tales of the dryads. How they claimed the souls of the dead. Where were they when I killed Julian Gathrax? Had they come to watch as I lost something else I cared about?

'You can't have her,' I shouted, making sure every single one of them saw the fury in my eyes. 'She is mine.'

'We do not come to claim the life of your bonded. We come to save her.'

The voice was both nowhere and everywhere at once. It echoed across every dryad watching. I spun my head around, searching for the single speaker only to discover it was every single one of them.

'Inyris saved many a life with her sacrifice. Allow us to provide our sister with a gift of our thanks. You can trust us,

Maximus Oaken of dryad blood. The dryad-born. Our child. Place your trust in us, as we have with you.'

As the dryads spoke, they moved closer. Roots slithered out from beneath them, like serpents hungry for rich earth, they gathered the phoenix's feathers as though they were magpies with rings, jewels and polished cutlery. Some reached for Inyris.

'Don't take her from me!' I shouted, snot and tears blending into one. 'Go away, all of you!'

'We simply wish to heal. You called for our help, allow us to provide it.'

I had called for Simion because he was a gleamer and could heal.

The sensation of roots unfurling over my mind had me pinching my eyes closed.

'These are the gifts we gave you. You called for a gleamer, but a gleamer has power only through our magic.'

There was no fight left in me as Inyris slipped from my hold. I watched, dumbfounded, as dryads wrapped her in the embrace of wood and root, lifted her from the ground and gathered her into their oaken flesh. Her limp, golden body turned around as though a spider spun her in a web. But it was no spider. Dryads cocooned her in their limbs, covering her in a layer of their own flesh until she hung between them.

'See the power with your eyes, dryad-born. Only you can recognise the power with sight alone. Dryad-born.'

I fisted my empty hand before the dryad's song ceased in my mind. My amplifier bit into my finger and the world exploded in light. Just as the dryad said, I saw the magic—the essence of every dryad pulsing down their roots into the cocoon that held Inyris. She pulsed inside like an infant in the womb, curled up as she fed on the healing that was offered.

A dryad came to stop behind me. I didn't move, nor flinch, as it settled itself into a static position that made the god look more like a tree than anything else. Its strong body pressed into my back until I was leaned against it. To anyone watching, I had simply stopped and sat with my back to a tree. But it was the aura of essence glowing around the tree that proved the truth of what it was. A god.

'This is your doing,' I said, eyes trained on Inyris. 'All of this, the fighting, the dangers, the battles. It is your fault.'

The dryad knew exactly what I spoke of. I recognised its understanding as the bark slithered behind me, branches bending around me in an embrace. *'You are not wrong to blame us. We have used your kind for years, creating an army strong enough to fight beside us when mother returns. It was never our intention to turn the mundane against one another, but, alas, we cannot control what humanity does, not entirely.'*

Exhaustion coiled over me. It was unnatural. Forced. As though the dryad lulled me into a false sense of security. If it could heal, could speak in my mind and read my thoughts, then it, too, could alter my emotions just as Simion could.

'This is not our battle. How can we fight beside you if we do not have the knowledge of what we are to face?' I fought the yawn, but it was futile. I felt myself slipping, pulled by the dryad into a spell of haze.

'Have we not shown you enough?'

Flickers of a vision passed in the dark of my mind. A world in ruin. A sky hissing with fire. An army of shadows, faceless and shapeless. Mutated souls. Damned souls. Then Lilyth. Mother of monsters.

'Your visions are not clear. Nothing is, but the truth that is coming—the impending doom that falls through our skies.'

The dryad did not tell me I was wrong about the doom, only about the visions. *'These are not visions you see, but moments in time. Stored, collected, gathered and remembered.*

I fought against the wave of tiredness, throwing my eyes wide until they stung with the need to be closed again. I looked skywards to the burning streak of flame slithering from the falling star. The same star my Heart Oak showed me in a vision, the one that brought Lilyth to Aldian and doomed us before we even knew. 'What... what does she want?'

'We can show you, if you are willing?'

My eyes closed again as another powerful pulse overcame me. 'Another vision?'

'No. Another time.'

'Yes,' I said, sparing a final glance at the pulsing beat of light that was Inyris's body within the knot of wood. If this was my chance for answers, I had to take it. 'Show me.'

The sensation that followed was akin to falling asleep, when your head hits a pillow, except you seem to fall further only to jolt awake. Except this time, when I fell backwards, there was nothing to stop me. I tumbled, back and back and back, into the darkness, until I landed in a different... time.

* * *

The sensation of jolting awake is what followed. I sprang forward, renewed with energy. I only got so far before my body snapped backwards, torn by a force at my waist like arms wrapped around my middle. My hands slapped down on rough bark, nails tearing at it until I made sense of what was happening. The dryad was still behind me, except everything else was different. It was dawn, the brilliant sky awash with pinks and oranges. The grass at my feet was not covered in feather and blood, but a dewy kiss that covered my boots in a glistening layer of water. We were no longer in the middle of the forest.

There was a sense of peace to the air.

'Where have you taken me?' I asked the dryad, hands gripping the branches as if I could pry them away. I fought the urge to scream for Simion, Beatrice... Inyris. Everywhere I looked there was no sign of them... of anyone. No song of battle, only the silence that came far before it.

'*Somewhere you must only watch, never partake. A moment in time, a place to witness and learn.*'

Fear spiked through me as the reality of the dryad's answer sank in.

'*Do not panic, Maximus. You have visited before and survived. Do you not remember what we showed you during the Claim?*'

'The vision...'

'*We have already told you it was not a vision, but a moment in time. Does the skin on your arm still not bear the mark to prove it?*'

It did. I didn't need to roll my sleeve up to know it. During the Claim, I had woken in the embrace of a dryad, similar to this. I had believed it was a dream. But it was...

'*A moment in time, after our brother Oribon first was freed out of the confines Lilyth placed him and his kin within. A prison of earth is the place most poisonous to gods who belong to the sky. Out of all her children, Lilyth distrusted the dragons the most. Or feared. She locked them up, just as she buried us deep in the earth. What you were shown was the day Oribon finally broke free, and we were there to witness it. As were you.*'

'It was real.' The mark on my arm, the sky full of dragons, the rumbling of a shattered mountain.

'*Very much so.*'

I inhaled deeply, delighting in the smoke-free air. Cool wind touched my skin, the song of bluebirds reaching us from a stretch of forest far off in the distance. This, too, was real, but this time, the dryad held on to me as though they wouldn't dare risk me being free to this pocket of time.

'What is it you wish to show me this time?'

'*Mother...*'

My gaze snapped skywards to find the same falling comet I had just left behind. Except this was not the same at all. It was closer, so much so I could make out the details of every lick of flame surrounding the falling object. I flinched back into the dryad as the sky boomed, a shock wave of power spreading outwards.

Birds scattered from trees. Even the earth beneath my feet seemed to tremble in anticipation. I followed the falling star until it crashed into Aldian, hundreds of miles from where I stood. I still felt the impact reverberating through every bone in my body.

The moment that followed was pure silence. As though every living creature held its breath for the arrival of Lilyth.

'This was when Lilyth first came to Aldian.'

'Weak and betrayed. Yes, this was the very moment in time.'

I swallowed hard as a gust of rancid air blew over me. It was the aftermath of the colliding star. It assaulted the back of my throat with its acrid scent, making me gag.

'But if Lilyth was the one to bring you to Aldian, how are you showing me this?'

The dryad paused, contemplating my question. *'Trees are the watchers of history. Even the most mundane of trees can stand by and watch as the world turns around them. They gather information and store it. As we connect with the earth we rule over, we are able to access these moments and call upon them. It is not a concept humans are unfamiliar with. You cut down trees, rip the flesh from their bodies and turn them into pages, all for you to write down your own histories. We are no different. This is all but a part of time stored when Lilyth fell.'*

'Why here?'

'Lilyth is an entity from a place even I cannot comprehend into words you will understand. I can, however, describe her in a way that your human mind can relate to. A leech. Festering in the darkest parts of a lake. Mother is of such desires. She passes from world to world, drawing the power and leaving them but empty husks always searching but never finding what it was she thirsted for the most...'

Always searching but never finding.

Five words that fit together but did not make sense. My mind flooded with questions. What did Lilyth thirst for? Where was she from? What made a being devour worlds? Thoughts came all at once until I wasn't sure which one to voice aloud. Except the dryad was part of my mind now, two of the same, joined as one. It chose what it deemed was worthy of an answer and gave it.

'*For the first time, some of her children resisted her. Ultimately, she won, but she was weakened. Forced—not to come to Aldian and drain it of its essence as she had the hundreds of other worlds she first visited. But forced to store us here, to keep us locked away in prisons of her making until she was strong enough to come and finish her one and only task. Except her control, what she needed to... use us, we took. In those last moments before—*'

'Annihilation.'

'*In every sense of the concept. Ruin. Raze. Devour. Destroy. Your language has many words that perfectly, adequately describe the one and only task mother wishes to complete. It is not, as you would say, personal. It just is.*'

A dark mass filled the sky, rippling outwards from whatever part of Aldian that Lilyth found herself in. Part of me longed to see her, to know what state she was in, to prepare myself for what was coming. But the louder part, the stronger part of me, turned my face to the side, closed my eyes and said, 'Take me back.'

'*Do you not seek the answers—*'

The weight of the world slammed upon my shoulder. I wore no crown, but as I took in this knowledge, I felt the constricting pressure of iron and steel lay upon my head. I wanted nothing more than the complacency of a time when I knew nothing of this. A time before my magedom, magic, dryads, death. 'Take—me—back.'

'Yes, my child. I see what it is you wish for.'

I sank into the dryad's body, smothered by bark and darkness. The air was stale and old, it filled my throat as though soil was forced into me. Then I was falling again, tumbling through time until I was snatched by unseen hands and forced back out into the light.

This time, I recognised the view before me. Gathrax manor. Seen from within the border of Galloway Forest, the view was so familiar a cry broke out of me. Sensing my need to break free, the dryad's grip on me tightened until I was practically fighting myself free.

We slunk in the shadows of Galloway Forest, staring outside the line of trees to a building that I would recognise no matter the time. The manor watched us, windows lit with candlelight until it looked like an all-seeing face with glittering eyes. It looked the same, if not with small differences. The vines across the brick walls didn't look as overbearing as I remembered. The gardens between me and the building, less well refined and manicured. Wooden scaffolding even hung to the side of the manor's far side, to a place of the building that was not entirely finished. Walls were half-built, windows glassless and open to the elements. Which was strange, because the west wing of the manor wasn't built until I was almost two years old, which meant... this was not the time I had left.

The dryad had taken me to another moment in time. One far from Simion but closer than the first.

'We are nearly there,' a familiar voice called out across the night. It wasn't the dryad who spoke but someone else. I longed to turn to see, but the dryad held me in place. I opened my mouth to speak, but a branch pressed itself between my teeth, smothering any sound I could make.

There would've been time to panic until I saw the impossible.

Deborah Oaken, my mother, raced past us. Curls of brown

hair flew behind her, the gleam of bright green eyes. In her arms she carried a bundle of cloth pressed to her chest. I didn't have time to see what it was she held as she shot past us.

The skirts of her dress were ripped and torn, her boots sodden with mud and grime. She had a limp in her left leg, causing her to slow as she gained on the outskirts of the forest.

I couldn't cry out for her, couldn't beg her to stop, turn and look at me, not with the dryad's limb in my mouth. Instead, as tears slid down my cheeks, I buried my teeth into the bark until my tongue was lathered with the taste of earth.

'You must not affect the events of this time. But you may watch, if only for a moment.'

And watch I did.

My mother, far more youthful than I ever remembered her being, stopped by the last tree before the cover of forest gave to the open gardens of Gathrax manor. I sensed her exhaustion as she leaned against the tree, slipped down and lowered her lips to the bundle in her arms.

'Maximus, we are safe.' She was crying, relief and fear unfurling into one as she looked between the bundle and the manor. It was then I realised who she held in her arms. It was me. 'I promised you a life you could choose—'

Another figure caught my attention. In the gardens, a glowing lantern of flame swayed in the hand of a cloaked man. Even with the dark smothering his details, I would recognise the gait, the outline, the presence.

'Hello?' My father called out into the dark. I would recognise him anywhere, in any time or place.

Mother startled, eyes widening as firelight graced the side of her dirtied face. She looked paler, as though the years had yet to be unkind to her. If I ever wondered how she got me from Wycombe to the South, it was proven in that moment. On foot.

'With our help, of course,' the dryad confirmed in my mind.

'I can hear you in there. King Gathrax will not take kindly

to those who want to run from him,' my father said, pacing closer to the forest's border. Mother clamped her hand over her mouth, stifling another cry. When Father didn't hear anyone respond, he shuffled closer and called out. 'Are you hurt? Do you need assistance?'

The genuine concern that filled Father's voice was the same as it had been before he died. There were some things time could not change.

I held my breath, refusing to blink as he gained closer to where my mother was hiding. Time stretched out, the sounds of the forest dulling to a faint whisper. I wanted nothing more than for them both to see me, to hear me. Blinded by selfishness, the need to be reunited with the family who were stolen from me, I managed a muffled cry. Mother's head snapped towards where I was held in the dryad's embrace. Father lifted the lantern, the firelight quickly shifting in our direction. Then, just before he held it high, exposing me to them, I was falling...

* * *

I collapsed forward, gasping for breath, feather and blood pressed beneath my palms. It was night again. Inyris hung above in her cocoon of healing, the phoenix's pulp beneath me, the dryads surrounding me.

It was not the limbs of the dryad that embraced me, but the strong, human arms of a man. I didn't register the voice that was speaking until hands cupped my cheeks and lifted my face to see him.

'I thought I lost you.' Simion stared at me with wide, unblinking eyes. His face was streaked with ash and blood, his skin cold to the touch. Seeing him, feeling him, was such a relief I fell willingly into his embrace. 'You called for me... I came to find you, but you were not here. Missing. Then suddenly you were again. Like I blinked and your body came out of the... Max... it came out of the tree.'

'Dryad,' I gasped, knowing what waited behind me.

I had to stop myself from digging my nails into his back, just to anchor me to this moment. There were no words I could form to explain what I had just witnessed, the places I had just been. It wasn't that the dryad forbade me from speaking, but I felt somewhat protective about the knowledge. A keeper of it, just as the dryads were keepers of moments in time.

I looked back to the dryad, only to find that the earthen god had slipped away. There stood the tree Simion had referred to. There was nothing mythical about it. I opened myself up to the magic, only to find the tree's outline dull and without the glow of essence—the life force of the gods.

It would have been easier to lie to myself and pretend it was all some dream, forced on me by delirium. But there was no denying the truth of it, not as my blood hummed with how close I had been to my parents. The ache within me was born only from seeing my loved ones again, but not being able to touch them.

'Max, talk to me. Where did you go?'

I looked Simion dead in his amber eyes, aware of the golden dragon who was perched on a branch beyond him, not a single wound on her body. There was no lying to the man who could reach inside my mind and pull out the truth. And I had vowed never to harbour a mistruth from him again.

'The past,' I replied.

CHAPTER 5

A city of tents had been erected within an hour of the battle ending. The plan was to keep moving, but there had been injured, many lives had been lost. A sombre feeling blanketed the camp, more oppressive than the blanket of ever-falling ash. I felt the grief like a familiar beast in my bones, waking to the atmosphere around me.

By first light we would continue for Gathrax manor, but until then a scouting party had been sent ahead. A handful of battlemages and their dragons, followed by gleamers who would conceal them from prying eyes. If this had been our greeting when reaching the South, I could only imagine what waited for us when we reached our final destination.

Gleamers raced between tents, the ground already torn up by the heavy footfalls. Sobs of the wounded carried on the faint breeze. Perhaps it was sadistic, but I couldn't help but rejoice in the sound. It meant they were alive. Not everyone had been so lucky.

Inyris could have been one of them.

The air was thick with smoke. It still slithered into the night sky, blanketing the stars from view. Most of the destruction came from Galloway Forest at the camp's side. My gaze fell back on the forest, to the glittering eyes of the dryads who waited within. If it wasn't for Simion who walked beside me, my arm hooked in his, I would've run back to them and demanded to be taken back to my parents.

Facing my past was easier than seeing the destruction around me. I had brought these people here, and they had died because of me. It was not a simple fact to swallow—it practically choked me.

'Nearly there,' Simion said softly, his voice a welcome distraction. He jutted his chin out to a tent that waited at the end of the muddied path. Firelight glowed from within, outlining the dark shapes of people inside. 'Just say the word, and I will get the answers you desire. There is no need to draw this out any longer.'

'I know you can. But forcing our way into his mind will not help.'

Just then, I heard another curse from the man inside the tent with Beatrice. He was one of the phoenix-possessed who was currently being interrogated for answers.

I stopped short of the entrance, cautious to go inside. From within, I heard Beatrice speaking in low tones, followed by the splashing of water over flesh, muffling harsh shouts. 'It doesn't sound like she's having any luck.'

Simion's frown deepened. 'Means must, when we are dealing with god-possessed humans who can spit flame with a thought.'

Like all the other phoenix-possessed we had encountered, the feather infecting them had been removed by our gleamers. But that didn't solve the main issue. The North were the enemies in the eyes of the South. History had conditioned the divide. Possessed or not, the man who waited inside the tent was not surrounded by friends.

I just had to prove otherwise.

Beneath my free arm I carried a wooden box. Simion knew what was waiting inside. He didn't voice his evident concern. Simion didn't believe this was a good idea, but I did, and thus he would let me try.

'I need them to trust me,' I said, as a violent cry broke out over the stillness. Inyris dove out of the forest's shadows, flexing newly healed wings. Seeing her made me catch my breath, as though I still expected my dragon to be dead. 'Breaking into their minds and stealing answers without their consent will only solidify us as the enemy.'

'Trust is earned, and it goes both ways.'

'Exactly.' I swallowed hard, drawing my attention back to Simion.

He towered before me, the metal of his breastplate coated in the remnants of battle. Piercing gold eyes flickered across my face as though he drank in every minute detail. I lifted a hand to his face, cupping the proud line of his jaw, fingers drumming his cheekbones. He leaned into me, warm and... real. It wasn't the comfort I expected. Since the dryad had snatched me from this time and forced me into another, the lines of reality were blurring somehow.

'We need to know who is continuing the spread of this possession if we hope to stop it,' I said. 'Camron cannot be blamed forever. Nor can a disbanded rebellion. Finding the person behind it means we can root them out and stop this, before we lose any hope of saving the South.' Speaking Camron's name aloud sparked a strange feeling. Conflicting. To my surprise, it was Simion whose gaze fell to my arm, half expecting to see the silver fast-marks twist like vines around it. Of course, they had vanished when Camron died, sacrificing himself to save us. His ashes had been scattered across the Thassalic, the very sea he had craved escape on. There was no coming back from that.

'Because we need them—the South, that is,' Simion replied.

I nodded, longing to just collapse into Simion's arms and refuse to ever let go. 'They need us, we need them.'

'Remember, our focus is saving the world. Not saving those who do not wish for the help.'

His words struck true. 'That is only because they don't yet know what is coming.'

Simion leaned down, metal armour clinking together, and pressed his mouth to mine. The kiss was brief and welcome. I closed my eyes, allowing myself the moment of enjoyment. He was the only person with such power over silence, where simply his presence could calm me.

'Anything I can say to convince you to let me join you?' he asked, as he pulled back.

I shook my head, hair falling before my eyes. Simion reached for a strand and cleared it back. 'Help those who need you,' I answered. 'Make sure the gleamers are ready to leave by dawn. We can't risk wasting precious time when we don't know what is happening with Leska.'

Simion mocked a bow, looking at me through a circlet of dark lashes. 'As you command, my King.'

The lightness of his tone distracted me from the severity of everything that had happened. I grabbed a fistful of his under-shirt and tugged him close to me. 'I told you, I don't like that title.'

'Well, you best get used to it,' Simion groaned through a mischievous smile, 'because that is how they will all look at you, no matter what side of the forest you stand.'

Simion's kiss was hotter, harsher. I snatched his lower lip between my teeth in punishment, conjuring a sharp hiss from him. Once we parted, I could tell just from the glint in his eyes that he would want to take me here and now, no matter what waited around us. 'If I'm the King, what does that make you?'

'Your throne.'

Simion walked off, flashing a smile over his shoulder. It took me a moment to understand what his response meant, and when I did, my cheek flashed with heat, skin stained with a flood of crimson.

Reeling from Simion's rather accurate answer, I pushed the flaps of the tent and entered. I steeled my expression as a furious, hateful set of eyes fell upon me.

'I hope I haven't kept you,' I said, shooting Beatrice a wary look as she stood on the other side of our prisoner. She held a pail of water in her hands, droplets falling from between the wooden slats. Her leather breeches were stained, her boots glistening wet.

Beatrice winked at the man before her, sarcasm dripping from every word of her reply. 'Oh, and I was just starting to enjoy his company. We were really starting to get along.'

'Fuck—you.' He sat, attempting to rock forward on the chair but failing. Not only was he tied down, arms behind his back and ankles to the legs of the chair, but the chair itself was anchored to the main pole of the tent. It wasn't with rope that he was held but a thin metal wire. Rope burned, but metal melted, which caused more discomfort to him than us.

Steam slithered over the man's bare shoulders as fire erupted beneath his skin. Before it sparked completely, Beatrice leaned in. 'Careful, with a mouth so foul you might give me the impression you're flirting.' She dumped the pail of water over his head, dousing any hope for fire to form.

'I will take it from here, Bea,' I said.

'Be my guest.' She hoisted the wooden bucket and threw it towards me. I caught it with my magic, connecting to the wood and discarding it carefully to the floor.

I took in the man, my mind piecing together what details I could. He wore deep azure trousers, coated in ash and grim. But the colour was a telltale sign of his origins. His home. If his shirt had not been burned to cinders, I was confident it would've been the same colour of his ruling Kingdom.

'You're from the Calzmir domain,' I said, holding the man's chestnut eyes in contest. He was handsome, for someone with a permanent scowl. Close-cut strawberry-blonde hair, a broad build; large, scarred hands. Where half of his chest and shoulder was marred by the burned skin caused by his possession, I could still make out that his forearms and neck were darker in tone than the milky pale of his chest.

He gathered spit in his cheeks and spat the glob at my feet. 'And you are Maximus Oaken, King killer, deserter, mage-fucker.'

I couldn't help but smile. Beatrice hid her grin behind fingers, waggling eyebrows at me.

'Original. I have to say, those titles are new, which will take some getting used to. I haven't heard those before.'

'Neither have I, but I think mage-fucker might be my new favourite,' Beatrice added.

I placed the wooden box before the man's boots and knelt before it. I was so close to him I could feel the heat radiate from his skin. 'Since you know my name, it would only be fair that I ask you yours.'

'What kinda interrogation is this?' he barked, throwing his head back with a howl. 'You're getting nothing out of me.'

Beatrice threw her head back with a laugh. 'He only asked your name, not what gets your dick hard.'

'Thank you, Beatrice.' I silently begged her to stop with the taunting. But, to my surprise, her choice of words was so vulgar it worked. I had already decided what type of man he was, and from the reaction he gave me, I was proven right. He narrowed his eyes, seemingly looking at me in a new light. 'Jameson Cork.'

My smile was genuine. 'I would shake your hand, Jameson, but yours seem occupied, and I don't like the idea of being burned. Been there, done that, didn't enjoy it. Can I offer you something to drink?'

His eyes fell to the forgotten bucket that had contained water. 'Little missy here has given me enough.'

'Not water,' I said, standing abruptly. 'Something stronger.'

His eyes widened. I took that as confirmation.

I found a jug of ale, the one I had requested be delivered to the tent before I got there. Pouring out three tankards, I handed one to Beatrice, kept one for myself and took the other to Jameson. Dryads knew I needed something strong to keep me going.

'I'll need my hands for that,' he said, mouth parting like a fish out of water.

'I don't trust you... just yet. But I hope that is something we can both learn before I leave.' I lifted the tankard to the man's mouth, carefully tipping the contents. Some of the ale dribbled down his chin, but most of it reached its mark by his groan. 'Better?' I asked.

He gasped for breath, tongue lapping the ale from around his mouth. 'A little ale isn't going to loosen me up. If you want me to talk, I will need more than that.'

'All in good time. First, riddle me this. How does a hard-working farmer become a fire-spitting warrior?'

Jameson's eyes widened. 'How did you know I was a farmer?'

'Yes, how?' Beatrice echoed.

'You know my name, so you know my story. I worked for the Gathrax family for as long as I could remember—'

I blinked and saw my mother racing through Galloway Forest with me as a babe, clutched to her chest. My father was there, his features illuminated above the glow of his lantern. It was so real, it was real. I had been there, watching. And they had heard me...

'—my father, no matter the season, would have the same marks on his arms and neck as you do. The sign of a person who spends his day beneath the sun. I'd recognise them anywhere.

The marks of a hard worker, someone who is not shy of grafting.'

'And what about it?' Jameson was wary but intrigued. I could feel the atmosphere shift, as could Beatrice from the impressed gleam in her eyes. 'It changes nothing. I am more than a land-worker now. I am powerful, powerful enough to stop the likes of *you*.'

The air hissed with a spike in warmth. I recoiled before Jameson started spitting flames. Beatrice wiggled the pail of water in warning, which seemed to subdue him.

'Believe it or not, but we are not here to conquer like the stories we've grown up on. We are here to help,' I said, trying to keep my features as soft as my voice.

'You killed King Gathrax,' Jameson spat. 'Rumours are your people killed Queen Romar too. What's next? Calzmir. Zendina? Two more Kingdoms to raze and you rule everything.'

'Jameson, you don't strike me as a man who cares much for royalty. What does it matter who has died because of me, or by me?'

'I care for who puts coin into my pocket—' His eyes widened as he walked straight into my trap. 'If you kill them all, what good are you to me?'

My eyes fell to the box. 'I can be very beneficial to you. But also, to every other hard-working soul. Everyone who has felt the oppressive weight of our Kings and Queens. Every person who has known nothing but graft... and for what?'

Jameson leaned forward as far as his bindings allowed. 'I don't do it for them. I do it for my family.'

'Then we are one and the same. Because everything I am doing is for mine.'

'That isn't what they told us—'

Beatrice stiffened beside me, mirroring the way every muscle in my body tensed. 'Who? Jameson, please, who did this? Who has funded this mutation? Which person promised you wealth and power to become what you have?'

His lips sealed shut, physically refusing to speak another word. It seemed that the ale had worked its trick, as did the familiarity of speaking to someone who knew hard work. We were connected, us workers, tethered by the common ground of belonging to someone else.

Silence hung between us.

Jameson's entire demeanour changed so quickly that it was jarring. His eyes widened, searching around the room for someone or something he feared. His nails scratched at the chair handles, his body shivering with unspent energy.

This... this was fear.

The burning wicks around the room grew taller as they fed off Jameson's essence. Sweat beaded down his already dripping wet skin. If he wasn't careful, he would burn out.

Before the room erupted in further chaos, I picked up the box from the floor. It was distracting enough that Jameson glanced to it.

'Never mind that,' I said, trying to divert the conversation, even though I was starving for the answer. 'I have something for you. A peace offering.'

'What's in there?' he asked, his gaze focusing on me once again. 'Something else to force me to speak?'

I paused. 'Jameson, I need you to understand that if we wanted the answers you hold close, I could easily get them. Outside of this tent are countless mages with the ability to enter your mind, flick through every thought, until we find what we want. But that isn't how trust is earned, is it?'

The lid of the box lifted, revealing the lump of wood within. Out of the corner of my eye I recognised the pulse of light, the glow of the Heart Oak's essence. This was a part of my mother's tomb, and being close to it was comforting.

Jameson tilted his head up, eyeing the wood down the point of his nose. 'Wood?'

'My version of coin. If that is the language you best speak, then so be it.'

'Is this some joke?' he barked.

'No. Not at all. We call it Heart Oak. Or an amplifier, but you will know it as a wand. Well, once you carve it into one.'

I watched every feature of the man's face soften in surprise. He even gazed at Beatrice, as though expecting her to say otherwise. She simply nodded and said, 'Believe my crazy friend or not, but that is certainly what he says it is.'

Jameson's neck practically snapped back towards my offering.

'You're not the only person who will be offered this. Every phoenix-possessed we save, every mundane human who dwells across the South. You'll be given a choice.' I closed the lid with a snap. 'But there is a cost, I will not lie to you.'

If I expected him to retort with another offensive line or laugh, I was wrong.

'What... cost?'

I smiled, knowing the temptation of power was far too great to ignore. 'When the time comes, you will fight for your kin. I am not talking about me, or the people you have been conditioned to hate. But your neighbours, your fellow labourers, family, friends. Dryads, even your foes. Do what is right, claim what should have always been yours, and stand beside me, not against me. I promise, it is the best of the two options.'

'It *really* is,' Beatrice chimed in.

Neither of us explained what exactly Jameson would one day face. But, regardless of the fire magic lingering within his body, we would need all the power in our arsenal to face Lilyth —even if I was still unsure what exactly we would face.

But I would find out, the moment I could get back to the dryads.

'Do we have a deal, Jameson?'

He stammered, eyes glued to the box in my hands, entirely entranced by the promise of magic that was kept away from the South. 'We do.'

Relief uncoiled in me, a serpent waking from a deep slumber. 'That is the right choice, Jameson. But first, I need you to tell me who bribed you to become a host for the phoenix. Who is continuing the spread of this burning plague in the South?'

Jameson levelled his stare back to me. For such a big man, the fear that radiated off him was so powerful that I took a step back. 'Devils.' The word rocked across the tent, causing the very air to become suffocating. '*Little* devils.'

Little devils.

Two words I never thought I would hear again. But they held so much power that a thousand years could've passed and I would still have understood them.

Them. Little devils. The name my mother and father used to describe two seemingly looking cherubs with orange ringlet curls, doughy faces and wide blue eyes. King Gathrax's daughters, the ones who had been exiled by Camron to... to the Calzmir estate. The same place Jameson was from.

I caught Beatrice's gaze and held it whilst Jameson lost himself to hysteria. Every soul in our camp would have heard his terrified screams.

'It can't be right, Bea.'

Although she shook her head, I knew she, too, felt the same knowing truth as me. 'They are children, Max. I know it seems connected, but I hardly imagine the Gathrax twins are behind this...'

I wished I believed her, I really did. But something in my gut told me Jameson was not the crazed man he presented himself as. Where there was smoke, there was certainly fire.

'And we know all too well the demonic blood that runs through the Gathrax family. Julian. Jonathan. Look what the phoenix did to Camron. It took in his passions and twisted them. Now imagine what would happen to two already twisted children whose family was murdered, and their lives ruined.' I choked for breath as the reality settled in. 'I hardly imagine it would take a phoenix much effort to manipulate such souls.'

If it was true, and the Gathrax twins were behind this, I could not exactly blame them for becoming monsters. They did not ask to be born into a family of danger and hate. They did not ask to be mutated by their surroundings.

Beatrice looked back to Jameson, her knuckles tightening on the end of her staff. He was mumbling under his breath, face flushed crimson, tears streaking down his proud face. 'It doesn't bear thinking about. I thought Queen Romar said the spread was occurring in Calzmir lands. Dryads, Jameson proves that.'

The blood drained from my face. I appreciated Beatrice's attempt to dispel my panic, but it was wasted. 'Camron banished Remi Gathrax and her twins to his manor. That is where they were sent after I killed King Gathrax.'

'Fuck, Max.'

I nodded, desperately needing to feel the fresh air on my skin. The urge to run and never look back was all-consuming. Besides Lilyth, who fell from the skies, threatening to destroy Aldian entirely, there was only one other name that haunted me. *Gathrax.*

'Until we know for sure, we can't waste the energy dwelling on it,' I said, as everything around me was coated in a haze of red. Gathrax red. 'A gleamer can enter Jameson's mind and confirm what we think is happening.'

'Then what?' Beatrice's question hung between us. 'What if it is them...'

'It will be time for a *family* reunion.'

CHAPTER 6

Simion held me from behind, his arms anchoring me to this realm. His breath tickled my spine, his lips grazing my flesh with small kisses that caused prickled skin to spread over me. Our tent was cold, but nestling into Simion was like being curled before a hearth. It was pleasurable, even if my mind spun with everything that had happened.

'Say the word, and I can help you sleep.'

That was the thing about Simion. He didn't need to enter my thoughts to know what I was thinking. I had attempted to feign sleep for what felt like hours, and I still couldn't find respite.

Every time I closed my eyes, I saw them—the little devils.

I rolled over, the pallet creaking beneath me. Simion shifted back, giving me enough room to face him. There was no light in the tent, only the blanketing darkness. But this close I could see him through the haze. His glistening golden eyes, the scar over his eyebrow and the boiling concern that had etched itself into his face after I had told him about what happened with Jameson.

'What about you?' I whispered. 'You're still awake.'

He forced a smile, one that didn't reach his eyes. 'You are my priority.'

I felt as though there was more to his answer, but he didn't elaborate. Instead, I shifted the conversation before the roots truly took hold. 'I don't think I will be able to sleep until I understand what you meant earlier about being my throne.'

The truth was, I didn't want to sleep, because then Simion would leave me as he had every night prior. I didn't want to close my eyes and face the Gathrax twins.

He traced his fingers over the curves of my body, his nail tickling over the mound of my hip, to my waist, over my ribs and up my arm. 'For someone who loves to read, I would have thought your imagination would have already answered that query.'

I leaned up on my elbow, staring down at him. 'As much as I enjoy sitting on you, Simion Hawthorn, you are far more important to me than simply that. Much more.' I kissed him, featherlight. It was brief. I wished I could've given into our connection more, but there was something I had to speak to him about. With everything else that had happened—the battle, Jameson, what the dryads had shown me—there was no point holding anything else back.

'Simion.' I paused, hating how serious I sounded.

'Yes, my love.'

I lay back down, resting my head on my hand like a pillow. 'Please, don't leave me tonight.'

'I—' Simion's smile faltered, his expression growing serious once again. His eyes broke my contact, looking at something unimportant behind me. 'I must. How long have you known?'

He didn't deny it. He never would. That was the thing about Simion. He wouldn't lie to me.

'Since our first night together when I visited the Mad

Queen. You thought I was sleeping, but I wasn't. I felt the bed shift and heard you walk out the room. You didn't come back. Every night since... I can't risk sleeping now knowing you will go and not come back.'

'I will,' he said quickly. 'I always come back.'

'Yes, but not until the morning. I'm a light sleeper, Simion.'

Simion's exhale was long and tempered. It was the sound of defeat, of someone who couldn't come up with excuses. He looked me dead in the eyes. 'I leave because I don't want to hurt you.'

I shook my head, dispelling his excuse. 'You would never—'

'Yes, I would.' His words were sharp, stifling mine. 'I can't trust myself, not with this power. We can pretend that it wasn't fire that tore your family apart, we can pretend that when you look at me, you see something other than the possibility of ruin, destruction. But I can't trust myself, not when I am sleeping.'

'And where is the evidence of this? How would you know when you leave at night and come back at dawn?' I knew this was why he looked exhausted all the time. It had nothing to do with his training, his attempts to control a power that was still a stranger to him.

'I dream, Max. Since...' He reached over his shoulder, muscles flexing, as his fingers brushed the spot on his shoulder where the phoenix feather was inserted and removed. 'Since the plague, I have these nightmares. Colourful, real. Sometimes, I hear the phoenix, remnants of a voice that was stifled when the feather was taken. And when I wake, it is to ruin. Sheets singed, walls dark with soot and ash. I can't risk it—I can't risk *you*.'

I can't risk you.

Now, the little devils didn't haunt the dark of my mind. Simion's words had conjured their image into our tent, filling the shadows. I knew they were likely possessed by the phoenix, thus being used like pawns just as Camron had been. But that didn't take away from who they were.

They got the nickname 'devils' long before a phoenix occupied their mind.

'This is simply another battle we must face,' I said softly. 'Together. Because I cannot possibly do it without you.'

Simion closed his eyes, the lines across his forehead smoothing out. 'When the others have been dealt with, we will sort this one. Until then, it is okay. I stay until you sleep, and I will be back by dawn.'

What could I possibly say to that? There was nothing to contest what Simion worried about. If anything, it made my love for him deep, iron strong. I cupped his face with my hand, delighting in his warmth but now understanding it for what it was. Destruction. Although I trusted him, Simion didn't trust himself.

It was up to me to help him, not hinder.

I swallowed hard, burying down all the reasons I needed him to stay, all the pleading and begging I was so close to doing. 'Where do you go... when you leave?'

It was a question I had wondered for days, but never had the chance to voice. 'Far enough away that if something happens, no one has the potential to be hurt.'

My mind travelled beyond the tent, out across the camp of mages and phoenix-possessed humans who gleamers worked to rid of the feather. I couldn't fathom where Simion planned to take himself when I finally found sleep. If I added that to my list of worries, I would never be able to close my eyes.

'Do not worry about me, Maximus. I cannot be a burden to you, that is why I do what I must.'

'That's easier said than done.'

Simion leaned in close, pressing a kiss to the tip of my nose, then my cheek, my forehead and finally my mouth. That kiss lingered until his warmth spilled into me, comforting every inch of my bare skin. 'Think about it this way, the sooner you get some sleep, the sooner I do.'

I narrowed my eyes on him, forcing a scowl. 'How dare you use you against me.'

That made him laugh, a sound I would happily listen to over and over again. 'Then make me sleep,' I added.

'Do you know what you are asking of me?'

I nodded. 'Absolutely.' It was more than wanting him to sleep. If Simion had left, thinking I was sleeping, I would have left the tent too. Not to follow him, but to sneak back into Galloway Forest to the dryads who watched over us from the shadows. I would make them show me my parents, take me back to a time when I could see them living and breathing. I didn't trust myself, nor my ability to refuse what I wanted.

'Close your eyes,' Simion said, his deep voice rippling over my naked skin.

I tasted the magic as Simion opened himself. Sweet as nectar, calming as the sound of wind through fields of reed.

'Can you do one thing for me?' I asked, as my lids closed and the world went dark.

Simion wiggled himself closer to me until his flesh pressed completely into mine. 'I would reach into the sky and snatch the very stars from it if you asked me.'

'Make me dream, give me something else to fill my mind than...'

He silenced me with yet another kiss. It was fleeting but oozed his emotion. When he pulled back, I almost leaned in for more. All the while my eyes were still closed, just as he asked. 'Good night, my love. Sweet dreams.'

I opened my mouth to reply, but his power burrowed through my skin and into the deep part of my consciousness. The world slipped away from me, replaced with images of something conjured.

It was Simion and me, back in the room of the Mad Queen,

surrounded by rumpled sheets, laughter and joy. There was no Lilyth, no little devils, no death or impending doom. There was only us, me and him, together with nothing but the worry of each other's pleasure.

'Now, my love,' dream-version Simion said, eyes alight with his joy. 'Care to come and sit upon your throne?'

CHAPTER 7

Two days had passed since the attack. Two days of preparing our numbers to fight again. Two nights of sleeping alone. Two days of agonisingly planning our next move carefully, knowing what would be waiting for us at Gathrax manor.

I had no doubt in my mind that the Gathrax twins were using Leska and the mages as bait. It was proven when our scouting team returned with news that Gathrax manor was entirely surrounded, but the phoenix-possessed were not attacking.

We had been monitoring the boundary since, watching as the phoenix-possessed just stood there, watching, immobilised —waiting.

In an ideal world, we would not be preparing for a battle after traversing the South on foot. Using Galloway Forest and the dryads' power as cover, we had made it to the outskirts of Gathrax manor by the third morning of reaching the South.

My nerves were practically on fire. My body shivered with the need for action. But if we had learned anything, it was better to be patient. And I had a plan to focus on.

As I slipped into Inyris's mind—seeing through her eyes as though they were mine, feeling the breeze brush over scales as though it kissed my naked skin—I couldn't help but compare the feeling to what I shared when the dryad took me to another time. It was an out-of-body experience, whilst also being purely in my mind. Physically, my body was in the belly of Galloway Forest, concealed by shadow and earth with an army of mages around me. Mentally, I flew above the line of clouds, concealed from anyone looking up from below.

Vibrant colours filled my thoughts. Inyris's keen eyesight was able to look through the haze of cloud to the impossible beneath it—to Gathrax manor, nestled in the middle of ruin.

It was as though the manor itself had been dropped from the dark abyss far above. Where it crashed into the ground, all around it was nothing. Burned, razed earth. My heart ached at what were luscious gardens tended by my father. The mark he had left on the world was now ash. Scorched earth, black as night, not a blade of grass left alive. Only from memory could I discern what had been there before the fire. Stone statues, manicured shrubs and bushes painstakingly cut into the shapes of bears and swans. All that was left was the manor itself—and barely.

It was one thing to have heard the state of the manor from the scouting party, and another to have seen it.

Inyris fed off my reaction. She pulled on my sorrow, my fury, allowing it to fester in her gut. I willed her to keep it contained, not to make a sound as she glided far above. Otherwise, the hundreds of bodies that stood around the manor—static as though they were statues—would hear her.

Phoenix-possessed. There were so many. Far more than the numbers we had hidden within Galloway Forest. Far more than we had been told in our report. Even with the dryads and the dragons, this time we were outnumbered. They looked towards the manor, unmoving and still. I did too, through Inyris's storm-grey eyes. I had to admit, it was a sight to admire.

Instead of the stone façade and windows that glowed like eyes in the night, it was hidden behind giant roots that rose from the ground. Entombed in earth, it was no wonder how Leska survived all this time. She had used the ground, lifting it over the manor, adding an extra layer of protection to those hiding inside. Some roots had been burned to blackened stumps, but others had been conjured to replace. This was great power —*desperate* power.

I snapped back into my own mind, calling Inyris towards me. The first thing I saw was Simion. He was knelt before me, his armour freshly cleaned, his skin glowing beneath the sharp rays of light brave enough to enter the forest.

The scar on his eyebrow flexed as it rose. 'Bad, or really bad?'

'Fucking awful.' My mouth was sand-dry. Swallowing felt like drinking from a cup of broken glass. 'Even worse than that.'

'How many?' Beatrice kicked off the tree she was leaning against. Her staff was out, gripped tight in her left hand whilst her short blade was in her right. She, like Simion and me, and every other mage around us, was ready for battle.

'Enough that we will need our distraction.'

'Starting with plan B is not a bad thing, necessarily.' Beatrice nodded, her eyes glazing over for a moment. It was one thing going into your bonded dragon's mind, and another to watch someone else do it. I might not have heard what command Bea gave to Glamora, nor did I need to. It was pre-planned and, frankly, our last resort.

I didn't want to admit it, but using our last resort before the battle even begun was not ideal. But that was the point of last resorts, wasn't it?

'I didn't see them,' I said from the corner of my mouth,

directly to Simion. 'The twins are not amongst the numbers of phoenix-possessed.'

He stiffened, muscles flexing in his jaw. 'Then they will be close.'

'I want to find them, before they find me. Are you ready?' I looked to Simion, as a bead of sweat formed on his temple. He looked more exhausted than he had last night. Although he had forced me to sleep when he was still with me, and was there when I woke, I knew he had not stayed. But I didn't ask him where he went. It was selfish not to inquire, but the answer would distract me. Today I had to worry about Leska, tomorrow would be for Simion.

'Born ready.' Simion took my hand in his, the cold caress of his power inching over the back of my mind. 'The connection is open, take it away.'

I relayed what Inyris had shown me, knowing the message was being broadcasted across every mage and fire-wielder in the forest. They all saw what I had. Hundreds of phoenix-possessed standing idly around Gathrax manor, staring expectantly at it. I had hoped for less, we all did. There were so many I had no doubt that they could've gotten into the manor if they truly wanted. But that was likely not their goal. Little devils. If the Gathrax family had anything to do with this, they did it for one reason.

To lure me here. To seek revenge.

Well. I was here. And, as always, I was willing to disappoint.

Before I released Simion's hand, I offered a final message to our regiment. The phoenix-possessed were not our enemies. They may have seen us as such, but we were here to help not kill. I wanted the death count to be minimised.

'*They* are close,' Beatrice called out, severing the connection. 'It is now, or never.'

The ground rumbled beneath my feet. I looked down to see

pine needles, twigs and debris jumping from the floor as though they had a life of their own—a stampede was heading our way.

Our plan B.

Simion drew me into his arms, gathering me up and resting his chin on the top of my head. Magic spoiled the air as the dryads joined us, concealing every single person in a blanket of their power. I didn't know what the stampede would see when they passed, but I knew it wouldn't be us.

I looked up as a shadow passed overhead. Then another. And another. Every dragon in our army flew towards Gathrax manor, no longer needing to use the element of surprise. It would draw the phoenix-possessed's attention skywards, as the true attack happened before they could realise.

Howls and yips sounded from every hidden shadow of the forest. The rumbling ground intensified. Then, all at once, we were surrounded by a wave of worcupines. Poison-tipped needles, maws dripping with saliva, growls of desperate hunger everywhere as the sleek bodies raced past us, following the direction of the dragons.

It had been Glamora who alerted Beatrice to the hordes of worcupines gathering within Galloway Forest. There hadn't been such a presence of dragons in the South since the Mad Queen flew over with her army to destroy the Southern mages. It had drawn the worcupines closer, and, instead of fearing what they would do, we used them.

Natural enemies to the dragons, they were still dryad-made creatures. And as I was trying to unite the North and South, it was time even monsters put their differences aside.

Show me. With a sharp tug, I was back in Inyris's mind, watching from great heights as the wave of worcupines burst out of Galloway Forest. The phoenix-possessed turned around seconds before they were overwhelmed. Needles broke skin, bodies fell down paralysed.

'Forward!' I shouted, forcing myself back to the moment. 'Gleamers first, go, go, go!'

The ground didn't rumble as we charged, it trembled. We followed after the worcupines, bursting out of the confines of the forest to join the battle. Charred earth crunched beneath my feet, smoke eased into my throat.

Simion and his gleamers led the way. Battlemages kept behind the line as the gleamers forced out a wave of mental decapitation over the worcupines and phoenix-possessed. Those who didn't fall to the paralysing poison on the worcupines needles stumbled beneath the force of our gleamers' attack.

Dragons circled the manor in formation. Their cries and calls were only meant to frenzy the worcupines, whilst alerting those inside the manor to our arrival. If we needed their help, they would know.

If the phoenixes joined this attack, there was no saying they wouldn't show themselves as well.

Just the thought of the gods of fire joining made me desperately want to banish Inyris away. She faced them once before, and barely came away alive. Luck lasted only so long.

Stick close to me, my love. Simion's voice filtered into my mind as I passed him. Battlemages flooded with me, threading amongst the line of gleamers as we entered the fray.

I had hoped not to face worcupines again. The memory of my last encounter was still fresh in my mind. But this time, my magic was not new to me. It was as familiar as an old friend.

I reached out, stabbing my essence into the earth around me, just as the other battlemages did.

There were three phoenix-possessed before me, fending off two worcupines. I melted the ruined earth beneath their feet, causing beast and human to sink ten inches deep. Simion followed behind, sending out a debilitating wave of mental force. It slipped around me, knocking the already struggling bodies unconscious.

My breathing came out ragged. The muscles in my legs burned, the exposed sun made the skin beneath my armour itch. A worcupine dove towards me, missing Simion's extended blade by mere inches.

'Max—'

My name was swallowed by the explosion of my power. I thrusted my hands skywards, playing the earth as though I was a conductor and it my musician. Shards of stone lifted from broken statues, piercing the worcupine's soft underbelly. I ducked, knees skidding over ash and mud, as the dead body of the creature tumbled to the ground. Inyris sparked in my chest, scolding me for risking myself. But it was all worth it as the dead worcupine fell in the line of a charging phoenix-possessed, knocking their legs from under them, forcing them to fall atop poison-tipped needles.

I offered Simion a quick wink, delighting in the impressed glow of his expression. Then on I moved, onto the next.

I fought as though I knew Leska was watching. She had trained me, forged me like steel into the blade I was becoming. This was for her. I buried the dread of everything that would come when I saw her, the conversations and secrets I would be forced to uncover. But for now, I took every emotion and fed it into my limbs, my magic.

The plan was working. Phoenix-possessed humans fell, most still alive. Our dragons continued to distract worcupines, enough for us to deal with them. Some fled, scarpering back into the forest only to be met by the dryads. Others saw that it was best to fight beside us, not against us—just as I hoped they would.

The tides were certainly changing. The forest shifted, trees moving as though dancing to the sound of battle. It was the dryads, doing whatever they deemed necessary to the creatures they had once created. Hope reared its head again, because it didn't take long for us all to stand side by side and fight as one. Hope that we were enough to face what was to come. We fought as a body of magic—

Fire flashed hot before me, so close the hairs on my arms singed.

'Hello, Maximus,' a woman said, her voice overlapping with something darker, something monstrous. Of course, I had never met her before, but she spoke to me as though she knew me.

'Which one am I talking to?' I said, steeling myself. Magic hummed over my skin, preparing. I saw the truth through her glowing eyes, like windows to the true being inside.

The little devils.

She laughed, a sickly giggle that belonged to a child. Or two. 'We have been waiting for you. Silly little, Max.'

It was the twins, using this phoenix-possessed as a puppet.

The how didn't matter. Not yet. I needed to know why.

'Then come out and face me,' I replied, fighting the urge to search for the true speaker. 'Show yourself, or do you see what is happening to your creations? Do you know what your fate will be?'

'Do not worry. We *will* see you soon.'

Fury billowed within me. They were toying with me, just as they had with my mother and any other poor soul forced to interact with them. In this moment, I had no doubt that Jameson was right.

'Where—are—you?' Lightning fizzed over my skin, crackling across the cloud-ridden sky. A wave of darkness passed overhead as it borrowed my essence and fed itself.

'Where you put us,' the voice within the woman said. 'Are you going to come and see us after you see your sister—'

The last word hissed like a snake, drawing out until my skin blistered with it. There was no room to ask how the phoenix within the woman knew about Leska, nor did it matter. Let them know, let them all know.

'—then will you come and see your other sisters? You will come, won't you, Maximus? We've changed so *so* much since you last saw us. Truly, you would be so proud.'

They were reading my passions, using it against me.

I leaned in as flames licked over the woman's skin. Her irises spun with the fiery glare of the phoenix poisoning her. The voices, the possession, confirmed something else for me. It was too late to save the Gathrax twins. They, like Camron, hadn't simply been possessed, but became the monster that infected them. This was their doing.

There was no saving them, unless they chose. From the sound of it, they were cemented in their hate for me.

Justified, I supposed. I did tear their family apart.

'Kill us then, I sense the passion in you. Do it. You are so good at killing, Max. Father. Our brother. Who will be next...'

A deafening thwack sounded, followed by the stifling of the flames. The woman's burning eyes rolled into the back of her skull before she toppled sideways. Behind her stood another woman. Ocean azure eyes, freckled skin, thin pinched mouth.

'Leska.' Her name broke out of me.

'About fucking time, Max!' She glowered, the usual demanding tone I had grown familiar with was as strong as it had always been. She held the leg of a broken chair in both hands—it was the amplifier I had made for her.

'Sorry I'm late,' I said, as the battle still raged around us.

'Fashionable, I am sure.'

I couldn't blink for fear this was some illusion.

'Now, are you going to stand there gawping, or are you going to continue impressing me?' Her smile was enough to fuel me. It wouldn't last for long, not when I told her everything that had happened after she stepped into Camron's portal. Instead, I turned back around and joined the battle. The fight was easier

to navigate than revealing to the woman at my side that her
—*our* father was dead, and she was my sister.

The phoenix-possessed tumbled beneath the pressure of
our fight. In the eyes of every phoenix-possessed, I felt the presence of the twins lurking. It forged me ahead. If they watched, I
might as well give them a show.

My magic billowed out across the battle, sinking earth and
entrapping the possessed. I didn't stop, not until every last one
was dealt with. Then I was left stood in the middle of the torn,
muddied grounds, looking around as our numbers swept
through and dealt with the remaining possessed.

We will see you soon. The twins' words had been meant as
both a warning and a promise. I scanned the scene for them,
wondering where they lingered. As if my mind conjured them,
on the breeze I caught the faint giggling of two little girls.

Little devils.

A hand clamped down on my shoulder, startling me. Lightning broke across the sky, lifting the hairs on my arms.

'Dryads, Max.' It was Simion, all wide-eyed and worried.
Behind him stood Beatrice and Leska, each of them looking at
me with ash-coated faces pinched in worry. 'Careful.'

'Sorry,' I said, breathless. It took everything in me not to
cringe against the memory of the laughter. 'I just thought I
heard something.'

'The sound of victory,' Beatrice added, clearing grime from
her blade by wiping it across her leg.

Simion took my hand and squeezed, anchoring me to the
moment. As if his touch dispelled the roaring silence in my
skull, I was suddenly very aware of the crying and shouts that
still raged beyond the manor's walls.

'Max,' Leska said, stepping close, seeing through the façade
that rose over my expression. 'You're looking at me like you've
seen a ghost.'

Seeing her stole my mind from thoughts of the little devils, and returned it to what remained unspoken for Leska.

Her—*our* father's death.

Lilyth.

All of it.

'Not a ghost,' I said, unable to take my gaze off her. I was too weak, too pathetic to speak the truth aloud, but that didn't stop it ringing in my head. *A sister.*

CHAPTER 8

Dread settled in my stomach like a stone, sinking deep into the pits of a lake where the bottom seemed to not exist. It sank and sank, deeper and deeper, until there was no hope of ever retrieving it. This was my reality now. This was what I had waited for, travelled the Thassalic for.

Leska. She stood before me, staring daggers deep into my soul. It was as though she looked at me and through me, all at the same time.

I felt small, inconsequential, in a chair surrounded by the colour of my former rulers. Red. Gathrax red. It was easier to drink in those horrifying details than watch as the truth settled over Leska like the first snowfall of winter. Or how her legs seemed to give out under her, the slam of her body hitting the chair, the creak of its legs as the force rocked it back.

Focus. Breathe. I tore my attention from Leska as Beatrice stepped in behind her, offering comfort in the form of a hand on her shoulder. I was selfish, pathetic, weak. But none of that mattered, not in this room where the ghost of my past lingered.

The last time I had been in this room it was to share a meal before my unsuspecting handfasting to Camron Calzmir. I had sat in this very chair, drowning in the red-papered walls, decorated with the gilded glass frames containing the dried palms of long-dead Gathrax mages. There was an empty chair beside me, tucked neatly under the dark-wood table with its velvet crimson runner and lit candles down the middle. Camron had sat here. I reached out and brushed my fingers over the seat. It was still warm. Of course it wasn't Camron's doing, but his presence was everywhere. Everywhere but the unmarked skin of my arm where the fast-mark once was.

'So, he's dead,' Leska repeated, drawing me back to the here and now. 'But if that was it, you wouldn't look at me like that. Something else haunts you, Max. So say it. Nothing can be worse than knowing my father is dead.'

Tears pooled in her eyes, as they did mine. I could not blame her for the reaction. And she was right, Cyder's death wasn't the only secret I kept. Had our limited time together made it so easy for her to read my emotions? Hoping for some comfort, I gazed to Simion who stood against the far wall. His arms were crossed, his thumb caught between teeth as he surveyed the unfurling conflict before him. The small flames from the candle licked across his jaw, accentuating the lines of his face, his mouth, his exhaustion. It had been hours since we took back Gathrax manor—hours since the phoenix-possessed had been gathered like cattle to be healed by our gleamers—and yet he still wore his armour.

You can do this. His voice filled my mind, grazing the outer limits of my skull.

It will turn her world upside down.

Simion paused before replying. If he was prepared to tell me I was wrong, he didn't. Instead, when he finally filtered his voice into my mind, it was to offer comfort in a different way. *As yours has. As all of our worlds will be if Lilyth completes her campaign. The truth may be painful, but it is also the key to healing.*

Resilient tears clung to Leska's bright eyes. She was thinner than I last remembered, due to a lack of supplies within the manor. Dirt caked her skin; her hair was clumped together in bands of grease. She had been offered food, the chance to bathe, but she had refused. Until those she had guarded were seen to, she would not eat nor wash.

I caught Beatrice's gaze from where she stood behind Leska's shoulder. Her hand had yet to lift from Leska's shoulder. Perhaps it would've if Leska hadn't reached up and placed her own above Beatrice's, keeping her rooted in place.

Comfort came in many forms; I was just glad Leska had it.

'You're my...' I choked, hand slapping over my mouth as my body attempted to stop me from speaking. The moment I told her, there was no going back.

Leska leaned forward. Her fingers grasped the velvet table-runner and gathered it up in her fist.

I closed my eyes. 'My sister, Leska. Half-sister...'

It wasn't gargantuan, but a weight lifted from my shoulders. Silence followed, only broke by the quivering break of a breath. Everything was so still, so quiet, I was forced to open my eyes just to confirm I was still in this reality.

A single tear slipped from Leska's eye. She sagged forward, her bowed shoulders shaking. When she spoke, it was to the table. 'Is it true?'

Her question was for me, and also for the universe—for the phantom of her father, for Beatrice and Simion.

'It is,' Simion said, offering me a soft smile in an attempt to calm the storm inside of me.

I didn't know what I was expecting to come from this revelation. I'd replayed this moment over in my mind, going through all the different possibilities like differing stories in a bound anthology.

Leska was the most important thing in my life. Something I never thought possible only weeks before. But here she was, my last family, connected by blood. Everyone else had perished, become memories that I would be haunted by. But she was real, flesh and bone, my sister.

Leska broke her silence with a sob. No. She lifted her face up, exposing a curved smile that lifted over a face cursed with grief. 'For fuck's sake, and here I was thinking you were about to tell me the world was ending...'

I was far too shocked to react to her words. That was part of the story she had yet to learn. There was no time to correct Leska as she pushed up to standing, paced around the table. She gathered the front of my shirt in two fists and hoisted me up to standing. Strong arms gathered me up, firm hands patting my back with two powerful claps.

It took me a moment to hug her back.

'Hello, brother,' Leska muttered into my ear. The words were meant only for me. My skin reacted, covering in gooseflesh as I melted into her.

'Sister,' I replied, using a word I never believed I would say. 'Sounds odd, doesn't it?'

'And for a moment you had me thinking I was alone in this world. Poor little orphan Leska, whose father was a sadistic zealot who believed in world-eating parasites. When the real truth was standing before me all this time.' Leska pulled me at arm's length, her eyes drinking me in as though it was for the first time. 'Yes, to answer your question, it does sound odd, but it feels right.'

I was speechless. Not because I didn't have anything to say, but what had to come out of my mouth next would ruin this moment.

'Beside the freckles, you don't look much alike,' Beatrice said from across the room. 'Or is that because you've rearranged Maximus's nose so many times, you've beaten the similarities out of him?'

'Dryads, Bea. Time and place,' Simion chortled.

She raised her arms up in surrender. 'What, we were all thinking it!'

Leska released me. I sagged backwards a step, no longer free of every burden I had to depart. 'That isn't everything, is it?' Leska asked, reading my expression.

I shook my head, my tongue swelling in my mouth with all the secrets.

'Turns out Elder Cyder wasn't entirely the crazed man we believed him to be,' I said, unable to use the title for the man. Father. He didn't deserve it. 'Everything he was doing with the rebellion, with creating a force of fire-wielding humans. It wasn't to take down the Council, not completely. It was his way of protecting the world—protecting you.'

Leska's smile dropped, the harsh lines across her forehead deepening. I opened my mouth and told her everything. Every missing detail, every piece of the puzzle she had not been on the island to witness. It all spilled out of me. Perhaps I said too much, shared information that didn't matter. But there was comfort in relaying the secrets kept between the Council, Simion, Beatrice and me.

By the time I finished, the light beyond the window was waning. We were all sat in our respective chairs, Simion beside me, Beatrice beside Leska. No one had moved, no one spoke. The floor was mine to speak and ruin what little peace Leska may have just experienced.

'Do we have a chance,' Leska finally asked, 'against this Lilyth?'

My heart thundered in my chest, beating against my ribs with the demand for release. 'We have to believe we do.'

I had just told her about the bounty of Heart Oak cuttings I had brought to the South with me. Already battlemages and their dragons were carrying away pieces of Gathrax manor. By morning, the rest would be shipped to the Zendina, and what was left of the Romar Kingdom. Captain Trelem had strict instructions, with a note to pass on with the bounty. I trusted her. If anyone could ride the ocean like a stead, it was her.

'The South has never had access to such power,' Leska confirmed what we already knew. 'It may help us, but we are still facing an unknown enemy, which puts this Lilyth a few leagues ahead of us.'

In the past, the South had only been four greedy mages, powerful people who wanted the magic to themselves. Now, I wanted as much of the Southern populous to have the chance to have an amplifier. Untrained mages were better than nothing, and we would need as much magic at our disposal to face Lilyth when she reached us.

'Which has to change. To have a chance, we need as much force to resist Lilyth—'

'To face an unknown enemy is to fail before you begin. If we do not know what we should expect, then we are simply sending people to their slaughter, Max.'

Leska was right, but that wasn't what mattered. 'And if we do not try, we die. I have seen a world that faced Lilyth and didn't survive. It is death and ruin unlike anything you could imagine. We have to try.'

'They need to know what they are facing.' Leska pointed to the door, towards everyone outside it. 'Otherwise, all of this, the passing out of Heart Oak, the creation of an army, it will be pointless.'

'Sparking mass hysteria now will only separate us,' Simion added, his hand squeezing my knee beneath the table. 'Until we can gather more information about Lilyth, then there is nothing to share. We believe my... my mother...'

I looked to him, watching the pain at the use of her title. A proud smile tugged at my lips, one I didn't bother to hide.

'... is believed to have some knowledge on who Lilyth is. My aunt is currently exhausting all avenues to find her.'

Beatrice kept silent, although I could tell from her expression that she still believed this to be a waste of time.

'I appreciate the sentiment. But what are we sitting around waiting for?' Leska stood, Beatrice joining her. 'There is a literal demonic entity falling through our skies. There are already questions about it. We need to tell those people outside this room, prepare them.'

'Finally, someone with a brain,' Beatrice said, arms crossing over her chest.

My heart had wormed itself into my throat, cantering wildly. 'And we will. I just need more time.'

'You've had time. Days. What has been stopping you from—'

'You,' I snapped, wide-eyed and breathless. 'My focus has been getting you.'

That stopped Leska for a moment.

'I know this is a lot to take in, believe me. But this is the moment we need to all stay on the same page, even if that page is only partially filled with information. I will continue to speak with the dryads. They will share their... memories.' That was a partial lie. I wasn't ready for the questions they would ask about the dryads' power to visit the past. I hadn't even started to understand it myself. 'I can try and glean as much information as I can, whilst we hope Celia Hawthorn is found.'

'Everything and everyone has a weakness,' Beatrice said. I was thankful for her calm nature; it settled me enough to gather my composure again. 'We simply need to find Lilyth's flaw and exploit it. If what Max has said is true, she was weak when she first came to Aldian. Weak enough to leave before she finished her task of damnation. Find out what and why, then we simply do that. History always finds a way to repeat itself. Instead of fearing it, let's harness it.'

'Not tonight,' Simion added, knowing he was keeping me from visiting the dryads. 'We all deserve to rest. Eat, sleep. The dryads can wait until tomorrow. There is still the issue of the Gathrax twins to deal with.'

'One hurdle at a time.' I placed my fingers over Simion's hand, delighting in his warmth. 'But Leska is right, Simion. It can't wait. I must go tonight. We need this knowledge. We deserve answers.'

'Then I will come with you.' Leska sparked some relief with her offer, one I did not refuse. 'Call it bonding time with the brother I have only just found.'

What I didn't tell him was the other reason I longed to visit the dryads. Being back here, in the South, a place I had called home for the majority of my life, made me crave my parents. Now I knew I could see them again, it was a drug I couldn't refuse.

Inyris had been quiet in my mind until I reached out for her. I understood Simion was protective over me, but I would be fine with my dragon close. I shook my head. 'Leska will oversee me. Inyris hardly strays far. There is something I need for you to do.'

Simion couldn't refuse me. Of all the power he had, that was not one skill he harboured. 'Anything.'

'Prepare a letter to King Zendina. Explain what we have sent to his land and what he is to do with it. It is best he is prepared for the shipment before he sees it and sinks it, and the Heart Oak, to the depths of the Thassalic.'

I moved my gaze to Beatrice. There was no denying her eyes kept shifting to Leska, waiting and watching. 'Bea. Can you see to the phoenix-possessed? Make sure they, too, are offered Heart Oak, as well as every civilian close enough to the manor. Until the reserves run out, I want amplifiers in as many hands as possible.'

To my relief, she nodded. Beatrice knew the importance of this plan. Although my mother was dead, her body formed into my very own Heart Oak, bringing the pieces back to the South felt as though she was here with me. This was Deborah Oaken's legacy.

'Leave the twins to me. I don't think we need to waste reserves finding them...' Their giggles haunted my mind even now. 'They are close. I am sure they will show themselves when they are ready. Until then, we use every second possible to continue our preparation to save our world.'

'And me, brother?' Leska asked, one sharp brow raised. 'Because unlike these two, if you ask me to simply rest after our visit to the dryads, I will break that nose again.'

I swallowed hard, the sound audible. 'They will need training. The basics. And I know of someone who has the ability to whip them all into shape.'

'We will need to know what type of mage they are first. I can help with battlemages, but gleaming is out of my skill limit.'

'It isn't out of mine,' Simion added.

'You need to continue your own training,' I replied. 'As will the other phoenix-possessed who agree to join us. Oversee that, help them to grasp this new power. I will find another to cover the gleamers' training, we have an abundance of skilled mages with us.'

'If we are going to ask the possessed to stand beside us, they deserve a title that fits their abilities,' Simion said, rolling his shoulders back.

'What do you suggest, brother?' Bea asked, chewing her lower lip.

'Sorcerers. A new name for those wielding a new type of magic.'

'Then it is agreed. Simion will train the sorcerers,' I said, overcome with pride. Simion was right, the legion of fire-wielders was great now. They deserved a title. They were not survivors of a possession, but gifted with magic just as us mages were gifted the power over earth.

'Spoken like a true King,' Leska said with a smile that sang of pride.

'Wait, doesn't that make you a princess, Leska?' Beatrice asked with a wink, knowing the stone she was turning over with her question.

I rolled my eyes. 'I am no King, Bea.'

'Tell that to everyone who is following you. You may not wear a crown, my friend, but it seems your bloodline is far too potent to pretend you don't have authority running through those veins. Dryad-born.'

Dryad-born. Yet another title to add to my ever-growing list, except this one I didn't mind as much.

I stood, forcing Simion's hand to fall from my leg. 'Let's save the world, then we can talk about King, crowns and princesses.'

My gaze fell beyond the window. The gargantuan roots Leska had wrapped around the manor blocked most of the view, but I still caught a glimpse of a streak of red far up in the darkening sky.

It was Leska who asked the final question. I hadn't noticed as she came to stand beside me, shoulder to shoulder, staring out at the same vision. 'Do we know how long we have, before our damnation finally arrives?'

'Soon,' I answered. Not because I knew the answer completely, but more that felt it in my bones and blood. '*She* is close.'

With that, we departed the room. There were endless things to do. It was agreed that Leska would meet me at sundown, allowing us all time to settle, wash and fix ourselves up after the battle. Simion was the last to leave me. He placed a lingering kiss to my cheek and whispered as though the room was not empty but full of people.

'I am proud of you, my love.'

'Don't say that too soon, I wouldn't want to shatter your illusion of me.'

He exhaled through his nose, fingers tracing the lines of my jaw. 'Impossible.'

I closed my eyes as a rush of his power slipped into my mind. It was comforting, but also distracting. If he continued, I wouldn't leave this room, wouldn't leave him.

'Meet me, later. Tonight. When everything you need to achieve is finished.'

His smile licked up the corners of his mouth, glittering his eyes with an inner light. 'Tell me where and I will be there.'

'The library,' I said, pulling back. 'I trust you remember where it is during your time as an undercover servant?'

'How could I ever forget. And what is it you wish to do in the library?'

Dryads, so many things. I pushed him away. 'Reading, what else?'

Simion shrugged, the flames across the candles sparking with more of his essence. 'Just what I thought.'

As light flared, I noticed there was something else lingering in those golden eyes. *Passion.* The poison left over by the phoenix feather, something that had seemed to build in him for days.

'Keep Inyris close,' Simion said, although the warning was palpable. 'And Leska even closer. If there are any issues, I will be there.'

'Between the dryads, Leska and Inyris, it would take a fool to sneak up on me. I think I can deal with two twisted children.'

Simion didn't seem to believe my dismissal of the twins, nor did I.

I left Simion, although his warmth didn't leave me. It followed me through the busied manor, as I passed rooms full of gleamers and newly healed phoenix-possessed victims. So many stones had been turned, secrets exposed. A cold chill crept over my skin as I thought about the Gathrax twins. Even the wind seemed to whisper a warning about them.

Little devils. Little devils. Little. Devils.

CHAPTER 9

I found Leska in the kitchens much later that afternoon. We had all been occupied with tasks, preparing the manor to house the new sorcerers we had relieved from their possession. I had visited Gathrax town, surveying the damage and helping the remaining townsfolk.

Simion didn't want me to leave the manor, for fear the twins would take that moment to accost me. But I found it important my presence was felt within the South. I wanted them to know I was here, that I had not turned my back on them.

It was close to dusk before I returned to the manor with supplies in tow. There was not a room without people in it. The building was bustling with activity—even the gardens had been turned into a camp for those who could not fit inside.

Dragons circled the sky, keeping enemies away whilst surveying for the two players in this game that had still not revealed themselves. The little devils. It would only be a matter of time, I knew that.

'Celebrating, or drinking your sorrows?' I asked, as I rounded into the kitchens.

'A little bit of both,' Leska said, lifting a dusty bottle of wine in her hand, the cork on the floor, forgotten. Her mouth was stained red with the liquid, her teeth darkened. And her gaze was lost, as it often seemed to be, to something unimportant.

'Care for some company?'

She didn't look up at me when she replied. 'Sure. Although I'm not up for talking about our feelings, Max. Not all of us can vocalise it so easily.'

I screwed my mouth, trying not to let the pain of rejection make me turn away. 'There is something I want to show you before I commune with the dryads.'

'It's late.'

I shrugged. 'I'm aware.'

Simion was waiting for me in the library, and I wanted nothing more than to run to him. But my desire for answers outweighed anything else, and as it was getting dark, it was the best time to enter Galloway Forest and find those answers.

'Then the bottle can keep you company, bring it with you.'

Her brows rose at that, so did her annoyance. 'You seem to be taking to the mantel of annoying sibling rather well. Like a duck to water.'

'You have no idea,' I said, hooking my arm in hers. 'I'm sure after you see what I have done, you would happily reconsider the offer of breaking my nose.'

I led Leska through the manor, knowing exactly where I was going.

'Where are you taking me, Max?'

The sorcerer I had asked to prepare Leska's surprise had brought it out here. I had found it an odd choice of place, but didn't question it. 'An old out-building that was used for prayer during the reign of the first Southern mages.'

'Sounds ominous,' she replied, hugging her arms around herself.

'I know.' I had asked for the gift to be brought to Leska's

rooms, but clearly that request was ignored. And there had been no time to rearrange it to be moved, not at such a late hour.

My breath caught when I saw the stone building in the distance. I had last seen it during my handfasting ceremony to Camron. She didn't know the importance of this building to me, but that wasn't what mattered. At least this exchange would drown old memories and replace them with new ones.

It had been as I last left it. Galloway Forest had engulfed the back of it. Inside, where I had stood with cords of blue and red tied around my arm, there was now a gaping hole giving view to the belly of a forest.

Walking up the aisle with Leska was strange. I took every step carefully, half expecting to hear Jonathan Gathrax announce his final play, to see Camron stand from the pews— which were now tipped over—and feel the shock as an unsuspecting crowd watched on. But we were alone. Me and the half-sister I never knew I had. Just as I had when I first entered all that time ago, my skin was not marked by silver fast lines.

The only thing different was the mannequin waiting at the end of the aisle. The gift was what it wore.

Leska stood before it, silent and unreadable. The bottle of red wine had smashed over the slabbed floor, glass spread out amongst the puddle of crimson liquid. I bit at the skin around my nails, unsure if I had made the biggest mistake. Waiting for her to speak was torture.

'You... you did this?'

I could barely look at the armour set without a wave of sickness rearing in my stomach. 'With some help. I like to think I'm talented, but this is beyond my capabilities.'

Leska crashed into me with force, wrapping her arms around me and squeezing. Dryads, she was strong. I could barely breathe. To anyone watching, it would seem like her single goal was to suffocate me, break my ribs and leave me in a crumbled heap on the floor. But I knew this was different.

'Thank you, Max.'

I returned the embrace, feeling partly strange to touch her but also revelling in it.

The armour was a replica of the one Camron had worn when he first infiltrated Wycombe. Red dragon scales over-lapped across a bodice designed for Leska. Amongst the red were flashes of gold and black. Inyris and Glamora had been adamant that they wanted to offer a part of themselves to Leska. I had commissioned it to be made during our journey to the South, and there were still alterations to finish.

Regardless of our shared blood, I had still taken something dear to Leska. Even if it was her father who orchestrated it, I had been the one to kill the man who had her heart. And I had no doubt that her being here, in the South, was a painful reminder to what she had lost.

'I may not be able to offer you something that belonged to Aaron, but I hope this helps make you feel closer to him.'

It was a risk, giving Leska something made from the corpse of her love's dragon. But unlike Camron, I didn't make it with ill-intention. I had used the scales that had been gathered, giving them a meaningful purpose.

'How did you...' Leska stepped in, running her hands over the polished scales, '... manage this? I mean, it is beautiful, but you didn't need to do this.'

'I didn't do it because I needed to, Leska. I did it because I wanted to. There is a difference. But, don't kill me, I may have snuck into your rooms at Saylam Academy and taken a set of clothing. The smithy Beatrice used to work in town were able to put this together based off those measurements. Of course, if it doesn't fit, then we can send it back for alterations, and it will take time to finish... but I wanted you to have it.'

Tears fell silently down her cheeks. Leska opened her mouth to say something, but choked. Seeing her reaction tugged at my heart. It was important Leska had something to remind her. And I no longer blamed Aaron for attempting to kill me. He was simply a weapon used by another—Cyder.

Don't blame the tool, but the person who wields it. It was a Southern saying, after all.

'So I take it from the tears that you don't want to break my nose?'

She half sobbed, half laughed, shooting me a stare. 'No, Max. This was... nice.'

'Nice?' I tipped my head to the side.

'Believe it or not, but I missed you. Perhaps it was my blood, calling like to like, but the time I spent within this manor, keeping the phoenix-possessed out, it was you I thought about. And... Aaron.'

'So I am not the annoying brother you expected?' What I didn't want to say was I would happily annoy her. Because that meant we were alive, together, privileged enough to piss one another off.

'Far from it,' she replied, 'and, anyway, you are King now, Maximus. I have heard it, through the Gathrax estate, amongst those I had been stuck with in the manor. Your name has rung throughout these lands, even though you've been far from them.'

My heart sank, deep and fast, jolting in my stomach with a thud. 'How do I tell them it is not a title I desire?'

Leska looked at me and nothing else. 'To desire power, Max, means you are not responsible enough to have it. The people need someone to look to, to know that their interests are kept in mind. You are that person for them. I see that now—'

The door slammed closed at our backs, silencing Leska. Icy fear crept over my skin as we both spun around to face it. Everything was so silent. Through the shadows I searched for them, hearing the scuttling of feet, the breathy giggles of something small. Then the sickly sweet tone of a young girl.

'Hello, *brother*.'

CHAPTER 10

The Gathrax twins separated from the shadows, one before the door, the other directly behind us. I snapped my neck just to watch them both, not wanting to lose sight of one for a single second. As the title of brother rippled across my skin, I drank them in. All ginger curls, lithe bodies and menacing fire-red eyes. Wings of pure flame—writhing reds, oranges and golds—protruding from their backs. These were not phoenix-possessed. No. Like Camron, they had become one with the creature inside of them.

Little devils. They had found me, before I found them.

It was pieces of a puzzle slotting together. The sorcerer putting the armour here, not where I had asked. But we had freed them of the possession, their mind should have been their own again...

'Passion,' one of the twins said. 'You may take our people away from us, but that doesn't stop their passions from being free to control. Silly, silly Max.'

'So you've finally got me,' I said, placing myself before Leska slowly.

'I told you we would find you,' the other twin stepped towards me, leaving her sister to guard the door.

My eyes snapped from her fire-red eyes to what rested on her head. It stopped me. A crown made not from metal but flame. The sharpened points were writhing tongues of gold fire, the band black as the night itself.

It was far too big for the little girl's head, sitting at an awkward angle. But even I sensed the otherworldly power radiating off it. I had seen it before, but in the shock of their presence... I couldn't place it.

'And who the *fuck* are you?' Leska pressed into my side, power radiating off her.

'The little devils I told you about,' I replied, magic flooding every bone and vein.

'He remembers us,' one sang to the other's delight.

'He does. He does. But does he remember what he took from us?'

Leska's shoulder brushed mine. It wasn't until then I realised she was without her amplifier. 'Max... behind me.'

Even without her magic, Leska was formidable. I knew that all too well, but still, when I moved, it was to place myself before her.

I couldn't speak as the reality faced me. These children, no matter what I remembered them as, no matter what they had become... I had taken something from them.

'Everything,' they answered in perfect unison. 'Our father. Our brother. Our home. Our power...'

That was why they manipulated the sorcerer to place the armour here. This was where I killed their father.

Giggles erupted as flames exploded from the candles around us. I flinched against the sudden heat.

'... but we have found new power now, haven't we, sister?'

'Yes, my sister. We have indeed,' the one wearing the crown said. 'A gift from your dearly departed husband. He left it with us, when he came to claim you from the North. We've looked after it ever since. Pretty, isn't it, sister?'

'Yes,' the other twin replied. 'Pretty *powerful*.'

They both chuckled, giggles scoring over my skin. Inyris was suddenly tugging on my mind, reaching across our tether, ready to—

'Ah, ah, ah.' One of the girls flashed with unnatural speed, stopping short of where I stood. A harsh finger pointed into my chest, making the material hiss and burn until her nail scorched skin. 'Do you not want to know what we are here for, before you send for your little beast?'

'Pretty golden dragon,' the other joined. 'I could make beautiful gowns with her scales...'

'Careful,' I hissed, attempting not to flinch from her nail. 'I may be able to command her away, but Inyris has a mind of her own. If she sees fit to come and feast on you, that is her choice, not mine.'

Fear was not something the twins understood. That was clear as they laughed off my threat, and even more so when they disregarded Leska's seething.

'Now, *little girls*, outside that door are countless mages, dragons and dryads. One thought and we would be overrun, one signal and this conversation will be over.'

'She missed something,' one twin sang as she skipped around us, circling like a hunter to prey.

'Yes, you missed the phoenixes. Because we have many waiting... lots and lots.' The crown flashed with heat and light, bathing my skin in the aching heat of fire. She tapped the crown with her nail, the sound making my skin cringe. 'And I control them, each and every one. I am their Queen. Would you care for me to prove it to you, *brother*?'

More phoenixes? We had barely survived fighting one, let alone more.

The ground shuddered with magic, a warning for the twins.

'What are you going to do about it? Kill us? No, no, no. That is Max's passion. He likes killing, doesn't he? It is in your poisoned blood...' She looked to the ground at our side, pointing at something that wasn't there now... but had been. 'Daddy died right there. Our *real* brother died outside in the forest, all alone. But you do not need reminding of that...'

'And I am sure you have not come all this way just to reap an apology from me, have you?' I tried to keep my voice steady, even if my entire body trembled. 'So, get to the point. What do you want?'

I couldn't take my eyes off the little girl before me. She was all-consuming, devouring.

'We want balance. Payment. Our daddy was killed by your husband, so we can't have him. Then there was your daddy, the one whose blood runs in your veins. We liked him... he was helpful, he wanted more phoenix-possessed, so he left us alone to make them. But then he died too. Then your mother became a tree, so we couldn't have her. That leaves one more person...'

'Finish this before it begins,' Leska snapped at my side. Even then I could barely take my eyes off the swirling pits of gold that was the little girl. She entranced me with her power.

'That leaves us with *her*.'

Whatever spell they held over me broke. Shattered. I spun around to find Leska, immobilised, as one of the twins hugged her middle. It was a strange thing to see. An embrace. Except, there was nothing loving about it. Not as the licking black flames of wytchfire slowly crept towards Leska's skin.

'No.' It was all I could manage. One wrong move, one wrong word, and it would be over.

'She will burn,' the twin at my back said. 'Unless...'

'Max, I am fine.' Leska's jaw tightened, but there was something peaceful in her eyes. 'Do not give them anything.'

'Lilyth is nearly here,' the crown-wearing twin sneered. 'She will be so proud of us. She will let us keep her crown and rule over the phoenixes. She will, she will.'

I forced her words to the back of my mind, ignoring how calmly Leska reacted to the destructive flames inching towards her. 'Lilyth will destroy us all,' I said.

'Wrong. She will love us. Because we will be the ones to destroy you. Dryad-born. But first we will melt the flesh from your dear sister. Unless...'

'Unless what,' I snapped, caring nothing about queens, crowns, phoenixes or Lilyth. I only cared about Leska.

Time stretched to uncomfortable limits. I waited for the answer, but they were toying with me. And I knew, before she opened her mouth to speak, that there was never another option.

'Maximus, do you know what our family enjoy most of all?' the crown-wearing twin asked.

I did. I heard the answer in my mind. Regardless, another creature lingered in my thoughts, waiting. I had to bide some time. 'If you harm her...'

'That would all depend on if you win or not.'

I refused to respond, caring only for Leska and how she closed her eyes, prepared for the flesh-eating fire to consume her. 'I am not here to play games that you have already lost.'

'Spoil sport.'

'Max,' Leska growled, cringing at the creeping black flame. I couldn't tell her to hold on, I couldn't reveal what was seconds away from coming. All I could do was hope she read my expression and the promise that I would let nothing happen to her.

I snapped, seething as though a fire boiled beneath my skin. 'Tell me what you want, no one needs to get hurt.'

'We do *love* the hunt.'

The hunt—a Gathrax family tradition.

'Did you give Julian that chance?' one of them squawked.

'Or our father!' spat the second.

'No.' The answer was simple. There was nothing else I could say to take away from the fact I had killed their family. 'If you want me, then take me. Not... her...'

'We do, don't we, sister. Killing you would be too easy. First, we want to break your heart. We want you to feel the pain you caused our family. That is a punishment worthy for you.'

A violent whoosh of air spread beside Leska. It blasted boiling air over the room. A feather was thrown into flame, opening a portal. It spun to life, spreading outwards in a disc.

There was no room to think, no room to counter their magic, as the little girl holding Leska forced them both into the portal. The other jolted towards it just as fury blinded me.

Beneath her bare feet, the ground split. Roots, the same that had killed her father, speared from the floor. She threw herself skywards, wings beating, scorching air blasting over me. My skin singed, but I fought on, trying to get through.

I couldn't see her, but somewhere through that portal, muffled by flames and panic, Leska cried out. My fist grasped feathers and pulled back.

In a final desperate attempt, too late, Inyris tore the stone roof from the building. Her jaw reached down, snapping towards the escaping girl. As ice magic built in her jaw, the twin gathered power too. Frost and flame crashed together. I was torn from the ground, thrown backwards, stopping only when the blunt force of stone smashed behind me.

I slumped, falling to the ground, pain radiating through my head. Blinking through the agony, as the corners of my vision darkened, I watched the final twin throw herself through the portal. It closed, as did my eyes. Then there was nothing but haunting darkness and silence.

* * *

Simion ran his fingers over the back of my head, healing the wound there. I closed my eyes, focusing on the soft caress of his magic. But nothing took my mind off the pain of knowing Leska had been taken.

My hair was matted with blood, my body bruised, and all I cared about was the feathers still gripped in my hands.

'This isn't safe,' Beatrice snapped, pacing a track into the ground at her feet. 'We can't just throw everything away without carefully planning our next move.'

I couldn't find the words; all I could focus on was the heart-beat in my fingertips and Simion's breathing.

'And I can't sit and wait for a plan to form, Bea. They have Leska.' A growl built in my throat, causing my entire body to tremble. 'If I don't go alone, they will kill her. The only way of succeeding is beating them at the hunt. I know the rules, we both do.'

No one could refuse me that. The threat was clear.

'Help me, Simion,' Beatrice said with a wave of her hand, continuing her pacing. 'He'll listen to you.'

'You know as well as I, Maximus will make his own mind up.' A firm hand rested on my shoulder and squeezed. A kiss followed, soft and steady, planted upon my cheek.

'So you are comfortable sending him to face unknown dangers? I'm not worried about the twins, I am worried about everything else lurking in the shadows in Calzmir lands. If what they said about controlling phoenixes is true, then that should be our focus. We don't even know where they have taken Leska—'

'I do.' My gaze was lost to a spot on the wall, staring directly into the painted eyes of Mage Damian Gathrax the Red. 'They called it the hunt, Bea. The Gathrax family always hosted it...'

From the glint in her golden eyes, I knew she clicked as to what I was thinking. Her gaze travelled to the stain-glass window, specifically to the forest lurking far beyond it. 'You think they are in Galloway Forest?'

I nodded. This was all part of their plan to get to me.

It was Simion who spoke my next thought aloud. 'You won't be alone.'

'Exactly,' I said, feeling the blood rush to my feet. 'I will have the dryads.'

'I don't like this,' Beatrice added.

'Nor do I.' I swallowed hard, trying to focus more on Simion's touch as he cleared my body of any mark left over from the attack. 'But I can't lose Leska...'

A moment before Inyris snatched me into her mind, I saw Beatrice's eyes glaze over with the same expression. Then I was spearing through the sky, cool wind tickling my scales. Ice built in my throat as the canopy of Galloway Forest itched my under-belly. Glamora was there. I looked at her—no, Inyris did—and the black-scaled dragon glanced back. In her bright eyes I saw Beatrice, a ring of gold to signify the shared moment.

Panic built in my powerful chest like a drum. It took me a moment to discern what it was that caused the dragon so much intense emotion. When I did, my human heart almost stopped.

The comet was closer than it had been before. All across the horizon the sky was spoiled in an ominous glow of red. It blanketed everything in the colour I hated most. It was as though the comet gave a warning to the entire world, bathing everything in the reflective glow of a trial by fire.

'Tell me.' Simion was knelt before me, my face in his hands. I snapped back into the room so suddenly I saw double. Beatrice wobbled on both feet, hands outstretched as she reached something to steady herself. 'What did you see?'

This was wrong, all so wrong. Yet I couldn't help but think it was planned.

'Lilyth,' I spoke the name with enough conviction to

conjure her myself. 'She has almost reached us. We are running out of time.'

Simion snapped his attention to his sister, who nodded in confirmation.

'How long?' he asked.

The world-shattering boom answered. As the comet entered Aldian's sky, it sent a powerful ripple out beneath it. It took a second for the window to shatter to pieces. Simion bowed himself over me, shielding me from the raining glass. My ears were ringing, everything muffled as though I was buried beneath water.

What followed was the most powerful silence I had ever experienced. There was nothing. All we could do was look at once another, a knowing understanding shared between us. Shards of glass fell from Beatrice as she stood, her face ashen with fear. Simion refused to let go of me, even with blood dripping from his ears. Even Inyris was quiet in my mind, refusing to share her emotions with me.

Everything stained with the red glow.

'*A sky on fire.*' The words tumbled out of me, still so faint my voice sounded strange. 'This is the same vision the Heart Oak showed me...'

Simion was looking to his hands, distracted. 'My power... the fire, it feels... stronger.'

I felt it too, an unnatural heat to the air, as though the comet was feeding Simion's power.

'She's close,' Bea said, 'We need to act. Gather the numbers, tell people what they are about to face.'

Even if we did not know what that was. I never got a chance to speak with the dryads, to glean answers.

There was something different in the air. A charge. Whatever power Lilyth had, it practically scratched over my skin.

'We are not ready...'

The world beyond the manor erupted into chaos. I was the

first to the window, gazing out as birds of flame flew across the sky, clashing head-on with dragons. The phoenixes—the very ones the twins had warned of. If the comet was affecting Simion's magic, it would be doing the same to the phoenixes.

They were using the charged power to attack now. The perfect moment.

I looked beyond the shattered window, taking in the grounds around the manor. They filled with fire as people ran out from conjured portals. Fire dripped across scorched earth, spreading like rivers towards the manor. Beneath the glow of red, my people joined the fight.

Mages. Sorcerers. As one, their battle cry loud enough for Lilyth to hear, they faced their enemy with no hesitation.

'Go,' I said to Beatrice and Simion, although I longed for them to never leave the protection of this room. 'Hold them off for as long as you can...'

Within the blink of an eye, Beatrice crossed the room and grasped me. She stared deep in my soul, eyes shivering as tears filled them. 'Don't you dare fucking die, Max.'

A choked sob forced its way out my throat. 'You too, friend.'

There was a moment of hesitation before Beatrice turned on her heel and ran from the room.

'You're not going to let me come with you,' Simion said, his essence flickering as his emotions spiked. 'Are you?'

'No,' I replied, placing one of the phoenix feathers on his palm, before I curled his fingers around it. 'I need you to stay here and keep as many people alive as you possible can. This is plain, the twins knew when to strike us. Fight fire with fire. We are going to need as many of the sorcerers to go against the phoenixes if we hope to have a chance.'

'Then I don't need to repeat what Beatrice has asked of you?'

I admired Simion's calmness. Dryads, what I would do to lose myself in it and not leave this room.

'I will come back,' I said, stroking the side of his face. 'I couldn't just leave and never come back.'

Simion caught his lower lip between his teeth, eyes flickering over me. He knew what I needed of him. But not before he gave into his own wants. 'Good. Because the promise of a night at the library still stands when this is over. You will meet me there. Promise me.'

I nodded, holding back my panic. 'I promise.'

His lips found mine as the world rocked in battle. Bathed in the light of the comet, with the backdrop of gods fighting gods, magic against magic, he kissed me. It was the type of lingering kiss that spoke a million words, and none at the same time. It was the type that drove a person mad with desire.

Come back to me, Maximus Oaken.

I could never leave you, Simion Hawthorn.

Flame sparked across his hand, curling around the phoenix feather. It combusted into beautiful gold tongues of fire, until it expanded outwards, revealing the doorway to darkness. I had no doubt the twins would be ready. In fact, I could almost hear their haunting giggles through the rushing air and flame, enticing me to find them. To play hide and seek.

To join *the hunt*.

CHAPTER 11

Beneath the overwhelming glow from the comet, I could see every detail in the belly of Galloway Forest. It bathed the trees, the ground, the wild fern and bracken. The forest was still a maze. A place a person could lose themselves, where lost souls were picked off by dryads.

I recognised this exact location, not through its features but through a *feeling*. The familiarity of the trees tugged at a memory, one I had buried for some time. This was where Julian had chased me. Where he had taunted me, forced his body on mine and held me down. This... this was where I had killed him.

One of the twins stood waiting for me, her hands crossed behind her back, a sickly smile sliced across her chubby-cheeked face. It didn't take much for me to notice she was without the crown of flames. It must have been with the other. 'We were beginning to think you didn't want to play with us.' Her pout was forced, the bottom lip extending outwards as she feigned the emotion.

'I should have known,' I said to the dark, 'of all the places you wanted to punish me, this would be it.'

The silence was heavy. Far off in the distance, I could just about hear the battle that waged on at Gathrax manor. It was a draw, pulling me back, knowing who I had left behind. The twin looked over my shoulder, lifting onto her tiptoes, fiery golden wings fluttering at her back.

'It doesn't sound good back there, does it, Maximus?'

I made myself focus on her, not the distant screams, roars and caws. 'What have you done with Leska?'

Her smile faded, revealing a scowl in its place. 'Well, if I told you that, then it would not be a fun game.'

'I am in no mood to play games,' I hissed, stepping forward, calling on my magic until silver cords erupted between me and every earth-bound thing around me. The dryads were close, but waiting, just as I had told them in my command. I couldn't risk the twins knowing I was not, in fact, alone. Not when Leska's life was at risk. 'How do I know she isn't already...'

'Dead?' the little girl said, harsh and sharp as a blade. 'Because that would be too boring. Too... how would Father have put it... predictable. Yes, that.'

I took another step, sensing the dirt and mud shift beneath her feet. One grasp, one move and I could engulf her. It wouldn't take much.

'Ah, ah, ah, Maximus. If you harm me, my sister will know. We see your passions, your wants. But if you wish to see your dearest sister again, you should listen to the rules of our game.'

'The hunt is simple,' I said. 'I've beat it before, and I will beat it again.'

'Then you are ready to begin?' She tilted her head, inquisitively drinking me in with fire-red eyes against porcelain skin.

'I am,' I said, preparing myself, unable to ignore the utterly thunderous crash of my heart and thrashing of anxiety.

It didn't need to be said to know what I was hunting. Leska. I had to find her. I hadn't traversed the Thassalic, hadn't done everything up until this point, just to lose her.

I would rather perish than fail, and from the gleam in the little girl's eyes, she understood that.

'Begin it then.'

'Oh,' she laughed, 'it has already begun.'

There was no time to contemplate why she bent her knees like a cat. Why she giggled at me as though I was the fool. When she spoke the word, it transported me to another time.

'Run.'

Black flame hissed towards me, spat beyond her thin lips. I barely had a chance to dive to the side before the heat crashed into a tree at my back. Wood erupted in wytchfire, completely engulfed until it stood as a pillar of black light.

I wasn't partaking as the hunter.

I was the prey. And so, I *ran*.

'Run rabbit, run rabbit, run, run, run...'

The taunt rose behind me as another bout of flame shot my way. I caught only a glance to know she followed. The twisted little girl flew through the air, wings beating boiling air against the ground, scorching everything beneath her.

Every direction I took was met with more fire. It spewed from her fingers, her tongue, her wings. My lungs ached with every inhale of acrid smoke and heat, my skin itched beneath my clothes as the forest became overwhelming.

I reached out with my essence, coiling magic around the heavy limbs of branches above me. One thought, one tug of my fist and they fell. The ground shuddered beneath the force. I hoped one would catch the girl, knocking her from the air.

They didn't. Any that came close exploded in shards of splinters and flame. Where they landed on the earth, more fires brewed, until it seemed the very earth was made from the element.

My body was different this time I ran through Galloway Forest. It was stronger, imbued with magic and training. I threw myself over roots, vaulting over anything in my way just to keep a distance.

'I'll burn you, little rabbit,' she sang, 'scorch the meat from your bones and feed you to the great mother. I am her favoured.'

I stopped dead in my tracks, turning back to face her. I reached up to the sky, ripping devil's ivy from the trunks of trees until they reached upwards like a web. Strands wrapped around the girl's ankles, yanking her backwards. She might have been able to burn herself free, but I continued to conjure more and more, tying her up, entangling her limbs in my power.

'If you think Lilyth will spare you,' I shouted, breathless, 'you are wrong. Lilyth has no favoured. She only ruins and razes.'

Vines hissed, burned apart by flame, only to be replaced by more. I wrapped them around her wrists, her legs, her waist until she was trapped once again.

'But you are wrong, for I am her Queen,' she seethed, fighting against my magic. 'Bearer of the crown. Her flame. She will never harm me...'

I could have ended her, but she was only a child. And doing anything to hurt her would lead to Leska's demise. Leska, who I had to find. Leska who, at any moment, would burn just as the trees did in the little girl's wake.

'If you are Lilyth's Queen, then where is your crown?'

That stopped her, just as I hoped it would. 'My sister has it.'

'Then that makes *her* the Queen, does it not?'

Every vine dissipated beneath the little girl's fire. Her wings flapped with vigour, turning every stand to cinders. I could have conjured more, but I hoped I didn't need to. From the look that pinched her face, the way her skin reddened with anger, which overspilled in her feral scream.

'I am the Queen, me. I am. Not her. I am!'

'There are two of you, and only one crown.' My heart hammered in my chest. It took everything in my being to steady myself. Something was important about this crown—I knew it. Still, my mind reached for where I had seen it before. Far in the corners of my frantic thoughts, the truth was just out of reach. 'Lilyth is close. If I was you, I would go and get that crown back from your sister before she arrives. Or else...'

That was the thing about children. Their passions were limited, selfish. I could not control hers, but I could use her for my gain. I had seen these girls fight over things before, scratching with nails as my mother forced them to share.

But the Gathrax twins never shared. Not anything and certainly not the promise of being a phoenix Queen.

She turned, aiming back towards the flame ridden forest. I knew, in that moment, she was running straight in the direction of her sister. Which meant that was where I would find Leska.

This time, I ran to follow her. She flew with a speed that was unnatural, powered by wings she shouldn't have. If it wasn't for the line of wytchfire left in her wake, I may have never found her.

'I am the Queen, give it to me,' she bellowed, her furious, jealous cry echoing around the burning forest. 'It is my turn, mine!'

It didn't take long to hear the response. 'But it is *my* turn. And I am older than you. It is mine.'

I almost laughed; the response was so juvenile. So pathetic. As the forest burned, as Leska's life was jeopardised and the mother of monsters fell from the skies—this was the argument that would decide the fate of nations.

Just as I had hoped, the little girl had led me to her sister. My heart skipped a beat as I saw the crown of flames sat at an angle on her skull. It was the same one I had seen Lilyth wear in the visions. That was why I recognised it.

I had seen it in my dreams, placed upon Lilyth's head, a crown of black and gold flame.

There was no time to question how it fell into the hands of the Gathrax twins.

'Give it to me,' the twin I had followed screeched, all-demanding and snapping teeth.

'No. I just got it.'

'I am the Queen, not you.'

We entered a clearing not far from where we had just run from. In a blink, the twins crashed into one another. The force was so great that heat blistered in the air, trees cracking from the shock of fire. I took my moment, peeled from the shadows and moved.

I found Leska immediately, my soul navigating towards her like a compass. She hung from a tree, her arms held above her, as wytchfire crept up its base. I knew this tree; I had seen this clearing twice before. It was the very one Julian had been impaled with, the mound of dirt at its base was where I had buried him. If I wasn't so focused on Leska, I might have drowned in the memory.

She kicked her legs, trying to give momentum to swing herself up. Even from a distance, I saw one of her arms come out of its socket. The pop radiated over the terrorised demands as the twins snatched, clawed and pinched at one another, dripping fire beneath them like tears from crying eyes.

It took little magic to sever the branch Leska was bound to. She fell, crumpled on the ground just shy of where the wytch-fire spread. All the while, the Gathrax twins warred with one another, fuelled by their own passions, with little need for me to intervene.

'Can you walk?' I said to Leska as the screaming girls tore at one another in the sky.

'Twisted ankle and a fucking useless arm, but yes. I can.'

I nodded, gaze settling on the crown that was now being pulled and tugged between both girls.

'The conduit controls passion and the gods who rule it. Take it, and it will stop this madness.'

There was no denying Leska had also heard the dryads' warning. I whipped my head around the clearing, catching the glint of eyes amongst the darkness.

'Let them have it,' Leska said, denying the dryad, already pulling at my arm. 'They'll soon kill one another over it.'

I resisted, rooting myself to the spot. 'The dryad isn't wrong. Leska, I have seen the crown before, I just hadn't remembered where. It belonged... to Lilyth.'

That name alone stopped Leska from demanding we leave again.

'Gathrax manor is under attack, and I think the only thing powerful enough to call the phoenixes off is that fucking crown.' The twins had already confirmed this, back before they abducted Leska. 'If we can use it, we could call the phoenixes off—control them.'

'Seems like a lot to ride on, don't you think?'

'Some risks are worth taking,' I said, as the smoke continued to grow, tendrils reaching skywards, billowing around us in an embrace of heavy smog. 'I know it means something, not only to the twins but to Lilyth.'

I couldn't explain it, we didn't have the time. But I knew, it was the key. A key to more knowledge, a key to more power.

'Give it back!' Fire dipped like liquid between the twins, continuing to spread across everything it touched. If they carried on like this, the fire would ruin the entire forest. There was only one way of extinguishing wytchfire, and that was by killing the phoenix who bore it.

But regardless of what the twins had become, they were still children.

This time, death was not the answer.

'I can fight with a twisted ankle,' Leska gargled through pain as she tried to stand. 'I can try and distract them, long enough for you to get in and take it?'

'But your shoulder is...'

She grasped her sagging arm, fingers digging into flesh. I barely blinked before she jolted it upwards, popping her shoulder back into its socket. There was no stopping as Leska reached for my belt and snatched the knife from it. 'Absolutely fine.'

She looked up to the fighting twins, her face aglow in the light of their fire. They scratched at one another, grasping handfuls of red curls until the other screamed.

'Hold the knife against me,' I said, eyes wide and urgent. 'Threaten me, that will distract them. All they want is to punish me for what I took from them.'

Leska did as I asked, grasping my neck with the clamp of her fingers, thrusting the cool blade beneath my chin. 'Then what?' she hissed into my ear.

'Leave *that* to me.'

Everything they had done, everything they hoped to do, was because of the family I took from them. Although the dead were long gone, I finally understood why the dryads were believed to have taken souls.

Because, whether it was real or not, they were the only beings who could conjure the memory of the dead. Glowing eyes flashed open all around the clearing. Leska didn't notice, nor did the twins. But I did, and I knew exactly how they could help. I sent the request out to the dryads, silently begging them to aid us. When I was met with no resistance, it was time to try.

'Sisters,' I gasped as Leska pressed the blade to my throat. Tears ran down my cheeks from the smoke, not sadness, but that didn't matter. 'Sisters, help me!'

One of the twins turned, then the other, and suddenly the crown was forgotten.

'You are not our brother,' they said in unison, voices overlapping, sickly sweet and dangerous.

'No,' I sobbed, feeling the earth shift as the gods moved closer, inching earthen limbs towards the twins to connect with them. 'But he is...'

CHAPTER 12

The dryads tore the twins apart. I knew, the moment the gods' magic enveloped the twins, it was not this time they would be witnessing. But another. Maybe the dryads showed them this very place, when Julian chased me down and I murdered him. Or maybe it was another memory. But the way their eyes glazed and mouths opened in a sob, it confirmed one fact.

They were no longer looking at me, but the phantom of their dead brother.

'Julian?' one cried out, her eyes glassy and distant. Her hand relaxed, dropping the strange crown upon the bed of pine needles. The ground hissed where it hit, smoke curling as it burned away at the earth.

'My brother,' the other called out for the man they could see. 'He is alive. He is alive.'

All around us, the fire diminished to cinders and smoke. It was as though a great gust of wind blew through Galloway Forest, extinguishing wytchfire as though it was nothing but a mundane flame.

Leska relaxed the blade from my throat. 'What is happening to them?'

'They are being shown a moment in time,' I explained, unable to fathom what this looked like as a bystander. I didn't contemplate what happened to my body when I left this time for another. It was vulnerable, left behind whilst my essence visited elsewhere.

I understood that Leska had countless questions. I did too. But this would only last so long. Fire still dripped from the girls; not as powerful as before, but still damaging. Through my bond to the earth, I sensed the dryads' pain.

I paced across the forest until the crown was beneath me. There was a reluctance within me as I knelt before it, reaching my fingers until they were inches away. Heat fizzled in the air, but still I was drawn to it.

It was in my hands in seconds. An odd, unsettling feeling rushed through my body, sending every vein ablaze with molten fire.

I felt a rush of something breathtaking overwhelm my body. It was a feeling I couldn't explain, a power I don't think I could have ever imagined.

'Stop.'

The command was final. The word was meant for the Gathrax twins, it was meant for every creature born from flame, every phoenix I felt in that moment, as though I held a leash to the collars around their throats.

This was power unlike anything... this was control.

'Max, your eyes...' Leska said from my side, but my mind was far too loud, the world so insufferably warm, that I didn't care. My fingers and palm ached beneath the warmth, but it was nothing I couldn't handle.

'Release them,' I said, speaking to the dryads. There was a fear in the way they regarded me, as though I held the power to destroy every last one of them in my hands—because I did.

The Gathrax twins dropped to the ground, wings limp and folded over their trembling, powerless bodies. They clutched at the earth, unable to call upon their fire, as I didn't allow it. In that moment, I quelled the creature they had become, leaving only the little girls they had been before the magic infiltrated them.

I wanted more than their defeat. I wanted their demise.

'Neither of you are Queens.' The words were tumbling out of me, fuelled by a heat I didn't know I possessed. Regardless of how they called for their dead brother, no matter how they looked at me with fear, they were still little devils. These girls were the ones who tormented my family, who tortured my mother. Their blood ran red, Gathrax red. It was in their very core to be a monster, just as it was in mine to cleanse the world of them.

'Please,' one begged, as she gathered her sobbing sister into her arms. 'We just want to see our family. Show us him, please. We are... scared.'

Were they frightened because they could recognise the doom facing them? Could they feel how heightened the magic was, how powerful and all-consuming? If they did, then they would know what I was going to do. Their fate had been written out, sealed with death.

'You tried to kill us,' I said, ire boiling over in my chest. 'You attempted to hurt those I loved. You are no different to your brother and father. Evil. *Evil* little devils.'

The dryads watched on, their trepidation evident in the very air. It was best they kept silent, if not my ire would turn on them too. Hot. So *fucking* hot.

'Maximus,' a voice warned. Leska. Leska who beat me to a pulp, Leska who broke my nose and punished me for a death that was never my fault.

'Stay out of this,' I hissed, my skin overboiling with heat.

I was so close to the twins now. My shadow cast over them, the world aglow in the red shimmer of Lilyth's comet. Dryads, I was prepared to face her. This anger inside of me, it was destructive. I dared for Lilyth to face me, I willed it. With the power of her fire in my hands and the earth in my blood, I would ruin her.

'Max.' A hand laid on my shoulder.

I spun to face Leska, lips curled over teeth. *Crack*. Pain radiated in my face as my nose was shattered by the colliding fist. The fury, the ire, the passion. It all faded, blown out until I was hollow and empty. I clutched at my nose, blood gushing in my mouth, agony radiating across every bone in my face.

'Get yourself together,' Leska said, as the little devils' wails built in pitch until the forest was alive with them. 'What the fuck were you doing!'

I couldn't respond without my mouth filling with blood. Nor could I stop Leska as she reached down to pick up the crown that had dropped. Instead, I kicked it with a boot, sending it just out of reach.

'It's the crown...' I spat, breathless, exhausted as though the unnaturally warm metal sapped my energy. It drank from me, body and soul, leaving a husk of panic. 'I can't control it.'

Even without touching it, the persuasion lingered in the back of my mind. A small voice, begging me to do what it was I desired. Phoenix magic was dangerous. A power that didn't belong to humans. It gave us the ability to control gods, to leash them. But not without the cost of our humanity.

'Mine,' the girls cried, as they clawed over the ground to grasp it. Their power was back in reach.

I unfurled my magic into the ground, softening it. The crown sank just before they could reach it, disappearing beneath layers of mud. Even the earth longed to reject it, pushing back against me. But I kept going, pushing it down until clay and stone engulfed it.

'You ruined everything!'

Leska placed herself before me, hobbling on a shattered ankle, as the twins righted themselves. I felt the weight of their attention scratch over my skin. 'And you are both making it extremely hard not to kill you.'

Fire licked out from beneath their hands, spoiling the little life the earth had left. It raced towards us.

Max, we are close. Simion's voice speared through my mind. He sounded panicked but just hearing him... knowing he was alive made everything better.

'I can show you your family again,' I pleaded, my energy waning. Every scrap I had left was used to keep Lilyth's crown buried. 'If you want, I can give them to you.'

That stopped them for a moment.

My skin shivered as I searched for Inyris, knowing she was flying towards us. I could feel the very air speed past her scales, her wings slicing through clouds. I didn't need to show her my location, she would find me.

'I told her I was the eldest,' the remaining twin said, giggling. 'Now I will be Lilyth's favoured Queen just as I said I would—'

The air snapped. Around us, the light grew a harsher, boiling red. But not from the fire. It was from the comet. I could hear it now, a song throughout the sky, as it crested over Aldian in a furious arc of red.

It was so close. Closer than it had ever been before.

It seemed nothing mattered as my eyes caught movement from behind the screeching girl. A shadow peeled from the floor. It unfolded from itself, corporeal, with hard edges and a body that distorted the view behind it. It was tall and deathly pale, with stretched limbs that lifted and snatched the twin by the hair. She turned, her scream scorching my skin before it was abruptly cut off. It lasted until more of the shadows peeled from the darkness, cresting over her in a wave before devouring her whole.

CHAPTER 13

I couldn't fathom what I had seen. A creature born from shadow, humanoid, with distorted, monstrous features. Teeth and claws, sharp as blades, but the edges twisting like live shadows.

'What the fuck is that?' Leska called, but my heart was a deafening thump. I could barely move, let alone speak.

'Sissy!' the remaining twin screamed, searching the moving shadows for her sister. But she was gone, snatched away by these unearthly creatures. That didn't stop her from thrusting out her flames, casting them in a wave of fire magic. Whatever she hoped to achieve didn't work. The fire did not harm the beast, but seemed to part the slithering shadows, revealing a pale, sickly body beneath them once again. Flesh hidden by an armour of shadows. Its shape wavered before settling back into its partially solid form.

'Now we have to fight fucking shadows?' Leska shouted, levelling the blade as if it could do anything to fend off these creatures.

I couldn't move, looking at the space the little girl had been, finding it empty.

'*Shades,*' the dryads cried out, lashing out with their ancient magic. I almost buckled to my knees beneath the weight of their godly power. '*Lilyth's damned souls. She is close. They have come to retrieve the conduit!*'

Conduit. The crown. We no longer just had the little devils to contend with, but shadows—shades.

Monsters.

'It's Lilyth's army,' I said, as more appeared. They encircled the clearing, drawing out the light until the world shimmered in a shadowy haze. 'Don't let them get that fucking crown.'

My heart rose in my throat, making my desperate shout sound more like a strangled cry. There wasn't a moment to contemplate what would happen if I touched the crown again. But whatever the outcome, I knew I could not let Lilyth's shades get it. It was her source of connection to the phoenixes. Whatever she did with their power would make the achievements of the little devils pale in comparison.

This, I knew deep in my core, was our chance against her.

I dove forward at the same time Leska and the remaining twin did. A wave of darkness followed as the shades rushed forward. Dryads pulsed earthen power, doing everything they could to draw the shades back. For a moment, I thought it was working.

'Mine. Mine. *Mine!*' the remaining Gathrax twin screamed, her little hand curling around the crown first. Fire erupted from her eyes before channelling out her back. Her wings screamed with renewed magic, blasting the shades backwards. Her magic worked against the shades this time, it actually hurt them. Those unfortunate enough to meet the force of her passion burst apart in wisps. Those remaining were overwhelmed by the dryads who rose, spearing roots from the ground, piercing the shades, keeping them in place.

'Get back here, you little shit,' Leska shouted, racing awkwardly on her broken ankle. The remaining twin was flying away, crown in hand, but stopped as Leska jumped up and grabbed her ankle. The sudden weight forced her back down, bodies hitting the ground hard. I made a move but was stopped as more shades peeled away from the ground, blocking me.

These creatures didn't have faces. It was just a mass of darkness with an awareness. Hollow spaces for eyes and a large split mouth full of pointed teeth. One tilted its head at me inquisitively. I lashed out, snatching any earthen debris around me and throwing it out towards them.

To my surprise, and theirs, the magic hit its mark. The creatures flattened, hissing as they fled my force. I continued throwing my magic outwards as more formed. Stones lifted around me, forged to spears. One thought, one push of my hand and the magic continued its onslaught. Every time the shadows were forced back, I aimed my stone-made weapons into the darkness and hoped it was enough.

But the more I took down, the more appeared. The wall of shades grew so thick I could no longer see through them. All that was left was the sound of struggle, Leska's screams turning from feral to agonised.

I threw everything I had left at them. Every ounce of power in my blood. Leska's shouts grew and grew, breaking into a sudden silence that cooled my blood to ice.

'Leska!' I screamed, trees breaking around me as I forced my power into them, using broken limbs of burned trees and ruined dryads as weapons.

Then I was falling—drowning in darkness, knowing little of what was happening beyond it. They were closing in, hands reaching for me, prepared to take me to wherever they had snatched the other little girl. No matter if I kept my magic up, pushing and pushing and...

My mind was snatched into another. Inyris. It was her way of protecting me from what was to come. Her desperation filled every ounce of my body, as did her strength. She gifted it to me, giving me the energy to hold off the shades just for a few more seconds.

Ice kissed my skin. I threw my eyes open to watch a pillar of frozen winds crash into the shades circling me. I raised an arm to shield my face from the shards of ice that flew at me.

Inyris landed within the clearing, snatching a shade between her jaws. Her tail thrashed outwards, knocking others out of the way, clearing the path between me and Leska.

I found her, lying on the floor, clutching her arm to her chest. Even from a distance I could see the damage. Her right hand was scorched to gore and bone, the remaining hand blistered and melted. The Gathrax twin stood above Leska, fire dripping from her like liquid. It seemed the shades no longer attacked her—there was no need, for she would go willingly with them, taking the crown to prepare for Lilyth's arrival.

Inyris placed herself between us, blocking my way with her muscular gold-scaled body. Cold steam huffed from her snout, her tail wrapping around me. I didn't care if she wished to keep me safe, I smashed my fists into her, begging her to let me go. She only constricted harder, refusing my pleas. I cut my palms open on the sharp edges of her scales, but that didn't stop me.

'Do not hurt her,' I screamed, as the Gathrax twin looked over her shoulder, offering me a smirk. Leska slipped out of consciousness, her eyes rolling back into her head as the pain overcame her. 'You won, just don't take her from me. I beg you!'

'But I told you, brother. I do love the hunt—'

Metal flashed behind her. I practically felt the tear as it sliced through flesh, bone and feather. Her mouth parted, her eyes widening, as a silent scream broke her face apart. When she tipped forward, Simion Hawthorn stood behind her, sword raised, blood dripping from the blade.

He had severed her wings, cutting her off from escape. The shades raced, darkness swallowing up her cry. Her pain was so great that she fell forward, the crown tumbling freely. Simion snatched it, before I could even offer him a warning.

Simion's eyes found mine, his skin smudged with ash, his eyes bloodshot. Then, without taking his eyes off me, he lifted the crown up and placed it upon his head.

No. I longed to close my eyes, to refuse what the overwhelming power would do to his mind.

But I couldn't look away, not as our eyes were welded to one another.

The crown pulsed. I watched, dumbfounded, as the black metal hugged his skull, the flickering flamed points raising in heat and height. His eyes flared a brilliant gold as he channelled the magic it offered.

A single line formed between his brow, deep and harrowing. Shades raced towards him, ready to take the one thing they had come for. Simion bowed his head, the air around him wavering as though his outline shifted. Inyris tightened her hold, anticipating what was to come.

When Simion looked up, pure and concentrated power rippled across the clearing. It shattered shades apart, it fizzed the air until breathing became unbearable. It was as though he harnessed the power of suns, brightening everything before me with such intensity that I was forced to close my eyes.

Time mattered little in the face of such magic. It could have been seconds, days or months before I opened my eyes. But when I did, there was nothing but ruin around us. The shades had all disappeared, banished back to wait for Lilyth to finally join them.

The comet was closer than ever, the sky still raging with the glow of crimson. Time was no longer a luxury we had.

'It is... over.' Simion stood before us, glaring down with swirling power like a tempest in his breathtaking eyes. It was like looking at a stranger. I knew the feelings he would have felt, the heighted passions as the crown manipulated his emotion.

For me, it had made me murderous. 'You are safe...' Simion said, his voice tempered and steady.

I couldn't think clearly. My body was exhausted, my power depleted. Even Inyris drew her lips back, snarling into Simion's face with warning. Her distrust echoed mine.

'From the shades, or you?' I asked, voice trembling.

'Both,' he answered, lifting a hand to his head and the crown. It dropped to the forest floor, forgotten. An afterthought. The only noticeable change was the resurfacing of his calm expression.

'How did you... control it?' I said, unable to fathom how Simion was freely able to wear the signet, use it and remove it. For me, it had ripped away at everything surrounding my passions and set it ablaze. I was far from control when I touched it, prepared to do anything, even if my conscience said otherwise.

But here Simion stood, eyes overspilling with power, the crown settling back from a raging inferno to mundane points of gleaming black metal. He drank me in as ash fell around him like snow. There was something so peaceful about the atmosphere. Then again, compared to the hell we had experienced, this was practically heaven.

'Because *you* are my passion, Max.'

Not power, not vengeance or retribution. Me.

I swallowed hard as the reality of everything settled over me. Inyris uncurled around me, recognising the lack of danger, trust echoing down our tether. Simion dropped to his knees. As Inyris allowed him the room to do so, I fell freely into his arms, delighting in his warmth, his scent, his tender touch. I refused to let go. He was my anchor; he was my warrior.

You are my passion.

My eyes opened, gazing over the clearing to where Leska lay. She was mumbling beneath her breath, eyes wide and staring up at the clear, star-filled sky. Beside her was a pile of ashes, what was left of the remaining twin as the crown turned on her.

'It isn't over,' I said to Leska, not believing my own words. 'Far from it.'

I waited, with bated breath, for her to reply. Leska's head lolled to the side, her distant and pained gaze falling on me as she clutched her ruined hand.

'No,' I said to Simion, the dryads—to any soul listening. 'It has only just begun.'

CHAPTER 14

The Gathrax library had barely changed since I had last been in it. But I was no longer the same person. After I had bathed in a brass tub, scrubbing my body of any remnants of ash, blood, shade and battle, I couldn't have felt more different to the Max who had last stepped foot inside of this place.

I was an imposter, or perhaps I was more my true self than this place ever made me believe possible.

I stood in the open doorway, distracting myself with the view. Rows of bookshelves were coated in dust, likely from a long period of time without me tending them. The portraits that once haunted me no longer held that power. Paintings of trees burning in black flame, faces of old Southern mages who fell before I was born. All stories that meant more to me than I ever would have imagined before.

It was strange seeing it, such a jarring reminder of the family who once ruled these rooms. Not a single shelf was left in the neat and tidy array it had once been. Books had been torn and scattered over the floor, pages ripped, spines cracked past the point of repair. I didn't expect to find the room in such a state, nor did I expect the arrow of guilt in my chest at seeing it in such a way.

If I listened carefully to the silence, I could have heard Dame's voice whisper from the corners. The lead maid, Dame, had been a large part of my life. And yet another person who had died because they got too close to me.

I could hear Julian taunt me, and remembered the warning my mother gave me about taking books and sneaking them into our home.

I had hated this place and loved it at the same time. Now I felt indifferent, because there was one soul who was waiting for me.

Simion.

He was nestled in a reading chair, his face tilted to the side as soft snores emanated from him. The battle had taken its toll on us all, but it was the deep exhaustion he felt from using the crown that really did him in.

Not wanting to wake him, but also needing his company, I closed the door harder than I should have. It alerted Simion to my presence. One golden eye opened at a time, resting on me. 'You look a lot better.'

I hobbled into the room. My body was marred with wounds that I hadn't noticed until the battle had ceased. The gleamers had done what they could, but all I wanted was for them was to focus on Leska. To help her.

To keep her alive.

'I don't feel it.' Any of it. I was numb, physically and mentally.

The open book on Simion's lap fell carelessly to the floor as he stood to greet me. Whereas his gaze settled on me, I could not take my eyes off the crown, the conduit that was still a mystery to me. It rested on the small table at his side, winking in the mundane light cast by the lit hearth.

There was nothing mystical about it now. It was as if its hunger for power had been sated by Simion.

'Dame would've had a heart attack if she ever saw a room in such a state,' I said, voice shaking at the mention of the Head of Maids. She had been a guardian to me, wise far beyond her years, until Aaron's dragon ate her alive.

'Do not concern yourselves with the voices of ghosts, but the living, dear Max.' Simion didn't look anywhere else but me. I didn't need to ask him what he saw, or why he looked equal parts horrified and worried. 'How is Leska's doing?'

'Breathing.' I had not visited Leska yet, knowing I was weak and couldn't face the damage. The scars that would forever change her. 'I am worried about her, and what has become of the Lilyth's shades. There are more questions than answers at this point, more we still do not understand.'

Simion's eyes flickered to the crown. I sensed his urge to reach out and pick it up. It sang in his eyes the same as his desire to reach for me.

'How... what does it feel like?'

When I had touched the crown—the conduit—I felt nothing but the overwhelming sense of my passion. It was like being dragged down a harsh ravine with no power to free myself.

Simion contemplated the question, chewing on his lower lip as he continued staring endlessly at the crown. 'It is like I am here, and everywhere at once. When I touched it, I was connected to the phoenixes. It's like the bond between me and my amplifier—but stronger. Far stronger and clearer. I cannot explain it, not in words that would do it justice. But... Maximus.' He returned his eyes back to me. 'It is power. A great well of power.'

My breath hitched in my throat. As Simion stepped in close, stopping as he stood before me, towering inches taller, I felt inconsequential. As though his connection with the crown still lingered, even after he touched it.

'It belonged to Lilyth. It is evil.'

'With the potential for so much good. Do not fear me,' he said, fingers carefully grasping my chin as he drank me in. Deep lines formed between his brow, his lips pursed, his golden eyes overspilling with anxiety. 'I am finally in control. True control.'

'Of yourself?'

'Of *everything*.'

Before I could ask for clarification, he silenced me with a kiss. It was tender and quick, a brush of soft lips against mine that sent shivers erupting over my skin.

'Now, what good is this power, if I cannot offer you some security.' Simion had drawn back, although his eyes had not stopped devouring me—undressing me. 'Forget the crown, forget everything that has come before. Unless you sleep, Maximus, you'll never be able to deal with what is to come tomorrow.'

'After that, I hardly imagine I will be able to shut off my brain.'

Simion raised his gaze to the door behind me. There was an expectation to his stare, as though the person who left so many marks across my body would come rushing in. 'Then I will need to help. Sit down.' Simion gestured to the reading chair. 'I'll tend to your wounds. Then you *will* sleep, Max.'

I didn't have the energy to refuse him. I wanted nothing more than to close my eyes and pretend nothing terrible was happening around me.

The little devils were dead. Lilyth's shades—the army the visions had shown me—had reached Aldian. Lilyth would soon follow. Leska. My mind whirled with these consuming thoughts until they registered as nothing but pain in my skull.

Simion took my hand, distracting me. He guided me to the seat he had been seated in. The plush cushioning engulfed me as I eased myself into it.

'If the Gathrax family ever saw me sitting in this, they would have my head,' I said.

Simion didn't bite at my comment, not as he began brushing my pained flesh with his fingers. His magic flooded over me in a cool sheen—mending bruises and fixing skin. In a way, I didn't want all the marks to be healed. It reminded me of what had happened. How was it fair my wounds would heal, but Leska's would never?

I blinked and saw the mess of her handless arm. It encouraged the sickening dread to thicken in my body. There was no gleamer with the ability to reconstruct bone, sinew, vein and muscle.

'The Gathrax family can no longer hurt you,' Simion said, studying my skin like a sculpture. He knew my body inside out. He understood how my bones should look, where my skin had marks and scars. As he worked on the cuts and bruises, he did so with care. 'No one can.'

'You sound so certain.'

He paused, the pads of his fingers warming the skin he touched. 'Of course I am certain. The next person to lay an unkind hand on you will burn.'

An intensity flared within Simion, circling his iris with a band of stark gold. It stole my breath away, lodging it in my throat.

It was not fear I regarded him with but awe. So much so, I couldn't form a reply.

'Max, I want nothing more than to stand by and support you. I never want to be in your way, tell you what to do, make decisions for you. But every time you come to me harmed, it is becoming harder not to.'

I bowed my head, unable to face him. 'There are things I must do, challenges to face.'

Simion knelt before the chair, taking my hands in his. My skin prickled in gooseflesh as his smooth thumb ran circles on the back of my hand. 'Please, confide in me. Tell me what *we* need to do.'

'Not *we*, Simion. Not this time.'

As Simion wished for me, I, too, wished for him. I vowed never to lie, not if I thought it would protect him, not if I thought it would protect me. The truth was freeing, even if it was the harder of the options.

'Talk to me,' Simion practically begged, looking deep into my eyes. 'I sense it in you, something you are fighting the urge to tell me.'

'It is about the dryads,' I spat out before I could change my mind.

'What about them? If this has got anything to do with the memories they show you, then you should not fear—'

'It isn't a memory the dryads show me.'

He looked to my arms as though expecting to find the marks he had just healed. 'Then what haunts you, Max?'

'It isn't a memory, but a moment in time. What they show me, what I can see. It is real. And I need now, more than ever, to find out the importance of that crown.' My eyes settled on it again, whilst the name the dryads used for it rang in my skull. *Conduit.*

I saw the question wet his tongue before he said it. How? Before he could ask it, I continued. He refused to look away from me. I felt his attention deep within my core, how his warmth graced my skin and his presence rooted me to this moment in time. 'Is this a burden you must carry alone, Max?'

I shrugged, feeling an ache in the back of my mind. 'Yes. Someone must. And if I have the means to try and find a solution, I will do it. How can I focus on anything else, Simion?' I didn't want to snap, but I couldn't contain my anger. I clutched my head in my hands, blocking out the light, but doing little to sustain the agony in my head.

'Allow me to help you. I do not understand any of it, but I

do believe we will succeed. But right now, in this very moment, I want you to focus on me. I promise you will think of nothing else...'

The tears that escaped my eyes were caught by his steady hands. Then he leaned in and kissed the place where the cool streaks were left.

'No more thinking. No more room for anxiety to rule your mind. We can spend time dwelling on the future, but we must take the opportunity to enjoy the present. Do you hear me? Inside these walls, right now, *this* is real. These shades will not attack in daylight, the dryads told us as much. And they do not think they will be strong enough until Lilyth finally reaches Aldian. So, in this room, nothing will happen. We are safe. I have you, you have me. You deserve peace, Max, and I know I cannot give it to you completely. But what I can do is offer you a moment in time of my own. A piece you can exist within, where nothing else should concern you.'

'Just me and you?' I asked, blinking back the tears, longing for his beautiful features not to be blurred behind them.

Muscles feathered in Simion's jaw, his eyes flickering across me. 'Exactly. Me and you.'

I exhaled the tension, giving into Simion's wish of offering me this. He was right, we did deserve this.

Simion scooped me from the chair. I was weightless in his arms. My hands clasped behind his head, my legs wrapping tight around his middle. He swept my fringe out of my eyes and leaned in close, stopping only when he was inches from kissing me.

'When I sleep,' I said, narrowing my eyes at him, 'promise me you will not leave. If you truly are in control now, there is no reason for you to leave.'

'I will never leave your side again. No matter the price.'

I smiled, an honest and all-encompassing feeling over-whelming me. 'Good.'

'Now, no more talk of the future, even if that is only moments away. Just focus on me.'

I nodded, recognising the fire building deep in my gut. A need. A desire. A *passion*.

Simion's mouth pursed as he guided us away from the chair. I didn't know where he was taking me until I felt the hard press of a bookshelf against my spine. A sharp breath escaped me at the suddenness of it. Instinctively, I put my hands out to counter it, but instead I knocked piles of books from the side, coating the floor in them.

'Simion, if you keep touching me like this, sleeping really will be an impossibility.'

Days of pent-up need for him could barely be contained. It was also my exhaustion, my panic that we would soon face a time when we really would never experience each other again. I needed him in every way possible.

Simion leaned in, mouth brushing against my neck. 'Tell me to stop and I will.'

Light flashed off the crown as it drank in the building passion between us. 'Actually, I forbid you from stopping.'

'Then you do this one thing for me. Every place I touch,' Simion said, his voice deep as the furthest oceans, as rumbling as a summer storm. 'You focus on it. Nothing else. Can you do that?'

The answer was simple. 'Yes.'

With my weight now propped up by the bookcase, Simion didn't need to hold onto me. With one hand he traced his fingertips over my neck, the other reached between us, grasping my crotch.

I bowed my spine, arching into him, urging him to grasp tighter, harder. All the while he kept me at bay, refusing the kiss I starved for.

'Do you want more, my King?' Simion asked, lust erupting from his stare. His hands were growing hot with his fire as it lingered in the layer beneath his skin. It made my clothes feel suffocating and insufferable. If he didn't kiss me, if he didn't use those hands to tear every item off my body, I might just scream.

'All... of... it.' I spoke each word with conviction, straining against his hold.

Still, he didn't give it to me, not until he knew that there was no room for anything else in my mind but him. When he was satisfied, he pressed his lips to mine and kissed me as though it was both the first and last time.

I dug my nails into his scalp, keeping me to him. My tongue lapped over him, my teeth nipping at his lip. If I could melt into him, I would have. There wasn't an inch between us. I devoured his taste, drawing him in, kissing deeper, harder. Simion thrust his hips into mine, one hand gripping at the back of my neck whilst the other fumbled to grasp the lower portion of my shirt.

We only broke apart long enough for him to pull it off. That second of distance was filled with desperate breaths and urgent eyes. Only once I was naked, with nothing but the thick air of the library to touch my skin, did we return to one another.

I grasped Simion's jaw and tilted his head upwards. His neck was on display, enticing me. As my lips pressed over his skin, he expelled a moan so great it had the power to rupture walls.

The empty hearth exploded in conjured fire.

The shock of it drew us apart. Before Simion could apologise for his lack of control, I used my body weight to turn him around. I stopped only when his back was to the bookcase. Lifting his arms up, I held them above his head.

Magic oozed from me, coiling with the essence in the wood of the bookcases. Strips peeled back by an unseen hand. My intention guided the strips until they tied around Simion's wrists, binding him, keeping his arms hoisted above his head.

'Better,' I said, dropping to my knees, as a delighted smile lifted Simion's mouth.

'I am not sure yet,' he replied, hungrily gazing down at me.

He was a fly in my web, willingly caught.

I snatched the buckle of his belt, undoing it with a forceful pull. Once it was free and thrown to the side, I worked on undoing the buttons of his trousers. Even though Simion's hands were... occupied, that didn't stop him from wiggling his trousers free.

'I am going to ask you to clarify what you meant when referring to yourself as my throne,' I said, taking his hard length in my hand, wrapping firm but careful fingers around his girth. 'But first I am going to take you in so far, so deep that there truly will be no room for anything else inside of me.'

Simion's jaw dropped, the tension in his cock hardening more so. He throbbed in my hand, tip glistening with his excitement. There was nothing with the ability to make my mouth water than seeing his seed.

'Take your time,' Simion replied, 'we have all the time in the world.'

It was a lie, but I appreciated his attempt for normalcy. We both knew what was coming, one look out the window would remind us.

'I need to tell everyone what is coming,' I said, not wishing to ruin the mood but needing to free the final thorn that all the secrecy had embedded into me. 'They deserve to know what they fight for. They deserve a choice.'

Simion closed his eyes, exhaled through his nose and nodded. 'There will be time for that. Tomorrow.'

'Is it always tomorrow with you, Simion Hawthorn?'

He laughed beneath his breath, hips writhing. 'Yes. Because the promise of tomorrow is a privilege not all of us have. By recognising a tomorrow, one is recognising a future full of endless possibilities.'

I was not the poet Simion was, so I came back with three

words that were simple, yet encapsulated everything I felt inside, 'I hope so.'

'Now, did I not warn you,' Simion said, as my face gave my thoughts away. 'Think of me, nothing else. Okay?'

I lowered myself further onto my knees, positioning myself just beneath this length. I held the shaft above my face, shadowing myself beneath it as my tongue moved towards his balls. 'Oh, I will try my best.'

'Good boy,' Simion groaned.

Dryads, help me. This man was not going to be my undoing, when he had already become my reckoning.

My mouth parted, my tongue extending, as I lowered his balls to it. As the soft, gentle skin settled, I got to sucking, trailing my tongue around each ball in turn whilst working my hand up and down his hardening cock.

Simion watched me, bottom lip caught between his teeth, groans trapped within his cheeks. At one point his eyes rolled back into his skull. It was such a loud, demanding sound I had no doubt every soul in the Kingdom would've heard it.

'Take me in your mouth,' Simion said finally, brows raised as he begged for me to shift my attention from his balls to his cock. 'Every inch. That's it. Show me just how good you are.'

'Who said I was good?' My mouth and chin were lathered with spit. I had salivated so much it was as though I hid an ocean in my cheeks.

'Bad, then. Terrible.' He attempted to force his hips closer, guiding his cock towards my mouth. 'Are you going to make me beg?'

'Patience, Simion.' I felt all powerful, just as Simion had described how using the crown had made him feel. He was my conduit, he was my well of power. Simion's lip curled, flashing teeth. His expression was mischievous, deadly. Smoke hissed around his hands as the wood binding his wrists caught fire. Ash fell around me, languidly falling as Simion broke himself free.

He cupped a hand to the back of my head, knotted his fingers in my hair and took his cock in the other. Carefully, he guided himself before my parted mouth, tapping his hardness on my outstretched tongue.

'You know, patience is a virtue I have never had,' Simion said, easing himself between my lips.

'I'll have to punish you for this,' I said, glowering up at him.

A beat of time passed between us, overspilling with unspoken desires. It was Simion who broke it. 'Good. Punish me. Edge me. Then, once I am ready, I will sit you upon me just as I know you want.'

Dryads, I did.

If my mouth wasn't completely full of him, perhaps I would have said as much. Instead, I showed him my need physically. I sucked Simion until his knees crumbled and he had no control of himself. He was large, so much that I couldn't take him all in. But that didn't mean I didn't try. Helped by his hand, I gathered him deep in my throat until I gagged. Tears pooled in my eyes, breath evaded my lungs. And all the while it was the most enjoyable feeling.

Simion pulled himself free, tugging my hair until my scalp burned. 'Careful...'

He didn't need to explain his warning. I tasted his cum all over my tongue, or the promise of it at least. 'Now let's see this throne you keep talking about,' I muttered, shrugging my shoulders as I pretended to search the library for it. 'Where is it?'

The corner of his lips peaked. 'Say no more.'

Simion took my hand and guided me to a place before the hearth. We stopped momentary, greedily kissing each other, hurryingly removing the final items of clothing left on his body.

'You are the most beautiful creature to exist,' Simion whispered, speaking to my soul. I thought the same about him. It was one of life's joys to look at him, to gaze at his muscles, his skin, his frame, his details. 'I am proud of you. The man you have become. The one who will guide us all to victory.'

'Would it be sappy if I said I would achieve nothing without you?'

'No, I would want to hear you say it over and over. You could scream at me, punish me, unload all your deepest dislikes on me, and I would relish in every moment of it.'

I paused, dumbfounded. 'Why?'

'Because it would be you talking, it would be your voice. I count myself lucky—blessed—that it is I who has found himself worthy enough to experience you.'

'Shut up and kiss me, you fool,' I said, stifling a chesty sob.

His smile stretched from ear to ear. 'With pleasure.'

Simion was right. With him, nothing else mattered. Perhaps one day I would ask the dryads to take me to this very moment, just so I could relieve how weightless and freeing it was to exist in the same time with Simion.

With his foot, Simion cleared the fallen books, giving us enough room for a place to lay. He did so first, stretching himself out on his back. I was left to stand beside him, watching, insides turning with excitement, groin aching with the need for touch.

'In my jacket pocket you will find what you need.' Eyes wide, lips glistening and his cock held to attention in his hand, Simion beckoned me to him. 'When you are ready, come and take your seat.'

Even if I wanted to prolong the moment, I couldn't. The need for him inside of me, the feeling of him filling me, I could never refuse it.

I rushed to his jacket, found the vial of lubricant stashed in the inner pocket. The contents emptied on my fingers, then dribbled down over Simion's length. I reached behind me, lathered enough over my ass and then positioned myself over him.

It was nice to know that Simion had been thinking about

this moment as much as I had. All those stolen, rushed moments, leading to this.

There was nothing stopping me from enjoying every second.

My knees popped as I lowered myself into position. Simion guided himself before my entrance, easing into me until he disappeared inside, inch by inch.

'Fuck, Simion,' I cried, as all feelings and sensations flooded me.

'Is this worthy for you, my King?'

Pleasure spread outwards, passing over my skin like a wave of flame. 'It is everything and more.'

By the time my ass met his hips, Simion, too, lost himself to pleasure. I began to rock, shifting my weight backwards and forth, up and down—delighting in the swell of him. His long fingers dug into my thighs. When the momentum was too slow, he lifted his hips and thrust into me.

I closed my eyes to find a field of stars. Colours exploded with every thrust. Gold light burst, spreading across my mind, down my limbs to the very tips of my fingers. Every inch of my body felt Simion and his presence. Not only physically, but mentally. I would have stayed, lost to the endless tumbling that was his sex, until his touch drew me out of it.

My cock was in his hand, wet from the lubrication. As he pounded into me, the rhythm growing harder, he moved his hand too. Up and down, encouraging me to run straight towards the edge of bliss.

The need for release built in me. And Simion sensed it.

'Not yet,' he said, forehead shining with sweat. He was breathless, as was I. I didn't notice my thighs and knees ached until he guided me from him. Soon enough I was back on the reading chair, laid out across it, legs lifted over Simion's shoulders.

His focus was on entering me again, but not before he

licked his fingers and rubbed fresh spit on his already glistening tip. When he entered me, it was world ending and world making. His muscles protruded from his form, veins covering his flesh like the riverways across the earth. It was one of the world's wonders, to watch him, skin shining with sweat.

I was back in his hand, leaving all my pleasure with him.

There was nothing needed of me but to enjoy it. I laid back, watching his pleasure build whilst he made love to me. Because that was what this was. It was more than physical, more than lust, it was a deep need.

'As much as I want this to never end,' he said, forehead creased in deep lines. 'I fear I can't hold myself back another minute.'

'Cum for me,' I said, knowing I was close too. Every jerk of his wrist, every slam of his hips and press of his cock against the delightful spot deep inside of me—I couldn't hold back. I was a mountain, ready to break. A volcano prepared to erupt.

There was no more permission needed. I gave up on controlling myself, just as Simion did the same. I didn't close my eyes. Watching him meet his desire was only encouraging me to do the same. There was no holding back.

For a second, there was only peace, then everything exploded.

Simion finished deep inside of me, his thrusts slowing as his breathing deepened. I came too, shooting the ropes of my seed up my stomach. A rush of sensitivity took over, but I didn't need to tell Simion. He slowed his wrist, carefully milking the very last dregs of my cum out of me.

Then he sagged forward, mouth to mine. I drew him in, pulling at his damp skin until he was laid atop me.

I simply wanted him—his touch, his scent, his presence.

Magic spilled from his touch, a warning as to what was coming. The cool brush of his mind mingled with mine. It was a fleeting moment, because he was exhausted and couldn't keep his eyes open. But when he knew there was nothing but him in my thoughts, he withdrew.

He had succeeded. Simion had taken my thoughts and made no room for anything else but him. And I revelled in it.

'I don't want it to end,' I said. Not the sex, because I couldn't go again. But this, him. Every night he would hold me and then he would leave me. 'As your King, I forbid you from stepping foot outside this room, Simion Hawthorn.'

He nestled in close, the chair creaking in protest at the faintest of moves. 'How can I refuse you?'

'Then you won't leave me tonight.' It wasn't a question so much as it was a command. 'We both stay here, stretch this moment out until the very last possible second.'

My surroundings returned to us. It was as though our connection had blinded me to anything around me, until I saw the scattered books, messy bookcases and disarray of the Gathrax library.

I had once taken books from these shelves full of smutty scenes, never once expecting I would make one of my own in this place.

I laid my head on his chest, gazing up at him. His eyes were closed, a smile etched onto his face, mirroring the one on my own.

Simion peeked at me through one eye. 'I already told you, my love. I won't leave you. Not now, not tomorrow. Not ever again.'

CHAPTER 15

'You have come for the truth, Maximus Oaken.'

The dryad's voice reverberated off every ruined tree around me. Although I got the impression it actually came from every tree, it was as though they spoke as one, filling my mind with shared power.

I stepped into the impenetrable dark of the Galloway Forest, disappearing into another world. My hands stretched out before me, brushing rough bark as I navigated the shroud. Inyris was beside me, her wings furled into her sides.

'I have come for answers,' I called out.

Specs of light burst to life around me. Small dots that hovered around me, spreading out in a wave of light until the forest was aglow with warm amber. Fireflies. There were thousands of them, if not more. The light caught on Inyris's scales, glittering as though she was made from solid gold.

Her jaws snapped, catching a few between her teeth. The rumbling groan she expelled sang of her thanks for the snack.

It was ethereal to see the forest pitched in such a wonderous glow. Especially after so much flame and destruction.

Stood before me were an arch of dryads. Their faces broke

away from bark, their limbs stretched out into humanised bodies. They were gods, and human. One looked so similar to someone I might see in the streets of Wycombe that I did a double take, noticing willow leaves falling from their head like hair.

'Tell us what you wish to know, Maximus Oaken, and we shall provide.'

I swallowed hard, my throat constricting as though my body wished to stop me from prying. But I needed answers. I couldn't see the falling star from my point within the wood, but I sensed it. Like a scent in the air or a faraway glare of eyes over my skin. Its presence was always known.

'The crown is important to Lilyth, I need to know why.' It was currently with Simion, being used to stifle the growing number of phoenixes who seemed to flock to him. Even after sleeping, he woke looking more exhausted. However, despite the dark shadows beneath his eyes and the ashen kiss to his skin, Simion's eyes were bright. Glowing with some strange new power.

'Lilyth's conduit. One of four. Have you come for answers, or come to find more?'

An unpleasant tingling spread across my back like wings. 'There are more?'

'As there are four gods, four found children, four elemental monsters—there are conduits to match. The last time we saw mother, we fought for the conduits. With them, we turned on her.'

'This was how she devoured worlds? But you resisted, and she was forced to leave you in Aldian. Show me why. Help me understand Lilyth's weakness, so we know how to beat her.'

'As you request.' The forest creaked and groaned as every tree shifted in unison. 'However, that is not all you wish to see, my child.'

There was no hiding my thoughts from gods. Especially not

gods whose essence ran in my veins. That didn't stop the creeping of discomfort from crawling up my spine like a spider. 'Don't toy with me, all seeing, all knowing. There is no need for me to tell you why I am here.'

It was a risk, speaking in such a way to the dryads. But I sensed they understood, which was confirmed by their response.

'Remember, where you go, you must be a phantom. A ghost. Do not speak, do not reveal yourself. For lurking in time is dangerous. Disruptive. The cost can be far too great. Another has paid this price before you, another gave themselves away in the hopes that the past would ease their broken heart. Do not repeat this mistake. One wrong action and you may not have a life to return to.'

Inyris huffed icy smoke from her snout before nudging it into my side. She was gentle when she nipped my shirt in her teeth and pulled me back. I gathered her in my hands, rubbing over the glassy smooth surface of her armour. 'I will be fine, Inyris. Just make sure I am safe when I am... gone.'

Gone. Because there was no other word for it. One moment I would be here, the next not. Simion had said something about my body reappearing in a tree. It was magic I was yet to understand.

'Come, Child of the Forest, find your answers.'

I stepped from Inyris, conjuring calm emotions to smother her worry for me. She blinked her storm-grey eyes, turned her gaze to the dryads and erupted in a snarl so vicious, it translated from beast to god.

'She worries for you, but there is no need. When you are with us, your body comes. Nothing is left behind for Inyris to protect. It is the dryad that protects you that will need protection themselves.'

Inyris flicked her head once in agreement. She understood this. 'What about her *shades*? They have yet to return for us—'

'*For the conduit, not you,*' the dryad confirmed. '*Lilyth's shades are only weakened wisps of what will be when she finally arrives. They will not waste their numbers returning now, not without Lilyth to regenerate them.*'

Frustration boiled within me, so sharp and sudden it took my breath away. How could we possibly face Lilyth, knowing nothing of what she was to come with? Her army of shadows. The destruction of worlds.

I looked up, past the canopy of tree, to a sky on fire. 'I am ready to understand. I need to, otherwise we are doomed.'

'*Then let us go.*' A taller dryad in the centre approached. It was covered in ancient bark that looked more like folded brass, with long limbs of spear-like branches coming off it in all directions, and a crown of twig and leaf. It opened what seemingly were arms for me in a welcoming embrace. I stepped into it, pushing caution aside.

'You said there was a price to pay if I affected time,' I said, settling myself into the dryad's hold. 'But until now, I have been kept behind a shroud. I didn't think I was physically there, only a watching ghost.'

Could I go back and see my parents? Not only see them, but hold them again, touch them? Warn them of what was to come and save them from death?

The dryad's warning rang out in my skull. *One wrong action and you may not have a life to return to.*

'*Body, mind and soul. The time can affect you, just as you can affect it. Be wary, Maximus Oaken. Heed our warning.*' Its voice filled my head, no longer sung throughout the forest, but within me.

I pressed my back to its body, legs crossed over roots that slithered beneath me. Inyris paced before us, spittle splashing from her jaw as she shook. There was no way she would leave me, even if my body did as the dryads suggested and just... disappeared.

Attempting to make sense of the magic, I focused on every sensation I could. The dryad folded its branches over me, gathering me up in its essence. Then all of a sudden, I was falling backwards, spinning into a dark abyss as a hole in the world opened up behind me.

* * *

I had been here before. In my dreams. Except this time, it was real. The ground beneath my feet was dried and dead. Dust billowed on hot winds, twisting it in cyclones until it thrashed against the army of shadows.

'*Dammed souls,*' the dryad corrected. It was behind me, shielding my body from onlookers. '*Servants of Lilyth. Her shades. This is what becomes of the souls who do not offer her the one thing she searches for. Sustenance. Fuel. For every world she infects, she gathers more, continuing to search for the very thing she desires.*'

Even at a distance, I could see they were wailing, faceless monstrosities. But where was Lilyth? The sky above was on fire. Instead of clouds, there was a sea of flame. From amongst it I heard them. The phoenixes. Bright birds of fire far larger than any I had seen. It was their wings that billowed hot air down over us, their flame that scorched the ground until life withered.

Sweat covered every inch of my skin within moments. The feeling was insufferable. I tried to turn, but the dryad held on tighter, gripping me in place, preventing me from leaving.

It was then I noticed the rest of them. A line of dryads stretched out, blocking the dammed souls from moving out of their formation. Dragons waited, sentinel, at their sides, watching from raised peaks in the distance. I caught a flash of silver, a body so large it could block out natural light. Oribon.

'*Our brother waits for the moment.*' I sensed the tension in the dryad's voice. '*We all wait.*'

'For what?' I whispered, my voice drowned by the calls of birds, the creaking of dryad and the wingbeats of dragons.

'*A chance.*' It occurred to me that I saw no signs of the nymphs. '*You will. Lilyth will come to despise them the most.*'

Something moved amongst the mass of darkness. A body, lithe yet powerful. Lilyth.

'Mother...' the chant began, the same I had heard in my dreams. Here, standing behind a cloak of time and shadow, I recognised that the language was not one I knew. Although I understood the word's meaning, the sounds were coarse and hard. 'Mother. *Mother.*'

There was nothing safe about this time, only the presence at my back. I had to rely on the dryad for protection, for shielding.

Lilyth swept her serpentine eyes over her army, admiring the destruction they left in their wake. I waited, holding my breath, for those eyes to fall on me. To find me. They burned red hot, each with a singular black line down its middle as though a dagger of shadow waited within. In place of legs was a tail, scaled like a snake's. Wings protruded from her back, spreading wide.

And there, upon her head, rested the crown. The same one I had seen in visions past. The very same one that Simion now protected back in Gathrax manor.

I searched her body, searching for other objects out of place. The air shifted around her edges. She opened her arms out before her, as though she could embrace her army. She was gathering them. Taking them *into* herself.

This was something the broken dream did not show me. Fragments of a moment in time. But I remembered one detail. Lilyth doing the same with the dryads, the dragons and the phoenixes.

'I've seen enough,' I spat as my heart broke into a furious canter. I could hardly hold my breath, let alone break free from this living nightmare. The panic of being separated from my time, my world, was terrifying. It took great effort not to scream, begging for this to end.

'*You wanted knowledge, so you must wait.*'

I didn't realise I held on tight to the dryad's branch until my nail snapped, followed by an explosion of pain. Blood blossomed in my cheeks as I bit down on my tongue to stifle my scream. I had never felt fear like this. Nor power. It was everywhere. I pinched my eyes closed, filling my head with my demand to go home. To go back to Simion...

'*Watch!*'

My eyes flew open in time to watch it all change. Something wet brushed over my feet. It was as though the ground was bleeding, expect it wasn't blood, it was... water. The world was flooding.

A piercing scream filled the world as the gods of water initiated their attack. They rose from the ruined earth, lifting out in a wall of ocean before Lilyth. She didn't have the chance to move. It overwhelmed her, crashing down over her body and the remaining shadows. Swept away by the force, Lilyth was left unharmed. It was never meant to kill her, only distract. As she lifted her clawed hand, drawing the nymphs out from beneath her, gathering them up in a glowing orb of blue and white—her next child attacked.

Something on her arm caught my eye. A flash of silver metal —strange blue gems winking down the length of a gauntlet I had not noticed before. There was no room to contemplate where I had seen it before. Not in the Heart Oak's visions, but another place. Somewhere rooted in my time, worn on the arm of someone I had seen.

'That is the conduit, isn't it?' I could barely speak from the anxiety lodged in my throat.

'*Yes. Watch carefully. This is where our betrayal began.*'

The nymph's essence not only reflected off the gauntlet but

twisted within it. Water swallowed Lilyth's arm until the gauntlet was almost out of view—

The sky boomed, splitting apart. It was so loud my eardrums felt they would shatter. Ringing filled my head, blood seeping down the sides of my face. I could've been screaming; I would never have known. A blur of silver shot past me, so bright and fast I almost missed it.

Oribon, father of dragons, the very same who flew over Wycombe before the Claim, the same who tested me with trials. He flew into Lilyth with such force the air rippled outwards. I was forced back into the dryad. The skin across my back broke, cut to shreds from the friction. Even through my tunic, I could feel the tender torn skin, and the spread of warmth as blood soddened the material.

Dragons filled the sky, clashing tooth and claw with phoenixes. The air grew hotter, boiling until my skin blistered around my arms. I smelled smoke and knew the dryads were feeling the same destruction.

Lilyth's cry was spoiled with her pain, a noise that could be understood across words, times, creatures. Not only the physical pain of jaws tearing into her shoulder, or the talons gouging her tail, which attempted to constrict around Oribon's body. It was the sound of heartbreak. Of betrayal from those who she loved the most.

The ground shattered as roots joined the fray. It was the familiar power of dryads. Oribon was cast aside, broken and weak. If there was anything human about Lilyth before, it was gone. The dryads continued the attack. Dragons fell from the sky like flies, as did the flames of the phoenixes who fought for Lilyth, not against. The crown pulsed with the phoenix's essence as she successful controlled them—just as Simion suggested he could.

That was the power of the conduit. It could not fall into her hands again.

'The gauntlet,' I said, breathless, inhaling so much smoke I was practically made up of it. 'It is missing.'

It no longer rested on her arm, revealing the pallor of flesh beneath. In that hand, she swung forth what could only be described as a wand with a circular tip that reminded me of a sceptre. My blood spiked at the vision of it, knowing exactly whose conduit this was. I sensed it pull at my soul, as though commanding me.

The dryads reached for it, attempting to separate it from Lilyth, just as the nymphs had successfully done. Except... the gauntlet was back on Lilyth's arm. I narrowed my eyes, leaning forward against the dryad's hold, trying to make sense of it.

'*An illusion,*' the dryad confirmed. '*A forced image conjured by the nymphs in their final effort to go against Lilyth. As are all the conduits you see, all but the crown. This was our chance to separate them from her, but we had to give Lilyth the impression we were weak. This is where we make her believe she has won. To give us a chance.*'

For every god that attacked, Lilyth gathered them up. Their bodies were drawn into glowing orbs, spinning as one above her hands. Once the nymphs faded, once the dragons were drawn from the fight, it was only the dryads and phoenixes left.

'If you had the conduits, why did you not just finish her then?'

Dark blood spilled from wounds across Lilyth. She was weaker, physically. But her power was still no match. She gathered the elemental gods up like toys, storing them for her own use. No matter the roots that pierced her over and over, she broke free, tears streaking down her cheeks, mouth drawn out in a scream of pain and heartbreak.

'*We tried, Maximus Oaken. But desperation led us to this moment. We learn from lessons of the past, preparing for success in the future.*'

'And the conduits?'

'*Were hidden away, taken with us from this moment and locked within the prisons Lilyth placed us in upon Aldian.*'

If the gods had weakened Lilyth, why not fight back? Why not finish her before she locked them away in their respective prisons?

'*Hindsight is a powerful tool, Maximus Oaken. At the time, we believed tricking Lilyth, separating her from the source of her control over us, was the most important task. We, too, were weak, drained, and knew that the time for continuing our battle was not to be at that time.*'

'So you thought you would just lump your fight on us?' I couldn't hide the anger that these gods had the power literally in their hands to finish Lilyth, but, instead, kept up their illusion of being weak just to separate her from the conduits. 'This was never our problem. Our issue to solve, until you decided the humans would make a good army for you.'

'*That is where you are wrong. Lilyth would stop at nothing, she would traverse world to world, conquering, all in search for the sustenance she requires. Aldian, this world, would have been in her line of sight eventually. And, now, we have given you a chance to fight back, instead of dooming you. Perspective is as important as hindsight. See this as a chance, one no world has had before.*'

The ground shuddered as Lilyth's body finally fell forward. I fought the urge to jump from this shroud, to throw myself towards her and finish it. As if sensing my plan, the dryad's limbs constricted around my waist, just as Lilyth outstretched her hand towards the dryads and called them to her.

'Let me end her.' I ripped at the branches holding me, as if I could tear free. 'I can finish this before any of it began.'

'Doing so will ruin the play of time. It will knot the threads of what will be, removing the possibility of you to have a life to go back to.'

'It would save countless people.'

'*No,*' the dryad snapped, the furious sound like a storm tearing through a forest. '*We warned you what playing in time would do. You must not affect events here.*' Before I could so much as move a muscle, I was jolted backwards into the silence of time. Cast away, my body no longer held by the dryad, I tumbled backwards, losing the one chance to destroy Lilyth at her weakest.

* * *

The ground came up to meet me. I barely had time to put my hands out to protect my face from hitting it. Agony tore up my bones, jarring them with the force. Vomit exploded from my body, spilling out across the dewy ground. I blinked. *Focus. Focus.*

'*You are safe here. Take your time.*'

If the dryad hadn't spoken, I would never have clawed my way out of the hysteria. It was then I noticed the details. Grass, green and luscious, very much alive. Light. I looked up to a sky of beautiful blue, hardly a cloud amongst it. Apples littered the ground around me. Some rotten, the smell deathly sweet. Others were so ripe, so red, I could've reached out and taken a bite.

'Why did you do that?' I tried to search for Inyris, but our connection was missing. Between the thundering ache in my head, the guilt of not acting when I had the chance, I could barely think straight. 'I could have killed her. I could have stopped all of this from happening!'

'*Ask yourself, Maximus. What world would you have to return to if Lilyth never reached Aldian? If we were never here? It would be a world without mages, a world without the greed of Southern Kings and Queens. The dryads would never have been here, Galloway would never have fallen in love with one of our own. Thus, the first dryad-born would never have been born. You,*

Maximus, would not exist. Nor would those you love. This is why I did not allow you to act on your desires. Yes, destroying Lilyth would free us, but you would never have existed. Being lost in time, in a place you do not belong, for the rest of your days.'

The dryad no longer held on to me. It was one of the only trees in the clearing. And, certainly, the only dryad. It was an orchard, one I vaguely recognised. But the panic, the chaos, it was enough to distract me from the world around me.

I sat back, throat burning from the acrid taste of bile. As the dryad's words settled over me, another wave of sickness spiked in my stomach. I swallowed it down.

'I understand now,' I said, breathless.

'Time is delicate. More so than the wing of a butterfly.'

Dirt caked my fingers, wedging beneath the broken nails. My skin was red raw. I wished I could have called it a dream, but the physical marks left on my body suggested otherwise. It was all real. I reached behind me, brushing my fingers across my lower back, recognising the ache of broken skin and the damp tunic.

'How do we have a chance, if gods cannot destroy her?'

'Unify. Lilyth is nothing without her... children.' There was something in the way the dryad said children that seemed odd. As though the word was unnatural, or had more of a meaning than I could comprehend. *'We were more than physical embodiments of stolen power, we were the source of her magic. Humans understand the term "fight fire with fire". But what time has forgotten is it is not only fire that requires a fight. It is every element. Water, earth, air and fire. To fight against Lilyth, we must do so united. God and human, side by side. Four elements joined, not separated. We have done what we could, tethering ourselves to you. But it will be the conduits that Lilyth will want, because no matter our bonds, we are powerless to stop her control if she holds the conduits again.'*

Pieces of the complex puzzle were falling into place. 'Then we must find them.'

'Yes, you *must*.'

I reached out for Inyris, but still couldn't sense her. Not entirely. It was muffled by something... I looked around again, taking in the view for what it was. We had not returned to my own time. This was different. The air was lighter, it was daytime. The woods sang with birdsong.

'You haven't returned me to my time, have you?'

'Maximus, you already know the answer to that.'

My skin prickled as I drank in the view again. The peace that filled the air, the lack of ash, the sky blue without clouds or scared by Lilyth's comet.

The dryad leaned forward, essence spilling off it in a wave of pure power. It reminded me, finally, that it was a god. This was an embodiment of one of Lilyth's elements. Vicious as she was. Old as she was. I could not help but respect her power.

'Maximus.'

My name carried on the wind, drawing my attention somewhere over the crest of a hill. The voice was familiar. I knew who it was the moment I heard it. No matter the time, no matter the place—I would never forget the dulcet tones of my mother.

'Go to them, watch, but do not show yourself. You understand now what toying with time will do.'

The dryad's warning was fresh in my mind, but everything else was forgotten as I pushed myself to standing.

'Maximus, will you be careful?'

My legs carried me, the dryad following behind. Although it did not restrain me this time, I knew it would reach out the moment I stepped out of bounds.

'That is close enough, child.' There was discipline in the dryad's tone, yet still something soft. Caring almost.

Over the edge of the hill, I looked down on a ravine cutting through an orchard. It was then I recognised where we were. In the far distance, Gathrax manor was nestled before a dark stretch of Galloway Forest. From here I could see the town beyond, even so far as the outer edges of the Kingdom.

But it was what waited for me below the hill that mattered.

My mother sat on the edge of a bank, her bare feet dangling into a stream of water. In her hand she gripped an apple, red as freshly spilled blood. And there I was. No more than three years old, little limbs padding out into the shallow water, chubby arms reaching down and plucking stones and pebbles to show her.

It wasn't a memory I could call upon, but it must've lingered somewhere in the far reaches of my mind for the dryad to know this is where I wished to go. I slumped on the ground, peering over the edge as I watched time play out.

I was laughing, my high-pitched innocence ringing over the land. Mother began to sing as I ran towards her.

'... run rabbit, run rabbit, run, run, run.'

It broke me. I longed for nothing more than to call for her, to demand that she saw me as I saw her. But the dryad's warning had been clear. And if I wanted access to times like this, I would need them to trust me.

'Thank you...' I said, tears falling into the grass. Despite the beauty of what I watched, how real the sounds of my mother and me were, how they warmed me, the sight of them... nothing could rid me of what else I had seen.

This is but one moment in time. A blessing of power our connection grants. What you see before you is yours to take, but if we do not save the world, it is not only lives that will be lost in the millions. It is history. Memory. Time. All of this... it will be gone.'

'I will do anything in my power to beat Lilyth. In time we will have the numbers, the power. The phoenixes did not fight with you before, but now we have their power.' Simion filled my mind as he always did. As did the growing number of people who had access to the phoenix's fire. 'We have dragons, we have dryads. It is only the nymphs we must convince to help us. They have done it once before, they can do it again.'

A heavy presence pressed down on my shoulder. It was the branch of the dryad, its twig-like fingers gripping me and squeezing. It was such a fatherly sensation—if I closed my eyes, it was as though Father was here with me.

'*Prove our doubts wrong,*' they said, '*you must find the conduits before Lilyth returns for them.*'

'Then tell me where they are. Help me.'

'*I am afraid we cannot. The knowledge of our conduit is lost in time... the location kept from us by another.*' Determination boiled in my belly. I looked back to my mother and me, feeling a guttural sense to protect them, and the memory. '*But there is one person who knows. A key to the knowledge.*'

'Who?' I said, desperate to know.

The dryad leaned into me, returning their earthen limbs around my waist. When they replied, just as the shadows of time crept into the corners of my vision, it was with the name I expected to hear.

'*The answer, as you already know, lies with Celia Hawthorn. Find her, and you will also find what you seek.*'

Frustration rose its head, like a serpent uncoiling within me. 'You think we have not tried? Celia Hawthorn does not want to be found.'

Darkness crept over my vision, blinding me. But the dryad's reply was as clear as daylight. '*You have simply not been looking in the right moment in time, Maximus Oaken. Do not give up.*'

CHAPTER 16

'The answer, as you already know, lies with Celia Hawthorn. Find her, and you will also find what you seek.'

It had been two days since the dryad had offered me this guidance, and still we were no closer to finding Simion and Beatrice's mother. There wasn't the time to look ourselves, even though we had sent word back to the North, to Elder Leia, to continue the search.

There were tasks still left to complete in the South. Tasks ever more pressing and important before Lilyth reached us.

I sat on the dais of the main-chamber room, using what once was King Gathrax's throne as my own. The smell of rot still lingered in the air, left over from the red-scaled dragon that had still been hanging from chains across the ceiling. The same red dragon whose scales were threaded into the armour I had commissioned for Leska.

Leska. Two days after the twins' attack and she had still not woken. Even with hourly updates from the rotations of gleamers attending her, it seemed her wounds had scarred her far deeper than the eye could see.

Guilt was ever the heavy burden to bear.

Distracting myself from images of Leska, unconscious, in bed with her wrist wrapped in gauze and bandages, I focused on the room before me. When I first entered, crimson scales had littered the floor like snow. Not a single one remained now. In its place was a sea of people. A crowd, as though most of the Gathrax Kingdom had come and filled the room, leaving not an inch spare. Even beyond the open doors, as far as the eye could see and even farther than my hearing could stretch, the South came to hear me.

This was the moment I revealed the truth. About gods and monsters, and the facts behind both. And it was not only knowledge welcome to those who flooded Gathrax manor to hear it. Letters had been flown to every major manor, town, Lord and Lady in the South. Not a single soul could be in the dark, not with Lilyth's arrival being days away, if not hours.

The sky was on fire. The comet ever closer. Whispers and gossip were far more dangerous than the truth. If we truly wanted these people to stand beside us in the face of peril, they needed to know we were honest with them.

Simion shuffled at my side, his broad frame made to look small beside the piles and mountains of crates filled with Heart Oak. Every possible soul would leave this place with a mage-mark on their flesh—if they wished to join us after knowing what they were to face.

As I stood from King Gathrax's old throne, it was so silent I could hear the heartbeat in my chest. The sea of people held in a collective breath.

'I see word still travels fast.' I finally spoke, stretching my gaze out across every face, recognising the mixture of distrust and awe in the crowd. 'But then, the South knows war well. It is written in our history, scored so deep into each of our lives that the promise of it still haunts our nightmares.'

I felt like an imposter, standing before these people as they whispered 'King', and yet I couldn't have felt more other. But, for the sake of inspiring them, I would pretend. Just like I had been made to become Julian Gathrax, this was all an act. 'War is upon us again. You have seen the skies filled with phoenixes and dragons. Fire and ice. Galloway Forest moves again, as though possessed by spirits, not dryads. And it is all for reasons even your nightmares would not be brave enough to fathom.'

Gleamers, who were stationed across the dais, chose this moment to step forward. Simion stood at the helm of them. I took a moment to look at him, admiring the focus across his face, the stern admiration for those who had come. And beneath it all, the hope that our plan to get them on board would work.

He was more King than me. From his posture to the kind glint in his eyes as he regarded the crowd.

I steadied my breathing. 'Although, as the South's misleading history proves, I am not here to use my words to convince you to put your lives on the line, to stand before an unknown evil far greater than anything possibly imaginable. So, if you are each willing, would like to show you.'

There were hundreds of people, if not a couple of thousand, in attendance for this announcement. Which was enough that the vision the gleamers would share would also spread by word, like a wildfire, throughout the South. Likely quicker than any of the letters we had sent out.

When no one stepped forward and refused my offer, I nodded to Simion. With a tense face, he nodded, taking the hands of the gleamers until they were a connected chain of power. I chose that moment to connect to my amplifier, fisting my fingers until the ring pinched into my tender skin. I watched the halo of essence wrap around the gleamers, oozing from their eyes like lanterns held up through heavy mist.

I did not need to share in the vision, for it had haunted me enough. Instead, I watched the faces of the crowd morph as Simion and his legion of gleamers broadcast the image of Lilyth, the scenes that I had been witness to during my jaunt in time with the dryads.

It was everything I had allowed Simion to see when I returned with the knowledge of the crown, and the three missing conduits. Although we did not share the importance of the conduits to the crowd, we did lead them into the vision hoping maybe someone would recognise them, perhaps some dusty heirloom left in an attic.

Besides the dryad's warning that Celia Hawthorn held the answers to the missing conduits, I did not even begin to know where to find someone who did not want to be found.

At least we understood why she had been missing for so long. She was the key to our complete success, or failure.

The atmosphere to the room changed immediately. As Simion severed his connection, that collective breath they all took earlier was released. I suddenly missed the deathly silence, as the entire room exploded into chaos and fear. Even beyond the manor, I could hear the cries and shouts. And, worse, the name of the monster who currently fell through our sky. *Lilyth.* It repeated on the winds, giving the monster it belonged to more power in my mind than she had before.

'Please,' I called out, arms lifted as though they had the power to quell the panic. 'Please, I understand what you have seen is enough to spark fear, but I would not have done so if I do not have the means to protect you.' It was only half a lie. I could not protect them, not completely. But I could allow them all to protect themselves, in hopes they then stood beside me as one.

'Who am I, if not but a stranger come to ask your aid? I understand that, and I also know I cannot and will not be like those who have come before me, commanding you to stand in the face of danger, knowing you may not walk away from it. But, for those who do wish to protect their homes, their loved ones, I will offer you something that will see the odds of success are in your favour.'

Simion approached one of the crates, his movements rehearsed. He placed his palm on the flat lid and pushed it open, revealing the neatly stacked piles of Heart Oak within. Clippings I had brought with me, knowing this moment would happen, but not with so little time left.

'Heart Oak. Magic. I bring to the South the very thing that we once had, but was kept solely for those who wanted control. I, as the King no one asked for, no one wanted, will give you access to magic. Do so with it what you will. Use it to protect your home, or protect your neighbours, towns, Kingdoms. I will not ask you to stand by my side and fight, knowing I cannot be the one to send you into the mouth of a monster. But, I will give you each access to the key that could tip the scales in the battle to come.'

Beatrice, not to my surprise, turned up at this moment. She passed through the crowd, gently moving people out of the way, her gaze fixed on me. There was something in the lack of blinking and the way her mouth was parted in anticipation—I knew she had news about Leska.

As much as I longed to finish this abruptly and leave for my sister, I knew I was close to getting what I needed from this meeting. I could taste it in the ever-changing atmosphere.

'Step forward, if you would be willing to stand, united, against a common enemy for the North and South. No longer do we need to be separated, we can be united. A front, not only protecting neighbours in your community but also those neighbours who linger far beyond the leagues of forest.'

No one moved. Not until Beatrice stepped up beside me, facing the same people she had grown up alongside, and said, 'So, who will be the first?'

It was my turn to hold my breath. I did so, watching the

crowd as they, too, watched themselves, waiting to see who would be the first person to start an avalanche of hope.

Jameson stepped forward, the phoenix-possessed man we freed. Before him stood a woman. They beheld so many similarities, I didn't need to be told that they shared blood. But it was the protective hand Jameson kept on her shoulder that told me was her father. That, and the gleam of pride and hope in his eyes.

'How... interesting,' Beatrice drawled, eyes fixed on the woman.

'I speak on behalf of only myself when I say that I stand beside you,' Jameson began, releasing the woman who continued to walk forward. Although his eyes were on me, his words were meant for the crowd. 'We have all been pawns on a gameboard of Kings and Queens we never asked for. You, Maximus Oaken, are different. I see that now.'

Every soul in the crowd listened to Jameson. Of course they did, for he was one of them. Just like I had once been. A normal man, someone who grafted and worked hard for an uncaring Kingdom.

'Thank you, Jameson—'

I stopped short as he bowed. It was a deep dramatic dip, his gaze pinned to the floor. 'I stand beside you, to fight for my family, my home and my Aldian.'

It was a wave of emotion swept out across the room. I couldn't look away as the entire room joined Jameson in his bow.

'No,' I spat quickly, racing down until I stood level with them. 'Please, do not bow for me. I am before you as your equal. Forget titles you have learned. Forget what you feel you must do for me. I only ask that we stand together, side by side.'

They did not listen. I watched as they continued to bow, a silence sweeping over the room. I caught eyes with Simion, only to find his glittering with tears of pride. I swallowed hard, longing to scream and tell them that I was not worthy.

But who was I to tell them what to think? Because that was exactly what this moment was. It was their choice, just as standing beside us, to face Lilyth, was also their choice.

Jameson was the first to straighten. When he did, it was with an honest and determined grin. 'For Aldian.' He beat his fist into the air.

'For Aldian,' echoed the room. Over and over. 'For Aldian. For Aldian.'

The song was so powerful it shattered against walls and glass windows, until the air hummed with the feeling.

It took everything in me not to smile. I took my place once again on the dais, feeling weightless. Feeling hope. And there she was again, waiting patiently, shoulders raised back. Jameson's daughter, no younger or older than me. Prepared to risk her life for the one thing that always mattered.

Family.

'And what would be *your* name?' Beatrice asked for me, the corner of her lip quirked upwards.

'Elaine,' she replied, gaze flickering between the floor and Beatrice's intense attention. 'Elaine Cork.'

Elaine was a striking woman, much like her father who watched on with an aura of pride. She had ringlets of tight blonde curls, deep brown eyes and a broad frame hidden beneath the white shawl.

Beatrice scrawled the name down without sparing a glance back at the parchment. 'Well, Elaine Cork. Please step forward. I trust you know what to do?'

'My father has made it clear, yes.' As quickly as the room parted for Elaine, they began to form a line. Jameson helped our gleamers with keeping order. My eyes pricked at the corners, a lump rising in my throat. I dared not focus on anything but Elaine. Except, for just a moment, I did look up. It was to find a line that stretched outside of the room, lingering through the corridors and out into the gardens.

'Then we begin.'

Elaine looked towards the crates, hunger overspilling in her eyes. She took a step up, reached inside one of the crates and pulled out a cutting of Heart Oak. My skin tingled as she touched it. It wasn't a possessive feeling, but one that came with knowing these people all touched a part of my mother. My Heart Oak.

'Dryads,' Elaine hissed her profanity to Beatrice's delight. I remembered the discomfort as my palms scorched with the mage-mark scar. Mine seemed to tingle now, and would likely burn by the time we were done here.

'The pain will pass,' Beatrice encouraged, placing the parchment beneath her arm as she went to help. She took Elaine's hand in hers, running gentle fingers over the new scar. 'Now, we must test what type of mage you are.'

Elaine looked up through long, pale lashes, waiting for the next command.

'We start off small,' Beatrice said, stepping behind Elaine. 'Eventually, you will be able to carve out your amplifier into the design you like. But first, hold it in your hand, focus on that stone right there.'

'What... what do I do with the stone?' Elaine asked, cheeks blushing red as Beatrice positioned herself behind her.

Beatrice replied by whispering into Elaine's ear, but I knew what she would have said. 'Move it.'

We all watched, waiting for the stone to budge. It didn't. 'Not a battlemage then,' Beatrice said, disappointment lingering her tone. If Elaine was, Beatrice would've been the one to train her, but that left one more option. 'Rules out an elder mage too. You must be a gleamer.'

Silence hung between them, but a faint light pulsed from

beyond Elaine's eyes as she focused on something only she could hear.

Mind-speak, no doubt.

'Tonight?' Elaine barked out loud, the word misplaced and strange. Whatever she was reacting to was in Beatrice's head. Yes, definitely mind-speak.

'Definitely a gleamer.' Beatrice gestured towards the mage who waited on the left side of the room. Elaine blushed as Beatrice leaned in, whispering something in her ear. Then Elaine was moving, throwing Bea a glance with a single raised brow.

'Shall we move on?' Simion interrupted, not without a knowing wink to his sister. He had not once left my side.

Beatrice nodded, her gaze never straying far from Elaine.

'I am proud of you,' Simion said, threading his fingers in mine as the crowd each stepped forward in turn, taking a piece of Heart Oak and moving to their respective sides of the room.

'Why?' I said, hoping only he would hear. 'I am sending them to their death.'

'No, you are wrong. You gave them an option, and they all have chosen.' Ice spread across my skull, alerting me to Simion's entry. *'They all have chosen to stand beside you. I sense their honour, their focus and desire to do as you have asked. And, above it all, their admiration. Something I share.'*

And on it went. Through the day and far into the night. We gave out Heart Oak in the same way that the rulers of this Kingdom once took taxes. There were no rules—the gleamers went to the left of the room, the battlemages to the right. Those who were elders stayed behind, but these were as rare as finding gold in a stream.

It would have taken days to complete the task, which we did not have. Because as night graced the sky, a strange roaring built beyond the manor. Everyone stopped at the same time, looking out the stained-glass windows as a flash of boiling red passed.

Inyris filled my mind, snatching me away from the room a beat before the inevitable happened.

It was not a word she shared with me, but a feeling. A horrifying emotion that stabbed into my core and buried itself. As the light passed from view, there was a moment of stillness before the comet hit the earth miles away, sending a violent boom through the night.

Mother is here. That was what Inyris was sharing. *Mother is finally here.*

PART TWO

THE BARGAIN

CHAPTER 17

There was not an inch of my body that didn't ache. My bones were worn and tired, my mind detached from days of barely any sleep. Evening was fast approaching, and with it, Lilyth's shades would arrive.

It was imperative we left for Wycombe before sundown.

'You look like shit, Max,' Beatrice said. She was the first to see me hobble down the corridor. Simion looked up slowly, standing as I came into view. From his reaction to my torn clothes, ash-coated skin and haunted eyes, he thought the same.

'I feel like it,' I replied, feigning a smile.

It had been the same routine for four days since Lilyth finally reached Aldian. The days were full of preparing as many Southerners as possible to travel through Galloway Forest—under the protection of the dryads—to reach the North.

The nights had been solely for battle.

'How many have we lost?' Simion asked. As I had requested, he had not left Leska's room door for close to four days. Day and night, he was positioned here alongside Beatrice, protecting my sister from the shades' constant attacks.

It was not only Leska I was protecting, but Simion. He had

the crown, he had the conduit Lilyth and her shades wanted returned. Keeping him in the heavily guarded manor was my only option.

'Between seventy and one-hundred,' I answered. Speaking the number aloud made me sick. If I had any food in me, I would have vomited it out across the floor. But four days of constant battle, moving between the manor and Gathrax town, helping against the shades—there was little time to eat, let alone sleep.

'It is getting worse,' Simion said, heat flickering around his broad frame.

'Which is exactly why we must leave.' If I could have grabbed them both and run out the manor in that moment, I would have. 'No more waiting. They will continue coming until they get what they want, which means our presence in the South will continue to be a threat to innocent people. Is she ready?'

News of Leska waking had reached me last night, but I had not had the chance to visit until now.

'Almost,' Simion said, 'but do you truly think you are in any position to travel?'

The answer was simple. No. But we have to.

It was not the screams of agony and fear that still haunted me, but the silence that followed after the shade's attack on Gathrax town that night. I blinked and saw the destruction, entire streets levelled. We had at least managed to navigate the shades towards the Green, attempting to keep civilian casualties to a minimum. But by the time we were able to slow it down enough to kill it, it had taken far more lives than I imagined.

What we had learned was that the shades could only attack in darkness. As long as a flame burned, banishing shadows from corners of rooms, we would keep them out of the manor. Light didn't destroy but weakened them, so they became vulnerable to steel.

'Dare I ask how many shades it took to murder so many innocent lives?' Simion added, practically every muscle of his being tense. I felt his eyes trace over me, inspecting the dried patches of blood across my leathers.

'One.' Every set of eyes on me raised. 'They are far stronger, now that *she* has arrived.'

'It's chaos,' Beatrice spat, nervously pacing. 'Imagine what could happen if we face an entire legion of shades.'

The thought alone was ruination.

But what unsettled me the most was Lilyth's silence. Her lack of presence. Since Lilyth's comet touched down in Aldian, we had not had the displeasure of meeting her.

Her shades, however, returned nightly.

Beatrice stopped dead, her nail caught between her teeth, whilst Simion continued to stare at me, the conduit of flames resting upon his head.

'Any news on Celia?' I asked the same question every time I saw them.

'Leia still cannot reach her. We cannot rely on finding her.'

I snapped, exhaustion and fury clawing up my throat. 'We must. Celia is the key, the dryads confirmed as much. If we have any chance in locating the final conduits before Lilyth, we need your mother to help.'

Beside the drawings on the parchments slotted into my pocket, depicting the three remaining conduits, we had no other information. I had drawn them from memory, snatched straight from the moment in time the dryad showed me. It was clear they were important to Lilyth, which meant, by proxy, they were even more important to us.

'Time is running out, I can feel it,' I said between chewing my lower lip.

Simion was before me in seconds, drawing me close to him. 'You need to rest, before we think about doing anything. We all do.'

'I will rest once this is all over. Until then, I cannot stop. Not for a moment.'

'Max is right,' Bea said. 'The moment we stop is the moment we allow Lilyth to get leagues ahead of us. I can't help but think she is keeping us busy, whilst she searches for the rest of the conduits.'

I looked to the closed door, more importantly to the woman lingering within. My eyes snapped to the brass handle a moment before it turned and the door opened.

Out slipped Elaine Cork. Her tired eyes found Beatrice first, offering a meek smile. Her white apron was marked with trails of russet brown. Dried blood. Her pale fingers were stained a faint pink.

'How is she?' I asked, breathlessly studying Elaine's face for answers. The crease of her brow, the way her eyes stayed on Beatrice, as though she gained strength from their wordless connection.

'We have done the best we can, with what was provided,' Elaine said, wringing her hands. 'Leska's vitals are strong. I am sure that doesn't surprise you.'

It took no time before Beatrice was at her side, arm wrapped around her shoulder. 'You've impressed me to no end, Elaine.' Beatrice planted a kiss to her cheek.

It transpired that Elaine had been a healer from the Calzmir Kingdom, so discovering she was a gleamer was not a complete surprise. Her father, Jameson, was already en route to Wycombe, using his new abilities as a sorcerer to help protect those travelling on foot. Elaine had opted to stay behind, said it was to help Leska, but I suspected it had everything to do with Beatrice.

I trusted Elaine because Beatrice did. There was a kinship between them, something more, in fact, and because of that Elaine had not left Leska's side in the past day.

But as I looked to Elaine, I knew there was something she

was not saying. A detail kept back because she either didn't want to share or wasn't sure how to.

A shadow slinked in behind me. Days of being alert almost made me reach out to my magic, but it was as depleted as my hope. A warm hand rested on my shoulder and calmed me.

'Is Leska comfortable enough for visitors?' Simion asked.

Elaine nodded. 'Yes, she has been asking after you all.'

My skin prickled as I looked through the door, a violent rush of gooseflesh over every inch of skin. My vantage point only showed me two gleamers huddled together, speaking in whispers. The air was heavy with lavender, masking the smell of blood and exhaustion.

'Thank you, Elaine,' I exhaled, feeling the weight in my shoulder lessen. 'I understand this magic is new to you, but staying back to help Leska has been valiant.'

Beyond the window, the sky was still pale from the cloud-filled sky. We would need to leave, and soon. Between Elaine and the two gleamers, we were all that was left in Gathrax manor. Once the sun set, Aldian would become a playground for the shades again.

'We plan to leave within the hour. Gather anything you wish to bring with you, and then we will begin our journey for the North. It is safer there, for all of us. Wycombe have a large number of trained mages, which we do not have.'

I was sure Elaine said something else, but I didn't catch it. Not as another voice rose from within the room. 'Are you going to stand out there, or come in and see me?' Leska's voice was full of vitality, and overspilling with the commanding drone I was used to. But there was something edged to it, a tension that seemed misplaced.

Beatrice nudged Elaine, wrapping a hand around her waist. 'Sounds like you really have worked your magic.'

It was meant to be a compliment, but still Elaine didn't smile. There was no pride in her eyes. Elaine worked out of

Beatrice's hold as the two remaining gleamers swept from the room. They all left, footsteps fading into the ruined manor.

'Go,' Simion said, his hand urging me forward. 'I will prepare our means of travel and make sure *my* phoenix hasn't been torn to shreds by Inyris.'

My phoenix. Simion had not only physically claimed the gods, but mentally.

In tandem to his comment, I caught the muffled grumble of my dragon followed by the chirping caw of our new companion. Simion's mount, claimed when he wore Lilyth's crown of fire— her conduit to the element she coveted so dearly. And the reason her shades returned beneath the cover of night, to take back what belonged to her.

'We will not be long,' I said, a beat before Simion's mouth found mine. I delighted in the calming kiss Simion gave me. It was heavy with emotion, lingering and soft. It was the only power that could clear my mind, if only for a moment. When I caught black-pointed metal across his brow, I remembered everything that had changed between us all.

'I will be here, waiting for you, as always.' He planted a quick kiss on my cheek, and dryads knew I wanted to melt into him. Days of no touch, days of short-lived moments, was taking its toll on me.

What I would give to carve out a place in time with him, somewhere no one would interrupt.

All thoughts and wishes seemed to deplete to nothingness as I entered Leska's room. It was bathed in overwhelming fire-light. It spilled in from the many windows, highlighting the rumpled sheets in the fourposter bed, the pile of bandages and the murky pots of water left by the gleamers. I hadn't seen her since the attack in Galloway Forest.

Melted candles took up the majority of the room's surfaces, even across the floor. All this to keep the shades banished, to keep Leska safe. I navigated around hardened puddles of wax, moving towards the woman who stood before the window.

Leska's outline was haloed by fading daylight. It caught the hard edges of her armour—the red, black and gold-scaled gift I had commissioned for her, which was now finished. Seeing her in it took my breath away. Relief almost buckled my knees, but I held firm. Her dark hair had been cut down to the scalp. I could still see the faint scars left from where the wytchfire had touched her.

'From what I have been told,' Leska said, speaking to the view beyond the window, 'you've had your hands rather full, protecting the world from our unwanted visitor.'

'Something like that,' Beatrice barked, half a choke and half a sob. 'Good to see you up and about.'

I still couldn't form words.

Leska turned her head, enough to catch the lines of her profile. 'You have got Elaine to thank for that.'

Pride flashed over Beatrice's face. Still, I couldn't find the words. I longed to hold onto the relief of seeing Leska out of bed, standing, dressed and well. But something was off.

'Max, it is not like you to be so quiet. Haven't you got anything to say to your favourite sister?'

The answer was no. What I longed to do was wrap my arms around her, hold her as though a faint breeze would tear her away. I opened my mouth to say something, anything. But Leska turned around fully until I could see what she hid from us. I released a guttural sob from the deepest parts of me.

Her hand, or where it once had been, was now an empty space.

'Do not cry for me, Max.' Leska raised her right arm up, showing the single mound of flesh that ended at her wrist. The skin was fresh and pale, stretched over bone where the gleamers had forged it in place. 'It could have been a lot worse than this.'

All the blood; the harrowing expression on Elaine's face; the way the gleamers rushed from the room. It all made sense now.

'I'm so sorry.' The words tumbled out of my mouth before I could stop them.

Leska ignored me, brushing off the apology with the wave of her arm. 'If you think this will stop me from breaking your nose, you're wrong.'

Her attempt to diffuse the violent storm in my mind almost worked. Almost. 'That is my fault. If I didn't—'

'Shut up, Max.' Leska paced towards me swiftly, her shoulders rolled back. 'You were not the one to conjure wytchfire and burn me. In fact, if my memory tells me anything, you are the one who came back for me. If I ever hear you take blame for this again, I will prove that I can still break bones. Okay?'

I nodded, biting down on my inner lip to stop the tears from coming.

'How... does it feel?' Beatrice asked, her face set in a grimace as she regarded Leska's wounds.

'As though I can still feel my fingers, even though the wytchfire ensured they were forever dealt with. It's a phantom ache, but nothing that will stop me.' Leska offered us both a smile, one that sang of her confidence. 'But, I am alive. If a hand was the price to pay for it, so be it. I understand this is a shock, trust me I know. But dwelling on it won't change the outcome. So, for me, please don't. This will not stop me... believe me.'

I swallowed hard, forcing down the sadness that wrapped around my throat and squeezed. But I did it, for Leska. With her shaved head, body garbed in dragon scales and the defiant gleam in her eyes, there would be no tears shed.

'We must leave for the North—'

Leska took a powerful step forward. 'Before the mother of monsters sends her lackeys to come after that crown again?'

I nodded. 'Exactly.'

'And Lilyth still hasn't shown herself yet?'

'Not as of yet,' Beatrice answered for me. 'Although I dare speak it into existence. There is tension in the air, a thickness that sings of the impending doom.'

'The calm before the storm,' I added. 'When Lilyth first came to Aldian, the journey had weakened her. I imagine she is struggling greatly this time as well, especially without the four conduits.'

'I would not call it calm, not from what I have heard every night. *They* are hell-bent on retrieving the crown. What do we know about the rest of the conduits?'

'Not enough,' I said confidently. 'Until Celia is located, we are in the dark.'

I withdrew the three pieces of parchment from my belt and unrolled my drawings for Leska. There was the dryad's sceptre, the dragon's shield and the nymph's gauntlet.

Leska scanned over the sketches, as so many had before. But unlike those who had, Leska paused on one of the parchments. 'This... I have seen this.'

To my surprise, it was the sketch of the gauntlet. Well, it wasn't entirely a surprise, since it was the sketch with the most detail. As though my mind found it familiar—from the silver metal to the blue gemstones.

'When?' Beatrice asked, voice full of anticipation.

'Yes, my father... he—'

It was then the piece of the puzzle finally fit in my head. I closed my eyes as a sharp pain passed through my skull. I was no longer stood in the room, but in a system of caves from the ghost of a man at my side.

Elder Cyder had worn it, concealing the gauntlet beneath his cloak as he had shown me where he held the nymphs that helped him to make an army of phoenix-possessed. At the time I had wondered how he had kept hold of such solitary gods, but if what Leska was suggesting was true, then he was the last one to have the conduit. The last one who could control the nymphs, make them do whatever he desired.

It all made sense.

'Are you sure?' Beatrice asked.

Leska looked at me, knowing I had just worked out the same thing as her. 'Yes. Cyder had it. That was how he made the nymphs help him. It was not from choice, but because he could control them.'

'Then we have a detour to make before we head back for Wycombe city,' Beatrice said.

My gaze snapped to the shadowed corner of the room. 'Don't say it. Anyone could be listening.'

Leska's lips forged together and she nodded in agreement. 'There *will* come a time we must face her. Best to do so whilst she is in a weakened state, no?' Leska said. 'The longer we wait... the higher the chance she finds what she is looking for...'

It didn't need to be said, what would happen. With the conduits, Lilyth would gain control over the elemental gods. Dryads would turn on us, even if they didn't wish to. The dragons' loyalty would shift in a heartbeat.

We wouldn't stand a chance.

'So, what do you recommend?' I asked, actually longing for someone else to call the shots.

'I say we pay this mother a visit, give her a good old Aldian welcome.' Leska straightened. 'But not before we check off the possibility of the nymph's conduit being... being where we think it was left.'

The hidden island where Cyder had housed his rebellion. It had to be there.

'I'm in.' Beatrice's brow waggled; a devious smile littered her mouth. 'I am practically gagging to meet Lilyth. I have a few choice words I would like to share.'

Panic constricted in my chest, tightening my lungs until my

breath was rasped. 'It will be dangerous. I can't make that call knowing what else is at risk.'

I couldn't stop myself from looking down to Leska's hand-less arm. She noticed my pity, but before I could claw it back with an apology, she spoke.

'Every second that passes only increases the chance of danger.' The glass shuddered at Leska's back, the light blocked as thick serpents of vines slithered across the windows. Even in my exhausted state, I recognised the taint of magic, the way her blue eyes shone with it, like lanterns glowing through mist. 'In the famous words of our dearly departed father, *"put can't in your pocket and pull out try".'*

The windows cracked like the soft shell of an egg. Leska's conjured vines wrapped around her back, folding over her scaled armour like wings until they wrapped down her arm, stopping where her hand once waited. Fingers of vine and root took place, flexing and testing themselves. She gathered the tendrils of earth into a fist, lifting it up before her, marvelling at her creation just as we did.

'Well, Leska, I didn't expect that,' Beatrice said through an impressed smile.

'I live to surprise.' From her belt, Leska wrapped her vines around the handle of her axe and lifted it before her. In one hand she held the sketch of the gauntlet, and the other access to her magic. The little devil may have taken her hand, but it only fuelled her spirit.

'For nights I have listened to you all battle her shades. I admit, I would be disappointed if I, too, don't get to join in on the fun tonight,' Leska said, twisting her amplifier with ease, the sharp metal edge catching the reflection of her deadly grin.

I smiled as Leska toyed with her earthen limbs, testing them, playing with their weight and balance. 'For the first time, I pity Lilyth.'

It was only partially true. Because unlike Beatrice and

Leska, I had seen the full might of Lilyth, and I knew what would become of Aldian if we didn't face her eventually.

Ice crawled over my skull, distracting me from the mother of monsters just at the right time. Slowly, Simion's voice entered my mind, filling me with the familiar kiss of his presence.

We are ready to leave for Wycombe, my love.

My love. Dryads, help me, those two words really had the power to undo and fuel me.

Slight change of plans, I forced out into my mind, knowing Simion was listening. I shared an image of the island, silently extending the thread of hope Leska had provided. *We have a short detour to take.*

CHAPTER 18

Simion Hawthorn was a vision most days. But now, as he stood before the towering bird of flame, slender fingers running through its plume of feathers, he was breathtaking. Lilyth's conduit rested atop his head, the points flickering like a mirage on a scalding day. Rays of light seemed to bounce off the otherworldly metal, casting his brown skin in a glow of pure radiance.

I stopped in the entrance to Gathrax manor, with the stretch of scorched earth between us. In tandem, both man and god turned to face me. Simion withdrew his hand, and I admit I felt a twist of jealous at their proximity. There was nothing more I craved in this moment than his touch, his attention.

Allowing my thoughts to wander to the library—which was now a cavernous space torn apart by talons and shades—I could easily lose myself to grief. That had been our hideaway, a place we could shut the door and only exist as two.

I suppose the time for such moments were lost to us, now the impending doom of the comet had arrived.

Inyris flashed in my mind, pulling on the tether binding us. It was brief, but strong enough for me to look upwards. Raising a hand to my brow, I blocked the light out enough to see the gold-scaled creature curled around the bell tower. Distrust oozed off her in waves. She stalked Simion's phoenix, *Erinda*, as though it was a mouse and she a cat.

No matter how I shared my emotions, Inyris had a mind of her own. And, in a way, I was thankful for it. The only thing stopping Erinda from turning on us all, scorching us to ash beneath the wytchfire hidden within its body, was the crown atop Simion's head.

'Come to marvel at me or Erinda?' Simion called, his voice loud across the silent, barren landscape.

I took a deep inhale, feeling the heavy stench of burning lather the back of my throat. 'You know the answer to that, Simion.'

His smile proved he did. It was him. It was always him.

I kept still, my skin tingling as Simion withdrew his hand from Erinda. He offered a word beneath his breath, then paced towards me. Behind him, powerful wings beat, feathers ruffled and Erinda was airborne.

I felt Inyris's scales brush over stone as she released the stone wall and leapt skywards. She gave pursuit to Erinda, circling the god of fire as though they played a childish game of chase.

'Are they ready to leave?' Simion asked, his eyes flickering to the manor as he stalked towards me.

It took effort not to become entranced by the crown. I focused on the gold of his eyes, knowing it had the power to anchor my attention. 'Within the hour.'

'A lot can happen in an hour.' A gasp escaped me as Simion's sure hands found my waist and held me.

'Is that you or the crown talking?'

'Would it matter?'

I swallowed hard. 'It is going to play with your passions.

Heighten them until it practically screams bloody murder into your ear. Careful.'

From the furrow in his brow, I could tell it took Simion considerable effort to release me. 'I can manage it.'

'I don't doubt it for a second.' I brushed my fingers down his cheek. The truth was we did have an hour and, dryads, I wanted him. But it would have to wait, like all good things. Because what I desired more than Simion was distance. Distance from Gathrax manor, from the threat of Lilyth's damned. 'Aren't you going to ask after Leska?'

'You say it as though it is something to be sad about.'

I blinked and saw her arms. 'She lost her...'

'Leska has lost nothing but time. Power is not in what we have, but what we do.'

'You're right.' But that still didn't take away from the responsibility I had placed upon my shoulders. If I had not taken Leska to show her the armour, if I had just left her...

'Of course I am right, Your Highness.'

Tingles coursed over my shoulders, spreading across my back like wings. 'Is that so, *Your Highness*?'

His mouth lifted at one corner, then the next, until his handsome face creased in the most awe-inspiring smile. Simion reached up, took the crown from his head and lowered it to his side. 'Is there ever going to be a time when I can exercise my new rights as King and find my own throne to sit upon?'

Heat rushed through my cheeks, staining them crimson. 'Time and a place, Simion Hawthorn.'

'I preferred "Your Highness".'

A roar distracted us from the building tension. We both looked up to find Inyris snapping her jaws towards Erinda, spitting frozen air. Simion's phoenix twisted and turned, moving with the grace of a dancer. Inyris was all power, no grace.

'They hate each other,' I said.

'Mortal enemies turned allies—it is a lot to swallow for such ancient creatures. Humans have history, but gods have eternity. It is going to take time for them to grow used to each other.'

'Ah, time. The thing we do not have.' I quickly shot Inyris a warning, not that she would listen. It was forbidden to attack Erinda or any other phoenix unless provoked. And from what I could sense, Erinda was simply toying with Inyris, enjoying every moment of their little game.

A gentle, warm hand rested upon my shoulder. As whenever Simion touched me, he had the ability to draw me out of my dark thoughts. 'I will not allow anything to happen to you.'

'It isn't me I am worried about, but everyone else. Lilyth is here. Her damned creatures attack us in the cover of night. We know nothing about her beside the scraps of knowledge the dryads provided. There are three conduits of power to find before Lilyth locates them.' My heart beat faster and faster, cantering until my ribs ached. 'Every time I think we have a chance, I feel it slipping away, like sand through my fingers. How can we stop Lilyth when we don't even know what we are going to face?'

What I didn't voice was I did, in fact, know what we had to face. Destruction. I had seen it, a world ruined by Lilyth before her children turned on her. And still she won. Biding her time to return and devour another world.

'Maximus Oaken.' Simion used my name as a weapon. It was both calming to hear him speak it, and scolding. 'May I remind you that you are not alone. We shoulder these burdens together. Me, Beatrice, Leska, Inyris—'

'Erinda?' I added.

He nodded. 'Erinda and the entire race of phoenixes are under my control. I have the crown. Which means we have one more conduit than Lilyth.'

'That we know of—'

Simion planted a finger to my lips, stifling yet another negative comment. 'We only focus on facts. One at a time. We have the crown. We know where the conduit for the nymphs was last seen. That leaves only those for the dragons and the dryads.' He didn't say it, but his mother's name lingered across his tongue. 'Lilyth's damned are barely shadows, no more bothersome than wasps. We beat them with light and, my darling, I have an abundance of it.'

He finally withdrew his finger. I took a deep inhale, allowing Simion's words to settle over me.

'All I want is to hide away in the Mad Queen with you,' I said.

Simion's expression softened, his posture opening to allow myself to fold into him. 'Me too, Max. And we will, I promise. There is so much I wish to do with you, I do not have the time to explain. But I promise, I promise with my entire being, that we will get there.'

I believed his promise because Simion's fingers brushed the back of my neck and the emotion behind it bled into me.

'I love you, Your Highness,' I said, my words muffled into his hardened chest.

Simion placed a long, tempered kiss into my hair. He held my face with his hand, the other grasping hold of the crown as though it was some mundane object that mattered little to him. 'And I love you too.'

* * *

From atop Inyris, I could see for miles. I searched the horizon for signs of Lilyth, to see where her comet had landed, but there was nothing but peace. No billowing cloud left from destruction, no ominous force acting as a sign of where she hid. To our left was a stretch of Galloway Forest—below us was the endless expanse of the Thalassic.

Wind screamed past my ears, whipping the hair from my face. Ahead, Glamora cut across the ocean, her black scales glistening with sea-salt spray. Beatrice rode at the front, with Elaine holding onto her waist. Inyris kept pace with the large dragon, wings gliding as her body cast a shadow on the ocean below. Every now and then I felt the tightening of Leska's vines around my waist, anchoring us together. I didn't need to look back to know my sister slept, I heard the raspy snores in my ear even above the screeching winds.

Simion kept to the rear, Erinda beneath him and a formation of phoenixes cast at his back, in the formation birds took when migrating to warmer climes. Every time I looked back to him, it was as though the sun shone behind him. Except it was his fire, the glow of it falling beneath the phoenixes like rain falling from clouds. As the day slipped away, revealing late afternoon, the light never left us. As the dark came, the phoenixes changed formation until they encased us in a circle. Inyris grew distracted, flashing teeth and hissing at any phoenix that got to close. The only noise Glamora made was the low-bellied rumble that sang of her amusement at the younger dragon's unfettered fury.

Simion. We should stop soon.

He was always there, waiting in my mind. *There is a small island not far from here. No more than an outcrop of rocks we passed on the way to the South. It will do us for the night. Beatrice is already aware.*

It didn't take long for us to find it. A stretch of rock protruding from the darkening ocean like a jagged tooth of some great, sunken creature. Clouds of a promised storm rose across the horizon, making it impossible to see the stars. The winds picked up, thrashing waves beneath us. By the time we landed, fine pinpricks of rain lashed down from the heavens, coating us each in its aching chill.

We trod into the gaping mouth of a cave, Simion leading the way with bundles of conjured fire in each hand. He cast the looming shadows away, exposing the cave's every nook and cranny. His fire needed no wood or kindling. It simply burned, allowing us each to make camp for the night and dry off our sodden bodies.

'I will keep watch first,' Simion announced, the outline of his body highlighted by a fork of lightning that cast across the darkened sky. 'Get some rest.'

'Gallant brother of mine,' Beatrice called from the place she was already laid, arms curled around Elaine who was nestled beside her. 'I won't argue with that offer. But when you are ready, wake me. I will do the next. We all need sleep, emphasis on *all*.' Her eyes settled on me, as though reading my mind, knowing what was to come.

'You can't do it alone,' I said, knowing there was no way I would leave Simion alone. 'I will join you.'

'Of course, you will,' Leska added, voice raising from her place against the stone wall. She was sat up, eyes closed, one knee drawn up. 'Let's hope the storm covers any...'

'Thank you, Leska. That is more than enough.'

Elaine's light chuckle was followed by Beatrice's deep rumble. 'However tired or... distracted you get out there, Simion, please keep these flames burning. I don't fancy a visit from the shades tonight.'

It was odd, because this was the first night the shades had not sprung forward at the first sign of darkness. I wondered about those we left behind and the army currently working their way through Galloway Forest with aid from the dryads. Would the shades leave them, knowing we have the conduit?

Either way, I could only pray—to whom I was not sure.

'Oh believe me.' Simion gestured beside him, burning the conjured flames brighter and hotter. 'There will be no room for shadows and shades tonight.'

My heart jolted violently at the suggestion in Simion's tone. I bade them all goodnight, placed my hand on Simion's shoulder and guided him outside.

A lip of stone rose over the cave's entrance, keeping the rain from falling upon us. Perched all around, Simion's phoenixes waited like sentinels of glowing flame. Darkness hung around them, an impenetrable sheet that seemed to have eyes and teeth. Were the shades watching?

I certainly sensed something, lurking just beyond the sheet of rain and night.

Inyris and Glamora were curled up not far from us, gold and black scales merged into one. I didn't dare disturb my dragon. It had been a long few days for her too, and I would need her at full strength.

'Max, I am a holding back a tidal wave of desires for you. Sitting up with me is only weakening my defences. Especially with this on.' He gestured to the crown atop his head.

There was no stopping my smirk. 'I know. Which is why I offered to join you with first watch. I may not be using the conduit, but I, too, have passions.'

'You do?' Simion leaned in closer, his arm brushing mine.

I turned to face him, laying a leg on either side of his hips. His fingers found my shins, trailed up to my thighs and held on. 'Do you think Lilyth watches us from the shadows?'

His golden gaze flickered to the wall of shadows, his grin faltering for but a second. 'I think Lilyth is always watching, especially since I am wearing her conduit as though it is mine.'

'It *is* yours, Simion.'

'What else is mine?'

I shifted closer, enjoying the bite of his nails through the damp leather of my trousers. 'Me.'

'You make controlling these desires of mine impossible.'

We couldn't get any closer. Simion had drawn me onto his lap, my body delighting in the warmth of his conjured fire, the power beneath his skin. His hands moved to the small of my back, encouraging me to arch into him. 'Then I give you full consent to have me, right now, in this moment.'

Who knew how many moments like this we would be allowed?

'Dryads, Maximus,' Simion growled, the gold of his eyes brightening with the unnatural power flowing through his body. 'You worry about Lilyth being our damnation, when it is you who will ruin me.'

I took his face in my hands, pressing his stone-hard jaw into my palms. 'Believe me, Simion. It will be you who is ruining me tonight.'

'Even with the promise of the world ending?'

I refused to pay that mind. Not here. 'Then take me, like it is the last time.' I looked skywards as another fork of lightning cast across the dark sky. This time it was mine, conjured by the sparking magic in my veins. It fizzed across my skin, raising the hairs on my arms. 'Fuck me, Simion.'

The growl that emanated from Simion echoed across the phoenixes. I looked up, noticing how their beady fire-gold eyes looked everywhere but towards us. I wondered if that was Simion's doing. As one, the phoenixes cried out into the night, a song of his burning passion.

'This time,' Simion added. 'I want to hear your desires. Tell me what to do for you.'

I took a deep breath, relishing in the way he drank me in. Then I spoke, allowing the command to slip out with ease.

'Bend the knee for me. *Now*.'

CHAPTER 19

Rocks cut into Simion's knees, but the discomfort clearly did not register. Not as his full focus was on me as I stood above him, glowering down my proud nose, eyes glittering. Simion's fingers plucked the buttons at the waistband of my trousers until the material was loose. He took his time, drawing it over my hips and thighs, which strained with muscle, until it pooled at my ankles.

Dryads. I found myself longing for his praise. My mouth ran with moisture, born from the riling storm of excitement in my stomach. It built and built, matching the rain that raged around us.

'How do I fair, kneeling before you, Max?'

'Perfect.' A tempest crashed in my chest, making my hands shake with excitement. 'Keep going, Simion.'

'I have no intention to stop, my love.'

His fingers had been hooked into the thin band of my undershorts, the heel of his hand brushing the stone-hard mound of my cock. Coarse, dark hairs crowned the top of my groin, trailing up to my bellybutton in a thin line. Simion took his nail, tracing it down the line until it disappeared within my shorts. He didn't stop until it connected with my concealed length. As soon as he touched it, regardless of the material that separated us, I leaned my head back and groaned.

Pleasure was a boiling, feral thing. This was power. It turned me into a creature of senseless sounds and cries.

'Unless you want to alert all of Aldian to my misbehaviour, I suggest you cover your mouth,' Simion said, muffled by the aggravated lashing of rain.

I looked back to him, his face glistening with water. He was drenched to the bone, as was I. The wind had changed, lashing it in our direction. It was warm, almost comforting.

'Are you going to just hold it, or—'

'The King still offers me commands,' Simion retorted, his voice tempered with lust and sarcasm.

'Do you not forget that it is you who bends the knee for me now?' I asked.

His hand snuck beneath my undershorts, grasped my length and pulled it free. It was so sudden that my eyes glazed over, my need for an answer forgotten.

Droplets of rain fell from Simion's nose, landing on my tense knuckles. 'You are not wrong.'

'I know,' I said through a smile. He guided the curved tip of my cock to his mouth, stopping only half an inch away. At this point, I wasn't sure if he was teasing me or himself.

I wove my fingers across the back of his head, teasing his curls. From the throaty growl Simion released, he delighted in the scratch of my nails across his scalp.

Simion was usually the one who experienced the perfect balance of tenderness and pain—it was the dance of pure bliss. I had learned from him. This change in giving and taking was thrilling.

'Fill that pretty little mouth with me,' I said.

His gaze narrowed, lips sharpening at the corners. 'Then

once your seed fills my cheeks, we will re-evaluate exactly what you would do when you're on your knees.'

Dryads.

Simion's passion was a boiling volcano, a chamber of molten lava spitting and frothing, begging for escape. It seeped from his touch, spreading over my length like a breath of hot air, unfolded across my groin until every part of me shared in it.

He took me into his mouth, spreading his lips around me. There was no stopping him, not until my cock found a natural end at the back of his throat. He gagged on it, encouraging me to tighten my hold on his hair, grasping him in place.

He worked his fist in a rhythm with his wet mouth. Rain continued to fall, lubricating my grith, making the movements easier, faster. Simion was large, in many ways. But in his hand, he made me feel paramount.

Focusing on my cock's crown, he weaved his tongue around it, wetting it, sucking. His knuckles tightened near the base of it, his spare hand cupping my heavy, full balls whilst he massaged them within his palm. It was a miracle I was still standing. I rocked back and forth, caught in the sway of wind and rain. Knees weak, body no longer belonging to me, Simion owned me flesh and soul.

Needing to catch my strength, I drew myself out of his mouth. I could see that his lips were swollen. Not once did his fist stop moving, to my delight. A hint of my passion seeped from the end of my cock, milky drips of seed that only promised of what was to come.

'Are you all right?' Simion asked, his voice soft, although his eyes sang of his want to take my cock again and pound with force until my cum lathered his tongue.

'Trying to control myself, that is all.'

'Good boy, always worrying about control. Give into me, my love.'

His praise ruined me, in all the best ways. 'So you *don't* want me to be good?'

'I want you to be terrible, Max. Your legs are shaking, your groans are so loud Inyris is stirring and all I can taste is your attempt to hold back from finishing. What's stopping you?'

My brows raised, fire-coiling eyes widening. 'I am not ready for this to end. But you are correct, I am close, I fear I cannot hold back for much longer.'

'Fill me then,' he snapped, lips curling over teeth. 'I want it, all.' His hand worked faster, harder. 'Do it, I dare you.'

I bent down, grasped his jaw in my hand, drawing him upward to meet my mouth. The kiss was all encompassing and passionate. It was fire and ice; it was peace and chaos. It was everything I could need and more, and dryads I wished this would last.

In that moment, hidden on an island surrounded by ocean and storm, bathed in the light of phoenix flame, I learned that we could carve our own place in the world no matter where it was.

'I love you,' Simion groaned into my mouth.

'Me?' I replied, fingers still on his face.

'Your mouth. Your mind. Your heart. Your soul. Your skin. Your voice. Your—'

I silenced him with my tongue. It slipped into his open mouth, catching his next words and drinking them in.

A new voice called out from the darkness. 'Maximus...'

My heart thumped in my chest. Simion jolted backwards. I scrambled to stand, facing the sheet of rain that had surrounded us. I quickly raised my trousers up, fumbling to buckle them at the waist.

I hadn't noticed just how heavy the rain had become until looking beyond it was impossible. A sheet of impenetrable rain.

'Maximus...'

I couldn't discern who spoke, but it was familiar. 'Beatrice?'

'Well, if there is one way to ruin a moment, it is my sister.' Simion stepped beside me, squinting into the darkness.

'Maximus.' The voice was harder, more strained with emotion. I searched through the curtain of rain, trying to make out Beatrice through it. There was certainly a shape beneath the phoenix's glow. But it was distant.

Simion moved before me. 'I will see if she is okay, then be sure that I am coming back to finish this.'

'Maximus...'

'We heard you,' Simion snapped, stepping into the rain until it swallowed him whole. 'Bea, you truly are insufferable.'

If she replied, I didn't hear it.

Panic thundered in my ears, suddenly left alone with nothing but rain around me. There were flickers of fire, as no rain could extinguish the natural flame of the phoenix. Inyris woke as I reached for her, my dragon raising her head in my direction. I could barely make out the glint of gold, but knowing she was close and aware was calming. But I felt suffocated, as though the rain was pressing in on me, further and further and...

Simion stepped slowly through the sheet of rain, rivulets running off his skin like morning dew.

'Is everything all right?' I asked, hands wrapped around my chest. Seeing him calmed me, until it didn't. Something was wrong. He was corpse still, his face void of expression. But there was something else... a lack of light to his eyes, which had me faltering. 'What is it, Simion? Tell me...'

'Where is it?' His voice was rough and loud. Almost too loud.

'Where is what? I don't understand?'

I pulled upon the bond between Inyris, but all I sensed was my dragon's calm nature. Even as my insides thrashed, my dragon was ready to settle back to sleep. I couldn't make out why.

Simion took a step forward. His outline shifted, as though

the rain blurred his body. His face morphed into a smile so quickly I almost missed the emotion that came before. It was as if he was always smiling, even though I knew it was not true.

'My crown, I believe I have lost it. I would like it back.' He came closer and still I couldn't move back. The rain dusted off his shoulders, bouncing as though it feared him. 'Will you help me, Max? Help me find it?'

The closer he paced to me, the harder the rain feel. It was becoming impossible to see a foot in front of me, let alone anything beyond. I lifted a hand to my brow in hopes I could make Simion out.

'Simion.' I reached out my mind, connecting with the ice-cold brush that was Simion's mind. The impression of his emotion crashed into me, and my stomach rocked violently with sickness. Pleasure. Enjoyment. It was the same feeling he had shared with me when my cock was in his mouth... except now it wasn't. 'You haven't lost it, it is—'

My words died in my throat. The amplifier on my finger pulsed as I drew upon my earthen connection. Magic spilled beyond my skin, melting into the stones at my feet. It took little effort to lift them. Countless bullets of rock and stone shifted out of view. One thought, one intention and they shot forward, directly towards him. But instead of catching flesh, they passed through him. Where my stones moved, Simion's body parted as though he was made from cloud and mist, only to reform.

'I have lost my crown, Maximus,' he continued, not noticing my attempts at magic. 'Help me find it.'

My magic reached to the rock bed beneath his feet, to catch him in a trap. But he continued to walk, undisturbed by my attacks.

Because he was not real, this was not real.

It was as though Simion was made of water. The rain. The unnatural storm. The voice. It was all fake—no, it was an illusion.

'You haven't lost it,' I said to the rain, to the being behind it. 'It has been taken from you.'

From *you*.

Simion burst apart, skin parting from his false frame like ash. The world seemed to stop. No longer did the rain fall, but stopped static in the air, hanging like diamonds on unseen string. I reached out for Inyris again, but my dragon was relaxed. A hand brushed over her scales, echoed over my skin. I allowed my mind to meld with hers, only for a moment. It was to find... me. A version of me, standing before Inyris, stroking her snout. But it wasn't me. Like this version of Simion, it was an illusion.

The phoenixes, although still close, did not flinch at the change in atmosphere. I did not have the ability to see through their eyes, or into their minds, but no doubt it was to find a presence that calmed them.

There was only one explanation. I thought of the tidal wave that raced towards me as I flew towards the rebellion's island, conjured by the nymphs' power. This was no different.

The magic, it was familiar.

'Lilyth.' I snapped back into my body. 'So you found the nymphs' conduit before we did.'

The mother of monsters emerged through the hanging droplets, brushing them aside with the back of a hand. I caught a glint of silver around her forearm, a cuff I had seen before— once on Elder Cyder's arm and the other on Lilyth's arm in the visions. Except the woman who revealed herself was no monster. She hadn't the tail of a serpent, the wings of a dragon or the horns of a demon.

Her skin glowed like milk; her raven hair was so black it blended seamlessly into the night. A gown of shadow hung to her body, clinging to curves and muscles, and by the dryads she had plenty of them. I had never been scared of beauty before, until the epitome of it stepped before me.

'You humans are smarter than I gave you credit for.' Lilyth's voice was soft as silk and as deadly as the curve of a blade. 'Many beings have faced me, many have fallen, and yet here you stand, and for the first time I sense a trial...'

Magic pooled into every rock, stone. It flashed across the night sky, forks of white light that echoed its energy in my very veins.

'Now, now, Maximus Oaken, the Lost Mage, the False Son, the Traitor Mage, dryad-born, King of Aldian. Do not waste your magic on me, you cannot harm me in this form. Did you truly believe I would visit you in the flesh?'

For a beat of time, she became transparent. I could see through her body as though she was a phantom, one conjured by the nymphs she now controlled.

'You have come all this way to see me, and yet that, too, is a waste. What you want, you will not get,' I shouted.

She stood still, hands at her sides, black nails tapping on her thigh. 'Oh, maybe I will not retrieve it tonight, but I will get it in time. Willingly, or not.'

'Then what do you want?'

My mind reached out for Simion again, only to face a wall of uninterrupted pleasure. I dared not think of the illusion she had conjured to distract him.

'He sees you,' Lilyth confirmed, 'or a version of you. The illusion hangs off the end of his cock. Except, in a way, it is me who provides him pleasure this time.'

A bolt of hot light shot down from the heavens, crashing into the spot where Lilyth stood. As she had warned, my magic was wasted, but that didn't matter. I could control everything but my fury, and her words tempted me.

'Leave him alone.'

'I shall,' she replied, 'once I am given back what belongs to me.'

I leaned closer, body trembling with unspent rage. 'Then you will leave this place sorely disappointed.'

Her laugh echoed through the darkness, as though the entire world sang with it. 'Brave words coming from an insolent life that will soon fall beneath me. I am surprised my treacherous little children have not shared their knowledge with you. The dryads, my collectors of knowledge, slippery little bugs.'

'They have shown me enough,' I spat, fists tense, nails slicing crescents into my palm.

'That they have. And you will know what I will do to your world. I will drain it of its power, its life. I will take your humans and gather their souls. The sky will burn, the lands will flood and not a single person will be left. Unless...'

'I am not interested in what you have to say.'

'No?' Lilyth tilted her head, inspecting me like a dog does a bone. 'You wish to save this world, do you not? I could give you a chance, a way to build a bridge of trust. No one truly wants to perish, do they?'

'Tricks. No different to this illusion.'

'A deal,' Lilyth corrected. I didn't want to, but I believed her. Sincerity rolled off her in waves. Perhaps it was magic, but I couldn't ignore it. 'You give me what I need. My remaining conduits.'

She slunk forward, a stalking cat moving cautiously around me. She was not real, just an illusion, but I knew what this creature was capable of. 'I don't need to listen to your desperate attempts,' I replied. 'Your coming here only proves one thing. You do not know the location of the final conduits. So, you come crawling to me.'

'I can see you are stubborn. It runs in your blood, dryad blood, which may I be the one to inform you means you, too, are part of me. For I am mother to the monsters, titan to those you call gods.' Lilyth stopped behind me, her cool breath brushing over my ear. For an illusion, she felt real. 'My deal is fair, as you will understand if you allow me to share it. Think, child, do you really have a choice? What would it take for me to ruin your little army of humans currently traipsing through the great forest? One shade, maybe two? And the city that awaits them... I have it surrounded. My shades are hungry, I am hungry. You... or your answer... is the only thing between ruin.'

'We... we have—'

'Have what?' In a blink, she was before me. 'A chance. No. I have shown you what I can achieve, even without the conduits. So, what will it be? We all have a choice. You have, perhaps, the gravest to make. Give me my crown, help me locate the final conduits and I vow to leave this world with my children. There will be no need for death, no need for ruin. We will leave. And I will continue my search for a new home.'

New home. The more she spoke, I felt as though I was grasping at answers I never believed possible. Everything Lilyth had done, all the worlds she had devoured before, was to find a home?

I didn't need to ask it, but something made me. 'And if I refuse?'

'You have already seen the outcome in your dreams. You know what shall come to pass. I will leave this deal with you, give you time to contemplate it. Though I suggest you keep my visit to yourself, otherwise there will be no deal. Tell another soul and I will come for your heart, take my crown and leave nothing behind.'

My heart. Simion. My family. My home.

I opened my mouth to reply, but stopped as a very real, cool nail slipped beneath my chin and lifted it. My skin ached beneath the press of the tip. All I could do was look in the pools of her dark eyes, recognise the seriousness to everything she had said.

'I am intrigued by you, Maximus. The dryads believe they

created a force strong enough to resist me. They are wrong, of course, but still—I am intrigued.'

'If I agree—'

'Which you will, because you know what will happen.'

My throat bobbed with the hard swallow, forcing down the lump into my chest where it settled. 'How... how do I find you?'

Her nail withdrew, her bare feet stepping backwards over the slick ground. 'Do not fret, I am always watching from the shadows, just as you first thought. There is nothing I cannot see. I do hope that the next time we meet with one another, it will be because you have made the right decision. I understand how difficult it can be, choosing where your loyalty lies, but I assure you, aiding me will only benefit you and this world.'

'And what of the other worlds?' All the ones that came before this, all those that would come after if I gave Lilyth what she wanted.

'Do not concern yourself with matters you could not begin to fathom. Look up to the stars. There are many places you can see, and many more you cannot. This choice is yours and yours alone. Save those you are responsible for, or *damn* them. Either way, I shall get what I desire. History is nothing but a warning of what shall come. Do not forget that. I will allow you five nights to decide the fate of this world. Give me the crown, prove to me you will help me, and I will spare the lives you are responsible for.'

Before I could conjure a reply, Lilyth was gone. For now.

The world rocked beneath me. I bent over, caught my hands on my knees and spilled the contents of my stomach out across the ground. I didn't stop until my lungs begged for air and my empty stomach spasmed.

But her deal lingered—haunting me, poisoning me, ruining me.

CHAPTER 20

I had woken the next morning to the soft brush of Simion's lips against the back of my neck. Instead of it urging me gently from sleep, it tore me out of the darkness. I was all too aware of his strong arm over me, the way my spine nestled perfectly into his chest. Before I opened my eyes, I steeled my mind, keeping gleamer magic out and Lilyth's threat within.

After she had visited, I found Simion, who acted as though we had never been separated. It was clear the illusion Lilyth cast was very real to him, which only encouraged my stomach to spasm. I had let him sleep until my eyes grew heavy, then Beatrice and Elaine swapped for the next watch. I was sure Lilyth wasn't going to make another appearance.

Even my dreams had been haunted by the search of the final conduits, and Lilyth's promise to leave this world. It would have been easier not to believe her, but something in me knew she spoke the truth.

New home. She was looking for a home, leaving ruin in the worlds that did not suffice for her.

And just like Lilyth had done with the nymphs' power, I faked an illusion of my own, forcing a smile across my face and making sure it reached my eyes. Until we left the outcrop of rocks, I had kept the need for conversation to a minimum, blaming my strange mood on being tired from the night before. Simion had winked at me, as though sharing in some secret joke. I had barely looked at him since.

We had no time to waste visiting the Hawthorn island now. But how could I explain that without revealing how I knew that the nymphs' conduit was no longer there? It was still almost a day's flight away.

So, I did the very thing I vowed not to do to those I loved.

'Inyris flew me to Galloway Forest before dawn,' I lied. 'I conversed with the dryads who have confirmed Lilyth found the nymphs' conduit before us.'

Heads snapped in my direction, eyes full of confusion and horror.

'Are you—they certain?' Leska asked, oddly calm. She looked at me as though she could see through my lie, but said nothing to combat it. *Yet.*

'Why didn't you wake me?' Simion nudged. 'With the threat of shades, leaving us alone was a risk, Max.'

'I know,' I exhaled. 'Ask your phoenixes. Glamora too. They will notice a shift.'

Simion's phoenixes sang in a barrage of squawks. I thought they fed off his emotion, but it seemed they were aiding my lie. 'It is true, the phoenixes sense a shift in the balance. A change in the... waters.'

We each looked to the calm surface of the Thalassic, thoughts drifting to the gods who dwelled within. Did they listen now? Was Lilyth watching?

'Then we move onto the next,' Beatrice said, nodding as though she tried to convince herself. 'Lilyth has one, we have the other. Everything will ride on us locating the remaining two.'

The shield and the sceptre.

I couldn't stop my eyes deviating to Simion's crown. It demanded my attention, just out of reach. Before I had looked at it as our means of power, now I saw it as the potential to save the world—though not by using it.

'Max, are you all right?' Simion's cool trace of power lingered in the back of my skull, testing my newly forged protection. He withdrew, only for his eyes to flare with fire. Something tugged in my chest, a knot of emotion around my heart.

'Stop it!' I snapped, suddenly overwhelmed by what he was doing. Simion was using his new powers and reading my passion, searching for answers. 'You are not entitled to just traipse around inside my head.'

Inyris had been watching from her perch, until my emotions spiked. Her long neck wove down, lips pulled back over serrated teeth, forked tongue flickering towards Simion.

'I didn't mean to—'

'Just because we share a bed, doesn't grant you access to every part of me, Simion.' I could see the reaction ripple over the group, mouths slacking, eyes widening. All but Leska who continued to watch, studying my expression. If I looked at her too long, I feared it would all come crumbling down. 'Don't do it again.'

Simion straightened, his shoulders rolling back, a mask rising over his shock. 'Don't worry, Max. It won't happen again.'

I hated how cold he sounded, and how sharp I was to create such a distant reaction.

Dryads, I couldn't even look at him.

'We are exhausted,' Leska spoke, drawing the attention from me and my outburst. I couldn't help but feel as though she was saving me from the attention. 'If Lilyth has the conduit, we must make out next move. We need to reach Wycombe, speak with the Council, ensure that those who travelled from the South reach the North safely. Then there is the matter of locating Celia.'

'It's going to be like searching for a needle in a haystack,' Beatrice added, her arm never straying far from Elaine, who nestled into her side. 'Even if we wish to find the rest, we are blind to know where to start.'

'Then we start by burning the haystack,' Simion glowered, his voice as hot as the fire in his blood. He turned on his heel, refusing to look at me, and moved for his mount. Feathered wings beat in symphony, until every phoenix was airborne.

'I guess that is another option,' Beatrice replied, as her and Elaine moved towards Glamora who, until now, had been curled into an obsidian ball, catching the final scraps of rest before the long day.

Leska didn't move until the rest of them were far enough away. Inyris ambled down towards us, talons digging into stone for leverage. 'Do you want to talk about what just happened?'

My blood thundered in my ear, the beat so loud it was deafening. 'If I said no, would you press me on it?'

'I would like to think you have whatever burden you woke up with under control.'

I forged my lips closed, swallowing whatever urge I had to slip the truth to her. When I did manage to speak, my dismissal was answer enough. 'We should get moving.'

Leska closed her eyes for a moment, exhaling a tempered breath, and shrugged her shoulders. 'After you, brother.'

* * *

Two agonising days. It took two days for the journey to come to an end. Two days of hardly uttering a word. Two days of lying to those I loved. But, most importantly, two days of no shade attacks. Lilyth was, if anything, true to her word.

It meant I had three more nights to solve the issue of the missing conduits, before Lilyth clawed through Aldian to find them.

From a distance, Wycombe looked like a shadow cast across the land. Pale light glowed across the city, giving it the impression of stars reflecting off the dark ocean. Such a peaceful view, when the potential for worldwide destruction was so real.

I leaned down into Inyris's neck, getting a better look. To our right, Saylam Academy pierced the veil of the world. Since I had broken Beatrice out of imprisonment with the aid of the Hawthorn rebellion, new stone had been laid. I could see the difference in the shades of the wall, where new Avarian stone met old. It was a symbol of a city rebuilding.

What would become of Wycombe if I didn't do as Lilyth asked? Would the city be flooded, the mountains beyond it crumble, bubbling and boiling with fire? When I had first looked upon Wycombe, it was in awe at the possibilities of so many lives. Now, it was with the possibility that it would become a feeding ground for Lilyth to claim more of her damned souls.

Dusk had fallen and we had been flying for hours. The insides of my thighs ached, the skin on my palm was rubbed raw from holding onto Inyris's spines. Inyris's exhaustion was bone deep. I thanked her for flying, filling my mind with images of wild boar and other creatures she would be able to feast on once we reached out destination.

It seemed the promise of fresh meat kept Inyris's wings beating with vigour.

I wondered what the people of the Northern capital thought as they looked skywards and saw specks of fire spearing towards them. The last time the phoenixes had been within the city, it was to destroy the late Queen's Heart Oak. Now, it was to bring the chance of a new power.

It was Simion who changed course, making us all follow. Erinda dipped low suddenly, casting a warm glow of power across the farm fields below us. I understood the reason for the change when a riot of dragons broke from the darkness, the silver armour of battlemages glinting from their backs. It was natural for my heart to leap in my throat, for the last time Elder Leia sent her soldiers after me, it wasn't a welcome party.

But Elder Leia was waiting for us when we touched down. Carriages waited alongside an entire guard of battlemages. Not only were the skies full of her protection, but they also covered the ground in neat formations. Ever prepared, always ready—that was Elder Leia.

'Welcome back,' Leia said, her voice carrying over the field as we each dismounted. She was garbed in an elaborate set of armour that was as white as her hair, with starbursts of gold across the bodice. An ivory cloak caught in the breeze at her back, making the emblem of the dryad ripple and distort. 'It is a relief to see you all in one piece.'

'Aunt,' Beatrice offered, stepping before Leia. Where there was once tension, now it was only warm, honest smiles and open arms. 'It's good to see you too.'

'Gosh, someone get a scribe and write that down.' Leia opened her arms, welcoming Beatrice into them. 'The feeling is mutual, dear girl. And who is this?'

Elaine stepped forward, tipping her head into a curtsy. 'Beatrice's friend—'

'That title has yet to be determined,' Beatrice corrected, as Elaine's pale cheeks flooded with crimson. 'In fact, I would go so far to say that I had unknowingly left my heart in the South and have finally found it during our visit.'

Leia took Elaine's hand in hers and shook. 'It is wonderful to meet you, Elaine. Welcome to the family.' Her silver brows peaked. 'And a gleamer. I see that Mage Oaken's well-kept secret has paid off.'

I almost vomited at the statement, but it was not Lilyth's deal that Leia referred to, rather that I had taken stores of Heart

Oak to the South and handed it out like coin. 'My mother always taught me that visiting a place empty-handed is bad manners,' I said.

'Good. Because of you and your little secret, we will be better prepared to face this monster who has decided that Aldian is the best playground for her power.' Her eyes settled to Leska, who waited just shy of my shoulder. There was no denying the wince as she saw Leska's arms, and the vines that wrapped around them. 'Leska, I am extremely happy to see my most trusted battlemage returned.'

'I had a duty,' Leska replied, back straight. 'I would do anything to ensure it is seen through.'

The unspoken topic of Elder Cyder hung in the air. There would be a time we spoke on it, but now was not it. 'I know you would,' Leia said.

'Forgetting about someone?' Simion said, crown atop his head, fire alit in his eyes.

'Forgive me,' Leia replied, stepping in closer to her nephew. She laid her hands on either side of his shoulders. 'But I am not sure I know who this is. When I last saw my nephew, it was as but a man, but now I see someone changed.'

'We all have been forced to adapt,' Simion replied, as his eyes flicked over to me. I looked down to my feet, unable to hold his stare.

'That we have.' Leia stood back, scanning her eyes over us all. Relief settled the lines across her forehead. 'There is much to discuss, and I fear we do not have the time for it. There have been... events during the evenings. Reports of shadows attacking our people, although those attacks have not persisted in the past two nights. All of a sudden, they just stopped. And since, no more attacks have been reported.'

Out of the corner of my eye, I recognised the group sharing a look of surprise. Leska was the only one who continued to stare at me, knowingly. Was it a coincidence the shades had retreated, or was it because Lilyth was proving her honesty? It was all more reason for me to trust her, to recognise this was my only choice. If I gave her what she longed for, she would leave us.

I had to hope as much because I had made up my mind.

'I sense this is something you are familiar with, this news.'

'There will be a reason Lilyth has stopped sending her shades to cause chaos,' Simion added, voice neutral. I longed for him to look at me, but he wouldn't.

'Well, let us hope they stay away for a little while longer,' Elder Leia began. 'We need all the time to recuperate. We expect those who left the South to arrive within the coming day. Anyone with magic has been stationed throughout the city to aid where needed. Since we have informed our people what they are to face, tensions have been high. Turmoil poisoning every home, every street.' Her golden eyes settled upon me, and for a moment, I felt the phantom ache of a crown on my head. Unlike Simion, I didn't wear one. But that didn't negate the pressure. 'I fear we are losing control quicker than the world is ending.'

'Which is why we must find Celia,' I pressed, doing my best to focus only on Leia. 'The dryads believe she is the last to have knowledge of the sceptre conduit. If we have hopes of finding it, we need her.'

'Everything is being done to locate her—'

'And yet she is still not found.' I didn't wish to snap, but the buildup of nervous energy was practically overboiling. 'Sorry, I am sure you are working hard. It is just important we find the conduit.'

'That we find my mother, you mean?' Beatrice asked, side-eyeing me.

'Yes, we will do what must be done, but locating the

remaining conduits is the only thing between us seeing an end to this, or losing.'

I will do what I must to protect Aldian.

'We have not stopped trying to locate my sister. But more on that after you all rest. Now, the carriages will take you all to Saylam Academy. Dragons can rest and feed at the Nests. Simion, your... phoenixes are welcome to stay close, but it is best they keep a sensible distance from the city. I fear their presence will only distract our people.'

'Understood.' Simion's jaw feathered, his teeth practically grinding together with such force I could hear it. 'Our focus now is protecting those we can... see.' *Not those who are lost to us.*

'There are some leads we have on Celia, I will share with you tomorrow. From the looks of you all, I guess there will be no refusing a good bath, a hearty meal and a comfortable bed?'

No one refused, because Leia was right—each of those were things we all craved.

'We will reconvene tomorrow. I will send escorts to collect you all by dawn.'

Simion turned on his heel before Leia had even finished speaking. He moved for his mount, running slender fingers over the patchwork of gold and amber feathers.

'Go to him,' Leska encouraged, her vines shifting on my back as she urged me forward. 'Never sleep on an argument, trust me.'

We had not exactly had an argument. That would have required a conversation, and there had been only silence between us in the past two days.

Simion seemed to hear Leska—his profile turned, his eyes catching me. But before I could take a step, he clambered onto his phoenix. Its wings beat, fingers calling across the trodden ground, warm air brushing over us all. Within moments, Simion was nothing but a dot in the sky, flying towards Saylam Academy, not once looking back.

The further he gained in distance, the lower my heart sank. I was unsure if it was because of the space between us, or the expanse between me and the crown he wore.

CHAPTER 21

A headache had settled in the far reaches of my mind. A volcanic throbbing that spread over my skull. Not even the tea I clutched in my hands could rid me of it. Only sleep would help, and last night I had not had much of it.

Our lodgings were within the newly built portion of Saylam Academy. Leska and I had been provided a room amongst the accommodation level, a place where novice mages would live during their annual schooling. It surprised me, after everything that had happened, that the Academy had opened its doors again. But as my mother would have once said, *'one can only move forward, not backwards'*.

I had woken the following morning, not long after I finally found sleep, to the bustle of students moving from their shared rooms, chattering about their daily lessons and the scraps of gossip I would expect from school life. And I was jealous. Jealous they could roll out of bed, their greatest worries being the next exam or trial they had to pass. Whereas mine was saving the world.

'Are you going to drink that, or wait for it to become too cold to enjoy?'

I snapped out of my exhausted trance, lifting my eyes to Leska. She stood before her neatly made bed, a nightgown hanging from her muscular frame. The dragon-scaled armour waited on a chest at the end of the single bed, where I had left it last night. I had helped her change, offering when she struggled to undress herself. Her shorn head flickered with new growth, caught by the silvery glow of Avarian stone walls.

As though to prove a point, I lifted the mug to my lips and tipped it. A cascade of mint and lemon infused water rushed into my cheeks, already ice cold.

'Happy?'

Leska screwed her mouth. I felt the instant urge to apologise for my attitude, but she spoke first. 'Listen, Max, I really am trying to fight the tide against having a stereotypical brother–sister conversation, but you are making it really hard.' Leska studied me as a sculptor would their subject. I could practically feel her unravel the details, piecing together a story in her mind. 'So, go on then. Talk to me.'

My fingers tightened on the mug, concealing the need to shake. 'You'll be pleased to hear there is nothing to share.'

'Bollocks,' Leska barked. 'Something happened with you and Simion when you took the first watch the other night. You both have been... distant since.'

Not between me and Simion. 'It is nothing.'

'Say that to the bags under your eyes, the pallor to your skin and the way you've bitten your nails down to the stubs. Something is bothering you. Plus, you owe me.'

'I owe you?'

She lifted her arm, flashing the empty place where a hand once rested. My stomach dropped like a stone, but Leska smiled broadly as though she was a spider watching a fly catch in her web. 'Get talking.'

I swallowed hard, knowing there was no way I could tell her the truth. But the crown, Lilyth and my inability to be in the same place as Simion without suffering, was not all that worried me. 'We are on the cusp of a battle I fear we cannot win.'

'That isn't exactly news, Max.'

'Then I have nothing else to share.' Needing to change the subject, I distracted Leska with the only subject that held the power to do so. I scooted forward until my feet were planted on the cool stone floor. 'Tell me about him... about our father.'

Leska's gaze dropped, her brow furrowing as though they became too heavy to bear. 'He was not always the man you met in the end. He was kind—distracted, but kind. I suppose now we know what occupied his mind.'

It was not hard to imagine. The man I had first met was welcoming and gentle. His smile was encouraging and, contrary to how it ended, he helped me when no one else dared to spare me a glance. 'He was right, all along. About Lilyth.'

'But he was not right about how he went about preparing to face her.' Leska stood abruptly, padding over to the narrow stained-glass window on the room's outer wall. She rested her forehead on the glass, staring far beyond. 'He allowed his focus to cloud right and wrong. He paid the price for it.'

I had not asked Leska about her mother, because there had never been the need to. But now, as I recognised the hollow space in my chest left with the death of my parents, I wondered if she sensed it too. 'You've never mentioned a mother before...'

'And for good reason,' Leska said, 'at least I thought so. My birth mother left us when I was very young. Father said it was because she could not find it in her to be with a family. Now I see it from another perspective. My father had his... focus. Perhaps she saw it, recognised his warped mind and could not cope.'

'Have you ever seen her since?'

Leska faced me, a deep-rooted torment drawing down at her features. 'The day her body was turned to the dryads. She died a year shy of my tenth birthday.'

'I am sorry,' I said, as another bond between us clicked into place. Leska and I, we were two lonely souls left to face a cruel world without the guiding force of a parent.

'Don't be,' Leska said, pausing for breath. Her posture straightened, her shoulders rolling back and chin raised high. 'Now our little heart to heart has ended, could you do me the honours and help me back into my armour? Leia said she would send an escort by the first bell, which is not even an hour away. Years of being a novice in the Academy has drilled the schedule into my bones.'

I placed my cup down, not caring for the chilled liquid and the lack of comfort it could give. 'Your wish is my command.'

Leska smirked at that. 'My wish is for you to be honest with me, Max. I may not be a gleamer, but I sense that you have yet to tell me what is truly haunting you.'

'Maybe I do not want to burden you with it.'

She shrugged. 'Perhaps. Just answer me one thing—can I trust you to deal with it?'

I couldn't speak; couldn't move. How could I answer the question when I didn't know? I would either help Lilyth, hand her all her power back and hope she stayed true to a promise. Or I would refuse, and put this world on the path to complete destruction.

'I will figure it out.'

'Maximus Oaken, I am confident you will make the right decision.'

My stomach turned, a wave of sickness rearing its ugly head again. 'And if I don't?'

Leska nudged my shoulder with hers as she passed, shooting me a warning glance. 'Then I guess I will be here to pick up the pieces, just as any good sister would.'

I forced a smile, thanking her silently with a nod. Only when her back was to me did I drop the false pretences. If I failed, there would be no pieces to pick up. No matter how

Leska wished to help, there was no fixing a world consumed by death.

* * *

'I have tried everything, believe me. No power can reach Celia, no message has been received. I am sorry. Beatrice, Simion, I swear this has been hard for me to come to terms with too.' Tears brimmed in Leia's golden eyes, making the rich colour swirl. Not a single drop spilled.

Beatrice sat slumped in her chair, her eyes staring off at some unimportant brick in the wall. Simion, on the other hand, paced the room, arms crossed, heat rippling from his shoulders as he simmered in silent turmoil. Dryads, I longed to comfort him. To stand up, take him in my arms and hold him close.

Empty plates from breakfast stretched before us, hardly a crumb left. We had lived off cold meat and cheese during our travels.

'Mother could not have simply disappeared,' Simion said finally. Hearing him made me release a breath I didn't know I was holding, although it did little to ease the tension in my chest. 'Unless what you are insinuating is that she is dead? Is that what you are skirting around, Aunt?'

'She isn't dead,' Beatrice added, sharp as a blade. 'I know that. You both do.'

'I wish I could tell you different, but that is a possibility.' Leia fiddled with the scroll on the table before her, nails picking nervously at the edges. She had not long listed off everything her and the Council had done to locate Celia Hawthorn, as though that made the terrible news easier to bear. 'Believe me, I take full responsibility of this outcome. It was my vote that... I was the reason you were broken apart and I am sorry.'

It was common knowledge that Leia Hawthorn was the deciding vote that sent Beatrice and her mother to their separate exiles. And from the way she looked, as though the weeks we had been separated recently had truly taken its toll, I believed she had faced her own punishment.

'And there is no one who knows where Celia was sent to? You all knew where Beatrice went, so there must be something to point us in the right direction.' I couldn't drop it. I couldn't give up on the hope that Beatrice and Simion had the chance of seeing their mother again. The hope that Celia held the answers we longed for.

I needed her. The world needed her.

Beatrice's chair squeaked as she righted herself. 'Our focus should now move to locating Lilyth. She, unlike Celia, is here. There must be other mentions of conduits, anything that suggests objects of power...'

We all knew the answer to that, I just didn't have it in me to repeat it.

'We are having the scholars and historians scour every source we have to locate any hint of a shield and sceptre of power. There is nothing I know of, but that doesn't mean we will not find some hint of the conduits in stories or myths. If Cyder found Lilyth's gauntlet, then we had knowledge at some point...'

'Knowledge my mother may have had, or Celia,' I added, refusing to drop this topic of the Hawthorns' missing mother. 'The dryads had been clear that she was the key. We have to believe them. If they say that Celia holds that knowledge, then she does.'

'Perhaps you are right, Maximus. But we have tried—'

'Try harder,' I snapped, unable to control my emotion. 'Someone has to know something. A retired Council member, anyone who was around during the dismissal of Celia. I hardly imagine the Queen exiled her and let her simply walk out of the city. She would have placed her somewhere, sent her on the way whilst ensuring she was at a distance she could not return.'

'That knowledge died with the Queen,' Leia said. 'I have asked, I have inquired. The only person who knew was the late Queen and she is—'

The thought came to me so quickly, it practically exploded out of me. 'I can find out.'

Simion stopped pacing. He turned to me, eyes boring into me. I held them for a moment, recognising that he knew exactly where I was going.

'I appreciate your desire to help, but I cannot see what you can offer that we have not already exhausted and more.'

'Take me to Galloway Forest. To the dryads. We must go, now.' My words came out broken and breathless, as though I couldn't keep up with my mind before I spoke.

Leia scanned over the group, from Beatrice to Leska and then finally to Simion. 'What good will that do?'

'Maximus can visit that time. He can find out for himself what happened to our mother.' Simion's voice was tempered, as powerful as his stare, which felt like hands tracing over my body.

Beatrice leaned forward, elbows resting on the table. 'Forgive me for bringing this up, but isn't playing with time dangerous?'

'I am with Bea on this,' Leska added, the roots across her armour slithering as it responded to her emotions. 'Something doesn't feel right about toying with a concept which is far more complicated than we can begin to understand.'

'I know the risks,' I said, knowing I only ever witnessed time and never partook in it. 'But I also understand what we could lose if I don't try.'

For the first time, Elder Leia was utterly speechless. There was a glint of hope in her eyes. A desperate need to see someone she, too, had long ago lost. I waited for her to refuse me or to barrage me with questions. Instead, she stood from the table and said, 'Ask of me what you require, and I will make it happen.'

My heart thundered against my ribs, almost pushed between my lungs. It was a nervous energy, but a desperate one. Because there was only one reason the Queen would wish to exile Celia to a place no one could reach her, and that was because she knew something that frightened the old Queen.

'Simion,' I said, 'will take me and guard me alongside Inyris and his phoenixes.'

There was no way I could tell them that Lilyth was no threat, not whilst I was her loyal hound, retrieving the conduits for her.

'And you expect us to sit around and wait in the meantime?' Beatrice asked, tilting her head. 'Because you can think again.'

'Those from the South will be arriving. See that they are unharmed—' I knew they would be, Lilyth had held up her promise so far '—then prepare those able to fight, armour, weapons, more Heart Oak. Before the shades return, we must arm as many people as possible who are willing to fight. It is better to face an enemy in dim light than complete darkness. And I have a feeling that, by tomorrow, we will know a lot more.'

What I didn't add was, by tomorrow, I would at least have the crown and the conduit to give Lilyth.

But first, it was time to discover the truth of Celia Hawthorn's fate.

CHAPTER 22

'I have done something to upset you.' Simion had held those words in all the way to Galloway Forest's border, practically boiling over with the need to say it. They had burst out of him as he dismounted Erinda, before his feet even hit the ground. 'And do not offer me some bullshit excuse or tell me everything is fine.'

I leaned into Inyris, thankful for my dragon's support. 'It isn't you, it's me—'

'By the dryads, Max.' He was before me in seconds, soft hands grasping mine, brows furrowed over tired eyes. 'Please, anything but that. Talk to me, give me the chance to make whatever I have done right again.'

Simion had not voiced it aloud, but he knew I was keeping him out of my mind for a reason.

'You haven't done anything.'

He hadn't; this was all on me. But how could I tell him the truth, knowing I was going to betray him?

'Talk to me. *Please.*'

Behind me, the forest creaked in the winds, trees celebrating my arrival with song. The dryads Simion had just blasphemed, watching from the shadows. I couldn't come out and explain to Simion what I was hiding. *Oh, by the way, I need you to willingly give me that crown so I can personally hand it over to the demoness who wishes to ruin the world, on the off chance she spares us?*

It was better he didn't know.

'Not yet.' Two words, it was all I could muster. I couldn't begin to explain what Lilyth had wedged between us. It was not only the lying, but the images of Simion being pleasured by an illusion of her creation. It sickened me. To my core.

Simion's shoulders fell forward, his chin dropping to his chest. 'I am going to ask one thing of you, Maximus. If I am to stop tormenting myself, at least promise me it is for a good reason. I need to hear you say it.'

'I promise. And I need you to trust me.' *Even if I don't trust myself.*

That stopped him. 'I always do.'

'Then you will allow me to do what I need to protect this world.'

'Yes,' Simion said, flustered, fingers slowly falling from mine. 'But remember this is our world, not solely yours. We do it together.'

And yet Lilyth had made the bargain with me. That had to be for a reason.

'Can I stay with you tonight?' My question was meant to distract him, and it did. 'Leska snores, and, not only that, but my body has grown used to sleeping beside you. Last night was...'

'Torturous?' Simion answered for me. 'Yes, of course. I trust you know where to find me?'

The Mad Queen, the tavern Simion had practically grown up in. 'Always.'

There was still a distance wedged between us, but we had to overcome it. Even if this was tricking Simion. Even if the thought of what I had to do sickened me to my core.

Simion's chin jutted towards Galloway Forest. 'It looks like we have a visitor.'

I turned, following his gaze, and found a dryad stood beyond the forest's treeline. It was tall, with willow branches for hair, a face of bark and leaf, and a knot of roots that slithered through the ground as it moved closer. I would never overcome the beauty of the gods of earth, but now I saw them in a new light. They, like the nymphs, could be used as weapons against us. One moment they could be our greatest allies, the next our greatest enemy.

'Go,' Simion urged as Erinda led a host of phoenixes to the clearing. They, like Simion, would protect me. Even through Lilyth had been true to her word so far, no harm had come to anyone since our deal was made. 'I will be waiting for you.'

'Simion.' I swallowed hard, wondering if my task was even possible. 'I'm worried I'm going to fail you.'

Hands wove around my waist, drawing me back. A soft breath fondled my cheek before the caress of a mouth settled upon my skin. Simion kissed me, brief yet powerful. It sang of his answer even before he spoke it aloud. 'You could never fail me, Maximus Oaken. Regardless of what you find, it will not change anything.'

'This is your mother we are talking about, finding answers as to what happened to her.'

'I know.'

'And this could change everything for you.'

'I know.'

And that was exactly why I was not prepared to fail.

* * *

I recognised the room immediately. The Queen's Heart Oak stretched skywards, as healthy as I had first seen it. Russet bark practically glowed with life; the canopy of leaves was so vibrant in colour. Birds nested amongst the many branches, filling the room with their lyrical song. The stone throne sat empty, half-swallowed by the tree's body.

'Why here?' I asked the dryad whose bracken limbs grasped onto me.

'*You wished to see what happened to Celia Hawthorn, and we were here to witness her fate.*' The dryad was one of many that stood on either side of the room; sentinel guards. I had seen them before, until Camron Calzmir had infiltrated the city and burned them all to cinders beneath his wytchfire. '*Not all of us perished that day, child.*'

Relief uncoiled within me like a fresh breath of spring air. 'Celia is here, but not in our current time?'

'*In a manner of words.*' The dryad paused, enough for me to notice the far-off patter of feet. '*Celia Hawthorn's presence is heavy here. Hush now, child. They come. Remember, do not interact with this time. Only watch. The price to pay is far too great if you do.*'

If I do? Price? 'So, it is possible?'

The dryad's limbs tightened, anchoring me in place. Imprisoning me. But they did not answer, not before the doors to the room slammed open. I watched from the concealment of the dryad's enchantment, as the Queen strolled into the room, and Beatrice followed behind.

No. Not Beatrice. Celia, her mother.

She was beautiful. The perfect blend of Leia, Beatrice and Simion. A tall woman with brown and grey hair woven into braids falling down her straight back. Her brown skin had a warm undertone, her eyes a paler gold, more akin to a light brown. And beside her proud posture, her hands were bound before her, pinching at the skin around her wrists. There was a defiance, an evident fury set in her eyes.

I recognised the power of that emotion for what it was. The scorn of a mother torn away from her children.

'Leave us,' the Queen shouted, her voice filling every inch of the room. I knew her command was meant for the group of battlemages who had followed them. The battlemages turned with military precision and left out the door they had just come through. The hollow clang of the doors closing itched at my skin, rippling over the deafening silence between the two remaining women.

'I will never forgive you for this,' Celia Hawthorn said, wide-eyed, jaw tense.

The Queen walked carefully towards her and, to my surprise, reached for the chains around Celia's wrists. They fell away with ease, melting into nothingness before my eyes. 'Nor will I forgive myself, but this is the right decision.'

'Calling this a decision suggests I had a choice in the matter. We both know I didn't.'

The Queen's forest green eyes—*my eyes*—flared open. 'Nor did I, Celia. You betrayed me, alongside Deborah. I trusted you both, deeply, and you took what I shared with you and decided to trick me.' Her aged hand, marked with liver spots, slapped against her chest. 'My heart will never be restored after your betrayal.'

Celia leaned in until her face was inches from the Queen's. 'And what of my heart? You have taken my daughter from me, discarded her to a place she has no means to survive in.'

'Beatrice will survive. In fact, I imagine she will thrive away from *us*.'

'I want to see her.' Tears pooled in Celia's eyes, brightening the light brown into a familiar gold. 'One more time, before *this*.'

The Queen contemplated the request but shook her head. 'When my child is returned to me, you will be returned to yours. I do not have the luxury of seeing him again, I do not even have the privilege of knowing his name.'

'And Simion? What of my son? He is sensitive, he needs me.'

'Your son will toughen himself up before you see him again. We will need him to, for what is to come.' The Queen reached down to her hip and withdrew a strange object. It took a moment to recognise the length of twisted wood, a knot of root forged into a ball at its top.

'The sceptre,' I breathed, seeing the object of Lilyth's earthen power before my eyes.

'Yes, but this story is yet to end.'

'Take it,' the Queen said, offering the sceptre to Celia with two hands, as though she handed over a child. 'Insurance, proof that I will return you to your children the day mine is given back to me.'

'That isn't wise,' Celia said, hesitating, 'I am the only one with the knowledge of Lilyth's conduits. Let me tell you what I have learned, let me help you with the same knowledge I kept from you.'

'No, Celia. The conduits must remain pawns off the board. That is this game we play. Until the right time. Not even I can know—if I do, it will only alert Lilyth. We need more time.'

'Time,' Celia scoffed. 'The very thing you take from me.'

The Queen didn't respond to her accusation. 'You understand the sceptre's power. It has been in my possession since my parents burned in wytchfire. Even to this day, I will never understand how the dryads found it amongst the ruins of the first Heart Oak. Should it not have burned too, I thought. It was believed to have been entombed with them, lost to time and history, only to turn up unharmed when I needed it most. Now, it is time to pass it over.' The Queen extended it again, hands shaking ever so slightly. 'Take it, Celia. Guard it.'

'And if you require it?' Celia took the sceptre, a gasp of breath escaping her as though a rush of something powerful flooded through her body.

'Then I know where to find you.'

Celia hardly took her eyes off the sceptre. Even from my concealment, I could feel the radiant waves of magic flowing from it. 'You really should not suggest you see that child as anything more than a source of essence for the Heart Oak. You do not love him, only what he can give you. He belongs with Deborah.'

Hearing my mother's name, lashed from Celia's tongue like a weapon, shocked me to the core.

Genuine, soul-shattering agony creased the Queen's face, ageing her before my very eyes. 'He is my world. As he is Deborah's world. I may not have carried him, but that is my child. My son. I understand you see it for something else, but whatever worm has been in your ear suggesting such things is wrong. My child may have been born to a dark fate, but that does not and will not negate the love I have for him.'

I didn't want to, but I believed every word.

'The only worm has been your mistruths,' Celia answered.

'My decision to share my truth has only been made with the desire to protect you all. You may not agree with the way I have gone about it, but you can agree that my intentions were never ill-placed.'

'Lilyth is real. You need the conduits now—'

'No, I do not.' The Queen's eyes dropped to the sceptre. 'I do not know when this being will come, but it will be one day soon. I hope not in our children's lifetime, but unrest is brewing. The dryads can only see then and now, I have no ability to see what will become of tomorrow, let alone the future.'

Celia attempted to hand the sceptre back. 'Which is why you should keep this. I do not like you for what you have done, but I do not see the need for me to keep such a powerful conduit when you may need it.'

'As I have already said,' the Queen stepped back, her bark-made armour rustling like the sound of fallen leaves underfoot, 'if I require it, I will find you.'

I jolted back as Celia turned in my direction. She couldn't see me, not in the protection of the dryad's enchantment, but that didn't stop my skin from reacting to her piercing gaze. 'Will anyone else know where I am... in case...'

'No. The knowledge of your personal exile will be kept with me.'

Celia's brow furrowed, her lips drawing down into a frown. 'Dryad forbid, what if something happens to you? What if the knowledge *dies* with you?'

'The knowledge will never die, not when kept by the dryads. It will simply wait until the right person discovers they can find it.'

My heart skipped a beat, my breath catching in my throat.

The Queen was talking about me.

Celia closed her eyes, the lines across her forehead deepening. But when she opened them again, she was void of expression. The familiar glint of determination filled her eyes, which turned back to the Queen.

'What... what is it like?'

The Queen placed her hand on Celia's shoulder and guided her towards the Heart Oak. She gestured for Celia to stand before it. I watched as the bark rippled like water around her, lifting as though a hand reached out and hugged Celia Hawthorn from the back.

'It is only but a moment in time. To you, it will feel as though little time has passed, for us years will have slipped by.'

Tears were falling from Celia's eyes now, dripping onto the sceptre she clutched to her chest. Grief. Grief of a relationship she would never have with her children. Grief for a life she had hoped for.

'Let me go,' I said to the dryad without truly knowing I

spoke. It was a command from deep within, the desperate panic of discovering the answer to Celia's exile.

'The price is too great to pay.'

In the distance, Celia asked one last request as she leaned against the Heart Oak. 'Keep them safe. It is your duty, since you have taken me from them, to make sure my family have a life.'

'I will. Until next time, Celia Hawthorn.'

Celia closed her eyes, clutching the sceptre to her chest. I refused to do so much as blink, staring at the Queen's back as she lifted her hands, commanding her Heart Oak to engulf Celia's body. 'You will be trapped in this moment in time, caught in a pocket where only my blood will be the key to reach you.'

My blood. As in the same blood that ran through my veins. 'Whatever it is, whatever the cost,' I pleaded with the dryad. 'Let me pay it.'

I had to help her, to free Celia from the inevitable. Not only for Simion, but for the sceptre she held onto. Because in our time, the Heart Oak was destroyed. This was my only chance.

'It is dangerous, child.'

I dug my fingernails into the dryad's bark, prying away their binding so I could step beyond it and interact with this moment in time. It was not a want; it was a need. 'If I do not retrieve that sceptre, it will endanger the world as we know it.'

It was in that moment I understood why Celia could not be reached by Leia and her Council. If Celia was hidden in the Heart Oak, trapped in time, the same one that had burned in Camron's wytchfire, it meant she was gone—dead in the present.

This was why Leia's gleamers could not locate Celia.

This was why she had never come looking for Simion and Beatrice.

The Queen had exiled her into a moment in time, only to be saved upon my return.

But here, now, she lived. And she had the one thing I needed. Blood pinpricked beneath my nails. Real, tangible blood. 'Free me.'

The scene had changed as I had been fighting to free myself. I searched for the Queen, but she had left the room. The Heart Oak looked unchanged, but I sensed what lingered beneath.

'What is the price,' I said, panicking, my breathing heavy. 'Tell me the price, let me decide if I can pay it.'

'Memories. We are the keepers of time, which is only a physical representation of such a concept. This, like the others you have been shown. You may watch on as we do, but if you are to interact, to step into the memory, it must be with a trade. One for another.'

'Then take it,' I said, uncaring. I had many memories I didn't wish to keep, many I would gladly eradicate from my mind. 'If that is the price to pay, I have more than enough payment for you.'

'Oh, child. It does not work in such a way. The longer you interact, the more we are forced to take. That is how our power tethers to you, keeps you safe whilst free to roam. Another paid this price before you, and the toll was great.'

'The Queen?' Of course. I could only imagine what moments in time she wished to see, to interact with, to pay the price of being selfish with such an otherworldly power.

'It changed her. Ruined her mind. Made her mad. If you do this, it will change you...'

Mad. The Mad Queen. Suddenly, I understood that title in a new light.

'My answer is the same. Release me, take what you need. Any memory is worth this.' Worth retrieving the conduit that, in my own time, would have been destroyed alongside Celia in her tomb.

'As you command, dryad-born.'

The dryad released its hold on me. I fell forward, palms slapping into the cold and very real stone beneath my feet. I was no longer a phantom watching from the shadows of their enchantment, but a physical and solid being able to feel and experience this place.

I hadn't the time to contemplate what was being taken. Not as I pushed myself to standing and ran for the Heart Oak. My footsteps echoed around the cavernous empty space. Any moment now I expected someone to enter the room, to grab me and discover me in a place I didn't belong.

But I did. This was my right, it was in my blood. What good is the power to change the course of fate if I could not use it?

'Quick, child.'

The Heart Oak towered above me. I lifted my hand and pressed it against the bark, feeling the beat of life course beneath my touch. I didn't know what I was to do, but the Heart Oak was a product of my blood. Like a key to a lock, it simply fit in and turned. I had touched it before, but this was different. It was as though I was searching for a door to something, where before I had no idea what to look for.

Where the bark had not long ago moved, it shifted again. Parting to reveal the form of a woman beneath. She was muttering to herself, eyes closed.

'Celia?' I said her name in question, hardly believing this was possible. 'Celia Hawthorn.'

Then her eyes opened, and she stared directly through my soul.

'Who are you?' she asked, although the pinch in her brow proved she at least recognised something familiar in me.

'The key to free you,' I answered, repeating the words the Queen had not long spoke. I took her hand in mine, feeling her warmth, how very hard and real her skin was against mine. The urge to reach out and take the sceptre was strong, but I buried it. For now.

Celia's eyes lingered from me, to beyond me, searching for the Queen who had moments before locked her within the Heart Oak.

'Come,' I said, my eyes fighting the urge to look at the conduit. 'I have a couple of people I think you would like to see.'

There was resistance in her grip as I tried to lead her down from the Heart Oak. 'Who?'

'Simion and Beatrice.' My body trembled, my mind wondering as to what I had lost to pay for this very chance.

Celia's eyes widened, then she took a step forward. 'Are they here?'

I shook my head, knowing the dryad lingered close. 'Not here. Somewhere else.' I took a breath, knowing there was no way of explaining what I meant without being sharp and to the point. 'The future, Celia. Lilyth is here and we need you.'

CHAPTER 23

It had been hours since I had last seen Simion and his mother. Beatrice too. I had heard my friend coming before I saw her. Breathless gasps, half-broken sobs and heavy feet, she had barrelled down the corridor beyond the throne room.

'Is it true?' she had screamed, wide-eyed. 'Max, is it true?'

I could only nod.

Beatrice had fallen into my arms, her full weight pressed on me. Perhaps Leska could not hear what Beatrice whispered to me, but they were words I would never forget. 'Thank you.'

Her thanks had haunted me since she had pushed into the throne room and left me to stew in my thoughts.

'I thought playing with time was dangerous, Max.' Leska voiced the very warning that the dryad had first drummed into me. No one had the capacity to ask it yet, not with the chaos that came of bringing a woman back who had been lost in time.

'It is, but this was different,' I replied, back slipping down the cold wall until I was sat on my haunches. 'Celia was purposefully imprisoned in time. She was left there for the Queen, or me, to find. It affects nothing of the future because, for all we would have known, Celia would've been left in the Heart Oak that Carmon destroyed.'

'So, Celia never existed in our time.'

I nodded, feeling a violent sickness sink claws into my stomach. 'Exactly. There is nothing to affect, her being here now only proves she perished in Camron's wytchfire.'

Leska leaned against the wall opposite me, eyes glowing with her constant use of magic, vines curling around her upper arm. I could see from the way her cobalt eyes fixated on an unimportant place on the wall, and how she worried her lip, that she was deep in thought. 'Does this mean you could—'

'No,' I said quickly, almost too quickly. I knew what she was going to ask, before she finished. It was the same question I had pondered over and over since I returned with Celia.

'But, Max, I am not suggesting you should do this, but what if we can go back... change things. Make different decisions.' A hopeful tear rolled down her cheek. 'What about Aaron?'

Aaron, the man I had killed in self-defence, the one Leska's own father had sent to murder me for simply being important to the Queen he opposed. 'There is a never-ending list of ever-changing possibilities as to what the future would behold if I went back and stopped myself from killing Aaron. So many I could not even begin to comprehend or explain. I don't understand it myself, but what if he did survive? Where would I be? Would we be having this conversation? Would Celia have been reunited with her children? Would...'

Would Lilyth be infecting my mind with her bargain, torturing me every waking moment with a promise that was feeling more like the double-edged blade it was. 'I can't do it again, the price is too dangerous.'

Leska looked to me, genuine concern overwhelming her other emotions. 'What price, Max?'

I swallowed hard, reaching into my mind to search for whatever memory I had exchanged for having free rein in that moment of time. Of course, I couldn't find it. Was that because I didn't know what I searched for, or because it had already been taken... ripped out only to leave an empty, hollow space?

'To play with time, I must offer my memories. The dryad made it clear. A toll, a tithe. There is no saying what will become of me if I continue on this path of meddling. It would ruin my mind, it could infect me with...

'Madness,' Leska said the word so firmly, it took my breath away. 'That is what would become of you. Madness, just like the Queen. She didn't get her name from the South, Max. It was given to her by those around her.'

The Mad Queen. I shook my head, knowing all too well the title she obtained, how it hung above the very tavern Simion called home. 'Exactly.'

'It was something my father once spoke about. How the Queen's mind was failing her. He explained it as a sickness, something that ate at her brain, making her erratic in moments and... lost. I blame her jaunts with the dryads. It is the only explanation.'

I didn't need to listen. I knew exactly what Leska was suggesting, and she was right. It made complete sense.

'The Queen toyed with time, and it ruined her.' My admission echoed around the arching ceiling of the corridor. 'She paid the price over and over.'

I might never know where the Queen went. What moment in time continued to call her back. I knew the draw, the ability to see my parents and watch them even beyond the limits of death. I was a moth to a flame. But what flame burned the brightest for the Queen?

Leska was stood before me in a blink. I stood, facing her. She didn't blink, hardly moved a muscle in her face. 'I forbid you from doing it again, Max.'

The rawness of her command rocked me to my core. 'I won't.'

'No, you will, because I know you. Which is why, as your sister, I command that you leave time alone. No more visits, no more searching for answers as to what Lilyth is. The past matters little when it is our future that is at risk.'

Her vines grasped my shoulder like a phantom hand. The grip of her power was strong—even her eyes emoted the mist that came with the overuse of magic.

The only noise left between us was the sound of both our breathing. I couldn't form a word, nor could I agree. Leska sensed that, so she used the last weapon in her arsenal and used my very weakness against me.

'I need you. You are my family, and I can't risk losing you too. As insufferable as you are, you selfishly belong to me and I refuse for you to chase this and lose your mind like my father, like the Queen.' Leska's vines continued to twist until her hold on me was iron strong. 'Look me in the eyes and promise me, Max. For as long as I live, you do not do it again. Say it. I need to hear you fucking say it.'

It was the easiest deal to make, far simpler than Lilyth's bargain. This required little thought, as it was my heart that guided me to my answer. 'I promise, as long as it is not required, not to meddle with time again.'

She sagged forward, leaning her forehead into mine. Then her vines released me, and we held one another, reminding me that she was right. Leska was my only family left, a family I had not even imagined possible weeks ago. And we were all we had left.

This all had to end before it was in peril. The dryad's sceptre and the phoenix's crown would have to be sufficient for Lilyth. When Celia shared the location of the final, I would gift that knowledge to Lilyth. If anything, proof that I was not against her. *We* were not against her.

At our side, the door creaked open. We both released one another, turning to find Simion waiting for us. His eyes pierced through me, looking deep into my soul. But it was the smile he offered me, full of joy and thankfulness, that almost knocked me to my knees.

'She is ready to see you,' Simion said, pushing the door open again.

Leska nodded, leaving me and Simion to stare at one another. Before I moved to follow, he stopped me with a question. 'Are you all right?'

I forced a smile. 'I am.'

He laid a hand on my shoulders, slender fingers squeezing gently. 'You know, I will never have the words to thank you, Max.'

'You don't need to do anything for me. I didn't do it for thanks. I did it for you.' It was only half a lie. I did, in fact, do it for Simion and Beatrice. But I also did it with the hope of finding the dryad's sceptre.

And I needed it. Desperately.

'I know,' Simion whispered before placing the softest of kisses to my cheek. Dryads, I could have melted into him. It was all I had wanted, his touch, his love. 'I will make it up to you in one way or another.'

There was no ignoring the desire in his words. 'Is that a promise, Simion Hawthorn?'

'You'll have to wait until we finish up in this meeting and get back to the Mad Queen. Perhaps I will start there.'

Bile rose in my throat at the mention of the tavern's name, especially now I knew the root of its meaning. 'Well, that is one way to make me wish the day away.'

I didn't enjoy lying, but my time pretending to be Julian Gathrax made it a skill that I was rather apt at.

Simion didn't notice, far too lost on a stream of joy. He leaned in and whispered something into my ear. Words allowed only for me. Heat unfurled in my crotch, spreading across my thighs and as far up to my lower stomach. I was confident the brush of his tongue was the last thing to retreat. I lifted a finger to my ear, confirming he had licked me when my fingers came back tacky with his spit.

'Really?' I asked, panting at the thought of what Simion had promised to do with me.

His brows raised, gesturing me to enter the room. 'You'll have to wait and see.'

I passed him, feeling as though I floated on air. Although I couldn't repeat what he had said to me, my mind wouldn't let go of the vision of the bar, me on my back and Simion looking up between my legs with a devilish grin that matched his devilish thoughts.

Dryads, forgive me.

* * *

Celia Hawthorn stared at the charred remains of the Heart Oak, hands clasped before her, a crowd stationed around her in a crescent formation. Leia stood at the side, a few of her most trusted Council members beside her. Opposite was Beatrice, shoulders back with a look of someone who still couldn't believe her mother stood before her. Not a single set of eyes looked towards me. All were pinned to the impossible woman they had searched for but could not find. A woman my own bloodline had imprisoned in time, left in a pocket, to wait for this very moment.

Although I had nothing to compare it to, there was a youthfulness to Celia as she turned to face me. Whereas Leia had lines at the corners of her eyes, Celia's skin was as smooth as polished stone. In a way, she looked more like Beatrice's sister, which I supposed made sense, since they were now close in age.

'Maximus Oaken.' She spoke my name with such gentleness I could have closed my eyes and conjured an image of my mother. 'The last I saw of you was in a bundle of cloth, held to

Deborah's chest as she ran through the shadows of Galloway Forest to get as far away from this very room as possible. Now, here you are, and look at you.' She paused for breath, taking a deep one as though this air was fresh and vibrant. 'I admit, I did not imagine it would be possible for you to look anything like Deborah, since she was only the vessel that carried you. But, I see something of her in you, a spark of her story.'

I couldn't help the tears. They fell freely, cascading down my cheeks, lingering into my collar where the material grew sticky and damp. Celia's words were my undoing. My mother's closest friend, her confidante.

'And from what Bea and Simion have explained, not even the universe could keep our bloodlines apart. You have found a heart in my children, and, even if you did not already have mine, you have solidified it.' She opened her arms, offering me the kindest of smiles. 'Come, Max.'

I was a five-year-old child again, broken down to a snuffling and sniffling little boy, as I willingly closed the space between us. Celia engulfed me in her arms, hands rubbing my back, pressing a motherly kiss into my crown. This time, I did give into my selfish desire. I closed my eyes, breathed in and imagined it was my mother who held me in her arms. It was not impossible to imagine.

'I feel like I should thank you,' I said, as I withdrew. Celia lifted a finger and cleared the tears from my cheeks slowly.

'Pray tell, what for? You are the one that brought my family together.'

'*Everything.*' It was all I had the ability to say, whereas my mind stormed with all the other answers. For helping my mother escape. For creating Beatrice, my closest friend. For Simion, the man who held my heart in his hands, who loved me with such a force that I would feel it across space and time.

'There will be time we can all thank one another, once we finally deal with our little parasite issue,' Beatrice added with her usual drawl. 'Lilyth may sense the sceptre is back on the table. I imagine, by nightfall, the shades will hit Wycombe in full force.'

No, I thought. *Because tonight I will end this.*

'My daughter is right. You brought me back for the sceptre, and the knowledge of the conduits. Although I see a lot has occurred since my departure, it feels as though it has been nothing but seconds since I last stood in this room. Many have perished, faces I will never see again. And more will perish soon, if we do not face the horror of the thing I fought to stop with Deborah and...' Celia lifted her gaze towards Leska, who watched from the shadows of a pillar, '... Cyder. Lilyth, the mother of monsters, parasite of worlds, has found herself back on our shores. We have no option but to face her, the very thing the Hawthorns had been set up for in the first place, even if they lost their way in mine and Deborah's absence.'

'We have a chance other worlds did not,' I said, reigning in my wild emotions and replacing it with the mask I had grown used to wearing.

'I have no doubt,' Celia said, reaching to the waistband of her trousers. 'So, you will be needing this. Since the crown and gauntlet has already been exposed, and you now have the sceptre, it is the location of the final conduit that you require.'

I would have questioned her on the final conduit, but my mind was utterly lost to the sceptre. I couldn't explain it aloud, but the sceptre she held to me oozed power. It was pulsing, much like the Heart Oak once had. Was that because Celia had been lingering inside of it, holding the sceptre in her imprisonment? All the cuts of Heart Oak stored for mages to pick emitted the same light, likely infected by the power of the sceptre in some way.

Instead of reaching for the sceptre, I kept my hands forced to my side.

'I am glad to see your hesitation,' Celia said, holding out the conduit to me. 'It proves that your intentions are well placed.' She couldn't imagine how wrong she was. 'You do not chase power, it chases you. Maximus, this is yours. You will need it for what is to come.'

I took it, for fear my continuous hesitation would only incite more questions. But as my fingers wrapped around the handle, a blast of power thrummed through me. Like when I took the phoenix's crown, I lost myself to the tidal wave. It was not my passion it grasped and controlled, but my mind. It opened me up, flaying my thoughts apart until I was fragmented—no, not broken, but shared between every dryad. I could not only feel them but *hear* them too. Voices in my ears, whispering the promise of knowledge. It was my name, spoken by every dryad, as they each bowed, knowing that my will now overpowered theirs. I controlled them, I willed them to do what I desired. Like Simion and the phoenixes, Lilyth with the nymphs. This was power in its rawest form; it was complete and devouring control. It was—

'Max.' I turned, drawn out of my mind, to see Simion stood at my side. 'Breathe, do not go against the wave but let it take you.'

I understood exactly what he meant. Simion had faced this alluring power and refused it. Instead of it controlling him like the crown did to me, he took the reins and controlled it.

So that it was I did. All that essence, those threads of earth and life that erupted, not only within me but around me—I took it. I gathered them to me, snatching each one until there was not a single frayed or loose thread left.

When I opened my eyes and faced the room, it was with the knowledge that my body was an encasement for power unlike anything I could have ever believed possible.

I was not simply controlling earth. I *was* earth. Stone, soil, bark and mineral.

'This calls for a celebration.' It was Leia who spoke, flooding towards her sister with a slight hesitation. I understood uncertainty; it was Leia's vote that was the deciding factor for Celia's exile. But what I now understood, from what was whispered in my ear, was Leia saved Celia from another fate. She used her deciding vote, her power, and saved her from execution. 'I will prepare a feast...'

'Dearest sister, oh how time has not changed you.' Celia wrapped her arm around Leia. Although she spoke like the eldest, she looked more like Leia's child than her sibling. 'Now, I desire nothing more than spending every moment of time with my family. Tonight, we survive any and all attempts at destruction Lilyth will throw at Wycombe. Tomorrow, we prepare to end this threat once and for all. Only after that, will we celebrate.'

'And what of the final conduit?' Every set of eyes fell upon me.

'Oribon.' Celia spoke the name of the dragon with trepidation and fear. 'I believe holds the answers.'

'Believe or have been told?' Simion added, eyeing us both.

Celia wrung her hands together, as if unsure what to do with them after so long holding the conduit. 'Deborah, Cyder and I searched everywhere for it. The only place we did not visit, due to reasons you can imagine, was the Avarian Crest. It is a dangerous place.'

'It is best we speak no more of this,' Simion said, looking into the shadowed corners of the room. 'We do not know who is listening.'

I faced the shadows in the corner of the room, knowing exactly who was listening, just as she had previously promised me.

'Then two conduits are better against Lilyth than one,' I replied.

Simion seemed to chew the words over, the crown glowing atop his head like a beacon. 'I will send the phoenixes out across the city. The shades are creatures of shadow until bathed in light. Leia, can the gleamers ensure the message is sent to every citizen, that they must make sure their hearths burn tonight? Light every candle. If they keep by the light, the shades can be harmed.'

Leia nodded, gesturing to her Council members whose eyes already began to glow with magic. 'Consider the message already en route.'

'If Lilyth comes looking tonight, it will be for the conduits. Max and Simion will need protection in case anything happens.' Beatrice wasn't wrong. 'Maybe it is best the conduits are hidden—'

'We will look after them,' I said, my knuckles paling beneath the grasp of the sceptre. 'Lilyth is weak, still. She will not risk coming for the conduits if we stay together.'

'Maximus is right,' Celia added, 'they must stay together. Although I can see that it will take much to separate those two apart.'

Heat flushed in my cheeks, but I refused to look away.

It was Elder Leia's turn to hand out commands. 'Simion, can you instruct your *phoenix-possessed* to station themselves around the dwellings in the city. Spreading out the power alongside the battlemages will be a benefit if any of the shades do come sniffing around. Best we fight side by side rather than from separate lines.'

'Sorcerers,' I corrected.

Simion leaned in close, his shoulder pressed firmly to mine. 'It was unjust to referring to those who *survived* the infection of this magic as phoenix-possessed. If we are to be equals, we need a name to match.'

Mages and sorcerers. North and South. Enemies to allies.

'I like it,' Elder Leia replied, showing a swell of pride across her expression as she regarded Simion. 'But if the sorcerers are our equals, they also deserve the same lodgings and treatment as the mages. I will see space is arranged within Saylam Academy.'

'Thank you, Aunt. It will do for now. But I have an idea for the sorcerers, one that can wait until the world is saved.'

Until the world is saved. Which, if my plan went ahead, would be by dawn tomorrow.

CHAPTER 24

Simion hadn't noticed that I didn't follow him into the Mad Queen. I found myself entranced by the sign that swung like a pendulum above me. With the sceptre grasped in my hand, I could sense every splinter of wood it was made from. My innate magic would have allowed me to control the wood, but this new power... it was different. Deeper. That was the only way I could describe it to myself. It was as if I could reach into the heart of the sign, tear it apart, reform it, mould it, manipulate it. The possibilities were endless.

It wasn't only the sign to the tavern that drew my attention, but everything around me. Buildings made from stone and wood, the ground beneath my feet, even the far-off whisper of wind gently caressing the branches of trees. I could feel it all as though the earth was my skin.

'There you are,' Simion said, looking out across the street. I snapped my attention to him, seeing how his back was haloed by the warm glow of a lit hearth. There was not the usual noise from the tavern behind him.

'Sorry, I'm distracted.' I looked to the sign a final time, trying to quell the feeling inside of me.

'You'll get used to it.' From the way Simion looked at me, I knew he recognised my distance. He was referring to the power, not my new knowledge of how the Queen got her infamous title.

'What if I do not want to?' I didn't deserve this magic and the possibilities that came with it. Holding it, finally sensing what Lilyth thirsted for, I understood how destructive it could be. But that was not the only possibility the sceptre offered. There was life too, thriving and healing.

'That is exactly the reason why you should be the one to wield it, Maximus.' His words helped distract me from the rushing beneath my skin. Simion cocked his head towards the tavern interior. 'Come inside. Nicho and Iria have retired to bed, though not without some questions. But it is not every day we have free rein in a tavern. Let's make the most of it.'

Simion was still high on the day's activities. Seeing his mother had opened some hope in him. I couldn't help but smile at his happy demeanour, knowing I was hours away from ruining it.

Before I followed him inside, I glanced towards the darkened street. Although I could not see Lilyth, I certainly felt her unwanted presence—watching and waiting.

Warm air riddled with dried ale filled my lungs with the first step inside. Simion shut the door behind me, then came to stand at my back like a shadow. 'Peaceful, isn't it? I don't think I have ever heard this place so quiet.'

'It is like stepping foot in a world only we are allowed within,' I said.

I scanned the empty room where stools were left upside down on recently cleaned tables. The floor sparkled, curtesy of the mop and bucket left leaning against one of the walls. My eyes caught the box resting upon the bar. To anyone else, it would have looked like a mundane crate hiding mundane items.

But I knew what power lurked inside.

Lilyth's crown—my focus.

'Fancy a drink?' Simion distracted me, moving my attention from the bar to something else.

'A small one.' I offered him a smile, moving to the closest table. Once I returned two stools to the ground, I placed the sceptre down. The relief was instant. Even my palm seemed to echo the ache, my knuckles and fingers sore from holding it so tightly. I could hardly take my eyes off it.

'I would not blame you if you wanted to spend time with your mother, Simion. You can leave me.'

His arms bulged as he pulled on the handle behind the bar. In his other hand, his fingers encircled a pint glass. Rich, dark liquid spilled into it, frothing at the top as he held it at an angle. 'There will be tomorrow. And the days after it. I wish to spend tonight with you.'

A prickling of gooseflesh spread across the back of my neck. 'I'm honoured.'

'And *I'm* beginning to feel like you would rather get rid of me.' Simion paced to the table, two full glasses in hand. He offered one to me, which I took gladly, then offered his up in cheers. 'A toast feels most appropriate, don't you think?'

I lifted mine up to meet his. 'What are we toasting to?'

'Family.'

Who knew one word had such power? I blinked, recognising the pricking in the corners of my eyes for what it was.

'Family,' I echoed, clinking my glass to his. The swig I took was hearty and deep. Froth lathered my top lip, spreading over my skin like the shadow of a clipped beard. Simion laughed at that, reached forward and cleared it with his thumb. He brought it to his mouth and licked it clean. All the while my stomach was doing summersaults.

'Lilyth has been awfully quiet,' Simion said, his timing strange.

I looked down to his glass, watching the condensation run down his fingers. It was easier than holding his eyes. 'She has.'

Simion's eyes narrowed as he exhaled a long, tempered breath. 'Do you need to be reminded that you can talk to me, Max?'

'I am talking.'

'No, you are deflecting. You are hardly saying a word. You can hardly hold my stare. I promised you I would not pry, and I meant it. But I am worried about you, dryads I am worried about everyone outside these walls. But I am trying to enjoy this moment of peace before the inevitable happens.'

Slowly, I returned my eyes to his. It was easy to lose myself to the gold of his stare. It was as though he had the power to draw me in and keep me hostage. No wonder the dragons in the tales I had read coveted the metal so protectively. With Simion, I felt the same urge to store him away from anyone and anything, keeping him to myself.

'I don't want to say the wrong thing and ruin the moment.' It was half a truth. Simion had just been returned with the mother he never believed he would see again. This was a day to celebrate, even if a monster hid in the shadows. Even now, I felt as though Lilyth was watching me. Did she sense the two conduits? Did it call to her like blood calls to a leech?

Simion traced a finger down the curve of my jaw, drinking me in with his eyes. 'Then we do not need to speak. I am happy to sit here in silence, if it means I have the privilege of sitting with *you*.'

I cried *again*.

This time, it was not from sadness, not from pain or fear. It was not a chest-wracking sob, but a single silent tear followed by another and then another. Simion reached across the space, took my shaking hands in his and drew me towards him. In a moment I was upon his lap, my legs held together by his arm, his other wrapped around my body. I sagged willingly into his chest, allowing the material of his tunic to soak up each and every tear.

'Here,' Simion said whilst he stroked me, rocking back and forth as he held me. 'Let me help you.'

'I wish I could tell you what I am feeling, but... I can't place it.' That was a complete truth. I glanced up to Simion through wet lashes, feeling his ale-coated breath brush over me. It wasn't unpleasant. It was real and for that I adored it.

He laid a palm against the side of my face. I leaned into it, delighting in the warmth of his skin, how his fire burned beneath it. But it was another feeling that overcame that, one of ice. Simion closed his eyes as he read my emotions, not my thoughts. My mind was still protected by my shield, and he wouldn't enter it without permission, but my emotions were an open book.

'Grief,' Simion said so suddenly the temperature of the room dropped. 'That is the emotion you are feeling.' He continued to hold my face, although his magic receded. 'It is understandable, after everything that you have witnessed today, that it would remind you of what you have lost. I am sorry if it has hurt you, I am sorry if seeing my mother has...'

I shook my head, knowing with complete certainty that his mother had nothing to do with why I was feeling like this. 'It isn't anything to do with your mother, Simion, I promise.'

'Then tell me what the cause is. Let me reach for whatever acts as this thorn of emotion and remove it for you.'

But Simion was right, it was grief I suffered with. It took me a moment to recognise the emotion for what it was, considering how familiar it was. But this was not from death. This was grief from the memory I had paid today, one that I could not even conjure to know what I had lost. Grief knowing what price was to be paid in a matter of hours. Grief for the relationship I would ruin by betraying Simion.

'I love you,' I whispered, unable to say anything else.

'That is not exactly the answer I expected.' His lips met my forehead. Simion held them there, kissing me, as the moment stretched between us. 'But I love you so much that simply telling you I love you would never begin to explain the levels of my love for you.'

I laughed, unable to stop myself as his mumbling words broke the tension over me. 'Simion Hawthorn, the poet.'

'I think you'll find I am a King now.'

'How did I forget.' My eyes faltered to the box upon the bar. 'To me, you have always been a person worth worshipping.'

'Is that so?'

This was it. The moment I betrayed Simion by using his greatest weakness against him. Me.

I manoeuvred myself over his thighs until one leg rested on either side of him. His hands moved to my lower back, holding me in place. I felt every drum of his fingers as he worked a rhythm upon my back. 'Take me. Have me tonight as though it is the last time.'

There's a high chance it will be. Not because the world would end, but we would—me and Simion. Maybe Simion would forgive me when he knew my betrayal saved us, but it would be one thorn he could never remove. One thorn that would always keep us apart.

Love was nothing without trust.

Simion didn't seem to notice the meaning behind my words. 'Only if you are sure this is what you want? Never feel obliged to—'

'Obliged? Simion, feeling your touch is one of life's many wonders. I care little for what has been, or what will be. With you, I think of nothing but the moment.' Something Simion said back in the Gathrax library sprung to mind. 'I focus on you, and only you. That is your power over me. And I willingly hand over my control to you, always.'

I felt every inch of skin that his eyes roamed over. His

fingers became firmer behind my back, urging me into him more.

'I look forward to hearing you say this to me, over and over, for as long as you want me.'

My hips rolled atop Simion. It took only a few subtle moves before I felt the press of his hardening length. 'I will always want you, Simion. No matter the time, no matter the place.'

He took his hand from my back, and for a moment, I thought he was going to stop. I was wrong. Instead, Simion rested his palm over my heart until I was aware of the steady beat of it in my chest. He didn't speak, because words mattered little now. Our bodies exposed what we wished to say, confirming the feelings we harboured for one another.

This time was different to all those that had come before. Between gentle, long kisses we undressed one another. Soon enough we were laid upon the floor, our clothes piled beneath us, the cool breeze of the tavern blanketing us. Our mouths hardly parted, our tongues in a continuous dance.

I refused to think of anything else. Whatever came when we finished didn't matter in this moment. I drank it all in—him, his touch, his smell and taste. If this truly was the last time, I would make the imprint so deep I would never forget a detail.

Simion was stretched out beneath me, his arms above his head. I sat on his hips, slowly encouraging his length inside of me. He was muttering my name, declaring his love in whispers as though the universe was not deserving to hear it. But I did. I heard every syllable and the meaning he placed behind it.

As I sheathed his cock inside of me, flames erupted across the tavern. Light flared alongside Simion's pleasure. Wicks upon candles exploded to life, the hearth spat out sparks across the stone floor, even the chimney became stained by dark plumes of soot and smoke.

I rode Simion, rolling my hips, lifting up as much as my aching thighs allowed. My magic reacted to my pleasure too. As he eased his cock against the sensitive point within me, it was as though the ground shivered with ecstasy.

'Come to me,' Simion encouraged, drawing me down to his mouth. His fingers wove into the side of my head, nails brushing over my scalp as he held me before his face. 'My darling, Max.'

'My Simion,' I exhaled, as he took over the movements, pumping himself with vigour into me.

Sweat beaded down his temple, mirroring my forehead. I reached down with my tongue, clearing his off, the salty tang exploding across my tongue. Dryads. It was not only the heat in the room that built, but the fire inside of me. Simion returned his hand to my bare chest, controlling the passion within me, guiding it like the banks of a river.

We held eye contact, refusing to break it. I hardly blinked, delighting in the creases of pleasure that wove into Simion's skin. His mouth was forged into a perfect shape, his tongue resting on his teeth.

I could not touch myself, not as my hands rested on either side of him, keeping me in place. But that didn't stop my cock from pulsing with enjoyment. I could feel the sticky seed of pleasure leaking out across Simion's muscular stomach, encouraged by every deep beat of his length inside of me.

If he kept going like that, it would finish soon.

'You feel so... entrancing,' Simion sang, using his hands to separate my ass cheeks until not an inch of himself could be wasted. 'I wish to bury myself in you and never leave.'

I flopped over him, stars exploding behind my eyelids with every pump of his length. 'You are always inside of me, Simion.' I tapped my chest, nail pricking just over my heart. 'Here, always here.'

'Dryads, spare me. You are my making and my ruin, Maximus Oaken.'

Simion suffered with the same affliction as me. I may not have been a gleamer, but I could read the nuances expression that gave away his emotions. He caught his lip between his teeth, his brows lifted into his hairline. All telltale signs that he was close.

I didn't want it to end. I wanted it to last forever and a day, preventing the inevitable from following. But I was weak. My deal with Lilyth proved as much. So, I tightened myself, drawing in the muscles, which broke Simion down into loud, rumbling moans. He was moving quickly, a desperate look shattering across his face.

'Come for me, Maximus. Mark me as yours.'

'Simion,' I cried out, his name forced from a shattered part within me.

'Say it again.' His eyes rolled into the back of his skull. 'I want to hear my name in your mouth.'

I rocked backwards, throwing my head back as another shout broke from me. 'Simion.'

For a man with so many words, he was reduced to only one. '*Fuck.*'

To aid him, and myself, I picked up my ass and worked it down upon him. Between his thrusting and my slamming, we reached our end. Together. A violent wave of power cascaded across the room, extinguishing every flame in a second. Cracks formed in the wooden panels beneath my hands, spreading out like a web beneath us.

Simion's pounding slowed as he came deep within me. I, too, recognised the spurting jolts of my cock as it expelled my seed across his stomach. One look down, and I could see that it pooled in his bellybutton.

I flopped over Simion, falling upon him to find his arms anchoring around me.

'Dryads,' he swore into my hairline, before pressing yet another kiss to me. 'You are one of life's miracles, Max.'

I rolled off him, lying by his side. My breathing was heavy, my lungs aching, as I attempted to catch my breath. Still, the pleasure rocked through me, threatening to be my undoing. But there, lurking in the corners of my mind, was the one task I had come here for. The sex left a bitter taste in my mouth, thanks to the betrayal that would follow. 'We should clean up and get to bed.'

'No,' Simion sighed through a smile. 'I do not want to move from this place. It may not be the library we left behind, but it now holds just as incredible a memory.'

My laugh was honest, my eyes as heavy as Simion. 'We can't just sleep here. What if Nicho and Iria come down?'

'Oh, from the way you were screaming my name, they know. I think you have provided them enough warning to stay away for the time being.'

Using one of the clothes I could reach, I cleaned the puddle of milky seed from Simion's stomach. After I sorted myself out, I could see that his breathing had evened, his eyes closed and his smile didn't once leave his mouth.

'Simion?' I asked.

He half grumbled in response. 'Yes?'

'You're tired.'

'I am. Lie with me.'

I did as he asked, positioning my body beside his. 'I love to fall asleep beside you and wake up to find you still here.'

My happiness faltered, like the drying flame of a candle. 'Rest, Simion. We will need it to face tomorrow.'

A tomorrow I will secure, for you, for Wycombe, for Aldian.

A gentle, encouraging chuckle emitted from him. 'With you by my side, I could face anything.'

I pressed a kiss to his cheek. To my luck, Simion didn't open his eyes. If he did, he would have witnessed the return of my tears. By the time I lay back down beside him, I stared at the dark ceiling, eyes wide, tiredness far from me. Hours could have passed, and I didn't move. Not until Simion's breathing evened and the familiar snores that I once hated had returned.

Only then did I stand and pull on my clothes as quietly as I could. I took the sceptre from the table, feeling the rush of untapped power return. Moving as quickly as I could, I grabbed the box containing the crown, turned for the door and didn't look back.

'Lilyth,' I spoke to the dark on the street beyond. 'I have what you seek.'

Droplets of rain began to fall from above, each cool drop a kiss against my skin. And in the gentle shower I heard it, the voice. *Find me.*

CHAPTER 25

Lilyth waited for me amongst the ruins of the cottage I had called home for a short time. Her deathly pale skin glowed against the night, as though a star was beneath her flesh. Perhaps it was—I still knew little of this being's origins.

From Inyris's back, I could see Lilyth like a beacon, guiding me to her. Shadows danced and slithered around her—not shadows but *shades*.

It was the army she promised, ready to strike if I did not give her what she wanted. I only hoped she held up her promise, long enough to leave Aldian intact.

The rain fell with vicious intent across the expanse of cliff and sea. Until Inyris noticed Lilyth's presence, my dragon had not been resistant to my panicked summons as I ran through Wycombe's empty streets. She had lowered her snout to the sceptre, sniffing it curiously, before blowing out a puff of frigid air. But that displeasure was nothing compared to her reaction to seeing Lilyth.

'Stop!' I commanded, both aloud and through the bond. 'Inyris, enough.'

Blue-white light crackled in Inyris's jaw as she prepared to unleash a pillar of ice down upon the mother of monsters. Lilyth didn't flinch, her wide smile never wavering. There was no fear, not in the face of Inyris. Lilyth had faced far worse than one dragon. She had faced them all, led by Oribon.

Admiration still grew in my chest, knowing my dragon would stand against the ender of worlds, for me.

I squeezed my thighs into her sides, pulling on Inyris's twisted horns as though I could steer her back in the right direction.

The rain fell harder, casting a sheet across the sky. Magic was everywhere, in every droplet that drummed against my skin, that made it into my mouth. Lilyth was toying with Inyris, preventing her from escaping the inevitable.

Sodden to the bone and trembling, I pointed towards the ground. 'Take me there, or I will do it myself.'

Inyris didn't need further explanation as to what I meant, because I showed her exactly my plan. The image I formed and delivered across our bond was one of me throwing myself off her side. Inyris might refuse me many things, but she wouldn't let me die. It was against everything that tethered us. Even if that meant delivering me to a world-eating monster.

If I expected Inyris to do as I asked with ease, I was wrong. She turned back to the glowing body of Lilyth, narrowed her slitted pupils and dove. Wind and rain screamed past my ears, slapping my face like the continuous stabbing of pinpricks. The ground rose up fast, too fast. Lilyth stayed immobile, watching with awe—almost enjoyment. Moments before Inyris's snout crashed into the ruins of the cottage, her golden wings flared out, caught the wind, and she stopped herself.

'How... entertaining.' Lilyth's laugh rumbled across the night. It only built as Inyris expelled the most vicious of roars inches from Lilyth's face, brushing her hair from her face and coating her in spittle. I found myself holding my breath, wondering if Inyris's behaviour would ruin any hope I had that this meeting would go the way I wanted... no, *needed*. I had only two of the conduits, not three. But I knew the location of the last. Lilyth wouldn't be pleased, but then again, I hardly imagined that she didn't already know.

I placed a palm on Inyris's neck, willing her to calm. As though recognising my attempt, she shot me a look that sang of her disappointment in me. That shocked me more than I expected, as did the wave of emotion she brushed over me.

Disappointment. Unfathomable disappointment akin to that of a parent to a child. It followed me, weighing heavy on my shoulders. Inyris would always protect me, but she didn't need to like me whilst doing it.

'Maximus Oaken, come to save his world.'

I slipped from Inyris's side, nicking my thumb along the sharp curve of one of her scales. Blood welled, catching Lilyth's attention. For a moment, all of her emotion was smothered from her expression, and in its wake was left the look of... hunger. Her plump tongue traced her lower lip, flashing four pointed teeth I had not noticed before.

Danger filtered into the atmosphere, making me regret coming. No longer did she look at me like a weak human, but like a feast.

'I come bearing gifts,' I said, silently begging for Lilyth to look at me as more than something she wished to wrap her mouth around. It wasn't until I reached back to Inyris's back and retrieved the box containing the crown that Lilyth's attention shifted. 'As you requested.'

Her lips drew into a frown. 'Strange, because I seem to remember requesting your help retrieving all three of the conduits, and you come bearing,' she pointed her long nail at the box, then the sceptre lodged in my belt, 'two.'

'As my mother would say, be grateful for what you have got and not what you haven't.' It was a natural defence for me to use sarcasm as a shield, even faced with a monster such as

Lilyth. Though the only monstrous thing about her was the way she studied the blood welling across my thumb. She still appeared to me without a serpent's tail or wings, human-sized, no taller than I was. But even in this form, there was no denying her power, not as the darkness around her shifted. The more I looked at the shadows, the more I could make out the shapes of bodies, limbs twisting, featureless faces watching me.

'Spoken like someone who has the privilege of being satisfied. Not all of us are driven in such a way.' Lilyth offered me a knowing smile, as though my storming thoughts had the capability of understanding the hidden meaning to her words. Then she looked around her, gesturing to the charred stone walls of the cottage. From the layout, I knew we stood in the middle of what was my mother's bedroom. The outer walls barely stood, the ground around littered with burned brick and shattered glass.

'You recognise the pain of losing those you love,' Lilyth said, sweeping her eyes across the remains of the room. 'I admit, you surprise me, Maximus.'

'Because I have so easily deceived my people?'

She shook her head, tutting with her dewy lips. 'No, because I would expect someone broken into so many pieces to be doing anything to put them all back together again.'

'I am not broken.'

Lilyth tilted her head, fighting a devilish smile. 'Are you not? Oh, I did not mean to suggest that being broken denotes weakness. In fact, I believe it is the opposite. You see, I, too, once had a home, a family, parents and—' She stopped talking, as though she longed to find the words in the darkness. If I was not so panicked, so aware that her shades surrounded me and Inyris, I might have focused on the sadness she revealed across her face. 'Children. But, as all good things are, they were taken from me. As you can understand, I, too, was broken. Shattered into so many pieces I was discarded by my people. But instead of allowing myself to be scattered to the wind, I found something that would put me together again.'

I swallowed hard, tasting the bile that crept up my neck. 'Ruin and destruction? Strange way to find solace in your heartbreak.'

'Do you know what becomes of a forest when it is razed to ash?' Lilyth asked almost too quickly, as though she was growing tired of my voice.

I gripped the box tighter, unable to speak beneath the harsh gaze.

'It grows back. Life. It returns and flourishes. New growth, new life, opportunity for... more.'

'I am sorry, I don't understand.'

'Nor do I expect such small minds to ever comprehend.' In moments Lilyth was stood inches before me. I could not place the smell that seeped from her, it was nothing I had ever experienced before. It was both stale and sweet, bitter and floral. It told a tale of a place she had come from, her home.

'Help me understand then,' I said, my body rigid as stone. 'If my being here proves I do not wish to be a threat. I want to find a peaceful way out of this, one without the need for destruction.'

'I am true to my word.' Lilyth raised a finger and placed the point of her nail beneath my chin. Her expression changed again, from boredom back to hunger. I didn't dare move, not as her nail pricked my skin, broke it and drew blood.

'Then you will leave, as you promised?' I asked, as a dribble of blood ran down my neck, into the collar of my black tunic.

Inyris expelled a trembling growl from the deepest parts of her. It rumbled over my skin, to the delight of Lilyth, who shot my dragon a pleased look. Then Lilyth released her gaze from me, brought her blood-tipped nail to her mouth and sucked it.

Pleasure erupted over her face. It smoothed the creases

across her skin and had her eyes rolling back into her skull before she closed them. Pure, undiluted ecstasy.

'What... are you doing?' The question fell out of me as disgust crashed in my stomach.

What kind of monster are you?

Lilyth opened her eyes quickly, parting her mouth so I could see the faint stain of pink in the corners. 'I am finding what I have been searching many a millennia for.'

Relief filled every inch of her face, widening her smile, brightening those otherworldly eyes. Even her shades chirped and sang around us, echoing whatever internal joy that explained Lilyth's change in demeanour.

The tide had changed, I felt it shift around my body like a corporeal force.

'Tell me what you see, when you look at me, Maximus?'

'A monster. A devourer of worlds.'

'I have been those things,' Lilyth said, smiling as though I had complimented her. 'To other worlds, yes. Everyone I have visited has gifted me with something powerful. Dryads, dragons, nymphs, phoenixes. These are—how would you say—tokens of my exploration.'

'You've been searching for something,' I said, echoing what I already knew. 'A home.'

'Oh, Maximus, you did not think I moved between worlds and realms destroying them for no gain? Yes, I have been looking for a home, but one that offered me the vital component of my kin's survival.'

'For power then.' My hand tightened on the sceptre, the box under my arm biting into my ribs from the tension.

'The power I have obtained was never my intention. Although it came in handy, as you have already seen.' There was something distant about her eyes, a way she gazed at me whilst seemingly not seeing me at all. 'Everything I have achieved, all I have done, was not for ruin and decay. It was for life, just like the forest I spoke of. It is to find...' Her eyes dropped to the blood dribbling down my neck. 'Sustenance.'

The sky could have split in that moment, torn in two by unseen hands. I stepped backwards, but shades hissed to life around me, blocking Inyris from view.

Lilyth lunged forward, grasped me by the shoulder and turned me around until my back was to her stomach. 'Allow me to show you. Perhaps you will understand my motives more keenly.'

She lifted her hand and brushed away the clouds. Rain parted as though she moved a curtain, allowing sunlight through a window. The sky that she showed me was clear and endless, with a prickle of stars winking across a sheet of obsidian.

'All those stars were potential places for me to discover a new dwelling. Not only for me, but for those I love. I would have continued searching, passing from one to another, looking for a suitable place that could house my kind but also... sustain us. You see, where I am from, we require something important to survive. A... nectar we long ran out of. Without it, we perish. I stood by and watched as my family starved. I was helpless, unable to do anything but watch as they shrivelled and expired. I vowed, as my child died in my arms, never to watch another family be torn apart. All I wanted was to find a place we could not only survive, but thrive. And, Maximus, I believe I have finally found it.'

My blood turned to ice. Inyris reacted, but too late. Lilyth's shades chose that moment to reach out from the shadows, snatching the sceptre from my belt and the box from my hands. I tried to act, but Lilyth stopped me. Her hand extended towards me, the gauntlet conduit glinting in the moonlight. There was no other way to explain it, but it felt as though Lilyth was inside of me, pulling puppet strings connected to my body. Not strings, but the water my body was made up of.

She was controlling... me.

Inyris snapped out, hissing ice, but stopped as Lilyth's shades overwhelmed her. A wave of darkness rose up so quickly, then fell atop my dragon, smothering her drawn-out cry.

Physical pain sliced through me, choking me where it lodged in my throat.

'You promised...' I forced out, my jaw stiff. 'You made a bargain to leave this world if I gave you the conduits.'

'The situation has changed, Maximus. I will put it plainly. I promised not to destroy the world, and that promise I will keep. But I will not be leaving. No, quite the opposite.'

One of the shades handed Lilyth the sceptre. As her long fingers wrapped around it, power flared in her eyes, green as the vibrant forest in the summer. Before my eyes she grew taller, slowly enough for me to watch. Her form shifted and stretched, like a snake shedding its skin. Fitting, because where her hips had met her legs, a serpentine tail now uncoiled, thickening with dark scales until she was lofted from the floor.

Inyris, leave.

It was not words that replied, but a feeling. *Never.*

I sensed her fighting the shades, knew she was alive. Gold shot beyond the knot of shadows, the force knocking my body out of Lilyth's control. At least, that is what I thought. Inyris crashed into Lilyth's enlarged form with such speed, the connection sent a blast out across Aldian. Talons clawed into her flesh, ripping away her human-forced mask and leaving behind the monster I had seen in the visions.

Inyris's attack lasted just a moment before another wave of shadow crest over her. It moved like a liquid wave, grasping souls wrapping themselves around my dragon until she was dragged to the ground and buried beneath them.

Her whimper pained me physically. This time, she was not getting free.

Before Lilyth could grasp control of me again, I reached out with my amplifier, snatched at every silver cord that connected me to the earth and sky, and pulled. My assault was desperate, but I threw everything at Lilyth and her shades before they could act. I had never drawn on this much power before, not all at once. The ruins of the cottage rose around me, lightning snaked across the sky, building to my call.

It all stopped when she pointed the sceptre at me. My power sizzled out like a candle in a storm.

'Dryad blood,' Lilyth sneered, her voice vicious. 'I control you, just as I command the very creatures who betrayed me. You belong to me, and you will offer my kin a new lease of life.'

She was not controlling the water in my blood. It was my blood itself she controlled, just like every dryad in Aldian and every nymph in the waterways. Lilyth controlled them all.

'I will fill this world with my people and give them the feast they have waited centuries for. The nectar we drank from before was not living, with no ability to reproduce and create more. But here, you... you and your humans will feed us for an eternity.'

I screamed, because it was all I could do. It was as though my limbs were being drawn apart, pulled from angles, as I was hoisted into the air. Inyris was forced to watch me, drowning beneath shadow, helpless to do anything.

Just as Inyris had smothered her pain when she fell from the skies, I did too. I cut off the bond, burying it deep, protecting her from the agony of my impending doom.

'Crown.' Lilyth's command was not for me, but her shades. Out from the darkness, the box was handed to her. She lifted it, talons scratching over the lid, the sound grating my skin. I held my breath, knowing the moment she took the conduit that all the phoenixes in Wycombe would be hers to control.

What have I done?

'Signed the fate of this world, and saved mine,' Lilyth answered, gleaning my thoughts freely now she held the power of the dryads in her hand. 'And soon you will all—'

She stopped, looking down into the box, her monstrous face breaking. Her cry was filled with horror and fury. It was the sound that came from the chest of a parent who held a dying child. It was, in fact, the same sound I had made when my mother had expelled her last breath in my arms.

Heat sizzled at my back, a bright light that cast away the shades enough for Inyris to claw her way free of them. I could not turn to face it, but there was no need. Not as the voice called out, snatching Lilyth's attention.

The box fell to the ground, and it was... empty.

A deep voice sounded behind me, filled with an ire so strong that it rocked against every inch of my skin. 'I will give you a chance to willingly relinquish control of my partner, or I will burn the fucking flesh from your bones, Lilyth.'

Simion.

He was here, haloed by the glow of black flame. It illuminated Lilyth's monstrous face, hollowing her cheeks and elongating her pinched lips and protruding bones. Her snarl broke, flashing the points of canines in her mouth, power rising in a wave as she prepared to attack.

'That belongs to me,' Lilyth snarled.

That being the crown Simion Hawthorn no doubt wore on his head. The crown he had hid from me, knowing I was going to take it and hand it over. I couldn't feel betrayed by his play, but thankful.

A warm, firm hand rested on my shoulder. I caught it from the corner of my eye, rich brown skin set against the gold of his armour. 'And *he* belongs to me.'

Lilyth snarled with the desperation of someone who knew they were about to lose. But it was in her blindness to the crown that she only noticed the first bolt of wytchfire that Simion sent towards her. Lilyth lifted a hand, waters drawing from sky around her to act as a shield... all the while Simion controlled another blast of flame, sending it crashing into the dryad's sceptre.

It erupted in the heat of black flame, wood burning to cinders, just as history described the destruction of the first Heart Oak.

Lilyth's keening scream was one born from loss. It ricocheted through me, turning my insides out as I watched the conduit slip through her talons, ash falling languidly like snow.

All at once I could no longer see her. My body was my own, but it was turned by Simion's hand. Fire erupted from his touch, swallowing me whole. I pinched my eyes closed, just as it engulfed me. If I expected pain, I was wrong. There was only peace and a powerful rush, as though I was forcefully moving from one place to another.

As Lilyth faded from view, her desperate cry remained. Even as we stepped through what I quickly realised was a portal, I could hear her. It was a call of fury but, more importantly, one of war.

CHAPTER 26

Wycombe was under siege. As we stumbled through the portal of fire, I heard the deafening screams of a city under attack. I had no doubt it was the shades, tearing through innocent people.

There was no time to contemplate as I took in the throne room Simion's portal led to, noticing first the crowd of faces. Leia and her Council; Celia stood with Beatrice and Leska; countless armoured battlemages surrounding them and a solitary dryad. They all looked to me expectantly. No, that was not the emotion. It was something else.

It was disappointment. It drew down at brows, screwed the corners of mouths into harsh lines.

Leia stepped forward, armour clinking. I didn't know what her outstretched hand was meant for until she spoke the two words that almost brought me to my knees. 'The sceptre. Did you get it, Simion?'

'Destroyed,' Simion said, just as the whoosh of air signalled the closing of his portal. 'It was the only option.'

They had this planned. All of them—the look they gave me, the way they all had been here waiting.

'But we needed the strength it gave, Simion.' Leska hardly looked at me as she spoke.

He stepped in beside me, shoulder brushing mine. I could hardly look at him for fear of what I would find. I had lied to him, betrayed him and still he stood rigid at my side. 'As did Lilyth. Now no one will have access to its powers. We do not require it to have the dryads fight alongside us.'

Leia levelled her eyes on me again. I refused to look away, even though everything screamed at me too. 'I expected more from you, Max.'

An eruption of noise sounded beyond the brightly lit room. Almost every head snapped towards it just as distant screams began. I chose that moment of distraction to disappear down my tether to Inyris, praying she made it free from Lilyth.

My dragon soared, seemingly unharmed, through the city's sky. Beneath her, people ran through the streets as shadows chased them. I watched, in muted colours, as bodies were dragged into nothingness, only for the wave of the shades to pass onto the next victim.

Wycombe was buried in chaos. Destruction was imminent. Inyris showed me a wall of shades careening towards Wycombe, all tooth and claw and pale flesh.

I snapped back into the room, but the pleas for help still rang in my skull. 'Lilyth has begun her assault on the city.'

'A perfectly understandable reaction to what you have done,' Leia snapped, from a place of panic, not anger. She could hear her city being torn apart by shades, she knew the damage that would follow. We all did. One shade had the power to murder close to a hundred mages. What could an entire army do?

'Sister,' Celia said, stepping in, hand on Leia's shoulder. 'Allow him to speak his side of the story.'

She offered me a reassuring smile, and I took it, allowing everything to come spilling out. I told them of Lilyth's bargain and how she visited me that night out on the cropping of rocks. I spared no detail, wanting them to know the lengths she went to speak with me, alone. I believed I had no choice but to accept.

Simion stiffened at my side, understanding why I had been distant. Leska and Beatrice shared a look, one that sang with their shared desire to tear Lilyth limb from limb with their bare teeth. I then divulged every scrap of knowledge I had gleaned from Lilyth herself. It was confusing to say it aloud, to tell a story about a woman who lost people she loved and vowed to find a new home for those she had left behind in her world. The gods were tokens taken from worlds she had visited and ruined. Except she no longer wished to do the same to Aldian, because we could offer her the very thing she had traversed the universe in search for.

'Sustenance,' I repeated the very word Lilyth had used. 'That is what she said.'

'And what does that mean?' It was Beatrice who asked the question, knuckles paling on the handle of the axe at her hip. 'What could we possibly provide her that other worlds have not?'

Lilyth had not explicitly answered the question, but it was the way she had looked at my blood, as though she hungered for it, that had me dragging up an answer. 'I believe the answer is in our blood. Us humans, she said we can provide... the sustenance, for her and her kind. An endless bank of whatever it is she has been searching for. She... tasted my blood.'

'Then let's go stop her. This blood-thirsting parasite has overstayed her welcome.' Leska was halfway to the guarded door, the battlemages naturally following her aura. 'I have a few choice words I would like to have with her.'

'Wait.' My word rang out across the room. I couldn't think straight as the pain in my head intensified. 'Lilyth needs us. I do not believe she will be in the city herself, but sending the shades to gather our people like livestock.'

I had to place my hope in this idea. It was all I had left not to break.

'Then what do you suggest?' It was Simion, gazing down at me with fire-filled eyes. The connection between us was open now. Thus far, he had not attempted to mind-speak. I took his silence as proof that I had truly ruined our relationship. I reached out, testing the tumultuous waters between us. *I am sorry for everything, Simion. It was not right, tricking you like I did.*

His gaze narrowed on me. *You, my darling, did not trick me. I saw it coming, I was prepared for what you were planning. If anything, I am sorry for not stopping you.*

When did you figure it out?

Passions, Maximus. I felt your desire for what you were to do. It was not like seeing your thoughts exactly, but reading between the lines of your feelings. Also, you did not think I would just leave the crown in some mundane box for any little thief to come and steal?

I took a deep, shuddering breath in, knowing the room waited for my initial answer to the first question Simion posed. *Thank you for not trusting me.*

It was quite the opposite. I trusted you. I did not question what it was that she made you do. As I read your passion, I knew Lilyth had also been truthful in her bargain. She meant it, until she understood what our blood could offer her. Instead, I followed your lead and simply acted as I saw fit.

By destroying the sceptre? Leia is right, we need its power to fight Lilyth.

Simion leaned in, his breath brushing my cheek, his fingers weaving through my brown curls, until he held the side of my head gently. *I know. And you have the means of retrieving it.*

'Simion, Max—perhaps there is another time you can whisper sweet nothings into one another's minds, but now is not it,' Beatrice scolded, hand on hip and lips peaked in a mischievous grin. 'We need a plan. And now.'

The sounds of terror only grew, each passing second, louder and louder, until the air of the throne room was spoiled with it.

I stared at Simion, knowing exactly what he was suggesting. 'It is dangerous, but there is something we can do to use Lilyth's store of power against her.'

'What is?' Elder Leia asked, mirroring the question on everyone's lips.

'Anything worth something comes with risks,' Simion whispered, 'It is up to us to decide if those risks are worth the end goal.'

I took a deep inhale, attempting to quell the building pressure beneath my ribs. It didn't help at all.

'What's it going to be, Max?' Leska added, still waiting at the door, ready to leave and fight for her city.

It was incredible, after everything I had done, that they all still looked to me to guide them. I once would have determined it as the blind leading the blind, as misplaced trust. But I did have a plan, faint, but it was still there.

'Survive. And, in the meantime, I will be going back and retrieving the conduits in the past, before Lilyth finds them in the present.'

Leska stepped forward, practically shivering with refusal. 'No. It is far too dangerous, Max. Time cannot be played with, we still do not even know the extent of the price you paid retrieving Celia. And you promised me you wouldn't do it again, Max. You promised.'

'I also promised to save Aldian from Lilyth, sister. I have to do this.'

'I agree with Leska,' Celia added. 'Going back and taking things from the past will only affect the present. By the time you are done, you do not know what you will come back to, or even if that is possible. Unless...' Her rich gaze faltered as her mind disappeared to a possibility.

Breathless, I asked, 'Unless what?'

'Unless you visit during a time when the conduit was forgotten. If it had no use in its timeline, then you should not affect the future, as long as you return it to its rightful place. That is the only way of ensuring the path of time is straight and without deviations. Like what the Queen did with me and the sceptre, we were both forgotten. Lost.'

'Then that is what we do. It is our only choice.' These were thoughts I had not contemplated.

'Perhaps it is,' Celia said, sorrow hanging heavy over her eyes. 'Which is why you must not take a conduit that has already had a part to play in this tale. Lilyth can have the gauntlet. Simion keeps the crown. But if we can find the shield before she does, then we are still two conduits more powerful than she is. The more gods she controls, the harder it is to fight her.'

And the sceptre? Simion's voice echoed in my head.

I steeled my expression, refusing to let Celia or anyone else know what was being shared between us. *I have a plan for that, but it is best they do not know yet.*

The universe had ways of testing, and in the next second, it chose us as its next target. Just as the morale was building and we were ready to spend the night in battle, Inyris yanked me back into her mind.

This time, my dragon was not watching the streets of Wycombe, but looking out across the Thalassic. If it was not for her heightened vision, I may not have seen what was coming. Blood cooled to ice in my veins, my heart practically stopping, as I saw the tidal wave racing towards Aldian's shores. Dragons cut through the night, gathering as one in the sky, barrelling towards the wave with magic building in their throats. Inyris joined, salt-water spraying her underbelly, the need to protect singing in her wolfen skull. Glamora was there too, her imposing frame moving with such ferocious speed it was almost impossible to determine her from the night sky.

It was the nymphs that Lilyth now controlled. And unlike the illusion this wave had last presented itself as, repelling us from the rebellion's island after The Claim, this was real. I felt the world rumble with the force, I watched as waters were drawn back, emptying the shallow shoreline as though the ocean had run from some great terror. It built in a wall, towering as high as Saylam Academy, with a vengeful roar.

Ice shot from the jaws of dragons as they attempted to quell the wave. Where the brilliant light of dragon breath slammed into the wave, it crystallised, the frothing crest freezing into static horses made of white sea foam.

'Maximus.' A palm connected with the side of my face. I blinked, unable to distinguish the throne room from the view of the Thalassic. It was as if I was in two places at once. The roaring wave was replaced with an endless scream. Not caring for my stinging skin, I snapped my head to Beatrice, whose face was crimson from the lack of breath as she expelled her cry. The glazed, distant look on her face told me she was witnessing the same thing.

'Lilyth...' I said, breathless as though it was I who flew through the skies, spewing molten ice from my jaw. 'She is using the nymphs' power, conjuring a wave that could sweep all of Wycombe away within seconds.'

There was a cracking in my tether, the feeling of shattered glass. Except it wasn't glass, but ice. The dragons were trying but failing to hold the power back.

'We need to find Lilyth and put an end to this.' I wasn't sure who said it. Not as I attempted to make sense as to what this play was for. Lilyth had made it clear we were important to her. Why would she then use the nymphs to drown every citizen? It clicked then, just as Beatrice sagged forward, back in control of her mind.

She caught my eyes, a knowledge shared between us. 'Oribon has been called. Glamora has shown me, he is sending every dragon from the Avarian Crest to our aid.'

Every dragon but Oribon himself. He would never leave, knowing what he protected.

The relief that was shared was short-lived. 'Lilyth is drawing the dragons out. She has no desire to flood Wycombe, she is making sure she creates enough of a distraction, something so large it will draw in all the gods.'

'Why bother?' Leia asked.

'Because she wants the final conduit. The shield,' I said, staring deep into her gilded eyes. 'Drawing the dragons away from the Avarian Crest leaves Oribon alone. Celia, you were right. Oribon has it and Lilyth knows that now.'

'We can beat her to it,' Simion said, heat radiating from his skin in undulant waves. 'I can fly on Erinda and reach the Avarian Crest before she can—'

'No, Simion.' I laid my hands on his chest, feeling my palms sizzle beneath the pure heat of him. 'You of all people must stay protected. The first chance she gets to take the crown, she will. You surprised her once, and I doubt she will allow that to happen again. We forget, Lilyth is not new to these games. She has played them many times, over and over, ruining worlds. She will always be one step ahead.'

He held my stare. 'Then we better stay one step behind her —in time.'

The mayhem from the city had reached new heights. It was as though the fight had made itself into the room from the sheer noise of it. A violent rush of wind slammed against the door, knocking it wide open. Horror spliced through me as I saw what waited beyond. Shadow, pure endless darkness, but it was not empty. The shades writhed amongst it, the stench of their rot and decay stinging my eyes.

'Keep back,' Leska shouted, urging the battlemages into a

new formation at her back. They protected us from the shades-filled corridor, which prevented any of us from leaving.

'Stay behind me too,' Simion said, placing his body before me. It would have been easy to give into his offered protection, especially since the red light brightened from his crown, making the shades hiss and retreat a little.

But this time I was not ready to hide behind him, or anyone. There was enough fury in me to wreak havoc, and dryads I longed for it. I hoped Lilyth was watching in some way, seeing exactly what we were all prepared to do to protect ourselves from her.

My fist gathered at my side, the air around it crackling. I pulled on my dragon bond, borrowing the power of air and sky from Inyris until I was made of the element. White light fizzed around my skin as I slipped past Simion and placed myself before the corridor. The hairs on my arms stood on end, the power overspilling from my eyes. I saw the reflection of it on the slabbed stone at my feet.

Arms of shadow reached out of the corridor, fingers grasping for me. A figure stepped in at my side, and another and another. The power unfurled within me, filling every place of pain I had ever felt, smothering it.

Fire brightened to my right. Simion gathered it in his arms, tongues of red and black. To my right, Leska stood. Her remaining hand crackled with the same lightning, but it was bluer, the snakes of power smaller. Beatrice was with us too, a dangerous smile splayed across her face. As one, we lifted our hands up.

Fire, lightning and earth cast down the corridor, banishing the shadows and the shades with it. Beatrice controlled the stone with her amplifier, creating blades of the element, which she sent piercing into every bit of milky exposed flesh of the creatures. Their short-lived screams were like nails being drawn down glass, only to falter into pure silence.

Sconces burst to life as Simion conjured fire in the metal brackets.

The magic fizzed out, but the feeling of euphoria remained. Drunk on it, drunk on the need to release more, to destroy more of Lilyth's shadows, I looked to Beatrice. Her expression was sobering, her dark brows knitted together.

'Max, I can't just leave Elaine out there to fight them alone. I wouldn't ask it of you, please don't ask it of me.'

I swallowed, not wishing for my friend to leave, but how could I refuse her? 'Go. But Bea.' I grasped her shoulders, holding on firm. 'Stay alive, okay?'

It was the same promise she'd made me give before.

The left corner of her mouth turned upwards. 'I have no plans for dying today, and nor should you.' She leaned in and planted a kiss to my cheek, before drawing back. 'Be safe. Don't fuck up our time.'

Before she took a step to leave, I asked her one more thing. 'No matter what happens, take care of Inyris for me.'

'I won't need to do that, Max.'

'Just, tell me you will.' A sob rose in my throat, but I refused to give it the power to suffocate me. 'I need to hear it.'

'Hurry back.' Beatrice grimaced, fighting her own wave of emotions. She knew that there was a chance we would not see one another again. 'Be quick, Max. The world literally depends on it.'

'I still don't like this,' Leska said, eyeing me with trepidation. 'Too much is at stake. The past is no safer than the future. Not to mention the effect it can have on—'

I stopped her with a look, shaking my head. Leska knew the price I paid, but if the rest of them found out, they would stop this before it began. This was our only chance. Leska recognised the expression and closed her mouth.

'Which is exactly why Max is not going alone.' Simion took my hand in his and squeezed.

'What?' My mouth was dry, my mind numb. 'You can't come with me, Simion.'

'You said it yourself, Lilyth will do anything to get the crown. But it will be impossible if I am not in this time. Not only can you keep me safe from her, but I can keep you safe— make sure you do not go changing anything too dramatically so that we have no home to come back to.'

I shook my head, unable to grasp onto the right words. 'No, Simion. I can't ask that of you.'

I closed my thoughts off from him, whilst screaming the last concern out into the void of my mind. *You don't know the cost it will have on your memories.*

His mouth found mine, devouring any hope I had to tell Simion he was not coming. I melted in him, hardly aware of everyone who watched on. All I knew was Beatrice took that moment to leave us. I didn't blame her, she was never one to see me and her brother kiss, especially not at the end of the world.

By the time Simion drew back, his kiss had weakened me enough that I knew I would not refuse him. He was right after all—we were safer together.

'Leska, Leia, Celia. You will need to protect our bodies and the dryad who takes us to the past physically, we will still have a tie to this time. I do not know what will become of us if we leave and something happens to us here.'

Focus sharpened Leska's cobalt stare, her shoulders rolling back as her posture straightened. 'No one comes in or out of this room. I can promise you that, brother.'

'All right,' I said, taking a deep breath in and filling my lungs. I couldn't admit it aloud, but I was scared. Deeply terrified.

'So, are you ready?' Simion asked, his smile as encouraging as it could be.

'If I say yes, would you believe me?'

Simion's gilded eyes flashed with fire. 'No, I suppose I

wouldn't.' He gestured towards the solitary dryad, waving his hand before him as though we were entering a dance. 'After you, my love.'

'Even in the face of danger, you are ever the gentleman.' I squeezed his hand tighter and we took our first steps towards the inevitable together. It was not the shield we were to locate first, but the sceptre.

To visit a time the dryad's conduit had become forgotten. A moment when history would not miss the sceptre from its timeline.

PART THREE

AS HAS BEEN, WILL BE

CHAPTER 27

'The price to pay is great, Maximus Oaken.'

The dryad's voice filled the dark of my mind. I had closed my eyes, hyper aware of every part of my body. Simion stood at my side, his hand forged to mine. The dryad had wrapped its wooden limbs around us, drawing our backs against its bark, which rippled and parted.

'I know, and I'm willing to pay it. There is not another choice,' I said aloud, refusing to open my eyes and see the wary faces of my friends and allies. Even without seeing, I could feel Leska watching on. 'Take us to a moment in time when the sceptre was forgotten. Please.'

'Do not forget, the last dryad-born to toy with time returned changed. The warnings of what will become of you are written in your history.'

The Mad Queen—I was aware of the possibility of that outcome.

'Watching history is different than traipsing through it.'

'It is not history that frightens me, but the very real prospect that we will not have a future.' I took a deep breath, aware of the way my body seemed to slip into the dryad, as though the god was devouring me.

'Then you understand what must and will be done.'

'I do.' I paused, filling my mind with my next question, not wishing for Simion to hear. *'And what of Simion, will he pay the price?'*

'There is one way to secure his mind, but it will only worsen the effects on yours...'

'Tell me, help me protect him.'

The dryad leaned into my thoughts and whispered the answer. They showed me what I longed for, in images and emotions, so powerful they pierced my soul, embedding into me like a thousand pieces of shrapnel. As they whispered the answer to me, I felt the bare skin across my arm tingle with anticipation.

'Shall I see that it is done?'

'Give me time to speak with him,' I replied, knowing what the dryad showed me was something I had wished to break not long ago.

Only in death, shall you part.

'Time, Maximus Oaken, is something you may not have if you continue to play in places you are not welcome, otherwise there will be no protecting the Hawthorn heir's mind from the same fate you will face.'

Fingers threaded with mine. I turned to follow the arm, finding Simion gazing down from my side. His mouth was taut with tension, and his eyes glowed with determination. The waring emotions made his face look severe, breathtaking. 'Are you ready?'

'If I said no, would you tell me we didn't need to do this?' I replied, settling my back against the dryad who communed through my mind. 'That we could find another way?'

'I would agree with you.' Simion offered me a smile, but it didn't quite reach his eyes. Instead, he closed them, leaning his head back against the dryad as his family watched on from the dais. 'But we know, we are all out of choices.'

I nodded, feeling sickness crash within my stomach. Bile burned my throat, but I kept it down.

'Keep as many people from Lilyth as you can,' I said to the watching group. My eyes lingered on Leska just a moment longer than anyone else. She knew what I would pay for doing this, and the haunted glint in her eyes suggested she struggled with the knowledge.

'Worry only of retrieving the dragon's conduit,' Leska said, eyes glittering with unspent tears.

'Until next time,' I said to her.

Her lips pursed, opening a beat later as though she would reply, but then closed. Her nod was the only thing I saw before the world slipped away.

* * *

Galloway Forest was bright with the most vibrant of colours. Sunlight streamed in through trees, catching leaves as though they were jewels hanging on branches. Dew misted the grassland at my feet, smudging my leather boots in a film of glittering droplets. I had been in Galloway Forest many times, but never had it smelled so fresh. I took a deep inhale, filling my lungs with unspoiled air, delighting in the taste of spring.

Beside me, Simion was doubled over, hands on my thighs, spitting the final dregs of his stomach across the base of a tree.

'Are you all right?' I asked, aware of how loud my voice sounded across the peace of the forest.

Simion shot me a look that answered my question. He cleared the back of his mouth with his hand, spat a final time on the ground and then straightened. It was as though every one of his bones clicked from years without use. Which, I suppose, in a strange way was true.

We stood in the past, in a time neither of us existed, where we were both not even a concept in someone's mind.

'I feel as though my body had been broken and put back together,' Simion replied with dramatic flair. 'How about you?'

Physically, I was fine, but mentally I toyed with the last thing the dryad had offered me. A way of saving Simion's mind from the same corruption mine was no doubt already experiencing. The dryad did not hold us in the protective cloak, but allowed us free rein here. Every second, the price for such exploration was being paid. Looking at Simion, seeing his beauty stand out against the dense woodland, the words lingered on the tip of my tongue.

'Fine,' I lied. 'I think it is easier for me to stabilise in this time because of the shared blood with the dryad.'

Another lie.

The dryad in question shivered, roots settling deep through the core of the earth's flesh. It was a different dryad to the one we had left in the throne room, but its consciousness was shared. That was the thing with dryads—it was one mind, one bank of history and knowledge.

Simion shot a look around the forest, drinking in the same beauty. He rested a hand on a mundane oak, the one he had just vomited across, and closed his eyes. 'It feels different. The air, it is lighter. There is more life here.'

'Then we need to be careful where we tread. One wrong step and we could alter the future until it is so unrecognisable that we have no place to return to.'

'Perhaps I am wrong for admitting this.' Simion stepped in close, his breathing tempered. 'But the thought of being stuck here, together, with no concern of monsters and dead worlds, is freeing.'

'I know.'

He gathered me against him, gilded eyes drinking me in. 'It doesn't sound so bad. Does it?'

'No, I suppose it doesn't.' I drew back, knowing we should get moving. 'But we don't have the luxury of such hopes and dreams.'

The more time we stayed here, the more we both paid with our memory. A swell of anxiety rushed up my chest, spreading its wings within me.

I had to do it, I had to protect Simion from losing his mind as payment.

My thumbnail caught my amplifier, twisting the ring around. Simion noticed, took my hand and lifted it to his lips. 'If you were a book, Maximus Oaken, I could read you with the lights off and the cover closed. That niggling little thought that bothers you, speak it.'

'I wouldn't exactly call it a little thought.'

'No?'

This had to be done. I looked to the dryad who seemed to creak in agreement and support. Then I dropped to one knee, tightening my hold on Simion's hand so he could not pull away.

'Max.' Simion's eyes widened, the heat in his touch flaring. 'Now isn't the place for getting down on one knee.' His head jolted in the direction of our dryad companion who watched on. 'We have company.'

A genuine, light laugh burst out of me. There was something so honest about Simion, how he couldn't possibly imagine another reason for me getting down on one knee. 'I'm not trying to seduce you, Simion Hawthorn. I have something to ask.'

Birds sung from the branches; small creatures scuttled over the forest bed. It was comforting to know we had witnesses to what was about to happen. Yes, perhaps I would never have contemplated this if the dryad had not given me the option to protect Simion. But if this was the price to pay, dryads I would.

'Hand-fast to me.'

That was it, the very way I could protect Simion from his mind being ruined.

My request hung in the air. I watched the words settle over Simion. His lips moved, tracing the statement as though it would help him make sense of what I asked. Then, all at once, the brightest of smiles broke over his face, ridding any tension that had been lurking on it.

Slowly, Simion joined me on the ground. He knelt before me, one hand in mine, the other pressed against my cheek. Joy spilled over my skin, seeping into my flesh, until it wrote itself out on my bones. 'I am sorry, Max. But I think I need you to repeat that again. Surely, my ears have misheard you.'

'Marry me,' I said it again, this time louder. 'Right here and now. Hand-fast with me, please.'

Please, because I love you. Please, because I must carry the burden that threatens your memories.

I held my breath, waiting for his answer.

Simion's smile widened even more so, if that was possible, until his gilded eyes overspilled with emotion. There was no containing it, he was forced to share it, ebbing his feelings into me through our touch. 'I admit, I am disappointed you beat me to it.'

'Well...' I exhaled, eyes flickering between his. 'Will you?'

Simion leaned in until his lips brushed mine. He stopped before, just shy of kissing me, so close my eyes crossed to focus on him. 'I had promised myself, that once this was all over, I would ask you the very same question. There would have been a time so perfect, a time when our future is secured and we no longer need to keep moving. A time when we could just stop and enjoy the now, without looking over our shoulders. I suppose here is the second-best thing, is it not? In this place, we only have our future to ponder. We have no past, no present. We are barely concepts in this time.'

'I am seconds from bursting if you don't answer the bloody question,' I scoffed, tears filling my eyes. 'Simion, I need to hear you say it.'

He placed a kiss on my lips, feather-soft. Then he moved to the tip of my nose, my forehead, my cheeks. By the time he was finished, there was not an ounce of skin free from the prickles of gooseflesh.

'I will answer you with a question of my own. Maximus Oaken, you are everything to me. From the moment I saw you, I had always dwelled on the past. It haunted me. Then, for the first time, I could look ahead and... allow myself to ponder the possibility of what was to come, not what had been. So, with that being said, will you do me the honour of securing this love? Will you marry me?'

I threw myself at him, knocking Simion onto his back until I was atop him—the soft bed of moss and grass beneath us, the shadow of tree and sky above. 'I do, Simion.'

'I do too, Maximus.'

The kiss was tempered and powerful. Two beings entwined, with nothing but the forest as our witness. In the back of my mind, another memory waited for me. I had stood in the chamber, surrounded by the faces of the four estates, Camron Calzmir before me. Cords had tied around our arms, silver marks etching across our flesh as our souls were bound by an ancient, coveted magic. I had done it before, because I was made to.

This was my choice. Simion was my choice. He embodied it from the very first time I laid my eyes on him in Julian's bedchamber. Even though, by handfasting, this meant protecting him from the corruption of traipsing in a time we didn't belong in, I still wanted it. Wanted this.

There was a real chance we failed at our task, and selfishly I desired the experience of being tied to him. I may not have contemplated it before the dryad had whispered it into my mind, but it was what I wanted.

He was what I wanted.

We stood before the dryad, our sleeves rolled up to our

elbows. I focused on the soft brush of his fingers against my forearm, how his smile drank me in. It was not coloured cords or ribbon that tied us together, but conjured vines that spilled from the dryad's outstretched arm like serpents. I delighted in the rough brush of their touch, how it tightened against my skin. Unlike when Jonathan Gathrax had read from his book, tethering me to Camron in both law and magic, this was different. The dryad sang in a language I could not understand, but the emotion that rolled from it was evident enough. All the while, I did not take my eyes from Simion.

'It is life's greatest honour to be bound to you,' Simion said, his proud eyes brimming with tears of love and joy.

'Even lost to time, you are ever the poet,' I replied, cheeks aching from grinning but unable to stop. 'And it is my life's greatest honour to be your greatest honour.'

'Even lost to time, you are ever the joker.' He winked, fingers drumming a tender beat over my forearm. 'That is what I love most about you, the way you use humour as a shield.'

'What can I say, it is in my blood.'

'As is my love for you, Maximus.'

I leaned forward just as the dryad lifted its bracken limbs over our heads. Petals of all colours fell around us, rich reds and blush pinks, smothering us like snowfall. They danced in the faint breeze, spinning around us until we were stood within a cyclone of the dryad's magic. It was an offering of privacy, for a moment where only we both belonged and nothing else mattered. I took it, delighting in the gift the dryad offered us, and I pressed my lips to Simion. The kiss was deeper than the rest had been. It was as though it beheld stories, hopes and wishes that I longed for Simion to feel.

'Only in death, shall we part.' I whispered against his mouth. Suddenly, the saying didn't inspire fear or dread in me. It was a pleasure to say it to the man before me.

'And in life, shall we thrive,' Simion added. 'Forever is a privilege with you by my side.'

Light sparked beneath the vines. It flashed over us, casting the forest in an incandescent glow. The petals stopped spinning and fell to our feet, dissipating like smoke as they touched the ground. By the time I looked down, it was to watch the vines sink into our arms. The green bled to silver, etching itself permanently into our flesh, binding us together as one.

The last time these marks had lingered beneath my skin I had hated them. Now, I felt nothing but pride. Come rain, snow, sleet or ice, I would proudly display my bare arm if it meant showing the universe the fast-mark.

Simion marvelled at the silver inking. It stood out against his brown skin, twisting from his fingers all the way up his wrist, his arm, to where his shoulder was still covered by his shirt. If the dryad wasn't stood beside us, I might just have torn his clothes off and inspected every inch of skin the mark touched.

'It is done,' I said, feeling an abundance of relief. Relief at knowing I was bound to the final soul I cared most about. Relief that came with knowing that Simion's memories would no longer be affected. If it meant I took all of this suffering for him, it was my pleasure.

'What next,' Simion said, brow peaking. 'Because forgive me if I am wrong, but consummating a marriage seems to be the standard.'

'Something to look forward to when this is all over,' I replied, although my stomach flipped at the promise of his sex.

'That is one sure way of me wanting to rush this, get home, destroy a monster and climb into bed with you when it is all over.'

This time, when I took a breath in, it eased the feeling in my chest enough for me to stop shaking. Simion pressed his lips to my knuckles, sending a shiver down my arm, the silver marks slithering as though it was a living thing.

'Just a few more moments of this,' Simion pleaded, lowering my hand but not letting it go. 'Selfishly, I want to think of nothing else but my husband. Just you, only you and nothing else. No Lilyth, no conduits.'

'I think we can spare that—'

A shrill, high-pitched wailing pierced the peace of the forest and shattered it. Birds flocked from hidden nests, spearing towards the blue expanse hinted through the canopy. This was not a normal sound that belonged in such a place.

'I suppose the universe has another plan for us,' Simion grumbled, hand flying to the hilt of his sword.

I looked to the dryad, unable to understand what we heard. 'I asked you to take me to a time when the sceptre became a forgotten thing.'

'*I have done as you asked,*' the dryad replied. '*Go, before your chance is missed. You wished to come to the time when the sceptre was forgotten. Displaced. Now is that moment.*'

I swallowed hard, focusing my mind on the task.

'Are you ready to steal a conduit, my husband?' I asked Simion, turning my back on the dryad.

Simion shot me a rather hungry look. 'Husband? I like the sound of that.'

'Good.' My stomach flipped a final time. 'Once we get this over with, I will make sure to say it over and over.'

'There is nothing more than I would like but to hear you scream it, Maximus.'

Simion lowered his hand to his sword's pommel, eyes flashing with the promise of his fire magic. We both didn't know what we were to face, it could be dangerous, so we had to be prepared.

A shrill cry lit the air again, spoiling the peace of Galloway Forest. This time, it was as though my mind could discern the truth of the noise. Because it sounded like a...

'Baby,' Simion said, releasing his sword. 'Is that a baby?'

It *was* the sound of a baby, taking its first breath in life, announcing its arrival. I had heard it enough during my childhood at Gathrax manor. I would recognise the innocent sound anywhere, in any time.

I nodded, unsure what we had been brought to witness. 'Come. Whatever it is, this is when the conduit is forgotten. We must hurry.'

There were no more words as we raced into the waiting forest, following the high-pitched cries to our bounty.

CHAPTER 28

We followed the trill of an infant until the forest thinned into a modest clearing. It was Simion who had stopped me from walking straight out and announcing myself, but my feet had been moving without much thought.

Quickly, as figures before us came into view, our dryad encased us in a blanket of time, protecting us from being seen. I gripped onto the dryad's branches, unaware of the tension in my grasp until my nailbeds ached and my teeth ground together.

The view before us was... strange. A man stood in the heart of the clearing, rays of brilliant light cast down upon him. He swayed from foot to foot, shoulders hunched over the nest of blankets he held in his arms, a soft song muttered beneath his breath. He had waves of long brown hair, a slender frame garbed in a strange fashion of loose trousers, an open necked tunic and an obscene amount of frill at his cuff and neckline. Until seeing him, it was easy to pretend we stood in a forest outside the boundaries of time, but his clothes proved we were many years in the past.

Which meant the sceptre was close, if this was the moment

it became forgotten in time. The dryad had brought us here for a reason, and this man was important to the story.

Our story.

'He is holding the baby, look,' Simion whispered, our voices muted by the dryad's concealment charm.

I narrowed on the bundles of blanket he held to his chest. There, hidden among the folds of yellow and cream, was the bright pink face of a babe. 'Yes. It hardly looks a day old.'

'Hours, I would wager.'

Growing up in the servant's quarters of Gathrax manor, I had seen many children come and go. It was not uncommon for the new mothers to give birth in their apartments, only to be forced back to work the following day.

I searched for signs of which Kingdom the man belonged to, but he was without the colours on his person. Not the red of the Gathrax, the blue of Calzmir, the white and grey of Zendina and Romar. Here, in the middle of the forest, this was the only place that claimed him.

'Whoever they are, they must have ties to the sceptre if we have been brought here,' Simion said, his eyes scanning in search.

'But who is *he*?'

The answer came from another. At the edge of the forest, the tree line shifted. No, it was not a tree.

'Galloway, my love.' The dryad stepped forward, wooden limbs extended towards him and the child. When he looked up, the most heart-warming smile broke across his face. It was honest and raw, his eyes widening an inch, glittering with awe and... love.

'Galloway,' Simion repeated, unable to take his eyes off what we saw. 'From the stories... and she is...'

'I heard her calling for her mother,' the dryad said, emerald eyes falling upon the swaddled baby.

The dryad was the most beautiful creature I had ever seen.

Hair made of willow, skin a multitude of green, browns and cedar. She looked more human than I had ever seen, except not. Moss covered her body, clinging to the curves of her figure. There was no denying the power of her emerald eyes, or the way the roots slithered at her feet.

Perhaps it was because I never expected to witness this, or maybe it was the first sign of the price of memories I had paid to be here, but the name did not register at first. Simion must have recognised it, because he swore beneath his breath. There was a niggling at the back of my mind, as though I reached for something just out of reach.

'Is it time?' The man, Galloway, replied. His expression had faded, the loving smile he offered the child no more than a phantom across his mouth.

The dryad shared in his emotion. She clutched the swell of her lower stomach, a place I had no doubt the child in Galloway's arms had not long ago been within. It hit me then, like a comet crashing to earth, who these two were.

Figures from stories, people from myths. It was Galloway and his dryad lover, the man behind the forest's name and the very beginning of everything I had come to know. My eyes fell back to the baby in his arms, the one he held protectively to him as though he never wished to release... her.

'That baby, she is the Queen. She is my...'

Galloway and the dryad snapped their heads in our direction. Panic glowed from their eyes, snatching the breath from my lungs. I shrank back into the shadows, but their eyes pierced through us. It was not us who they had heard.

Simion held his breath, his fast-marked hand tightening around mine. Unnatural warmth spilled around him, likely a reaction to a sudden spike in his own worry. 'Stay by my side. Something feels off.'

I looked back to the scene, watching as Galloway and the dryad fussed with their belongings. The child, all the while, was peaceful in sleep. Not aware of the danger that was coming for them.

'Give me our child, I shall get her to safety.' The dryad extended branch-like limbs to Galloway. Simion and I released a collective gasp, knowing in that moment that they had both not seen us.

Then who?

'Your chance to act will be now, Maximus Oaken. Be quick,' our dryad companion warned. *'I will not be able to hold onto this time for long, soon it will be severed from me.'*

'But where is the sceptre?' I asked just as Galloway handed over the infant Queen to the dryad. He then wrapped his arms around them both, gathering them close. I felt a twinge of emotion in my chest, like the snapping of string.

Simion raised a finger and pointed. 'I think I see it.'

Beside the base of a tree, amongst nectar-stained sheets, a bag and other mundane objects, was the very thing we had come for. Leaning against the trunk as though it was nothing more than a walking stick, the sceptre waited.

'Quickly,' our dryad snapped, a force pushing at my back. *'Time is of the essence.'*

I slipped from the protection, stepping back into the moment. A twinge echoed in my skull—was it the dryad plucking my memories away? Did I feel it more keenly because it now took a greater price?

Leaves rustled beneath me, my breathing intense and laboured. I waited, back pressed behind a tree, feeling my heart-beat in every tip of my fingers and toes. Although I could only partially see Galloway and his family, I could hear him clearly. Anxiety echoed in his every word. Yet I still had not known what caused such a reaction, even though the story of Galloway was coming back to me, there was a part missing.

'I can protect you both. Nothing *they* can do will stop me from doing my duty as her father, as your husband.' Emotion was a storm of fury and determination behind Galloway's words. There was no doubt he meant everything he said.

The dryad reached up and laid finger-like appendages against Galloway's cheek. There was a calmness about the moment, a knowledge of what was to come. 'It is not safe. I must hide our daughter from them. If the jealous discover the product of our union, there will be no telling what they would do to her.'

'Okay, my love. Okay. Take her,' Galloway said through gritted teeth, ire tensing his face. 'But promise me that we will see her again.'

'The dryads will take our child north. There she will be cared for until we can ensure her home is safe. Then, and only then, will she return to us, Galloway. It is the way, it is the only way.'

In the silence that followed my mind filled in the blanks of the story. It was like pulling at yarn, waiting to find the right string that would unravel it all. Although I knew the tale, it was still hazy. But I couldn't focus on that, not yet.

I peered around my tree when there was a long beat of silence. I saw Galloway's back as he faced the dark forest. His arms were empty of the child, and the dryad was gone. The dark forest he watched must have been where they went. He could hardly stand still, so when he finally traipsed into the shadows after them, I moved.

This was my chance. A time when the conduit was forgotten, because Galloway's attention was entirely locked on another. His daughter and wife.

I knelt on the ground, pressed my hands against the damp earth and connected my power to it. It was easier to see what was around me with my eyes closed. I allowed the earth to inform me, to fill my mind with the map of its layout.

My focus was the conduit.

Galloway and the dryad were close, but far enough for me

to act quickly without being seen. Before I severed the connection, I felt something more. Feet, ten of them, slamming against the ground as people ran... towards us. Galloway's dryad had been right, people were coming.

Breaking the tether to my magic, I kept it close enough to reach in case I required it. The most important thing was to get to the sceptre and back to our dryad, without being seen, without leaving a mark in this time.

But there, eating away at the back of my thoughts, was a question.

Why had the sceptre become forgotten here? Was it because of the child, had she been a great enough distraction? Or, perhaps it was the people who ran towards this very place. People I knew deep in my mind that I should know, but still could not grasp.

This was the price I was paying for playing in time. Double-fold, my memories were being sapped away like roots embedded in my thoughts... drinking and drinking.

To my luck, it was easy to snatch my bounty.

I moved quickly on light feet, something I had done for most of my life in the halls of Gathrax manor. Connecting to my amplifier, I softened the ground beneath my feet, muffling the sounds of my movement. I was a field-mouse, moving swiftly. Instead of risking myself by entering the clearing, in case Galloway and the dryad returned, as I knew they would somehow, I used my magic. The sceptre was made from the very element I controlled. It was forged by the dryads and given to Lilyth to spare them from her ruin. They had handed over the leash to control them, to save themselves. And here I was, taking it from the past for the second time.

It levitated from its resting place, shooting through the air until its handle clapped against my waiting palm. As soon as I touched it, a spark of immense power flowed over my mage-marked palm. It stopped me dead in my tracks as the euphoric rush overwhelmed me.

I was vaguely aware of someone shouting, the unearthly screech of a dryad in panic. But I couldn't open my eyes. Warm hands grasped my shoulders and drew me out of the trance.

Simion was there, panic creased over his face. 'We need to go.'

'Galloway!' another voice shouted, this one manic and gleeful. 'I know you are hiding here. Come out, we just want to speak with you and your little... *pet.*'

I turned my head towards the shouts, feeling every vein of earth and life. My essence was stretched everywhere, in every inch of earth surrounding. I was the tree on the furthest branch of the tallest tree. I was the deepest root of the oldest flower. There was no denying that if Simion had not left the protection of time, I would have never moved. It was too... distracting.

Our dryad waited with open arms, as more shouts grew in pitch. They wrapped their branches around us, snatching us roughly into their protection, just as four robed figures raced around us.

One red; one blue; one white; one grey.

'It's them,' Simion exhaled, breathless from the rush.

I wanted to ask who, but finally I remembered the story and knew. 'The first four mages.'

'We must leave before—'

I clutched the sceptre, drawing on its power. Where I should have felt guilt for controlling the dryad protecting us, there was nothing but a need to stay. 'No, not yet.'

Even if our dryad wanted to refuse me, they couldn't. I used the very power of the sceptre to control them, no different to Lilyth using the magic for selfish desires.

The four figures stood in the clearing, blocking the path between Galloway and the dryad from reaching the place he had left the sceptre. It was then I realised how it had become forgotten. It was not by choice or distraction—Galloway simply never had the chance to take it and use it. In the story it was told that the dryad gave Galloway the gift of magic by giving him the first wand. Now I knew the truth, I grasped it in my hand. It was the sceptre, all this time. It had belonged to him, and now...

'Far away from the safety of your homes, are you not?' Galloway said, standing sentinel beside his love. A light breeze caught his length of brown hair, enhancing the curls lost amongst the length. For a moment, I saw my face in his. He was my ancestor after all, they both were. The familiarities were uncanny.

'Leave.' Galloway's dryad swirled with magic, but there was something knowing in her green eyes. Eyes the same shade as mine. 'You are not welcome in my domain.'

It was a red-robed figure who stepped forward. Hands lifted and lowered his hood, revealing a mass of autumn red hair and sickly pale skin. There was no doubt this man was Gathrax born and bred, the hateful desire rolled off him in waves that I could feel even in the strange limbo where we were concealed.

'There will be no need for trouble,' the Gathrax said, voice a sickly sweet tone. 'Just give us the wand we have come for, Galloway, and we shall all be on our way home.'

There was no denying Galloway's gaze flicker in the direction his sceptre had been. Did he see it was missing? Did he sense the empty part of him, knowing I held it in my hand? 'You already know the answer, Gathrax.'

The blue figure stepped forward, hood lowered, revealing a woman with gold strands of hair, a sharp nose and familiar eyes of the darkest coal. Calzmir. 'Give us the power. Why should you be the one to harbour it all to yourself?'

'Because I never wanted it,' Galloway answered with his chest. 'Whereas you starve for it. Undeserving.'

More power swirled around the dryad. ' Unworthy. All of you are.'

The Gathrax gestured to Galloway's empty hands. 'And where is your little stick of power now?'

Galloway's brown eyes narrowed, wincing. They knew he didn't have it, otherwise Galloway would have already been holding it against them.

'Max, we really should leave.' Simion's voice whispered into my ear. 'We know how this story ends, there is no need to watch the inevitable.'

I didn't know how to explain it to Simion, but I did need to watch it. That is why I refused to answer him, why my eyes did not stray from the scene.

'We each have been patient with you, Galloway. We have asked nicely for the same power you have, we have grovelled and begged, and yet you still deny us,' the Gathrax ancestor said. 'Now we ask you and your little... dryad one more time. Give us magic, allow us to help change this world. And before you answer, please do so carefully...'

Roots and vines shifted over the forest bed, slithering towards the dryad who called them. The trees swayed around the clearing, leaves falling and twisting at their backs, encasing the four people in a wall of fury, giving them no way to leave.

'It was given to Galloway, kind of heart. I saw into his mind and found a human to trust.' The dryad moved before her lover, magic swirling around her, twisting in a cyclone of leaf, debris and stone. 'Do you wish to know what I see in your minds? Or perhaps you already know the answer to that.'

It was the Calzmir mage who replied. 'You see potential. You see what we will do with the magic, instead of the wasted parlour tricks Galloway does. Surely you are embarrassed by how he uses your gifts when he holds the power to shape a future?'

'I have nothing but love for him,' the dryad replied, voice full of the power of earth.

There was no denying the flashes of fear in the four figures.

They recognised the power before them, and the promise of danger overspilling in the dryad's emerald eyes. And I knew she was providing Galloway with a distraction, enough for him to claim the sceptre.

He didn't, because he couldn't. The sceptre was in my hand now.

How did this story end in the way I knew it too? From my vantage point, it showed the power on the side of Galloway and the dryad. But that was not the story history had carved out.

'One last chance,' the Gathrax mage shouted over the roaring power of the dryad. 'Give us what we have come for, or we shall take it for ourselves.'

He unsheathed a sword from his belt, flashing dull metal. What good was metal in the face of a god? How did they win this?

The dryad's laugh was everywhere. It filled the earth and rumbled with it. The trees groaned with her humour. If the four did not feel fear before, they would have in that moment, as the very earth itself laughed at them.

The red-robed man lifted his sword and pointed it towards them. Did he not recognise he had no way of winning against the pure force of a god? But it was not in surrender, but in signal. The sword was not pointing at Galloway, but at someone far behind him. A player of this game yet to reveal themselves.

'No,' I breathed, as my eyes wandering from the clearing to the dark forest beyond.

'There were more than four attackers at this meeting,' Simion added, shock in his tone. 'There were five.'

I had sensed ten footsteps when I connected to the earth. Not eight. But ten. Which meant there had been another person, someone concealed from history, a name forgotten— perhaps purposefully?

A woman waited in the shadows of the forest, a bow raised, the arrow no longer notched in her fingers. Because it was embedded in Galloway's back. Shock creased over the man's face, before the mysterious archer lifted another arrow to the bow, drew it and released.

Each impact shook me to my bones. It took five arrows to bring Galloway to his knees.

His dryad's magic dissipated, and she fell to the ground with him, collecting his dying body in her arms whilst the attackers swarmed like wolfs to a lamb.

'The choice was given and you chose,' the Gathrax man said, laughing to himself as the four of them circled the grieving dryad and the... dying body of Galloway. The silver marks that had wrapped around her arms faded, bleeding away in colour until nothing was left. Marks I had not noticed until now, marks the same as on my and Simion's skin.

'Only in death shall you part,' Gathrax spat as the archer joined them in the clearing. Another woman dressed in red, a winning smile across her face. Another Gathrax ancestor, someone the stories had forgotten.

'Your power belongs to us,' the archer seethed, hissing in the face of the dryad. 'Oh, for I do love the *hunt*.'

'Perfect aim, my daughter,' the Gathrax man said, wrapping his arm around the younger woman.

Time and history collided with itself a beat before the part of the story I knew well. Just as I had held my mother's corpse in my arms, the dryad gave into her heartbreak and expelled a blast of her godly essence. A root speared forward as the dryad loosed a scream so violent it would be felt in years to come.

This was the creation of the first Heart Oak. The four robed figures dove out of the way, but the scornful Gathrax daughter was not so lucky. A root speared through her chest, directly into her heart, snatching her life away within seconds.

I watched the Gathrax man's eyes flare wide, a violent scream clawing from his throat for his daughter.

Dead. She was dead within seconds, just as she had been the one to murder Galloway.

'*That is enough,*' our dryad said, using my distraction to regain control. '*This part of history is painful even to us. No longer must we stay and watch a story we know all too well.*'

'Wait,' I sobbed, longing to reach out. If I could just step free, punish the killers, I would stop years of suffering by the hands of the four ruling Kingdoms born in the aftermath of this very moment.

But it was ripped away from me as the dryad yanked us back into the folds of time. Darkness surrounded us. The only sound was the explosion of essence that was the Heart Oak being created, as the dryad's desperation entrapped her and Galloway together, forever.

CHAPTER 29

Stepping into a different time was not as smooth as it had been. We were forced by uncaring hands. Spat out from the mouth of time as though we were spoiled food. I felt the dryad, in the back of my thoughts, rummaging around for memories to steal from me. It was an odd sensation, like constricting roots around my skull—but there was nothing I could do to stop it.

This was the price I paid. I just hoped it was worth it.

To our luck, it was a blanket of snow we landed upon. I fell awkwardly, the sceptre squashed beneath my ribs as I had no time to catch myself. Pain radiated through my chest, echoed in the sharp inhale I took. Simion released a grunt, his body rolling to a stop, leaving a mark in the snow where he had tumbled.

'I am... sorry,' the dryad said, their voice hoarse. 'It is one thing to remember that moment, and another to visit it.'

I gathered my bearings, nodding at Simion to check he was okay. Flushed, yes, but unharmed, which was all that mattered. Behind Simion was a stretch of snowscape, a familiar mountain range set in the distance like a crown. Pillowy clouds thick with snow released its bounty across every inch of the land, blanketing it in an endless stroke of white. It made the concept of distances difficult.

'The Avarian Crest,' I said, shielding my eyes from the large flakes that fell upon me. It was as if no time at all had passed since I had been here, claiming Inyris as my dragon. But there were some physical differences. 'The mountains look different to what I remember them to be.'

'Because they are whole,' Simion added as he stood, dusting himself off and offering me a hand up. I didn't notice how cold I was until he touched me. It was distracting, the oozing comfort that bled from his skin. A thin curtain of snow fell upon us, small flakes that dissipated the moment they landed upon my skin. Whereas I fought a shiver, steam slithered off Simion's frame, the cold banished away by his claim over fire.

I turned to the dryad who already was coated in a layer of snow. 'This is the moment before Oribon broke out of the mountain, isn't it?'

It took a moment for the dryad to reply. They were weak. Exhausted. I sensed it just from reading their posture, and the way their eyes could barely remain open. *'You asked this of me. To take you to a time when the dragon's conduit was forgotten in time. But I am afraid the leap has taken its toll on me.'*

A strange sense of annoyance rooted inside of me. Did it take great effort to remove my memories, one by one? What possible toll could be worse than losing one's mind? That seed of annoyance promptly became one of panic, burrowing in my chest, sinking itself deep into my core. 'Then we will find the shield and return soon.'

I didn't have the time to waste.

'Not soon,' the dryad responded. *'I need time to regenerate my essence. During this time, the dragons were not the only ones of Lilyth's children to be imprisoned. We dryads had not long clambered out of the bellows of the earth. Our grip on this time is*

weaker than others. I fear I have taken you too far, the time to take the shield is yet to begin.'

How far had they taken us?

'When do we act?' Simion asked, worry etched into his brow. 'Some guidance will help us not cause ripples too great during this time. I trust we all don't need reminding as to what our being here threatens.'

'Time,' I answered, knowing it wasn't entirely the truth. 'The future.'

'Exactly,' Simion replied, side-eyeing me whilst waiting for the dryad to speak.

We both waited with bated breath for the dryad to respond. Their silence stretched, drawing thin. Every beat between their reply only made my heart ache, roots of panic stretching further in me.

'You will know when the time to act is upon you.'

'What if something happens,' I barked, nails embedding themselves into my palms. 'What if I—we need you.'

The dryad shivered, leaves shaking free from the snow and frost that had quickly settled. *'Maximus, you have the power to control me—you hold it in your hand. You used it before, do not play coy with me now.'*

There was no denying the hurt in the dryad's tone. They were right. I had used it against them, commanding them not to take us from the scene of Galloway's death and the Heart Oak's birth.

Guilt was something I was familiar with, but the feeling was still as sharp as it ever was.

'Do not just leave us here. Not without any guidance of protection from...' Simion's heat flared as the dryad slipped into slumber.

We blinked and it seemed the dryad became no more than a mundane tree, standing out in the field of snow, a solitary being left alone. It was only when I laid my hand upon its barren skin that I sensed the sentient presence within. Like called to like, the essence of the dryad humming through the sceptre in my other hand.

But it was no more than the faint fluttering of butterfly wings, weak to the touch.

'I don't like this,' Simion said, drawing me in close, as though his arms would protect me from the world.

'Nor do I,' I said, trying to organise the chaos of my thoughts.

I could not understand what I had been made to forget, but perhaps that was the point. How could I know what memories where missing until I stumbled blindly into those waiting gaps in my mind?

'Stay by my side,' Simion said, scanning the view of snow, field and mountain with an intense glare. 'We are far too exposed.'

Simion practically blended in with the expanse of white, the snow and light reflecting off the planes of his silver armour. I stood out in my black training leathers, which did little to stop moisture from seeping through. Without Simion's heat, I would have been frozen to the core.

'We must focus on what we know. As long as we do not leave our mark in this time. We keep hidden and get in and out before we screw anything up.'

A shiver passed over my skin again as the intensity of the cold built.

Simion noticed, and the world around us became a second care to him. 'You are shaking.'

'I'm fine,' I attempted, but my teeth chattered, and the tips of my fingers were going blue. 'I just want to get this over with.'

'Here,' Simion said, folding me into his chest where his arms encircled me. 'I can help before that. Then we get out of this downfall before it truly becomes nasty.'

Warmth blanketed me until it pushed out the deep ache of

chill. It was only a quick fix, nothing that would last. We had not left our time dressed to face the harsh terrain of the Avarian Crest.

'Better?' he asked, lips pressed into my crown.

'Much,' I replied, although I spoke only of the warmth. His power could not take away the toll this jump had taken on me. I couldn't explain it, not yet, but there were pieces missing. I was... confused. My mind a bucket with holes.

'If what the dryad said is true, we have some time to rest ourselves,' Simion said, more of his fire casting over me. The snow beneath our feet began to melt, leaving the hint of stone and grit beneath it. 'Once you feel ready, we need to find shelter, then we can form a plan. Somewhere a little less open would be ideal.'

He was right. It would take little to be seen. I scanned the view, drinking in the familiar elements from my previous visit to the Avarian Crest. A wall of trees waited about a mile east of us. *The Endless Forest.* The name came in the form of a small, distant voice that filled my head, reminding me what it was called.

Dayn, the young boy who sacrificed himself for me during the Claim. Even here, hundreds of years before he was born, his spirit lingered in my mind.

* * *

With the sceptre in my hand, my magic capabilities had increased a hundredfold. The possibilities were endless. Simion had been intent on finding a cave or some similar natural cover, but I was impatient and was beginning to not feel my toes through my boots. Instead of blindly searching for somewhere safe and dry to rest, I faced a wall of rock, reached out to my power and made one.

Stone practically melted beneath my intent. It was as soft

and malleable as clay, breaking away until I faced a perfectly carved mouth of a man-made cave. This magic was incredible. I could feel every stone, blade of grass, even the raw metals my mind sensed leagues beneath my feet. I knew, if I wanted to, I could have created an entire city with my mind, drawing it out of the ground.

It was one thing having the blood of a god, it was another having the raw power of one. No, not one, a collective. All the dryads, all their possibility and magic, was literally grasped in my hand.

Was this how Simion felt when he wore the crown? Could he draw down the heat from the stars in the sky, or from the core of the earth? I had no doubt those were small feats with such power.

'I suppose it will do,' Simion praised, urging me into the cavernous space I had worked out of the rock wall. He placed a warm, guiding hand upon the small of my back and urged me inside.

I knew, first-hand, just what dangers lurked within the Endless Forest. Facing a barubore now would not be ideal. At least here we could wait out the brewing snowstorm.

Once we had entered the cave it was to find smooth walls and a floor as levelled as clean-cut marble. If we were to leave this place, I would have to destroy it. No natural force would make such a place.

'We shouldn't let our guard down,' I said, as Simion conjured fires with the wave of a hand. They burned without the need for wood as fuel, although the shadows under his eyes told me the cost it had on him. 'There is no telling when we will need to act. Our focus must stay on finding the... the shield.'

'Say that again without your teeth chattering, and maybe you'll convince me.'

I gritted my teeth together until my jaw ached. There was

no stopping my body's reaction to being cold to the bone. My clothes were sopping, my limbs aching and mind torn apart.

'Get these off, Max.' Simion's command was firm.

'Is this all one elaborate way of getting me naked, Simion Hawthorn?' I asked as his hands trailed over my bare shoulders. He began taking my sodden shirt off, laying it against the warm rock face for it to dry. I didn't stop him. His touch was a blessing, and I couldn't feel my fingers enough to do it for myself. He was already down to his undershorts, the firelight casting the sharp planes of his body in shadows, highlighting the deep groves between his impressive muscles.

'If you do not allow your clothes to dry, you will catch your death before we even get the chance to return home.'

I snickered under my breath, glad for the lighter atmosphere that seemed to follow us into the cave. 'I take that as a yes to my initial question.'

Smooth lips pressed down onto my shoulder, sparking shivers down my arm. I watched them ripple over me, hairs standing over the silver vines inked onto my skin. Simion enjoyed the power he had over my body. He encouraged the reaction, brushing the tips of his fingers down the length of my arm, until they spread across the back of my hand and threaded with my fingers.

'It is one of my greatest pleasures to see you naked, Max. But my reason for stripping you down is only to warm you up.'

I turned on him, neck curving up so I could get a better look. His gilded eyes reflected the red and orange tongues of fire around us. Laying my hands on his hardened chest, I delighted in the warmth of his skin. It would take little encouragement to stay pressed to him for hours, if it meant sharing in what he could offer. No matter the place, no matter the time, he, too, was my life's greatest pleasure.

'Hello, husband.'

Simion's brow peaked, the left corner of his lip turning up. 'Say that again, I like hearing that word on your tongue.'

'Husband,' I repeated, brushing my mage-marked palm over the mage-mark scar on Simion's chest. I left it, just over his heart, as my other hand explored the silver fast-mark inked on his arm. It spread from his hand all the way to his shoulder and up to the base of his neck.

I closed my eyes as Simion dipped into me, head tilting, mouth meeting mine. It was a tender and calm kiss, one that I could melt into. His exhale tickled my face. It sang of his wants and desires, but also his restraint.

When Simion pulled back, I seemed to lean in more, only to his amusement. 'I wasn't finished with you.'

'I am not going anywhere,' Simion replied, guiding both our fast-marked arms up. 'We are bound together, forever. You can have me whenever you desire, no matter the place or... time. After seeing what became of Galloway and his dryad, I want to hold you and never let you go.'

What we had witnessed, although it was a story I knew, haunted me. Likely it would forever. It was the moment Aldian was split in two, a North and South. Much pain and anguish would come from the divide, but it was a rift that would be healed—one I had helped heal.

The death of the Gathrax daughter only added to the families' hate towards the North. Whereas the death of Galloway and his dryad lover stoked the Queen's disdain for the South.

If I had stopped it, intervened, nothing that came afterwards would have happened. Dryads, Simion and I would never have met. But in the moment, I could not have contemplated the consequences. There was only action.

I would have to be careful going forward.

'Take solace knowing their story will never be forgotten. Without the price they paid, we both would never be here. It is because of Galloway and the dryad that we were both on the path that led us to one another...' I stopped, my thoughts of Simion stopping at a wall in my mind. Deep pain radiated across my chest, my skull aching as a sudden pressure entered it.

Because I couldn't remember the rest. There it was, that fucking hole I expected to find. And now I was falling and falling into it, with no ability to stop myself.

'Max.' Simion grasped my hand and squeezed. It anchored me, stopped me freefalling into dismay. I looked up to find him studying me, a frown cast over his expression just as I pulled away from him. 'What is it?' he asked, as I turned my back on him. 'Maximus, talk to me.'

Soft hands grasped my shoulders, thumbs working circles into the sudden tension in my muscles. My teeth bit down hard on my fingernail, drawing blood as I picked at the skin.

How could I say it? How could I turn around and tell Simion that I remembered nothing of how we met one another? It was like reaching for a memory that no longer lingered in my mind.

Sharp pain thundered across my skull, intensifying. I tried and tried to locate the memory, my gaze lost to a place on the cave's wall. But no matter how I stretched, no matter how I searched, I found nothing.

In truth, there were so many gaps beginning to show themselves. I remembered the Gathrax manor, I remembered a time before, but the faces and names were hazy. The furthest memory I had of Simion was on dragon back, flying over Galloway Forest, as he told me the very story we had just witnessed in the flesh.

I knew two things in that moment. If I told Simion, gave him any indication of the inherent madness seeping into me, he would be powerless to save me. Knowing what I paid, knowing the effect this heist had on my mind, would ruin him. Because he couldn't stop it. I couldn't ask him to choose between me or saving the world.

We both knew which answer it had to be. I also knew, without a single doubt, it would break him just as it shattered me.

So, I did the only thing I was well tuned at, something no forgotten memory could take from me, a skill that practice had made my body attuned to. And I pretended. Some would call it lying, or acting—I saw it as protecting him, Aldian's future and me.

'I am just tired, that's all,' I said, as I faced him again, feigning a brilliant smile. 'And after what we have witnessed, what we have left behind, it is all just too much for me. That and I am worried about everyone we have left behind.'

There was relief in his face, the way the lines across his forehead smoothed out and his mouth parted in an exhale. He nodded in silent agreement, believing my excuse. What I had listed was enough for anyone to suffer.

'I understand. We should really try and get some rest. Even an hour or so, it will help clear our minds, renew some energy for whatever we must face next.'

I couldn't tell him that sleep would be impossible, not whilst my memories warred for space in my mind. But I nodded all the same, pretending, because that was my only option.

We laid out across the ground, our bare bodies pressed to one another for warmth. Simion refused to let me go, bleeding his warmth and offering me comfort. His arm was beneath my head, giving me a soft cushion to lay on. His other was draped over me, which I held onto as though it was some child's toy with the power to protect me from the darkness.

I stared into the dark before me, focusing on Simion's breathing. If I didn't fixate on him, I would have continued excavating my mind until it, too, was a hollow cave. The longer we stayed lost to time, the more my memories would slip away. It was no wonder the Queen had grown mad. I could feel such a thing lurking in the corners of my being, waiting to truly latch on in place of the missing memories.

Hours passed and, as expected, I could not find sleep. Simion's breathing had evened out a while ago, his snores tickling the hairs on the back of my neck.

'Simion,' I whispered, as tears of desperation fell down my cheeks.

He mumbled a response, likely from the interrupted dream I had just entered. He didn't wake, or stir long enough to truly hear me. But I spoke anyway.

'Promise you will never forget me.'

Silence hung between us as a response. Simion's heart beat across my stomach, echoing over my skin. I closed my eyes, focusing on his touch, his sounds and scents. If my mind would forget him, I would ensure my body never did.

'And... forgive me if I forget you.' I held onto him tighter, pinching my eyes closed as I focused on him, now, this moment, not the ones I was losing. Although my mind may scrub him from my past, there was no way my body would forget the touch of him, the press of his body and the way his flesh brushed over mine with every shallow breath he took. Dryads, our story was etched into my skin now with binding, silver marks. 'Because I will always love you, Simion. That will never change, no matter what happens. If I am lost, it will be you who finds me, always.'

CHAPTER 30

'Something is wrong.' I laid my hands on the cave's floor, feeling the imprint our warm bodies had left after sleeping. From a dreamless sleep, I had startled awake as though the ground had jolted. Because it had. Simion's face had been inches from me, and for a moment, I didn't recognise who he was. Anyone else would blame the confusion on exhaustion, but my reason was different. I almost sobbed when he opened his eyes, blinking sleep away and my mind caught up with me.

We were somewhere in the Avarian Crest, buried far in the past.

And he was Simion, my Simion.

Relief at remembering him was short-lived, as the ground trembled again. Dust fell from the ceiling, coating us as we rushed to put our clothes on.

'What could it be?' he asked whilst he tugged his shirt over his head, threading his arms through each sleeve with ease. I caught a flash of silver on his skin, thanking myself for the physical reminder of him. If... when my memories gave out and I lost myself to madness, at least my body would be marked by Simion.

Knowing that gave me some semblance of calm. I still had time to spare, a chance to get the shield, get home and still remember him.

'It is like something, or someone, is demanding my attention.' I couldn't explain it, but the earth was... moaning. It was as though the ground strained against my hands, echoing some far-off pain that lingered in the distance. When I had woken to the grumbling, it was faint, but since then the noise had built into what only could be described as the banging of fists against a locked door.

Even without the sceptre in my hand, I would have felt the tremors.

Simion hurried to get his boots on and then came and took my hand. 'I think it is best we get out of here before the entire place comes down.'

I nodded just as another tremor rocked the cave. It wasn't exactly an image the sceptre showed me, but an imprint. Like the lines on a map, except those lines were buried beneath earth and... moving.

'Simion,' I practically shouted, breathless as realisation sank into me. 'I think it's Oribon.'

I couldn't explain it, not entirely, but the sceptre was showing me what lurked within the ground and there was a presence—no, presences—that didn't belong. Beings, imprisoned... and they wanted *out*.

'But he would still be trapped in the Avarian Crest...' Simion stopped himself, his eyes glazing over for a moment of silent thought. 'He is going to free himself, Max. This is what we are here for.'

I knew Simion was right, because that was what the stories told. But there was a seed of doubt inside of me, something that had grown roots when Galloway's story was not what we first believed. Somehow, sounds echoing through the ground did not sound like success. It sounded like desperation.

'Not everyone can say they witnessed the mountains split apart,' Simion said, urging me towards the cave's exit. There was no denying his thrill, and I wished I share in it. But the impending doom was a far louder call. 'Let's go and watch history, my love.'

The way he used those words reminded me of Galloway and the dryad. It was both beautiful and haunting.

It took a while for us to find a path towards the mountain range. Unlike my first visit, the Endless Forest did not shift and move, keeping those unfortunate enough to find themselves within it locked in a maze of tree and bark. Nor were there trials to pass for Oribon to guide us to his dwelling.

The sky was coated in dark clouds, but not a single flake of snow fell. Although the brisk wind that tore around us was powerful and as cold as death itself, it seemed to urge us towards the mountain, not away from it. As though the air wanted us to go—needed us to.

We reached the field with our dryad, who waited for us in the same place we had left them. It was comforting to know our way out was close, in case we needed it.

'Dryad-born, the time is here.'

I didn't require the dryad to tell me. 'The shield is close?'

'Very much so, but to reach it you must do what is required.'

Do what is required?

'Is there any chance you can be less foreboding, and more helpful?' Simion countered. His attention fixed on the swirling mass of clouds that spun around the mountain's top. It was at such a distance that if anything happened, we would be safe, but still close enough to watch.

'Time is not a linear concept, Simion Hawthorn. It is push and pull, it is tide. What has come to pass, will come to pass.'

'Again, dryad.' Simion took a step forward, sheltering beneath the canopy as snow finally began to fall. 'That does not help. If you know where the shield is, tell us so we can get it and be gone before—'

A violent ripple shook through the earth, followed by a tremendous boom. There was no warning before another contraction rocked beneath us. I fell forward, smacking the ground with a thud.

Simion fought to steady himself as the air screeched around us. 'Max,' he called, attempting to reach for me. 'Are you okay?'

'It is time,' the dryad repeated with more urgency. 'You must act.'

You must act.

'Oribon isn't trying to break out.' I pushed against the icy ground, attempting to stand, but something distracted me. Just as I had connected with the earth in the cave, I did so again. 'He is begging for—'

One moment my consciousness was looking at Simion reaching a hand for me, the next I was... everywhere.

Deep in the belly of the mountain, the winged god clawed against stone. His powerful frame slammed against the walls of his prison, scales breaking, armour shattering, all whilst the final dregs of air were being exhausted. Black flame bubbled beneath him, thrashing upwards—wytchfire—I felt the power like an infection beneath flesh. Surrounding Oribon were hundreds—thousands—more dragons all waiting for freedom or death. Their bodies pressed against the earth as though it was my skin they touched.

I snapped out of the power, although the feeling didn't truly leave. 'It is the phoenixes, Simion. I think, I think they are trying to burn out the entire race of dragons inside of that mountain.'

Simion was kneeling before me, hands on my arms, urging me to stand. 'We should leave, Max. This isn't safe for us here—'

I grasped his hand and pressed it to the snow-coated

ground. It melted where his hand touched. 'Do you feel it, the fire?' I asked. 'Do you see?'

His eyes widened, the crown flashing bright atop his head. 'It is. I—I can—' His brow furrowed in concentration. 'I'll try and keep it at bay for as long as I can.'

But that didn't stop the dragons from being stuck.

Was this Lilyth's favoured children, making a play for the conduit? I knew the stories, the myths, which told of the tension between the phoenixes and the other three gods. Until Simion took hold of the crown, the phoenixes were always going to be against us.

This time in our history was no different.

They were here to suffocate the dragons in wytchfire. My mouth was dry, my head aching with the desperate slams of Oribon. I knew, without a doubt, that the dragon was never going to free himself. It was not in his power. Lilyth would not have put the gods of air in a prison of stone if she knew they could one day break free.

'They're going to die, Simion.' Power flooded up my arm the tighter I held onto the sceptre. 'Oribon is not breaking out of the mountain, he is begging for someone to free him. He is calling to *me*.'

Confusion rippled over the strong planes of Simion's face. A wrinkle formed between his dark brows, his mouth turning down. 'But you can't help them, Max. Not only do the rules put before us prevent it, but we do not have the power to break mountains apart.'

'Says the man holding back the wytchfire, Simion.'

He gave me the look of a man who had realised just how wrong he was.

I lifted the sceptre up, just as Simion's eyes dropped to it. 'I can do it. Focus on the fire, hold it back. I will help Oribon.'

What I meant to say was, 'I had to do it,' because if I didn't, the dragons would die. The ground trembled again as Oribon slammed his powerful body into the belly of the mountain. Urgency was everywhere, the need to act.

When I looked to the dryad for answers it was to find I already knew them. *'You must do what is required. It is time.'*

'If I do this, will it change anything?' I had to shout over the building storm and screaming mountains.

The dryad shivered, its roots creaking as the ground beneath it swayed with Oribon's physical plea. *'What must be done has been done before and will be done again. Time is a snake, chasing its tail. You are not permitted to effect change, but that does not account for what you have already done before.'*

I wanted to scream, to demand that the dryad gave me clear instruction. What I have done before? 'What is that even supposed to mean?'

Simion laid a hand on my shoulder. 'I think this was always supposed to happen. You being here, doing this. It isn't affecting time if you always did it.'

'Simion Hawthorn understands the truth.'

'I don't understand,' I shouted, feeling myself being pulled by what was right and what I was warned against. What added to the impending doom was the knowing that with every second that passed the tremors were slowing. Not because Oribon was giving up, but because he was dying—they all were.

And if we didn't help, they would soon burn.

But... in our present time, the dragons were free. So, they had broken out of this somehow. The dragons do survive.

Time is a snake, chasing its tail. You are not permitted to effect change, but that does not account for what you have already done before.

'My actions here have always happened,' I said, realising. 'Think of it from the perspective of Galloway. He had access to the sceptre, he had the power to destroy the four men and woman who came and murdered him. But he never did, because he couldn't—the sceptre was not available to him... because I took it.'

... you have already done before.

I stammered, sweat beading across my head. 'If time is circular, are you saying we were always meant to be in it? Our presence, both in Galloway Forest and here, was always supposed to happen.'

'What must be done, has been done before and will be done again,' our dryad repeated.

I'd take that as a yes—no matter if I didn't truly understand it.

'The wytchfire, Max... I cannot hold it much longer.' Simion faced the mountain as another avalanche of loose snow and ice fell down its side, billowing clouds behind it. 'You must do it. What if it was always you who opened the mountain for Oribon? But like Gathrax's daughter being the one to murder Galloway, what if nobody told this part of the story? If time is a snake chasing its tail, that means it is connected.'

I was shaking, and not from the cold. Power was building beneath my skin, as was the urgency to act.

Still, something was stopping me.

My body was frozen in place, kept from moving as his words settled over me. But there wasn't time for contemplating as a final, monstrous boom carried through the ground.

'But what if it ruins everything?' I shouted urgently, urgent with the need to help Oribon, urgent because I feared what would happen if I didn't.

'Then we will be stuck here, to live out the rest of our lives, alone. As much as it would pain me to leave it all behind, knowing you would be with me makes it all better.'

'Freeing them does not change the future, because in the future the dragons are free. A snake chasing a tail.'

Simion took my shoulder with his spare hand, the other still pressed into the earth, tendrils of smoke dancing between his fingers. 'I believe in you, so believe in yourself too.'

He released me and I dropped to my knees. One hand grasped the sceptre, the other laid flat out against the stone.

There was no more time to allow for hesitation. I had to act.

I believe in you.

Cords. I grasped every single one of them, the bright silver bonds that tied me to the element of earth. *Visualise.* My mind conjured an image of the mountain, filling it with how I had seen it when I entered it during the Claim. Split down the middle, as though a sword was cleaved down from the sky to break it in two. *Intention.* There was no longer a single inch of my being that harboured disbelief in myself. The sceptre drew on the dryads, those who filled Aldian, and those yet to find themselves free of their bindings. I called on them, taking their power until it was mine. Was this how they, too, freed themselves? Heeding my call, sensing my need for their power enough to draw themselves out from the belly of the earth?

So believe in yourself too.

And I did.

Magic thrashed inside of my being. It built until the roar was so fierce that there was no force in the world that could stop me. I held onto it until my skin trembled and my lungs ached. My eyes flew open, my focus locked onto the mountain and those desperate gods who had begged for my aid. Finally, I released every ounce of myself into the ground, felt it race towards the mountain and...

Crack.

CHAPTER 31

The Avarian Crest broke in two. And dragons poured from it. All of them. Small and large, they exploded into the sky. In seconds, the sky was full of their song, their freedom and joy. Ice crackled against the horizon, lightning built within the clouds, until the tension tickled over my skin. But, underneath it all, it was Oribon I sensed.

I was vaguely aware of Simion sagging backwards, followed by a rumbling explosion of black flame chasing the dragons skywards.

'You did it.' Simion's overwhelming relief unfurled in my blood. 'You fucking did it.'

Breathless and high on the use of magic, I couldn't take my eyes off the scene. As horrifying as it was, there was no denying the beauty of freedom. 'We did it, Simion. Together.'

As I broke my connection to my magic, I sagged backwards into waiting hands. Simion was there, gathering me to him, legs on either side of me. My eyes rolled back into my skull, as a rush of pressure released. He snatched the sceptre from my hand, discarding it on the ground. This power, what Lilyth desired more than anything, was not only destined to destroy and ruin.

It could move mountains, shatter them apart like glass in uncaring hands.

Beautiful and overwhelming; it was the power to mould life itself. Which was exactly why, when we were done with it, it had to be destroyed. I spared a moment for the miracle before me and gazed down at the sceptre. Laying in a bed of snow, it looked no different to a mundane stick. How could something so plain be so powerful? To anyone else looking, they would not think anything special about it.

'You are miraculous,' Simion mumbled, awe overspilling his tone. 'A maker of miracles. My miracle.'

I locked my eyes back on the mountain as every dragon cawed in unison. Talons ripped into the stone, drawing out the final dragon. Oribon clambered from his imprisonment as every dragon flying about him called out with their encouragement.

The father of dragons was as large as I remembered him. When he was free, he perched himself on the two tips of the broken mountain, his body moving so slowly due to its sheer size. His thick neck rose to the heavens, his wings flared wide at his side until Aldian was cast in his ominous shadow, and then he roared.

It was a sound of warning to Lilyth that he was finally free. It was the sound of joy and relief. And, even from the miles between us, as Oribon's eyes settled on me, I knew the roar was also of thanks.

I blinked and was transported. Not to a different place or time, but into the mind of Oribon. Just as I had conversed with him during the Claim, Oribon's ancient voice filled my soul. The air around me rippled, blocking Simion out, who had stopped moving completely. The dragons in the sky were the same. They looked as though they were suspended, wings static, yet still they remained airborne.

'I sense what it is you want from me, Maximus Oaken.'

I swallowed hard, feeling the entire focus of the dragon on

me. Even from our great distance, those vast eyes devoured me. Although I could not see the conduit, I certainly sensed it was close. Oribon recognised that too.

'Will you grant it to me?' I asked.

'You understand the power that comes with it. Will you abuse it? Will you take control, as one has done before, and use us?'

I shook my head, speaking from my heart and soul, without thought. 'I only wish to stop Lilyth. If you do not give it to me now, she will come for you one day.'

'Is that a threat, human?'

I shook my head, begging for the dragon to see the truth of what was in store for him. 'It is a promise. Lilyth will come for the conduit. You either keep it and face her, or provide it to me. I swear, once Lilyth is finally dealt with, you will have it back.'

'No,' the dragon's inner voice boomed. 'Destroy it. Such power does not deserve to exist. Lilyth wished to have it. She would send others to end us, just to retrieve the power we took back from her.'

'And yet I saved you.'

'So you have.'

'Please. I only desire to borrow the shield. To finish what you tried to finish.' Oribon was in my mind, tethered to me just as Inyris was in our future. He sensed my honesty, and knew that I would give it back.

'Destroy the leech. Then you must destroy the conduit. Promise me that, dragon-blessed.'

My heart thumped heavily in my chest, almost stopping me from breathing. I looked through the strange wall of air, seeing Simion had not moved a muscle in all this time. But the promise was the easiest to make. 'I promise, once Lilyth is dealt with, no other will control you again.'

Time caught up with itself. Around me the air roared; Simion jolted back into action as though nothing had happened.

Oribon was no longer in my mind, but still he perched himself atop the Avarian Crest. Rearing up his long, scaled neck he expelled a cry into the sky, expelling every ounce of stale, mountain air from his lungs.

Oribon then twisted his neck downwards and brought his jaw to his chest. It was a strange movement, almost awkward for such a creature. His jaw split and he caught a scale between his teeth and ripped it free.

A flash of dark grey caught on a glare of sunlight as he held it on his jaw. Then he faced us, fixing those ancient eyes on us and bowed.

I returned his bow, as did Simion. A sign of mutual respect. Connecting to my amplifier, I used my magic to lift the sceptre from the ground. Oribon noticed it, just as I slipped the dryad's conduit into the band at my waist. Sudden winds flooded over us when Oribon began to beat his wings. He flew up into the sky, climbing higher and higher, until his frame got smaller and smaller.

Then, Oribon dove.

His wings folded into his body, and he speared through the sky, directly towards us.

Neither Simion nor I moved, because there was some sense that nothing would happen to us. And we were right. Because as Oribon's shadow gained, he flew directly over our heads. Before he reached us, something dropped from the sky, falling from his mouth.

It was the scale, the one he had plucked from his hide. My eyes trained on it as it cascaded to the ground, meeting it a short distance from where we stood. The... scale glinted like pure metal, standing out against the white blanket of snow. I looked back to Oribon, as though he would offer an explanation. He turned back around, flying towards the Avarian Crest, to the dragons who were dancing once again, this time with more vigour.

'*Be quick, dryad-born. Take the shield, we must leave.*'

My eyes settled back on the scale, seeing it for what it truly was. The conduit. I took a cautious step forward as something else fell from the sky. It cracked into the earth.

'Fuck, Max. Move!' Simion shouted from a step behind me.

Something warm fell on my face as I looked to Simion to find out the cause for his panic. Before I could lift a finger to the droplet, Simion barrelled into me, his shoulder catching my middle and knocking me to the ground.

His body fell on me as we rolled over and over. Another hard crack hit the earth, followed by the spitting of snow, stone and... scale, just where we had stood.

A dragon laid out on the ground, broken and bloodied. Its green body was bent in angles no being should be in. And the blood that seeped from beneath it, casting the ground in rivers of obsidian, matched the droplet I cleared from my cheek.

Simion was already helping me up from the ground, fire flaring around him. He used his power, casting it in an arch of fire above us from his crown as another dragon swooped down. Its pained howl caught in my soul as Simion's wytchfire ate from the creature's flesh.

The dragons were attacking one another. I looked up and found them warring in the sky, a scene I had witnessed before. Oribon was amongst them, casting rivers of ice and lightning from his jaw, sending his children careening to the ground.

'It's the shield,' I spluttered, as another horde flew in our direction. Except their hungry eyes were not on us, but the shield Oribon had dropped. 'Oribon is giving us time, turning against his own—'

'Go and get it. I will hold them off.' Simion barely finished shouting before he drew on his fire and sent another wall out. It rushed over the ground, melting snow and scorching the stone beneath, until it slammed into the four dragons that speared through the sky.

I was up, feet moving, legs pumping, my only focus on the conduit. The atmosphere had changed the moment Oribon gave us the shield, because it meant he no longer held the power of his kin.

This was the moment we must take, the time when the shield was forgotten whilst the dragons warred with one another on instinct.

A shadow of gold scale cast above me. It almost caught me off guard, but I dove to the ground, hands grasping the shield. Lightning blinded the darkness in my mind. It was momentarily disabling, until I opened myself up to the power.

'*Stop.*'

The dragon who reached me did just as I commanded. It paused, staring, and emitted a growl that told of the promise of ice. But it did not attack—it couldn't, not as I held the power.

Considering the shield was as long as my torso, it was featherlight. Made from not only metal, but the combination of dragon scale, it emitted a power that made the gold-scaled creature bow to me.

Too much power, this was too much.

Simion held his fire at bay, eyes watching me, mouth gape. Flames licked at the ground beneath him, casting his face in shadows.

Three conduits, we had three.

'It is time to go,' Simion said, extending a hand for me.

But before I took a step to him, I faced back to the sky full of dragons, all watching me with such intent I could have sworn I could tell them anything and they would have done it.

So, I did just that.

'Forget us,' I said to the dragons, using the conduit as a leash and ensuring my command seeped deep into their cores. 'Forget we were here, forget what we have done. Oribon is your King, do not fight, do not war. We will need you.'

Power pulsed from the shield, a blast of air that rippled over the world until every single living dragon heard it. It was easy to give into the overwhelming capabilities. No one person should covet such power, such control.

Not Lilyth, not me.

And as I promised Oribon, I would see it destroyed.

'Maximus,' Simion shouted again, catching my attention. Just as it had when I woke early that day, my mind seemed slow in recognising him.

He was slipping away from me.

I sprinted to his side, taking his hand as though physically grasping him would stop the memories from fading. Guided by him, we ran back towards the dryad.

'Take us home,' Simion commanded.

I expected them to refuse us, to tell us that our effect on this time had ruined the future. The dryad didn't. Instead, they opened their branches to us, encouraging us to step into the concealment of their power. This time, I willingly sank into the darkness of existence out of time, the peace of it.

As it stole us, the shield hoisted on my arm, the sceptre lodged in my boot, Simion and his crown beside me, I felt a sense of success. But as the dryad spat us back out into the time we had vacated, victory never felt so far away, as we were faced with what we had left behind.

Chaos.

The air was tinged with smoke and tension. I blinked away the past, recognising I was no longer in the Avarian Crest. Although it took a moment for my mind to inform me of where I was.

Wycombe. In the castle. Except it was different. Because before me the castle wall was torn apart—ruined. The first thing I noticed was the view beyond it, a bright sky coated in the clouds of destruction. Entire streets levelled and homes flattered. But what truly sparked horror was the countless bodies of people, unmoving, left motionless upon the blood-stained street.

CHAPTER 32

I doubled over, spilling the contents of my stomach across a stone-slabbed floor. My muscles ached, my head throbbing and my lungs aching for breath. It was almost as though I had been held beneath a body of water—except the water was time.

How much had I lost? Besides the need to breath, the burn of vomit filling my cheeks, it was the one real thought. Overwhelming. All encompassing. It was day, at least I believed it was, but thick clouds coated most of the sky.

'Dryads,' a deep voice near me swore. I recognised it, but couldn't place it. 'What has happened?'

'Utter carnage,' another voice responded. 'Two nights of constant barrage. You've returned in time, just before Lilyth returns again tonight.'

I was vaguely aware of movement around me, but everything hurt. The pain clouded my senses. I gripped at my stomach as though that would stop my insides feeling like they were going to burst out of me.

'You did it,' came that exasperated voice again, followed by a face. A woman with bright sky eyes and shorn hair stared at me. She was enough of a distraction that I thought of nothing else. 'Max, you actually fucking did it. This is the chance we need—'

I narrowed my eyes at her, attempting to place her face. 'Who are—'

She wrapped me in a hug, forcing the words to suffocate in my throat. No one could hear what she said to me next, and I supposed that was the entire point.

'It's me, Max. It's Leska. I swear to the gods, if you don't remember me, I'll break that nose of yours again, just to remind you.'

Leska? That name, it was so familiar. But my head was screaming. I squeezed my eyes closed, glad for the dark. In the dark there was no confusion. Slowly, ever so slowly, it came back to me. *Leska. Leska...*

'Leska,' I practically shouted, eyes flying open. Relief was a wave that washed me away as I leaned into my sister, allowing her to take my weight. It was foggy, our story, but I could grasp scraps of it.

There was a sense of deep-rooted guilt that came with the memory of her. As though I had taken something from her. It was the type of feeling that came with expecting disdain in a person's eyes, but she only looked at me with pure relief.

'I should never have let you go,' she whispered into my ear, arms grasping me tighter.

She knew about the cost I paid to move through time. Leska was the only one who knew this truth. And seeing the reaction to knowing it has taken its toll on my mind.

'It was worth it,' I said, unable to look away from her as more noise flooded the room.

'Was it?' She drew me back to arm's length. 'What good are you to us, if you don't remember what you are fighting for?'

I scanned the room, or what was left of it, beyond her shoulder. There were so many tired-looking people stood around us in a formation. Towering walls of stone that glowed with veins of light barely stood upright. A large tree waited near us, the bark burned black, the branches no more than skeletal arms reaching at the air. My eyes fell on a flash of gold amongst it, a winged serpent with storm-grey eyes perched at a great height, watching me.

'Inyris,' I spoke her name as a feeling of familiarity plucked within me. It was a tether, a cord tying me to the dragon in the tree. The connection was made not of words, but a feeling that could only be described in one human term.

Mine. Mine. Mine.

'Inyris has helped protect us,' Leska said, following my line of sight. 'Although even if we could have made her leave, your dragon would have refused. She hardly allowed a single person to get close enough to your bodies to check for a pulse...'

Your bodies?

My head snapped from the dragon, back to the room. I hadn't realised I was missing something else until I began searching. I looked between the faces, trying to discern the piece that my soul called out to.

The skin on my arm shivered as my eyes fell upon him.

'Simion, it is good to see you too,' Leska added.

The man... Simion. It was Simion. I repeated his name in my head, praying that it would stick and not slip away like sand through fingers. He stood with the aid of his... mother. Yes, Celia Hawthorn. Her face was clearer than the rest, as she was a newer memory. Beside them was Elder Leia, dark circles cast beneath bright eyes.

'Have you told them?' I asked Leska, keeping my voice to a low whisper, trying not to reach and touch my temple.

'Not yet,' Leska replied, helping me stand on legs that did not feel like my own. 'But if you look at me like a stranger again, I will.'

'What's done is done.'

'I can see that.'

Her eyes fell back on the shield still grasped in my hand, made from metal and scale. Then to the sceptre hanging from my belt.

'Looks like we've missed a lot,' I spoke to the room this time, trying to pretend I wasn't struggling with placing myself in this time. My mind was slow and tired, filled with holes and missing information. If someone didn't distract me from it, I feared I would give into the madness that crept at the edges of my vision.

'Two nights and almost two days,' Elder Leia replied, all the while Simion didn't take his eyes off me. 'Dusk is upon us, and with it, Lilyth will return to the city for another evening of assault from her damned. As you can see, we will barely survive it.'

A harrowing expression pulled at her features, drawing the lines on her face into deep groves. Elder Leia looked to the floor. 'Many have been lost. Many more still missing.'

I choked on the idea of death, hardly able to look at the bodies beyond the ruined wall. Gleamers dressed in ash-and-blood-stained tunics raced between them, searching for the living.

'We will be ready this time.' There was fire in Simion's tone. The crown of flames flicked upon his head with renewed vigour. The power reflected in his eyes, a result of him connecting with his phoenixes.

At once, they rose in song beyond the castle, informing us that they were still guarding what was left of Wycombe.

'It is not good.' The weight of defeat slumped Leia's shoulders. 'Since you left, we have not left your side. Our only information from the city comes from the gleamers who have... We dared not leave your side, but some of our numbers were forced to aid the city. This is all that is left.'

I swallowed hard, my knees giving out at the thought of how many might have died. It was in that moment I remembered the other person missing from this room. Beatrice. Simion must have shared the same thought, because he practically screamed for her.

'My sister... is she?'

'Alive. Beatrice is alive,' Leia confirmed, but that words did not offer me the relief I expected. Because from her expression, dryads, Leia looked as though being alive was a curse. Celia had to hold her son back as the atmosphere shifted.

'Where is she?' Simion glowered, straining against his mother's hold.

'*Gone.*'

Not a soul missed the crack of his knees hitting the ground. Nor the pulse of radiating heat that burst from the crown, echoing over the room in a cloud of hissing air.

That one word had never been so hard to understand. Even as the throne room was bathed in silence, I still could not focus on what it meant.

'Gone... where?' I didn't realise who asked the question until I felt my mouth close.

No one replied. It was a few seconds of strange glances, but those seconds stretched on so long I felt every muscle in my body weaken. If it was not for Leska at my side, and the shield in my hand, I would have fallen.

'Someone better explain what the fuck is going on,' Simion stammered, attempting to hold onto some calmness, even though the stone beneath his hands had charred with unnatural heat.

'There is some hopeful news that comes with Beatrice's disappearance. As you remember, she left to aid the city.' To find and help Elaine, my scrambled thoughts reminded me. 'Lilyth has not only been killing those her shades have attacked but taking them somewhere. We have been unable to locate them. Casualties are low. It seems Lilyth requires them for a purpose. We believe it is tied to our blood, as you have previously explained. It is our only explanation at this time. And Beatrice—'

'*She* has Beatrice?' I leaned on the shield, knowing if I did not control myself the power it held could destroy Wycombe entirely. 'Lilyth has her!'

'I would say that Beatrice is the one who gained the benefit in this turn of events. Yes, Beatrice is currently occupied in whatever hellscape Lilyth is arranging for herself. But it was Bea who followed Lilyth's shades, and because of it we have been able to locate her.'

There was something she had said to me, a relief that flooded those serpentine eyes, as she spoke of what she had been searching for, and finally found.

Lilyth needed us. Not Aldian, but what it offered. Humans, and, more importantly, their blood.

Sustenance.

Another wave of sickness rocketed through me, burrowing into my gut until it twisted into knots.

'Then what are we waiting for?' Simion shouted, fire glowing in his eyes.

'You.' Leska's voice had the power to calm the room. 'That and Beatrice gave us specific instructions not to act. Not until you returned, successfully. The last message Leia gleaned from Beatrice proved that she was safe and well. She has gone under Lilyth's radar... as the monster has been rather distracted.'

'Distracted how?' I asked, although I almost knew the answer.

Leska's eyes fell to the shield again, awe glittering in the cobalt orbs. 'Turned out she found out that Oribon did not have the shield she went searching for. Perhaps he never did, in this time, since you have it now. All of Aldian felt the tremor, we do not believe the welcome she received from Oribon has been very warm. Since then, the father of dragons has been keeping her occupied, allowing those left in the city to get to safety.'

'Until Lilyth is destroyed, no one will be safe.' I stood taller, recognising the weight of the shield in all senses. 'If Beatrice has infiltrated whatever place Lilyth has taken up residence, we *should* go. And now, before Lilyth scampers back. We have two conduits. The crown and the shield. Lilyth has the gauntlet. Simple maths proves that we have a better chance against her now...'

I reached for my belt, knowing a third waited there.

'If we want to win this, we need a plan,' Elder Leia said, her eyes scanning the room. 'A solid one.'

'I have one.' And I did. It formed slowly in the back of my mind, gathering in the place of missing memories. I faced Leska, lifting the shield up in offering. 'You need to take this.'

What I didn't add was no one person should hold the power of two conduits.'

And I already have one.

Leska stepped back, her arms raised to her side in refusal. 'Max, I can't. I shouldn't—'

'Someone I looked up to once told me that to desire power means you are not responsible enough to have it.'

Her dark brow peaked. 'Those were my words.'

'Exactly, so take it. Use it.'

There was a hesitation, but also a draw between Leska and the dragon's conduit. I expected her to refuse again, but that was not like Leska. She lifted her arm, the vines coming alive where her hand once was. They reached over the space between us, slithering beneath the metal straps.

There was a relief that came with the lack of the shield's weight as Leska took it from me. Her eyes flared with silver, a band forming around her pupil. Inyris released a pleasured purr from her perch above us, followed by the very air shivering with anticipation.

I knew if Leska desired it, she could draw every bit of air from the room, from our bodies, from the sky. That was the power in her hands, her chance to prove to Oribon himself that she was worthy.

We all watched as Leska reined in her power, smothering it down to the far reaches of her being. When she blinked again, the silver band sank into her eyes. 'No wonder Lilyth desires this power. It is...'

'Intoxicating?'

'Dangerous,' Leska replied, her eyes drinking me in. They devoured me from head to toe, both in relief that I was here, but something else. Then, they settled on my free hand and stopped. A knowing smile slowly crept over her lips. 'And what have we missed, brother?'

I looked down and found what had caught her attention. Silver fast-marks wrapped around my skin, bright and proud. My stomach jolted and I fought the joy down, because it didn't feel right to experience such an emotion during such a time. Then my eyes found Simion's across the room and I couldn't help but drown in him.

'I think a congratulations is in order,' Leska announced, looking to Simion and finding the same marks on his arm. 'You went looking for conduits and came back with a husband.'

Husband. What a glorious word. No matter the reasons why I had joined Simion in such a way, I had still wanted it, wanted him.

Simion was smiling, bright and proud. Celia whispered something, then kissed his cheek, pure elation across her face. Even with the wave of elation, the undertone of bitterness still lingered. When Celia faced me, I could have sworn my heart skipped a beat. 'I wish Deborah was here to see this. Our sons are bound... words cannot describe. This brings light to a dark time, and I am so proud of you both.'

Would you be, if you knew why I did it? To stop time from eating away at Simion's memories, as it is with mine.

I was glad my mind was closed off to prying, because that

was a secret I would take to the grave. 'It is my honour. Simion is my world.'

'World seems too small of a word to describe how I feel about you,' Simion said, eyes boring through my soul. 'Universe seems more apt.'

'And there will be plenty of time for congratulations when we deal with Lilyth once and for all,' Elder Leia said, although the grin she fought to suppress was impossible to control. 'First, Aldian needs to be saved.'

'You are right,' I said, swallowing down hard. 'This must end.'

'Then, Maximus, care to tell us about this plan of yours?' Elder Leia asked with a glint of respect forged into her golden eyes.

I took the sceptre from my belt, delighting in the surge of power that speared up through me from the ground beneath my feet. Shock rippled over their faces, because no one expected to see it again. It was a part of the heist I had not shared, and for good reason. 'I am going to need you to keep an open mind,' I said, scanning the room of allies, friends and... family. 'Because you are not all going to like this.'

And they all listened, eyes widening a fraction as mouths dropped agape. No one interrupted me. Not until I stopped and faced the silence that followed such a suggestion.

Simion seethed, practically radiating his desire to refuse me. But he never would. He would follow me blindly over the edge of the world—that was his weakness. My weakness was encouraging him to take that last step.

'There must be another way,' Simion said, his lips pulled taut as he fought to say more. 'Tell me there is another way.'

'We do not have the time,' Leia said. 'I do not like it either, but it is a solid plan. It could work.'

'It could, but you are not asking your heart to walk into the line of fire, are you?' Simion snapped, swinging his burning eyes to me. 'Do not ask me to agree to this, Max. Please. I cannot agree, knowing the risks. I cannot—'

'If you have another suggestion, my love, I'm all ears.'

He opened his mouth, closed it again and looked to his feet.

'This is madness, Maximus,' Leska said, though she didn't refuse me either. No one did. 'But sometimes, a little madness is exactly what is required.'

I looked at her, skin crawling at the word that was more apt than she knew. 'You have no idea.'

'I think I do.' Leska side-eyed me knowingly. 'But Leia is right, it is a good plan. If it works, we save thousands.'

'We save the world,' I corrected.

I worried at the insides of my cheeks with my teeth until the flesh tore. Copper lanced across my tongue, burying the previous bit of vomit and bile. It would have been easier to shy away from the stares. To turn my back on this moment before we faced death herself with little knowledge if we were to succeed. But I couldn't leave this room without saying the one thing that sparked in my mind.

'There is no chosen one in this story. Not one single person who will stand before uncertainty and face it alone.' I swept my eyes over the room as I spoke, making sure I remembered these faces, the people I fought for and fought beside. 'This story is about family—family of blood, or one we were lucky enough to find along the way. We do this together, or not at all.'

The beat of silence that followed was heavy. I felt the urge to hold my breath, expecting someone to clap or perhaps laugh.

'Well, I'm impressed.' Leska patted a hand against my back. It was firm and powered, as though the air that followed it propelled her, giving her more force. 'That is certainly one way to build up morale, brother.'

I smiled at her, knowing that Leska would stand by me no matter what, because I would do the same for her. Then I looked to Simion, whose eyes glowed with worry for me, for his sister. But he had always encouraged me to be the blade, to be the one to use my strengths to face my enemies. His face softened into a smile and he nodded. There were no words he offered, but, as he raised his fast-marked fist and placed it over his chest, I knew just what he thought.

'I will be okay, Simion. We will see this through.'

'I know we will,' he replied, practically whispering, his words meant only for me. 'Because if not, I will raze everything Lilyth desires. It will not be her hand that destroys Aldian, but mine.'

The heat in his words, the twisting flames coiling amongst his golden eyes, proved he was being truthful. The thought of such destruction was frightening, but there was something in Simion's honesty that sparked its own fire in my belly.

'Then let us hope it doesn't come to that.'

His expression didn't waver, the crown pulsing heat and his skin practically radiating a passionate glow of red and oranges. 'Indeed, my love. We can only hope.'

'No, we can act.' I ran my hand down the side of his face, delighting in his sharp jaw and smooth skin. I would take the memory of his touch and keep it, for as long as my mind allowed.

'Before we face death itself, I have a gift for you...' Leska said, a glint of something mischievous in her eyes. It was enough of a distraction to draw me away from the man who held my heart in his hands.

She stepped aside, gesturing to the base of the Heart Oak. I didn't notice it before, but familiar armour waited there. Armour I had last seen the Queen wear, made from bark of the dryad, with the face of one across the breastplate.

Unexpected tears welled in my eyes, a sting that I was barely able to hold back.

'Go on,' she said, 'see if it fits. It's time for us to go to war.'

CHAPTER 33

I stood in an empty field a mile outside of Wycombe city. It was impossibly dark, the night sky full of nothing but stars ready to witness the power of gods clashing. The ground was sodden beneath my feet, mud already squelched across my boots.

The armour I wore was surprisingly light. It fit my body perfectly, with a little magic to shift the shape of the bark and wood. Atop my head sat a crown of ivy, thorn and branch. It was intended as a signal to the being we were about to face. There was something comforting about its presence, how it would taunt Lilyth as she laid her eyes on it.

Leska stood tall at my side, the shield hoisted in her arm, the other grasping her amplifier so tightly I could hear her mace creak beneath the tension. In the sky above us, dragons circled, their bodies blending in with the obsidian night. Every now and then I caught the flash of gold. Inyris was close; just knowing that eased my anticipation.

There was a tension to the air, a power. It laced up my skin, causing every hair to stand on end. The static charge was palpable, as if I could reach out and grasp a handful of it. As we waited in the almost quiet, my mind lingered on Simion. He would be leading the city's remaining battlemages through whatever portals the shades created, just as Beatrice had, but this time it would be to retrieve her.

'She is coming.' Leska broke the silence, her eyes flashing with a silver band of power.

I took her in, as if it would be the last time. The possibility was high. It was in that moment the first smattering of rain landed upon my cheek. It began slowly, until a thin sheet of ice-cold water blanketed the world in a wash of nymph power.

Of course, we both knew that Lilyth would not physically come. Not until she understood what she was to face. She'd made that mistake once, she wouldn't make it again. And we banked on that.

I felt oddly powerless without the sceptre. My fingers relaxed at my side, unsure what to do with themselves. But I couldn't reach for it, not yet. Lilyth knew we had the shield, that much was confirmed when she visited Oribon to retrieve it. But the sceptre was still destroyed in this time, and it would stay that way until we required it.

'Are you ready?' I asked, finding myself stepping closer to Leska, to the comfort of her presence.

'No, are you?'

I shook my head, rain falling from my skin as though it repulsed the nymphs' power. 'No.'

Her hand slipped into mine, cool fingers threading together, knotting. I squeezed her hand, glad for the anchoring sense it gave me, the knowledge that we could never be alone if we had one another.

'No matter how our story began, Max, I am glad we made it here. Together.'

I choked on her quiet admission, knowing I could not tell her I didn't remember how our story started. But she was right. It didn't matter. What mattered was having her, knowing her, standing by her side in the face of a world-ending danger. 'Family. The one thing that has driven Lilyth here will be the very thing that destroys her.'

'I hope so.' Leska faced the dark, watching the world be swallowed by the downpour of rain that raced towards us. 'I really do.'

The sound that came next was the telltale sign of Lilyth's shades.

Born from the darkness, they roared over the grassland in a wave of reaching limbs and faded, featureless faces. I found myself holding my breath, expecting it to overcome us. And they may have if Leska had not slammed the shield into the sodden earth before her. A blast of air and lightning rushed out before her, stark blue light like a vivid wave. It met the shades, the blast banishing them away in whisps of nothingness, only for them to slowly reform. My eyes fell on the woman who followed behind them, stepping carefully over the ground that withered beneath her feet.

'Looking for something?' Leska called out.

Hope seemed like a distant concept in the face of Lilyth.

'Yes, and I have finally found it,' Lilyth replied, the dark shivering against her voice. 'However, I gather you have not drawn me here to simply hand it over.' Her serpentine eyes fell on Leska, then her head tilted to the side, like a puppy setting their eyes on a bone. Except the bone was the shield held before Leska. 'I have not met with this one before.'

'How unfortunate,' Leska replied without showing an ounce of trepidation. I admired her ability to save face, as though she didn't face a world-ruining monster.

'For whom, me or you?' Lilyth's smile confirmed she enjoyed the bravado.

'That is yet to be determined.'

As Lilyth stepped closer, she drew the water and life from the ground and gathered it around her body in a dress of shifting silks. The gauntlet flashed along her pale arm, power winking along its edges. 'Go on then, tell me what it is that fills that mind of yours.'

I lifted my chin, unable to focus on anything else but this illusion of Lilyth. We just needed to draw her to this place physically. 'Leave. Leave Aldian of your own free will, just as you previously promised.'

'I see it is your turn to offer bargains in moments of desperation,' Lilyth said, this suggestion humouring her, as we all knew the answer.

I refused to reply. Refused to give her any words to show that we were open to being toyed with.

'And if I refuse?'

'We will destroy you, leaving only your bones to remain here.' Leska was quick to answer. Her eyes flared silver and the air thickened with bolts of hot light. 'The decision is yours.'

'But I cannot do that,' Lilyth raised her arms to her side, as though in defeat. 'Did the dryad-born not inform you as to what I am here for? Why would I continue searching the stars when I have finally found exactly what it is I desire? Nor do I believe your conscience would allow me to simply leave, knowing the ruin that would follow in my wake. The danger that lingers in those eyes of yours does not frighten me.'

'Does it not?' Leska spat. 'Then why not come here yourself? Shed this pathetic illusion and let me see you in the flesh.'

The rain shivered, slowed and then stopped. It was clear this projection of herself was not real, but she had to be close. When Lilyth spoke again, it was something I was not expecting. 'I have something I would like to show you.'

'We are not here for discussion, Lilyth.' I stepped forward, feeling the sceptre itch within my boot. 'What will your answer be—'

Lilyth's voice rose in pitch, interrupting me. 'Allow me to show you exactly *why* I am here. I have a feeling it may help sway your stance on my presence.'

Before I could refuse, the rain began to fall again, this time harder, with the taint of sickly sweet magic in it. It was as though reality rippled, parted like curtains and revealed the scene through a hidden window beyond. Suddenly, we no longer faced Lilyth. The illusion of the world-eater was replaced with another.

A woman stood over a bed made of straw. I recognised her to be Lilyth, but there was something different about her in this vision. She was younger, her eyes hollow with sadness. Her body leaned over the bed of straw, arms grasping the two bundles of flesh laid on it. My stomach rocked violently as I realised what she showed me. Children, two of them, with ringlets of blond hair set around gaunt faces. Piercing red eyes blinked slowly up at Lilyth who cried over them. She drew her thumb nail over her forearm, peeling her skin apart until blood bubbled through the cracks. She hovered her arm over the children's gasping mouths, allowing the droplets of blood to fall in. Tongues lapped up the pathetic droplets until there was nothing else for them to... drink. Then a terrible, shattering sound tore out of Lilyth's lips as the eyes of her children finally stopped blinking up at her. Lips stained with blood, pale skin almost transparent in the dark light. And although they stayed open, they looked at nothing of importance.

It was the long and endless gaze of death.

'Starved,' Lilyth's voice explained from beyond the illusion. 'My children starved to death because our home could no longer sustain them. Their little, innocent bodies withered to nothing because I failed them. My one task was to protect them, and instead I brought them into a world that killed them.'

I watched the scene change. Although the vision of Lilyth never let go of the two dead children, one boy and one girl, it was their corpses that proved the change in time. They sank into themselves, skin peeling over bone, chest caving inwards.

Shadows seeped through their open mouths, coiling around Lilyth's hands as though she controlled them.

Shades. Those children had become her shades.

'I was not the only one to lose my heart. What joy is there in ruling whole worlds if I cannot even ensure the life of my own children?' There was no denying the cracking in her voice, the heavy pain that came with sharing this.

When the scene shifted again, I was glad to no longer watch Lilyth's children wither in her arms to nothing but shadowed souls and peeling skin. This time it showed Lilyth standing upon a balcony. The sky was crimson-stained obsidian, and not full of stars. A moon of blood red hung above her, so large it was as if she could reach out and touch it. Instead, her focus was on the sprawling city before her. Her arms were outstretched, more shadows coiling around her hands as though it tethered her to the streets far below. But it wasn't until the scene changed again that I saw the truth. Bodies lined the streets, corpses of other beings clutching the bodies of starved, hollow people. Shadows seeped from their eyes, drawing up to where Lilyth stood, crying upon her balcony, coiling the souls in her hands.

This was what was left of her people. I sensed the grief in the vision, as though it belonged to me. What followed was the heavy weight of responsibility forced down on my chest. I clutched at it, fighting the urge to close my eyes. It didn't belong to me. It belonged to Lilyth.

It slowly clicked together in my mind; a picture being forged. Her shades were souls of those she had gathered in her hands in the vision. They were not simply a power she could command, but the very reason she was here. Her people, her kin, or at least parts of them.

And she had brought them with her, to find them a new home. A place that could sustain them with our blood.

As quickly as the illusion was conjured, it washed away as the rain continued to fall. All that was left was the taste of the memory in my mouth, the strange sense of death that hung in the air.

'You see why I will not leave your home?'

'The universe is cruel,' I said, wishing I didn't sympathise with Lilyth, but that vision touched something deep within me. 'Your world, ours, however many other lives linger in the stars—there is no denying how painful, evil and cruel it is. We have all lost something, some of us have more to lose, but that does not change how this will end.'

Lilyth's sadness was short-lived. Her face contorted into one of pure disdain and desperate anger. 'I do not need your permission to take this world, Maximus Oaken, nor did I require permission from the others I have been to before this.'

I shot Leska a look, one of knowing, a signal that only she would know. She looked at me for a moment, before focusing entirely on Lilyth. 'Then we work together, to find a way of living in peace,' Leska said, stepping away from me. 'There must be a way out of this, without the need to battle and lose any more of those we love.'

'Leska, no.' I went to reach for the shield, but it was taken out of my grasp. 'Don't do it.'

She spun on me, fury peeling from her eyes. 'It is and never has been your sole responsibility to save the world, Max. This is our home.' Leska lifted her amplifier, levelling it at my feet. I knew the ground could swallow me down before my feet shifted and I lost my footing. 'Lilyth,' Leska asked, 'if I give you the shield, help you retrieve the crown, do you offer me your promise that you will not ruin us?'

'Don't do this!' I shouted again, until my throat burned, eyes snapping to Lilyth, seeing the glint of pleasure in her eyes—the *want* in them.

'Have you not learned? I have no desire to destroy this world. I need it. But if it is a painless transition you ask for, that depends on your next actions.'

Above us the dragons roared, mirroring the panic that crashed within my stomach.

'Leska, please.' I called her name, but it was as if I wasn't there. I knew she heard me, but she chose to ignore me as she walked closer to Lilyth. She lifted the shield and thrust it into the ground before the illusion of Lilyth. I felt the echo of power a moment before it dissipated as Leska withdrew her touch and stepped away.

'Take it,' Leska cocked her chin to the conduit. 'It is yours.'

My blood hammered in my ears, raging like a storm in my skull. Every inch of my body was immobilised as I watched Lilyth look down at the shield with the hunger of someone starved. It was as though the world held its breath, waiting for action.

'I understand the pain of losing someone you love,' Leska continued, stepping back, producing room between her, Lilyth and the dragons' conduit. 'I understand how it drives you towards action, placing hope in even the darkest of thoughts.' Then she turned to face me, eyes widening only a fraction, enough for me to notice. 'Max, I am sorry, but there is no beating this. Sometimes, knowing when to give up is a person's greatest asset.'

She was right.

Because those were my words—words I had given her to say in this very moment.

Tears filled my eyes, my breath lodging in my throat. Lilyth's laugh started small, like the broken chirps of a bird. Then they morphed, filling the darkness until the rain began to fall harder. Where she had stood was now nothing but empty shadow. Beneath my hands I felt the slithering shift of earth as something large moved across the ground. The mother of monsters was close—her true form was coming.

Leska did not notice the presence, but I did. From behind my sister, the true Lilyth revealed herself. The monster. She parted from the wall of her damned, elongated talons clinking excitedly on the gauntlet she wore. As she settled her eyes on the shield, as though nothing else mattered, I reached into my mind, to the piercing cold presence that had never left me.

She is here. Lilyth has taken the bait.

Keep vigilant. One step at a time. Simion's voice opened in my skull like a flower budding beneath the sun. *See you shortly.*

'Lilyth,' I shouted, forcing as much pleading desperation into my tone. It was not that I didn't want her to take the conduit, I needed her to. The illusion of Lilyth couldn't touch it, which was always the plan. 'Lilyth, please! It does not need to end this way.'

'Yes, it does.'

Lilyth barely looked at me as her thick tail slithered, moving her closer to the shield. Leska had slipped back just as a flash of gold scale broke away from the dark, snatching her silently from the ground.

'So be it,' I answered, almost too calmly. 'But don't forget *we* gave you a chance.'

As Lilyth reached out to take the dragon's conduit, I slipped my hand into my boot to the sceptre that waited for me. Leska was far enough away to be safe, but close enough to withdraw her earthen magic from the bindings around my feet. The moment I wrapped my hand around the dryad's conduit, I released every ounce of power it offered me, rupturing the earth apart. The shield was the first to tumble into the deepest belly of the earth, directly into the waiting hands of the dryads who lurked beneath it. As their roots coiled around the conduit, drawing it away from Lilyth, she dove, her arm reaching into the ground as though she could reach it.

That was her next mistake.

I gathered the earth around Lilyth's clawed arm, burying the gauntlet beneath the hardened soil. I didn't stop, not until I no longer existed in my body, but in the earth itself. I became every stone that forged through the meaty flesh of her elbow, every root that wrapped around Lilyth, keeping her in place.

Lilyth pulled back with all her might, but she was mine. She had fallen for our illusion and now she was caught on the hook of my plan. It was working.

If the scream Lilyth expelled at the death of her children was world-shattering, the noise she made next had the power to carve apart time and space itself. She was rabid, pulling at her arm as the damned thrashed around her. But in a moment of silence, of stillness, every shadow in Aldian would have heard her flesh rip, her bones break and the gasp of breath as Lilyth came away from the earth without the gauntlet—and without her arm entirely.

CHAPTER 34

There was only a moment of stillness before disarray unleashed. I watched, power poised at the tips of my fingers, as Lilyth stared down at her torn limb. Blood pumped from the mess of flesh and bone, spilling over her pale skin, making it almost black in colour. Realisation sank into her. I watched it break over her expression like the tide breaks over a shore, slowly drawing out her features until she wore a mask of agony, disbelief and surprise.

The latter was the most enjoyable.

Her scream split the sky in two, opening the dark up until it heeded her call. It was not the nymphs' power that responded to her call. Not this time. Instead, it was the shadows. Darkness spilled from her back like wings unfurling to great spans. Out rushed the creatures of her creation—twisted souls with teeth and claw.

Lilyth was not powerless without the conduits. This was a creature who had overcome worlds long before she even had access to the power of the four elemental gods. And as she levelled her crimson eyes on me, I saw it—the monster made from a broken heart—before she disappeared behind a wave of shades as they poured out to meet us.

A wall of pure, impenetrable darkness raced towards me, bringing with it the stench of rot and ruin. Together, the four gods represented life. Lilyth was the moon in contrast, she was pure death. Darkness eternal, hunger incarnate.

I drew up, magic humming from the sceptre and my amplifier. It cast out a powerful ripple across the ground. The closer the shades came, the louder their snapping teeth sounded. The scratching of their claws against the flesh of earth felt so real. Even if I longed to find her, I couldn't amongst the chaos.

The need to finish this was a boiling star in my chest.

As my magic met them, it rose high up in a wall of clay, soil and stone. Dragons swept down from the sky, casting pillars of ice and lightning amongst the horde of death. But the assault was great, and out the shades poured in their thousands.

Simion. I called out to his icy presence just as the damned breached over my wall, clambering over with the desperation of a starved being. *I need you.*

Inyris dove from the blackness, gold scales flashing, Leska leaned forward with amplifier held at the ready. I continued moving the shield and gauntlet beneath the earth, pulling it through cracks of soil until they were far out of reach. If given the chance, I would have taken them both, but I didn't have the chance. The ground was crawling with the shades. Inyris was calling down our bond, commanding me to reach her. And I did, just at the last moment.

I turned my back on the shades and ran. Inyris swept low, the cool winds beneath her wings disturbing the damned that gave chase. Out of the corner of my eye I saw Leska atop my dragon, reaching out with her tendrils of vines. I met them with my own arm, feeling them wrap around me with vigour. Then the ground fell away and I was airborne, sweeping over the landscape that was crawling with the shadows of death.

'Now, Max!' Leska cried over the roaring winds.

I scanned the ground, searching for Lilyth, but she was nowhere to be seen. Her presence was everywhere and nowhere, as though she embodied every damned soul she controlled. This power... it was violent. 'I don't know where she is!'

'It won't matter,' Leska said, 'she is wounded. Act now.'

Something was wrong. Simion was silent in my mind, and he was not there. I couldn't explain it, but I sensed the change in the atmosphere. With the other two conduits buried deep in the ground, Simion and I were the only ones left with the power to harm Lilyth. And unless the damned were banished with firelight, there was no way of finding her.

I could see Wycombe in the distance, a far-off smudge across the landscape. Beside it was the shadow of Galloway Forest. So many lives, so many people we had to protect.

It was Leska who drew my attention back to the battlefield, pointing a finger to the ground. 'There. Max, look.'

I followed her finger, watching as shadows spewed from darkness like the ravine of a waterfall. The creatures billowed out, unending and fast, clambering over one another. There was no doubt in my mind that this is where they were being conjured from. Which meant Lilyth was close.

We played a game of want and desire. Lilyth had wanted the conduit, she had come forward to claim it. That was our chance to use her weakness against her. And now this, as the shades rolled over, unbothered by the dragons who cast frost and storm down upon them. Their attentions shifted to Wycombe, and at once they rushed towards it.

'Get me there,' I shouted over the screeches and roars. '*Quickly.*'

Inyris repositioned, fuelling her limbs with the panic we shared. We flew until we were in front of the raging tempest of damned souls. I did not need to offer the next instruction because my dragon was already spearing towards the earth. She had barely slowed before I threw myself off the side, landing hard on my side and rolling to a stop. The fall was softened as I used the sceptre to liquify the earth until I fell in a puddle of melted soil and grass.

Dizzied and aching, I regained my composure. The air had been knocked from my lungs, and it pained me to try and retrieve it. Quickly, I stood, watching as the shades noticed me and raced in my direction.

I was alone, the only thing stood between them and Wycombe—except that was not *entirely* true.

Inyris and Leska attempted to disturb the front line, calling down lightning and frozen winds, giving me a moment to act.

My knuckles gripped the sceptre tighter, the magic flashing through my body. This time, it was not the element I longed to control, but the gods. A violent tremor shook the earth beneath my feet, spitting stone and debris, breaking apart the top layer of the ground. From either side of me, the dryads rose. A formation of sentient gods, creatures of the very element that gifted us. I did not need to turn back to know that every possible dryad had heeded my call. It was as though Galloway Forest had moved itself, placing a wall of protection between Wycombe and Lilyth's shades.

My own army stretched out at my back.

The clash of power would have been heard from beyond the stars. As death and life met, it was with a force so shattering every bone rattled. But I did not shy away as the shades reached us, nor when the dryads unleashed bouts of pure power out across Lilyth's army.

I joined them, giving into instinct. Any shade lucky enough to get through my guards of earth met my magic. Stones severed their fleshy chests, leaves turned to blades and sliced the beings apart.

Although I could not see Inyris, I *sensed* her. My jaw

echoed hers, as she plucked shades from the ground, snapping shadow-coated bodies beneath the power of her teeth. I knew Leska was close too, because lightning cast down from the sky, smashing into the earth and breaking apart groups of the damned. Without the light it offered, we would not have banished the shades' natural armour enough to ruin them.

The air was full of the smell of singed hair and flesh and the screams of dead things truly meeting their end.

Small shapes shot past me, distracting me from the handful of damned I battled. It wasn't until I saw the creatures pounce at our enemy, that I knew what they were. Worcupines. They flooded through the dryads, passing them like yapping, loyal hounds. This, I understood, was not only our fight. Every creature joined, wishing to protect the world from an unfortunate end.

As I fought, conjuring boulders of rock to knock through walls of shades, I wondered if this is how all the worlds fought against Lilyth. Did they stand up against her, only to fail beneath the wrath of a being desperate to find a home for her kin?

Exhaustion was a far-off concept, as my body was fuelled by my element. Somehow, I knew if I relinquished the sceptre, I would fall to my knees, drained. So, I held firm, refusing to allow room for weakness.

It could have been seconds we fought, or days. I had no concept of time, not in the face of the present. Here, the past meant little and the future meant everything. I focused only on winning.

But the shades continued to come. I was being forced back, noticing the splinters of wood beneath my feet. In a moment of distraction, it was to find dead gods I trod over. Not every dryad had survived. Some lay buried beneath masses of shadow that had torn at their earthen flesh with teeth and claw. I fisted my hand, reaching to the crackling clouds far above, drawing down some of the dragon's gifted power. A fork of lightning clashed into the mound of shadows ahead of me, dissipating them in clouds of smoke and flesh. It was in the flash of blue light that I saw more dead dryads.

So many—too many.

Whereas Lilyth's army continued to return, ours was slowly being thinned.

Simion! I shouted his name louder. Perhaps I even called it aloud, because my throat ached and lungs burned. *We need you. I need you.*

Time slowed to a stop as another wave of shades raced towards me, the dryads trying to fill in the gaps left by their dead kin. I watched them come, gathering a storm of splinters before me, using the dryad's dead bodies as weapons in a desperate attempt. The energy buzzed beneath my skin, so powerful I truly believed I would burst. But then I lifted the sceptre, levelled the knotted tip at the shades...

'What is...' I breathed, narrowing my eyes in a moment of distraction.

It was not a wall coming towards me, but a creature. A monster. Something born from nightmare and fear, a creature fuelled by impossibilities beyond my mind.

It was horrifying.

The shades gathered in a physical mass. Out from the shadows, a beast had emerged, part-dragon, part-wolf. It mimicked the world around it, but far larger and more imposing. It shook its mane, expelling a skin-flaying growl that overspilled with the promise of ruin.

Foul fog expelled from its snout. Eyes made of darkness levelled at me, finding me amongst it all. A crimson-scaled dragon broke from the sky, a roar building in its throat, only to be silenced by one snap of the beast's shade-made jaw.

My bones reacted to the crunch of the beast. The shattering of scales was like frail glass. There was no stopping this creature. Inyris was there then, a flash of gold, spearing towards the beast.

'Inyris,' I screamed, panic fuelling me, knowing how this would end. 'No. Stand down.'

Perhaps she didn't hear me. Maybe she did, but she chose this moment to ignore me. Because Inyris knew that if she didn't act now, I would next face the jaw this shadow beast.

So, I acted first. Gathering the bodies of fallen dryads, the splinters of corpses that littered the ground, I, too, created a monster of my own making. It rose before the shadow beast, matching it in height and build. It was not a case of using my essence, but gifting it my power, filling it with a soul for itself.

Inyris wove off course, just before my creation rose in her way.

'Down, *dog*,' I spat, skin quaking with the pure force of such power.

This was magic unlike anything I had expected. It was strong and unyielding, a force that was intoxicating enough to lose myself forever. But I grasped onto reality, taking it by the fist as I animated the creature of wood and stone.

The shadow beast pawed at the earth, gouging deep groves beneath it. Dark mist seeped from its nostrils. Then, without warning, it raced forward.

Both monsters clashed. Mine rose on its hindlegs, kicking out at the shadow monster. A jaw full of broken shards opened and wrapped itself around the shadow beast's neck.

Severing my connection, allowing the essence to rule my creation, I forged forward hoping it would be enough to even the playing field.

But creating my giant of earth was not without a cost. My body was sluggish, my muscles strained and aching. Using essence was one thing, but giving it up was another. No matter if I grasped the conduit, I was still human. Dryad-born, yes. But that only made up for so much.

Splinters screeched through the air, smashing into the damned, so many that it was as though the sky rained arrows, piercing shadow and flesh. I readied myself again, preparing for more, when fire flashed at my side. A flash of heat scorched the air, intensifying the stench of death. But when I turned, squinting against the flare of light, it was to find a man at my side.

Simion Hawthorn was bathed in wytchfire. Even the crown upon his head twisted in points of black flame. It reflected in the pools of his eyes, making the outline of his body glow in a halo of otherworldly light. As he lifted both his arms, I felt my skin grow cold. A shiver began within me, drawn out as any heat in my body was leeched out by Simion's power. Then, like the snapping of a band, he cast out his wytchfire, fuelling it with the power of gods as it raged out across the army before us.

Suddenly, the world was coated in the light of day. Except it wasn't day that crest over Aldian, but a swarm of phoenixes. They flew overhead, breaking apart the damned with the fire spewing from beneath their wings.

It was no wonder the phoenixes were Lilyth's favourite of the gods. It was the power that had the chance to truly stand against her shadows. She favoured them out of necessity and fear. That is why they were never imprisoned like the dragons in the mountain, the dryads beneath the earth and the nymphs locked to the water.

And now we used that power against her, shifting the tide of battle once again.

'I thought you were not going to come.'

'As did I,' Simion said, turning to me as a wave of wytchfire continued to race at his back. I pressed myself into him, wishing to feel the support of his presence, his touch. When he lifted his thumb to my cheek and cleared something from it, I melted into him.

'What happened?'

'It was terrible, Max—'

That was not the answer I was expecting. I drew back from him, eyes searching for the truth of what kept him. But all I saw when I looked into his eyes was fear. Simion was haunted.

'—I heard you calling, but I couldn't come. What we found with Beatrice, it was terror. It was evil. Just bodies and bodies.' He pinched his eyes closed, practically sagging into me. 'I have never felt pain like it.'

'I have you, Simion.' It didn't matter that he was late. All that mattered was that he was here, by my side. 'The gauntlet and shield are away from Lilyth. She is wounded but throwing everything at us. If we don't destroy her, this will never stop.'

'Then *we* came at the right time,' he said, lifting back his thumb from my cheek until I saw the smudge of blood on it. I hadn't realised I was hurt, not until he brought attention to it. 'But Max, killing Lilyth is not the end of this. She has been...' Simion stopped himself, as though the words were too much. I saw the haunting in his eyes, the look of a man who had seen something so terrible that words were impossible to use. 'She had a plan too, and it has already begun.'

Before I could question him, more fire flashed around us. Simion had said we, and I finally understood why.

'Did you reach Beatrice?' I asked.

Simion's face dropped, as though I had brought up a ghost. His complexion drained of colour, his eyes dropping from my face to something unimportant at his feet. I grasped his cheeks, lifting him up, forcing him to look at me.

'Tell me.' I was shaking, my fingers trembling from panic and unspent power. 'Did something happen?'

'She is okay, Max.' Relief rushed through me, almost knocking me to my knees. 'In fact, Beatrice is currently tearing through hordes of damned.' Simion placed his forehead to mine.

Sparks of warm light filled the space amongst the dryads. It was then I saw them, people with fire dancing in their palms, joining the fray.

Sorcerers. Humans once phoenix-possessed but now blessed with their divine power. Some wore the armour of battlemages, light reflecting off the metal like dancing gold. Others, most in fact, wore the mundane clothes of civilians. I saw familiar greys and whites, even some dressed in the rich blue. These people were from the South.

'How?' I breathed, unable to fathom what I witnessed.

'You were not the only one with a plan, my love.' Simion smiled knowingly. All around us portals opened. I was so focused on the swarms of fire-wielding humans that I didn't notice Simion reach into his pocket until he held something aloft between us.

'What good is the power used against us, if we don't harness it ourselves? Camron taught me this little trick, I did not want it to go to waste.' Simion reached into his breast pocket and pulled something out. A feather. He turned the phoenix feather slightly, the plumage rippling like living fire. 'I made sure that, alongside the letters accompanying the Heart Oak you sent throughout the South, these also distributed with a single request. *Keep the fires burning, and when I call, you come.* This was never just a single person's fight, or responsibility. It was everyone's, and only together will we succeed.' He took my fast-marked hand, threaded his warm fingers with mine and lifted them up between us. 'Fight beside me, husband. Let's protect our home, so we can finally have one together.'

I could have wrapped my arms around him and suffocated him with my love—my thanks. Simion had just changed the tide of war.

'As if I needed any more motivation to win,' I said, unable to look away from his deep eyes. I leaned in close, lifted onto my toes and pressed my mouth to his. As dryads fought alongside phoenixes, dragons alongside sorcerers and the battlemages graced the sky with their power, I took Simion's lips to mine and held them. He exhaled through his nose, his arms catching me to keep me pinned to his chest.

'I love you,' he said the second we drew apart.

'I know,' I replied, winking.

'Are you not going to say it back?' Simion pouted his lower lip as the sound of battle waged around us.

I looked beyond him, feeling a new sense of energy overwhelm me. 'When we are done here, I will say it. Over and over until you are sick of hearing it.'

'I hardly imagine that would be possible.'

Before I could reply, agony tore at my chest, causing me to double over. I pressed a hand to my ribs, expecting to find blood pumping from a hole caused by something unseen. Simion's face split apart in worry, coming to grasp me as I fell to my knees. But his words meant little, not as I stared at my chest, expecting to find blood but seeing nothing.

It was then I heard it, the cry of agony, the soul-tearing roar of a dragon. I looked up to the sky, knowing exactly where I would find her. Inyris was falling from the sky, wings barely able to beat. Blood fell from a wound across her breast.

Both my dragon and sister fell into the waiting arms of Lilyth's shades.

Suddenly, I was running, legs pumping against the ground as my name was called out from my back. Simion chased at my heel, whips of fire flashing out around him, keeping shades at bay.

I could no longer see them, not as they were drawn into the reaching wave of shadow creatures. The shades reared up, snatched my golden dragon and dragged her beneath their hold.

The pain dissipated as Inyris severed our bond. I don't know if sharing her agony was worse than the impenetrable silence that followed. But I kept running, knowing Simion was chasing at my heel.

'You can end this,' the shadows sang in unison, although the voice belonged to another—Lilyth. 'The power is in your hands. Do you allow them all to die or all to live, beneath my rule?'

'Don't listen to her, Max,' Simion said, half a scream, half an exhausted exhale. 'Focus on me, only me—'

I couldn't. Lilyth parted from the shadows, blocking me from reaching Inyris and Leska. The shades moved around her like a curtain. In her remaining hand she lifted something up as though to show me. My heart stopped, my chest aching.

It seemed Lilyth had reached my sister before I could. Leska, all wide eyes and calm demeanour, dangled from Lilyth's grasp. She no longer held her amplifier, instead she kicked out, hissing as talons sank into her shoulder.

'It is my turn to give you *one more chance*.' In the pause, all I could hear was my thundering heart. It devoured all sound, drowning out the raging battle and Simion's warning screams. 'Give me what I desire, and I will give you what it is you want. *Or* she dies.'

CHAPTER 35

The time for negotiation had long passed. I admired Lilyth's attempt, but it was wasted. One swift look into Leska's eyes—defiance overspilling from them—and I knew what was to come.

Her jaw gritted, eyes narrowed, and the furious scowl that I was all too familiar with.

Leska nodded. It was a signal. Whilst Lilyth's entire focus was on me, and the sceptre in my hand, she didn't pay heed to Leska. That was a grave mistake. Leska didn't require an amplifier to inflict pain.

I lifted the sceptre, knuckles white from tension. Lilyth's devilish eyes followed, which gave Leska the chance she needed. With a great hoist, she reared her fist up and drove it into Lilyth's face. Even from a distance I heard the fragile bone of her nose crack. Blood spewed from the mess of flesh, filling the monster's mouth as she bellowed.

We charged as one, towards Lilyth, in her moment of distraction.

Simion with his crown, wytchfire flaring out like serpents. A roar outmatched the cry of Lilyth's fury. I followed it to find a shape part from the night. A dragon, born from black scale and ire made flesh. Glamora. A flash of silver caught my eye, drawing me to Beatrice upon her back. Lightning flashed behind her, mirroring the thrash of energy inside my chest.

Lilyth gathered a blast of dark energy—corporeal shadow drawn from the night sky—and prepared to cast it out towards us. But Glamora reached her first. The black-scaled dragon smashed into Lilyth, sending the blast of shadow back into the fray of damned and mages. I heard screams of terror but focused ahead. More would suffer if we did not end this.

I didn't see where Leska had landed, but Lilyth no longer held her. I only hoped Leska was safe.

Simion ran before me, whips of flame shooting from his arms. He thrust them forward, clearing a path through the damned who flooded over to help as Lilyth and Glamora clawed at one another. Beatrice clung to Glamora's neck, trying to hold steadfast, but Lilyth and the dragon were thrashing so violently it was impossible to tell where the dragon began and the monstress ended.

A violent chill burned over me, itching the skin beneath my bark-made armour. It took a moment to realise it was Simion, drawing another blast of flame but using the heat from bodies to conjure it. Even the stars seemed to burn brighter in the sky above, as though he pulled on their warmth from leagues away.

Lilyth fixed her gaze on him, just as her talons buried deep in the fleshy underbelly of Glamora. One hand discarded the dragon, the other swept towards Simion.

I acted. The earth split at my command, sending Lilyth off kilter. She fell into the hole, forced to scramble at the edges of the precipice. That gave Simion the chance to send a wall of pure, unending wytchfire out towards her.

It was in the light of his fire when I finally saw Leska. She was lying on the ground, unmoving. Her body was between

Lilyth and the fire. I acted in a breath. Instead of breaking the earth apart, I reformed it, drawing on the deepest stone and mineral buried in the soil. My own wall rose before Simion's creation, just before the wytchfire met Leska.

As the two met, the blast that rippled over Aldian had the power to flatten mountains. I was knocked backwards, torn by the force of power. All I saw was the blur of stars, the spinning of darkness followed by the harsh thump of my body against the ground.

I opened my eyes, pain reverberating through my body, to see more shadow. No. shades. They overwhelmed me, piling atop my body until I was confident that this must be death. Nails scratched over skin, teeth burrowing into the hard casing of my armour.

Without it, I would have been torn to ribbons. I curled into a ball, pressing the sceptre to my chest, screams erupting from my throat without control.

Max. Close your eyes.

It was so dark, I wasn't sure if my eyes were open or not. My answer came as bright red fire speared through the mass of the damned atop me, splitting them apart. It passed through like a blade, then again and again until the weight of Lilyth's monsters lessened enough to see through.

Simion stood atop me, face pinched in anguish as he swung a blade of pure flame. It burned in his hands, casting the planes of his face in shadow. It glowed off the dragon crest upon his breastplate, making the gold seem otherworldly.

Seeing him fuelled me, providing my muscles with the last drop of energy they required. Even though I felt the soft buzz of blood race over my exposed skin, and saw the reaction of horror in Simion's face.

But I took that pain. I took the pain, the panic for Leska and the unknown of Inyris and pushed it all into my power.

A snake of lightning fizzed over my hands, crackling like

living serpents. I saw the shades who attempted to reform, and cast my energy out.

Pale hides melted upon impact, singeing beyond the point of return.

'I almost had her,' Simion breathed, coming to step by my side as the lightning sparked out.

'It was... Leska,' I stammered as Simion's sword dissipated in a puff of smoke and he took my hand. 'She was in the way. I couldn't let the wytchfire touch her.'

'You did the right thing,' Simion said, wide-eyed and breathless. Dryads, he was beautiful. If a battle didn't rage around us, I would have happily melted into him. Somewhere deep down I understood this passion was a result of his overexertion of power, but it didn't matter.

'Let's finish this,' I said, seeing Leska and Beatrice attacking Lilyth in tandem. It was a scene that deserved to be painted on walls and retold in tales. Two warriors fighting against a world-devouring monster. Leska called down lightning whereas Beatrice fought with earth and steel, both with a vengeance.

For a moment, I thought Lilyth was distracted, until her blood-red gaze lifted and fell upon us. Her lips drew back in a snarl, her mouth moving in words I could not hear. Then she cast out a hammer of shadow, knocking Leska and Beatrice out of the way as though she had simply been entertaining them this entire time.

'Simion,' I gasped, taking his shoulders in my hands. But I was too slow. Before I could turn him, before I could place myself in his way, Lilyth conjured a weapon of her own from the shadows. A spear of obsidian launched through the air with speed.

The sound of it piercing Simion would haunt me forever.

We both looked down to the tip protruding through his stomach. There was a moment of confusion on his part, before he was yanked backwards, torn from my grasp. The spear Lilyth conjured was jointed to chains of shadow, which she pulled back towards her. Simion was half dragged, half bounced over the ground and into her arms.

I was running again, throwing every ounce of desperate magic at them, but Lilyth made sure to keep Simion's body as a shield. This time, he did not call upon the fire to aid him. He didn't move. Discomfort tore over my fast-marked arm, and I refused to look down at it. I refused to see if the marks still covered my skin or not.

Beatrice tore forward from the side, blood smearing the side of her face, blade raised. But Lilyth had already taken the crown from Simion's head. Fire blazed outwards, mirroring the laugh that echoed over the battleground.

Panic spurred down my bonds, echoing over the dryads and into the gold-scaled dragon conjoined to me. I had not felt her since she was overwhelmed by shadows, and sensing her now did not give me comfort.

It could only mean one thing.

Inyris speared between Beatrice and Lilyth, just before the ball of flame was thrown. Ice met fire as Inyris parted her jaws, using her body to shield Beatrice. Lilyth looked sideways, hardly bothered by the blast of frigid air.

I gathered the magic of the gods in my hands, filling every fibre of my being. Lilyth levelled her eyes with me, smiled and then focused her attempts beneath her. I cried out as her fire tore the ground at her feet, twisting in a cyclone as it burned deep into the crust of the earth. I was so connected to the ground that I felt every scorch of power. It blinded me, forcing me to sever my connection before the agony overwhelmed me.

There was no telling what Lilyth attempted until she stopped, her grin widening into the expression of satisfised longing. She leaned down into the charred hole, reaching for something unseen. Broken, scorched roots snapped with ease as she worked her way deeper. It was then I knew what she wanted, why she had fought so hard to hold her ground.

Because beneath her, just where I had left them, was the gauntlet and shield I had buried. And now she had them.

Three conduits.

The power over three gods.

CHAPTER 36

I looked nowhere but Lilyth. As power flooded through her body, the intoxicating rush of water, air and fire, she closed her eyes and released a pleasured moan over the world. I felt the tide of change shift in that moment. Even through my bond, Inyris turned. I felt every second of the shift as Lilyth regained control.

'My conduits are made from my blood and bone, the conjoining of my control to the element. Did you truly believe you could keep them from me?' Lilyth glowered, enjoying that she had won. 'Give me the sceptre. It is mine as much as it belonged to the dryads.'

'You're not deserving,' I spat, taking my last chance.

Celia Hawthorn had not only held the knowledge of the conduits, but also how to destroy them. I took that and utilised it, knowing my window for action was slowly closing.

My gaze fixated on it—a shield held together by Lilyth's bones, which overlapped with the scales of dragon, forged together. As the crown could destroy the sceptre, fire to earth, it was my sceptre that could destroy the shield.

There was no chosen one in our story, but if we were to work as one, I had to give them a chance.

One last *fucking* chance.

I called upon the dryads, knowing that in seconds they would turn beneath the phoenix's wytchfire and be torn apart by hateful dragon jaws. My power was earth, it was stone, root, vine and dirt. I gathered it to me, drawing on the essence—the energy in every living thing. The ground at my feet withered as I collected it, storing it within my body as though I commanded lightning.

But this was not lightning—it was *life.*

I cast it out, the force ripping out of my chest, barrelling down my arm and through the sceptre. It was silent and sharp, a single blast of pure, undiluted power. It glowed a green hue, flashing through the thick air before meeting its mark.

Lilyth raised the shield, ready to block the power from reaching her. But it never was meant for her flesh. In fact, my attack was meant for the very thing she thought would protect her. The dragons' conduit.

The shield cracked in two. Scale and bone shattered apart, sending debris deep into Lilyth's gut. Just as Simion had destroyed the first sceptre, I took another conduit out of play. Immediately I felt Inyris again, her relief, her freedom. Every dragon was now unleashed from the bindings that Lilyth had forged over them all those aeons ago.

I did not see where the remains of the shield went, or the gauntlet. Lilyth pressed her bloodied hand to her stomach as gore oozed through hundreds of gouges and cuts. Her crown of flames flared—brighter and fiercer—mirroring her scream of anguish and pain.

Simion was still unconscious before her, moments from being crushed beneath her thrashing tail. I reached into the metal of his armour, using the sceptre to tie with the minerals that made it up. Just as Lilyth had yanked him to her, I pulled. Simion's limp body was thrust towards me, until he thumped into my chest. The force of the impact knocked me to the ground, but I took him in my arms and arched my body over him.

'I've got you, Simion.' I pressed my trembling fingers into his neck, feeling the faint pulse of a heartbeat. My hands were covered in blood. Whose, I could not tell. Simion's breastplate was mangled, a mess of metal flaps and blood. He needed a gleamer, and quickly. But time was not of the essence as Lilyth bellowed my name out, flames licking at the world around her.

Leska was once again in Lilyth's hold. I couldn't see where Lilyth's talons where, they were buried so far in Leska's shoulder to keep her in place.

'In all the worlds I have taken, never has one been such a thorn.'

I held onto Simion tighter, wishing for time not only to slow but to stop completely. I couldn't form a word, knowing what was to come.

What happened next occurred without thought. Lilyth, red eyes burning with desperation, sank her teeth into Leska's neck. Blood erupted, smearing over Lilyth's mouth. It sounded as though the universe screamed, except it was my throat that burned.

I had once watched a fox tear out the innards of his catch, using teeth to rip away flesh as though it was paper. That is what Lilyth did to Leska. She wrenched her jaw back, pulling out a chunk of Leska's throat.

Blood was everywhere.

My heart did not crack, for it was already in pieces after losing so much. But the threads holding those pieces together started to snap, one by one, as I watched the inevitable. Leska was discarded onto the battle-trodden ground. Gore pumped over her fingers as she clasped at her neck, as if her hand could fix it. Nothing could fix this. Phoenixes cawed out as one, feeling the helpless grasp of control as Lilyth used their conduit to leash them.

The sky was full of gods warring, the ground trembling as mages, sorcerers and dryads attempted to stave off the damned that attacked with renewed vigour.

We were losing. I knew it. Even with one of her conduits destroyed, Lilyth would still win.

'I would do anything for my family, Maximus Oaken.' Lilyth was drunk on power, her phoenixes flocking in the sky above her head where they swarmed in a circle. Dark red clouds billowed outwards, spreading like a stain over the world. This was it; this was the nightmare I had seen so many times. 'Your efforts are wasted. Your attempts far too late. The convergence has already begun, a world where my kin can not only survive but thrive. Death is my domain, and in it I shall be victorious.'

'You... need us,' I screamed, breathless and useless.

'No, I need your blood. When my kin return here, they will have centuries of sustenance, but you, Maximus Oaken. You will be mine. I will drain you for everything you have to offer, just to remind you that you were never going to win....'

Lilyth didn't notice the additions to the battlefield. I almost didn't. But, out from the sodden ground, two children rose. Lilyth's gaze was fixed to the ball of wytchfire in her upturned palm, and the accompanying song as the phoenixes turned against the dragons and dryads.

I couldn't take my eyes off the back of the children.

Full heads of blonde ringlets, piercing red eyes, skin pale as milk. One was slightly taller than the other, both reaching up towards Lilyth as though they desired her to hold them. These, I knew, were her children. Except all questions of how they were here faded. It was when the two children spoke, the language not something my ears could understand, that Lilyth stopped her victory speech and looked down. It was clear she had not expected them, but it was the very thing that reduced her to a puddle of unprotected weakness.

The fire in Lilyth's palm died as she laid eyes on the children before her. She muttered something beneath her breath, an exasperated groan that I translated as hope. Disbelief. Joy. Tears pooled in her eyes and her face, still smeared in the blood of my sister, broke into a smile. And when she wrapped her arm around them, she fazed right through them.

An illusion—I had worked it out just a moment before Lilyth. And a moment was all that was required.

'You really should have left Aldian when we gave you the chance, *bitch*.' Beatrice stepped free of the shadows. They parted around her like wisps, gathering at her feet.

Beatrice held something in her hands, golden eyes wide and wild. The whisps of Lilyth's children still held on, but they no longer mattered. Not as Beatrice rose the strange object up. It was then I recognised it, or at least what it had been, as it caught in the glint of fire and lightning.

The shield—or what remained of it.

Lilyth barely snapped her head around to find the broken end of the conduit smashing towards her neck. Beatrice used all her force, screaming down at Lilyth as spittle flew beyond her lips. Once, twice, seven times the dragon's conduit rose and fell before it sliced clear through Lilyth's neck.

As it fell from Lilyth's bloodied shoulders, her head tumbled over the ground where the illusion of her children had just stood. The crown rolled off and stopped at my boot. I was so entranced by the suddenness of it, I couldn't fathom what I watched.

Lilyth, the remains of her severed body, tumbled forward. The thud of her corpse shuddered against the ground.

Then the screams began.

The shades wailed in unison, aware that their mother was dead. It was the frantic cry of loss, followed by horrific screams as gods and magic-wielders continued their assault around us.

Beatrice was panting. Her eyes were moon wide, the white stained red. Her armour was coated in black blood—even the bottom half of the shield was now shadowed with it. She stared down at the limp and headless body with expectance, her entire body lifting and falling with her heavy breaths.

'The gauntlet,' I screamed to Beatrice.

She looked up at me with vacant, wide eyes, blood smattered across her face. When she replied, it was as if she was physically stood before a mangled corpse, but mentally somewhere far away. 'I do not have it.'

'But—'

Someone had conjured the illusion. If it wasn't Beatrice, then who?

I couldn't make sense of what had happened. It was too fast. Then my gaze fell back to Leska. Her chest rose and fell, almost too dramatically. The ground beneath her was swimming with the blood that continued to pump out of her neck. And her arm was outstretched, fingers grasping something made of bright metal and blue gem.

The nymph's conduit.

Reality clicked into place.

The children, the sudden appearance of them, was an illusion. It was Leska who conjured it.

'Healers!' I shout as the battle raged on. Beatrice continued to look down at Lilyth's corpse, just as the lifeless eyes seemed to peer back up at her. 'Gleamers, I need you. Look at me! Simion is hurt.'

It took a few more screams to get her attention. Beatrice broke out of a trance, dropping the broken and bloodied shield at her feet as though it disgusted her. When her eyes settled on me, it was to see her crying. I wanted nothing more than to wrap my arms around her, but I couldn't. Not yet.

'Please. Make sure he is okay.'

There was no exchange of words as Beatrice took Simion from me and gathered his limp body into her lap. Only his long, drawn-out groan filled me relief, proving that he was still alive. It was all that encouraged me to leave him for another.

My feet pounded across the ground, boots slapping up mud and blood until my calves were drenched with it. I threw myself to where Leska was laying, finally seeing the true extent of the damage to her neck.

It was ruined. Through the fountain of blood, I could see bone and muscles, raw as freshly carved meat. But it was the way she looked at me, sniffling and broken, that was the true horror.

'Don't you dare die on me, Leska,' I said, unable to steady my breathing. I pulled her into my lap, coating my hands with her blood. It was everywhere. Leska blinked rapidly up at me, her skin the colour of snow. I pressed my hand to her neck, feeling flaps of broken skin brush against my palm. 'I swear I will never forgive you, never.'

Leska opened her mouth, but only rasped words came out. Her jugular was a mess, far beyond repair. I could hear every rasped breath bubbling through the dark space Lilyth had left in her neck.

Rain fell down upon us, casting a blanket across the battle scene. It muffled the sounds of war, coating the roaring flames and rumbling sky. I looked upwards, feeling the gentle kiss of droplets against my face. I tasted the magic, knowing another illusion was sweeping over me.

'I did... what had to be done.' Leska looked up at me, offering a smile that didn't reach her eyes. Rain washed away her blood, revealing healed and unmarred skin beneath. And yet she still lay in my arms, gazing up at me with wistful eyes.

'How are you...' I said, pulling my hand away from her neck to find not an ounce of blood across my palm. Then I saw it, just out of my peripheral. The nymph's conduit glowed, the blue gems winking into life one by one. 'This isn't real, is it?'

'No, brother. It isn't.'

The harder the rain fell, the deeper the magic penetrated my vision. Leska had conjured an illusion to distract Lilyth from her death, and now she conjured one to distract me from hers.

'Please.' The word was more a sob of pure desperation. 'Please, Leska. Don't leave me. I forbid it. There are gleamers here, so many who can heal you.'

Her hand reached up, brushing a tear from my cheek. It felt so real, her touch, the brush of her calloused hand, that I leaned into it, stifling my words.

'It's too late, Max.'

'No,' I bellowed down at her, holding her stiff body tighter. 'It isn't too late. Hold on. Just don't leave me.'

'I will never leave you,' Leska replied, her voice a smooth lullaby. 'Not truly.'

I lifted my head to the sky, no longer able to see dragons and phoenixes, stars or smoke. And when I spoke, it was not to Leska but the universe. 'Everything I love crumbles to dust. What have I done to suffer so much loss? When does this debt I seemingly owe end?'

'Max, focus on me. Nothing else, okay?'

Part of me longed to refuse her. As if the more I looked away, the longer I could keep her with me. Refusing to accept she was dying, refusing to look meant I could pretend she would survive.

But when she asked again, I could not refuse her. 'Please, brother. Look at me.'

Tears blinded me, blending seamlessly with the rain. I blinked my eyes free, chest aching, feeling as though I was being torn to shreds.

'Tell me it is over.' Her hand dropped, the vision wavering.

In a blink I saw her coated in blood again, then the rain shifted and Leska was once again healthy. 'I need to hear you tell me she is dead.'

'Yes. Lilyth is... she has failed.'

Leska exhaled a long breath, smiling up at the darkening sky. 'Then we have won.'

She was not wrong. But it felt like we had lost. In fact, I felt like I had lost everything. 'Which is why we need to find a gleamer, someone to heal you up so you can be by my side when we celebrate.'

'No, Maximus.' Leska blinked, her words becoming a faint whisper. 'I am tired.'

'So am I. Dryads, Leska, I am fucking exhausted.' My hold on her tightened. Even through this illusion, I could still feel the warmth of blood on my hands, the faltering of breath against my chest.

'I am so proud of you—'

'No. Leska. Don't you dare. There is so much we haven't done. It is my right as your brother to have you by my side, to tease you, annoy you, anger you. Dryads, Leska, if you just hold on for me, I promise you can break my nose for eternity. Just—don't—leave—*me*.'

Her laugh was the most beautiful sound. 'Do you know, I always felt like there was a part of me missing. I filled it with anger, I allowed Aaron to take residence in that space. And then when he was gone, it was larger than ever before. And it was you. You were what was missing. My brother, the other part of my soul that I had never known existed. Do not grieve the memories we will not make—treasure the ones we have. Take them with you.'

'You saved this world, Leska.' Without her using the conduit, without her distracting Lilyth with an illusion of her children, Beatrice wouldn't have had the chance she needed.

Leska deserved to live. 'Fight for life. Enjoy a life made from your actions tonight. Don't go.'

The blood was back on my hands, the illusion slowly slipping away. Not only could I feel it, but I saw it. I refused to take my eyes off Leska, catching flashes of her ruined neck, her ivory skin and dark, tired eyes. 'I did it for you, Max.'

'No, stop talking like that.' I firmed my hold on her body, noticing just how heavy it was becoming. 'Please, I can't hear you speak like that.'

'I...' The pause between her words grew longer. The silences felt like a punishment. 'I leave you all with a heart full of love, something I never thought would be possible after Aaron was taken.' She blinked, staring at something beyond my shoulder as a mumbling barrage floods out of her lips. 'I think I see him, Max. He is waiting.'

I could have begged for her to stay. I could have demanded she turn away from death and stayed with me. But I couldn't allow the last interaction we shared to be one full of anything but the love I had for her. Leska blinked slowly, the rain smattering over her face, her illusion slowly washing away.

'You were right, Leska. I will never forget you or the impact you have had on me, this world. You deserve your peace now.'

Her eyes settled back on me, occasionally shifting over my shoulder as though Aaron truly did stand behind me. I closed my eyes, sinking the word, the tone, the love behind it, deep into my bones, to a place no madness or time could scrub away. 'I love you, sister.'

Silence followed.

I opened my eyes, expecting to see her smiling, preparing to reply. There was nothing of the sort. I waited for Leska to say something. Her mouth parted, her tongue shifting into a position to provide me with an answer. But there was only silence. The illusion washed away with the rain, revealing the empty-eyed stare of my sister. But she was smiling up at me, that was never an illusion. And knowing broke me.

A tempest of pain rebounded through my body. I gathered her up, rocking back with my head tilted to the sky. And I screamed. I screamed as the gauntlet slipped from her fingers. I screamed when Leska's breathing stopped.

There was no elation that came after a battle. There were no cheers or joy, eruptions of celebration. The shades still raged around us, but they were dwindling in their numbers. Without Lilyth alive, there were no more souls to call upon, no more dead to aid her.

I gently laid Leska to the ground, tears falling freely. There was no feeling left in my chest to suffer.

Although she had died—left me—Leska's soul deserved to witness how this ended.

I left Leska's corpse behind me, passing Beatrice who still cradled Simion's limp body whilst staring endlessly at Lilyth's remains. Inyris landed before me, the ground trembling beneath her golden limbs. Like me, she was covered in wounds. A body mapped out in this battle.

Inyris nestled her snout into my side, expelling a low whimper that seemed to echo in the clouds above us.

My grief was her grief.

Except I was an empty, void, cavernous hole of space. I was without parents, without siblings. I was a man who had lost almost everything he loved.

So, I filled it, that space, with the magic that I had long ago hated. In a way, I still did. It caused all of this. But what was hate if not an emotion to harness and use, not waste. And by the gods, every ounce of it would be used to finish this.

I settled all that focus, all the hate and fury and grief, upon the shades that remained. Chaos ensued across the battlefield. Even if I longed for gleamers to come and aid, there was no way they could reach us. Fury built in me, the pounding quickening in pace—the drums of war.

Inyris stepped in behind me, roaring with equal might.

Then there was no thinking, no room for thought or contemplation. Only action. Only magic.

Only destruction.

CHAPTER 37

We fought until sunrise. Without Lilyth alive, it seemed her shades had nowhere to retreat. So, as the brilliant golden light of dawn rose over the Avarian Crest, spearing bright beams of light across the world, we won.

The remaining shades erupted, shadows exorcised by the light, their pale bodies piling into ash. All across the battle-ground puffs of death exploded. I had just pierced three damned with a conjured root as the light crest over their skin. I watched as their red eyes widened, their jaws of pointed teeth parted in silent screams. Then silence. Pure, endless silence as humans and gods alike settled into the realisation that it was over.

I don't know how long I stood in the centre of the field, surrounded by ruin and loss. It could have been hours. I barely had the energy to stand, but my gaze had been fixed to a disc of boiling heat as it cast its kiss of warmth over my skin.

Inyris curled herself around me, soft whimpers caught in her throat. I would not remember who came and brought me away from the field. All I knew was, by the time I left, a forest of tents had already been erected.

The battle truly was over.

It was all over.

I was taken to a tent in which Simion was being tended to by his mother and aunt. It took time for the wounds to heal, for any internal damage to be rectified. I had paced grooves into the ground beyond his tent, waiting for news whilst staring at the fast-marks on my arm. Any moment they would fade, that was what I convinced myself would happen. Because everyone I cared about died. Perished. Anyone who was unfortunate enough to see me as family—found or blood—met an untimely end.

Simion would be no different, I believed that. I prepared myself for it. So, when the news came that he was okay, that he would make it through, my knees finally gave out.

I lost hours to the pain. The grief. I knelt on the ground, pouring out tears until I was blinded, sobbing until my lungs couldn't hold breath. It was like that until Simion called my name through the tent's entrance, beckoning me beside him.

The first thing my eyes fell on was the pile of blood-splattered metal. Simion's silver, golden-trimmed amour had been cut from him. I caught it from the corner of my eye, resting against the gleamers' station. A perfectly carved hole pierced straight through, the breastplate a mess of jagged edges and bent metal. Seeing it transported me to the moment Lilyth pierced him. I found my mind full of holes, reality and memory becoming a strange blend of the same thing. Perhaps it was exhaustion, or perhaps I was just mad now, but if Simion hadn't spoken again, I was confident I would have replayed it over and over.

'Mother wanted to get rid of it,' Simion said, his voice a broken whisper. 'She believes it will be a painful reminder, and maybe it will. But when I look at it... I see the price I paid to save you.'

I tore my gaze from his armour and finally looked at him. Until now, I had done everything not to.

He looked so small in the cot. His chest was wrapped in gauze, a faint stain of brown spreading in the centre. I traced my eyes over his skin, noticing the ashen hue to it. It made the silver fast-mark stand out. I found myself reaching for my own, longing to feel the press of his skin against it. Dark circles hung beneath his vibrant gold eyes—eyes that hadn't once left me.

'Do I really look that bad?'

My forehead ached from tension. 'You look like death, Simion.'

'No, I have seen death, and I thought it was far uglier than me.' He offered me a smile, but I couldn't return it. Simion made a move to sit up, wincing as the muscles in his arms strained. I rushed to his side, scolding him for doing anything but lying there.

'You need to rest,' I said, plumping the pillow and repositioning it behind his neck. All the while he still didn't stop looking at me. 'I need you better. I need you to be okay.'

Before my hand withdrew, he snatched it, threading his fingers in with mine. 'Maximus, it is over.'

I didn't believe him, I couldn't... wouldn't. How was any of this over? I didn't feel relief or joy. The need to celebrate was far from my mind. Aldian had paid a terrible price to free itself from Lilyth. If I took the sceptre from my belt and held it, I would've sensed the damp soil coated in the blood of innocent people. Even without touching it, my skin still prickled with the echo of the feeling.

'Leska is dead.' Three words with so much meaning, though I felt hollow when I said it.

'I know.'

I swallowed down a sob, almost choking on it. 'My sister is dead.'

Simion's grip tightened. I knew it was not possible, but I

wished he would tell me I was wrong. I wish he told me that the gleamers found a pulse and were able to bring her back from the brink of death. But he didn't. Instead, he repeated himself. 'I know.'

'What... what am I going to do?' The flood gates opened. More tears, more breathless lungs, more of the agonising constriction around my chest.

Simion, as I already knew, did not have the answer. At least not one I needed to hear. Instead, with the little strength he had, he tugged me closer to him, using his actions to give me a command. I didn't resist because, truthfully, I desired nothing more than being with him. So, I climbed into his cot, fully clothed, my earthen armour making it difficult for me to position myself on the sheets beside him. The cot creaked as I laid on my back, staring up at the peaked tip of the tent's ceiling. Cool tears slipped down my face, clearing paths through the ash and grime that coated me.

'Maximus, I wish I could be the one to tell you this will all be okay. I wish I could give you the answers to relieve the grief you feel, lessen the load upon you, but I cannot do it. But what I can do is promise you that tomorrow is ours. And the day after, and the day after that. *She* made that possible. Her legacy. And by the dryads, we will make a world that Leska would be proud of. We will...' Simion paused, clearing his throat as emotion assaulted him. When he spoke again, it was with the gravel of sadness. 'We will forge ahead, in the memory of who we left behind. Just because she is gone, does not mean she is forgotten.'

'I could never forget her,' I lied, even though I knew my memories were fickle. How long would it take for the confusion to scrub Leska from my mind? But even if I forgot, against my will, I would ensure every other living soul didn't. 'I want Aldian to remember Leska. Every living person in Aldian and beyond will know her name.'

I would write her story into the history, forging her tale as

Galloway's story was. Not a single soul would be without the knowledge of Leska and her sacrifice.

'Mother told me what Leska did. That her last moments in life were used to turn the tides back in our favour. Even faced with death, she faced it with everything she had left.'

'She did it for Aldian,' I said. 'North or South, she saved us.'

'Yes.' I rolled my head to face Simion as he spoke, tears staining the pillow beneath me. 'But she did it for you. She saved you. That was the mark she left on this world, and by the dryads it is the largest mark possible.'

A spark of something kindled in my chest. I pressed a hand over my heart, taking a moment to recognise it for what it was. Pride. Swollen, burning and all-encompassing pride.

Simion reached for me, running the tips of his fingers down the length of my arm. It took me a moment to know that he was tracing my fast-marks. 'Leska made it possible for us to have a tomorrow, let us make sure we do well with the gift she has given us.'

'There are a few more tasks to complete before we can enjoy that,' I said, not wishing to ruin the moment, but it was true. We still had the issue of the three remaining conduits to deal with. And, from what the Council had debriefed me on, dealing with the horror Lilyth left behind. I couldn't spare a thought about it without feeling another surge of grief.

'Have you seen Beatrice?' Simion asked.

'No. She just left.'

After the battle, Beatrice had fled on Glamora's back. She had been the one to deal the killing blow, but there was something detached in her eyes as she drove the shield over and over on Lilyth's neck.

Simion took a deep inhale, his chest rattling. 'She has gone to collect Elaine's body.'

My heart stammered. 'Elaine is dead?'

'She is.' Simion withdrew his hand, rolling onto his back

again so he glared up at the same point of the ceiling I did. 'It was why we were late to come to you. Lilyth... the people her shades had taken from Wycombe... it was...'

'Take your time.' I felt sudden weight in the air, the horror of something seen but not spoken. 'We have an abundance of it now.'

And Simion told me, *everything*. I listened, not thinking it possible for something else to exceed the horrors I had just experienced.

Beatrice had willingly given herself to the shades, only to follow them to the location they were taking people.

'Voltar?'

'It seemed the phoenixes had been preparing for Lilyth's arrival for centuries. They created a castle of sorts, a dark place of burrows beneath the earth, hidden from the chambers of molten fire. That is where we found the ones Lilyth took. Bodies lined up on stone slabs. We believe she was... drinking from them. Their bodies were entirely emptied of blood. Their necks a mess of teeth marks. There wasn't a single one of them left alive.'

A new wave of pain encompassed me. The thought of Beatrice finding Elaine, laid out as though she was sleeping on a stone slab. Drained of her blood.

'Lilyth had said she came because we could offer her sustenance.' I remembered her looking at my blood in awe, tasting it and moaning. The way she ripped into Leska's neck... 'What do you think it was for?'

'Strength, maybe? Power, more likely?' Simion grimaced at the memory. 'I hope we won't ever have to find out.'

'How many did she...' *Kill, feed off?* I couldn't find the right way to finish what I was asking, but Simion understood.

'Almost three hundred, but the final number will come soon.'

My mind chose that moment to fill my thoughts with something Lilyth had said. *Your efforts are wasted. Your attempts far too late.* It was not only her words, but the look of victory across her face, as though she had already won before it was truly over. *The convergence has already begun, a world where my kin can not only survive but thrive. Death is my domain, and in it I shall be victorious.*

'Aldian will never be the same,' I said, numb to the core.

'No, it won't. Aldian will be changed, but that is what it has needed for years. We will be united, a nation not separated by Galloway Forest, by lies and twisted history. We have all paid a great price, some more so than others. That alone joins us together. Binds us. I believe this is the beginning of a new future.'

But there was still so much to do. And for that, I still had something to do. My own price to pay to secure our future.

I was conflicted, thinking about the final trip in time I had to take. Would I return with these memories? Would I even remember this conversation? Simion? Whilst a part of me panicked at the thought, another more selfish part almost desired to forget. Forget the pain, the loss, forget it all. Then I gazed to Simion and imagined how impossible it was I could ever truly not know him.

'I should go,' I said, although my body didn't move an inch. 'The sooner the conduits are destroyed, and the sceptre is put back in the past, the better.'

'Lay with me,' Simion said, hope glittering in his wide, amber eyes. 'Just a few more hours, just me and you.'

'I really need to—'

'It can all wait. All of it.' He pouted, my eyes flickering between his stare and his mouth. 'Give me this moment, with you, the peace.'

'I don't feel like I deserve the peace,' I admitted, voice breaking.

This was not over yet. Only but a moment of borrowed

time, until I took my final trip to the past and returned the sceptre.

'Come here, husband.' Simion encouraged me into the crook of his arm. I nestled myself carefully into his side, ensuring I didn't hurt him. I delighted in the kiss he pressed to my hair, the exhale that spread like cool wind over my scalp. 'Just me and you. Now. Tomorrow. And every day after that.'

I closed my eyes, wishing I could believe him. Still, Simion didn't know what I paid when I went in time. And I couldn't tell him now, it would ruin this moment he so craved.

'I love you, Simion Hawthorn.' I closed my eyes, feeling my sentiment reverberate in my chest as it too filled the quiet of the tent. 'Do not forget that.'

'And I love you, Maximus. The future is ours, that was the gift Leska gave us, let us not waste it.'

I didn't dare open my eyes for fear what Simion would find in them. I kept the shield in my mind up, knowing if, given the chance, he would see that the future was still not certain, at least not to me. Because if he knew what would become of me the next time I visited the past, he wouldn't allow me to go. But I had to, because if the sceptre was not returned to its time, our future would fade away before we had the chance to experience it.

Leska paid the greatest price for a future, and I had to ensure her efforts were not wasted. That her death *meant* something to Aldian, as well as me.

* * *

Another day had passed since the battle's end, and still I heard the cries of those in pain around me. It was a sound that would haunt me for an eternity and beyond. Gleamers would be working for weeks, if not months, to patch up everyone who needed it. Wycombe wouldn't be the same, not ever. This place would be looked at with fear, remembering what was lost here.

I stood before Lilyth's corpse whilst the battleground became a sea of tents full of gleamers tending to the wounded. Those who had perished in the battle were picked from the ground by dragons and phoenixes, under the instruction to take them to Wycombe for the necessary treatments. Inyris took Leska's body, because I wouldn't allow another to go near her. I could still feel the phantom pressure of her lying in my arms, and my hands were still stained pink with blood. When I was done I would go to her.

But there was something I had to do first.

'My love.' A hand rested on my shoulder, fingers drumming a familiar soothing rhythm that I felt through the bark-made armour. 'Are you ready?'

'Yes.' *No.*

Laid out before us, on two cloths, were the broken remains of the gauntlet, crown and shield. My body still ached from using the sceptre to destroy the final two. In some way they were bound together, likely the use of Lilyth's essence, which used the bones of her children to tether her power to the power the four gods. All that was left was the sceptre. In our time, it was destroyed, but if it was not put back where we found it, everything we knew would fade. Just as the dryad had warned, something I had not stopped thinking about.

'The gods have agreed to each take a part of Lilyth's corpse and guard them until she is nothing but a faint memory,' Elder Leia announced, gazing out across the bloated remains of the monster who almost ruined us all. 'Now they are free from any potential control, the gods each wish to help us willingly as they had before.'

I nodded, hearing the words but not truly taking them in. Beatrice was watching me, her eyes not leaving us for a second. She had returned hours before, the whites of her eyes red. I had held her in my arms whilst she broke down, offloading her loss on me. I was just thankful to be able to have a moment with her, to feel her touch, to be a pillar for her as she has been for me.

We had been interrupted by clapping. All across the camp we had watched as battlemages, gleamers, sorcerers came out and looked at Beatrice. She was the one who killed Lilyth. She saved us, and everyone knew it. Since then, eyes never strayed far from her. There was always a whisper of thanks following her, and I watched her eyes brighten, the weight on her shoulders lessen.

'I'll say this again. You don't need to come with me, Simion.' I looked at him out the side of my eye. The colour had returned to his cheeks, his eyes brighter and stance taller. He was not completely healed, but he held enough strength to stand by my side, dressed in dark leathers. Every part of him was ready, where I was not.

'I would never allow you to face this alone,' Simion replied as the dryad positioned themselves behind us. 'Never.'

Deep down, I was thankful that he would come with me. It would give me the chance to tell him the truth, before we returned, and I likely forgot him—maybe everyone.

Before the dryad offered their open limbs to us, beckoning us to step through time for a final time, I took Simion in my arms and kissed him. It was deep and all consuming. It sang of my love for him, my desire and need. And I hoped, if anything, he remembered it when he needed it the most.

'What was that for?' he asked through a smile as I pulled away.

'Something for you to remember me by,' I said, unable to stop myself. There wasn't a flash of concern over his face. And why would there be? He had no idea what the kiss was truly meant for, and he wouldn't until the sceptre was placed back in time.

'I could never forget you,' Simion said, winking as he took

my hand in his and faced us towards the dryad. 'Now, let's get this over with. There is a cool tankard of ale and a warm bed beckoning for us to enjoy upon return.'

My chest warmed at the thought of the Mad Queen tavern, of his attic room and the memories we had created together. There was comfort knowing he would remember them all, even if I might not.

'Please take us to the moment in time before the sceptre was no longer forgotten in time.'

The dryad bowed, their branches shivering as leaves fell like snow around us.

'What has been, will be again.'

There was no time to question the strange sentiment as Simion led me to the dryad. We positioned ourselves amongst their roots and fell backwards into time.

CHAPTER 38

Soil had caked beneath my nails by the time I finished burying the sceptre. The quiet of Galloway Forest was jarring. Not two days since we faced Lilyth, and here we were again, except changed. There was a sense of peace here. The type of silence that came with a gravesite, a place of death. Except it was not haunting. In fact, Galloway Forest had never felt so welcoming. Although we walked through a time years before I was born, I felt a sense of belonging.

Birds sang from branches above us; in the undergrowth I could hear the subtle shifting of bracken and leaf as creatures watched from the shadows.

Simion stood just shy of me, his shadow casting over where I knelt. Light glanced off his outline, the hard lines of his shoulders glowing in an armour of elegance. And he was smiling. The type of smile that came from knowing we were standing at the last hurdle, ready to pass it and start a new life.

I wish I had felt like that. And not such a deep-rooted anxiety.

'Are you ready to leave this all behind?' Simion asked, drawing me from my moment of contemplation.

'I am,' I said, despite the aching in my head, the empty void. To Simion, my moment of silence would have looked like a sign of respect. When truly, it was me attempting to piece together this story. My story. There were so many moments I could no longer remember, which added to the painful confusion I had become prisoner too.

But what I knew was the sceptre was returned back to the time before the moment it would be found again. I had heard the Queen recite to Celia how the conduit was discovered when the Heart Oak was burned by wytchfire. How until then, it had been completely forgotten in time.

When the truth was, it was never *forgotten* just simply not here. Borrowed. Taken. Used to save a future whilst solidifying a past.

Strange how time always caught up with itself. Like a snake chasing a tail, one continuous loop. Galloway's fall to the four mages of the South, the breaking of the Avarian Crest that freed Oribon and his children. Stories I had known all my life, and now it seemed I always had played a part in them.

It was a concept I would never truly understand, but I had no plans to ever meddle in time again.

Simion laid a hand on my shoulder, his warmth a welcome distraction. He didn't offer me any words, nothing but his touch, which was exactly what I required.

Before I stood, I laid a hand on the rough flesh of the first Heart Oak, wondering if the souls of Galloway and the dryad sensed the return of the conduit. I knew that soon Galloway Forest would be bathed in wytchfire and history would continue as it always had. A misguided war between the North and the South was inevitable. Knowing how such a peaceful place would become a scar on Aldian's history was strange.

But then again, I supposed not all scars were bad. Some were necessary.

Simion helped me stand, by body still aching from the

battle. He took my hand in his and guided me to our dryad companion who waited. It wasn't until we were stood before the god that I noticed the lack of welcome.

'The sceptre has been returned to its rightful place in history. We are ready to go home,' I said, hoping to encourage the dryad to open their arms and swallow us back up in time.

'No,' the dryad said decisively.

Simion stiffened, his hand tightening in mine. 'We will require more of an explanation than a one-word answer.'

'I cannot take you home, as there is no home to return to.'

The feeling of impending doom I had woken to for days finally stepped from the shadows and revealed itself. After Lilyth had died, I had not felt a sense of victory. It was always out of reach, and this was why.

'What do you mean there is no home to go back to?' My voice shook so violently it was a surprise the dryad could understand me. 'The conduit is back where it was taken from. History can play out as it always had.'

'I am sorry, Maximus Oaken.'

I am sorry. Not, this is what you have done, or this is how you can fix it. Just, I am sorry. A dismissal, a wave of a metaphoric hand.

An upsurge of uncontrolled fury exploded out of me like an arrow, my target the dryad. There was no thinking about who stood beside me, whose sensitive ears would hear my admission. 'But I have paid the fucking price. I have forgone my memories and given you the cost. The tithe is paid, the sceptre has been returned, so take us home—'

'Max?' Simion spoke without emotion. My name had never sounded so empty in his mouth. 'What do you mean you have paid the price?'

That one question, the very thing I had hidden from him, had finally been forced out into the light. Instead of offering me aid, the dryad closed their eyes and fell back into slumber.

In a blink, the god was no more than a tree and we were alone.

'This wasn't how I wanted to tell you,' I said, looking at him through tear-blurred vision.

'Tell me what?' he asked carefully, both arms raised in surrender beside him.

I dropped to my knees, unable to hold myself up. Tears of anguish and failure tore down my cheeks, caught by my hands as I buried my face in them. 'I'm sorry, Simion.'

He was deathly still. I didn't need to look at him to know he hadn't moved a muscle. In those drawn-out moments I wondered what I had done wrong. Had I buried the conduit in the wrong place? Was I supposed to do something else with it? The dryad's guidance had been clear.

Return the conduit to its place in time, and all shall be well.

I had done that, and now we were stranded in time. My actions had ruined our future. All those lives taken, all those souls lost, and it was for nothing.

'Talk to me, Max. Please, tell me what you mean about paying a price.'

I snapped at Simion, unable to control myself. 'None of it matters. We are stuck here. Whatever I have done wrong has cost us our future, Simion. It doesn't matter what price I paid.'

His jaw feathered with tension as he looked down at me. Then he knelt, joining me on the pine-covered ground. 'Yes, it matters. It matters to me, Max.'

I held his gilded eyes, allowing myself a moment to contemplate how bad it would be to be stuck here with him. Just us. Dryads, there was no saying how long I would even remember what I left behind. I could close my eyes and wait for time to swallow my memories one by one until I was all but a shell.

The longer I spent playing in the past, the more damage was inflicted on my mind. Staying here would lead to a state more severe than madness.

'Magic comes at a cost, Simion.' I began, taking a hulking breath as a wave of calm washed over me. I realised it had little to do with my own control, and everything to do with the fact Simion touched me. His fingers brushed the back of my fast-marked hand and drew away the anxiety, bleeding it out of me. 'We couldn't just step back in a place we didn't belong, without paying the toll to cross it.'

'I have gathered that.' Simion drew in his lower lip and bit down hard before he spoke again. 'But what is not clear is what you have given to be here.'

I took his hand and lifted it to my temple. His fingers rested against the soft brush of my skin and I could have given into his touch. Instead, I opened my mouth and told him.

'My memories. That was the cost. Every time I have visited another moment in our history, the magic has taken parts of my history from me. At first, I didn't know what was missing. But the longer we stayed, the more I have grown... confused.'

Simion's eyes slipped from mine and I knew that he wondered if he paid the same. 'I have been beside you for the majority of this and my mind is untouched. Why would you only be the one to—'

'I did what was required. To protect you.'

His gaze fell back to our hands, specifically to the fast-mark bindings around our skin. 'Max, tell me you didn't do it for that.'

I couldn't tell him he was wrong. Lying now would be pointless, so would excuses. Only the truth had the power to set me free, it Simion accepted it. He had all the right to know. He deserved as much.

'I hand-fasted to you because I love you. I did it to protect your mind, conceal it with the magic that bond holds, but I also did it because there is no one else in this world who I would wish to be with. Two birds with one stone.'

Simion didn't smile. Instead, he withdrew his hand, and

placed his palm on the side of my face. 'Darling, what good is this love, if you do not have the ability to remember it?'

'Protecting you was my priority. That is proof enough of my intentions.' The tears had not stopped falling, now they fell with vigour. I closed my eyes, allowing my body to react to his touch. How soft Simion was, how gentle, as though he held broken glass. In a way, my mind might forget him, but I didn't know how my body would ever disregard the imprint Simion had on it. He was as much a part of me as my soul or flesh.

'As loving you is mine. Nothing of worth is free to take. Just as you have given parts of yourself to save our world, I must do the same for you.'

My eyes opened at the tone in his voice. 'But it is all lost. I have done something wrong, and it is over.'

'No,' Simion looked over my shoulder, his eyes falling upon the Heart Oak. 'It is not what you have done, but what you *haven't*. Dryad.' Simion's voice was rich with authority as he called for the god. I half-expected them to stay in slumber, but its emerald eyes opened one by one. 'You have taken us to the moment before the Heart Oak was burned by wytchfire. You are the keeper of history, tell us when the phoenixes come.'

The dryad chewed on his command for a moment, before replying. 'No phoenixes will ever come to this place.'

Resolve hardened Simion's expression as he worked out a puzzle in his head. Perhaps I could not follow due to the gaps, but even his question confused me. 'Why would the phoenixes come here?'

Simion loosed a small gasp as he stood above me again. 'How did the Heart Oak burn, Max?'

'Wytchfire,' I asked, almost laughing at the relief that I knew the answer.

'And who set the wytchfire ablaze? Who burned the Heart Oak down?'

I opened my mouth to reply, but I couldn't. The answer did

not come to me, it was far out of reach. Panic seized me again, intensified, as black flames began trickling over Simion's hands.

'What if it was never the phoenixes? All this time, we were told it was their wytchfire that destroyed the Heart Oak because only the gods of fire could conjure such a flame.' He looked down to his hands, which were now wreathed in black flame. 'But that is not true, is it? Our other visits to Aldian's past have always seemed to be create the history we know. Perhaps this time is no different.'

'*As has been, will be,*' the dryad said, almost in confirmation to whatever idea Simion had grasped onto.

'There is no future to go home to, because the Heart Oak has not burned. That is the catalyst for all that *has been.* It is what drew the Queen here, what sent her on a rampage to the South to eradicate the mages. Without the destruction of the Heart Oak, without it being blamed on the phoenixes, it would not have ignited the war between gods.'

Pain radiated in my head, the faster Simion spoke. I longed to understand him, to catch up, but it was becoming harder with every passing second. 'What has this got to do with us?'

'What if our presence here was never to just return the conduit? Just as our taking it resulted in Galloway's death. Just like you were always the one to free the dragons from their imprisonment. *As has been, will be.*'

Every time the dryad's saying was repeated, it seemed to make a little more sense. As did the urgency in Simion's wide eyes, the unblinking gaze that was set on the Heart Oak. Then Simion was smiling, a frantic grin with moon-wide eyes reflecting the whistling fire in his hands.

'It is... a risk,' I stammered, clearing the tears from my cheeks with a swipe of a hand.

'I told you, everything of worth comes with risk. Max, we were meant to come here, because we were *always* here.'

There was no stopping him. Even if I wanted to, I couldn't.

Simion stormed towards the Heart Oak, footprints of fire left in his wake. He laid his hand on the Heart Oak, heat sizzling the air before black flame rose in a pillar up and up.

It rose in vigour and power, engulfing the tree completely in seconds. Leaves curled, fading to cinders. Bark cracked beneath the devouring heat. Fire dripped from reaching branches, falling around Simion like snow. Where the fire touched, more wytchfire sparked.

More and more, until it spread like a disease.

By the time Simion turned around, bathed in his unnatural fire, I felt a weight of relief lift in my chest. He refused to take his eyes off me, but when he spoke it was to the dryad. 'Is there a home for us to return to now?'

The roaring of fire, the spitting of kindling wood nor raging death could smother the sound of the dryad's reply.

'Yes.'

Simion took my hand in his and guided me forwards. I stopped him, not knowing what would become of me when we left the past behind us.

'I may not remember you, Simion.' Black flame crackled behind me, devouring the Heart Oak with vigour. 'This could be the last time I—'

He silenced me with his lips, forging himself upon me as though it truly was the last time. But it was not sadness he regarded me with when his eyes opened, but boiling determination. 'I will remind you, every minute and every day. Love exists far beyond mortal boundaries, Max. Time doesn't matter in the face of it. Forget me, and I will be with you to remind you. That is my promise to you.'

I couldn't breathe, couldn't think beyond Simion's promise. It was the honesty of his words that struck me.

Simion then lifted our hands up until our fast-mark came into view. 'If your mind forgets me, your body never will. I am imprinted on you, as you are carved into me. One and the same. Past, present and—'

'Future,' I answered, drowning in the gold hue of the man I love.

'Come on,' he said, wrapping his arm around me. 'Let's go home.'

CHAPTER 39

I woke from a dreamless sleep to the soft sound of snoring. As I opened my eyes, I found the light of dawn blocked by the hulking mass of muscle lying before me. Broad shoulders of beautiful brown skin rippled with each breath. My gaze settled on the puckered twisting of scars upon the shoulder blade, telling a story I remembered in parts. But what filled my body with relief was knowing who I woke beside.

From the ache in my arm, I had been on my side for too long. As I repositioned myself, it woke Simion from his slumber. His snoring gargled together, followed by an air-quaking yawn. He rolled over, sleepy gold eyes blinking away tiredness as he faced me. There was no ignoring the flash of concern that drew down at his brows as he proposed his question. It was not an offering of *good morning* or *how did you sleep*, but another question, one I imagined I had grown used to.

'Do you remember me, my love?'

I nestled in close, my nose brushing his. 'I do.'

Simion closed his eyes, a smile cresting over his handsome face. He exhaled a long breath from his nose before draping his arm over my body, anchoring me to him. 'Good, that is good.'

It was. That was the thing about my memory. It was like standing on a ledge, without the knowledge of how I got there, or how I would get down. Some days I woke knowing who Simion was, other days I did not. My memory was a wild thing, shifting towards and away from me. Sometimes the gaps were sparse, other times they were wide ravines. And the worst part was, it was never the knowledge of how I obtained this aliment that was forgotten. I knew that truth. And I knew that I struggled, almost like a knot of worry lodged in my chest. The mornings were never the hardest part of my day. It was the evenings, when I tussled with my mind. It was a way to torture myself, because every time I would close my eyes at the end of the day, I would wonder what I would wake up missing.

Or *who*.

But Simion was always there, waiting. He could not offer my memories back, but he could use his magic to calm me whilst he used his words to fill in the gaps. But today, a rare and celebratory occasion, his touch didn't need to be anything but a touch. A physical connection we could both enjoy.

There was no telling what tomorrow would bring, but after everything that had happened, I had learned to dwell in the present and not fear what would come tomorrow.

'Can we send a message to the Council and ask for today to be called off?' I asked, whispering beneath the sounds of the busy tavern beneath us. Through the floorboards I could heard Nicho and Iria fussing, preparing for the day's festivities. There was the far-off scent of apple-baked goods and the familiar rush of winds beneath dragon wings in the sky.

Simion's eyes drank me in, roaming over my face with no inch spared. 'As much as I wish I could make that happen, we have one day to face, then we can squirrel ourselves back here, together.'

'You're no fun,' I said, pouting.

Simion's strong arms snaked forwards, entrapping me

before drawing me onto him. Although he kissed my head, exhaling a pleasured breath, I felt the kiss on every inch of skin. 'I can be. I can be very fun. Do you require a reminder?'

'If I said yes, would you call off today?' I gazed up at him, staring through my lashes in hopes that my doe-wide eyes would be his weakness.

'One doesn't just call off a coronation, Maximus Oaken.'

'One doesn't, but the King can.'

He smirked. I could tell from his reaction to the title that Simion had not got used to it yet. 'I am not King yet.'

I lifted my head from the pillow that was his muscled chest, looking at the two wooden manikins draped with our outfits. On the left was my dryad-made armour of bark, twisting metal vines and sharpened leaf designs. Beside it was Simion's newly crafted silver armour with the twisting gold dragon engraved on the breastplate. Although it had been close to a month since the battle with Lilyth, I still expected to find the gaping hole within Simion's armour. Sometimes, I dreamt about the spear of shadow and bone piercing his chest. Other nights would be full of Leska, her body bleeding out in my arms. Though most nights my dreams were empty and peaceful.

I drank it all in, knowing this would likely be the last time we stayed here.

'I hardly imagine the Council are going to allow us to stay here, Simion.' I forced my body over his, straddling his hips with nothing but the thin sheet to cover our modesty. Not that there was much of that left. Simion was practically stone-hard beneath me, which to my delight only grew as my ass sat upon him. 'This isn't a place for a King to live, is it?'

Simion leaned up on my forearms, forcing his face as close to mine as possible. 'Perhaps not, but there is no saying we cannot sneak here during the nights and be back in the castle for morning. How does that sound?'

I rocked my hips, not dramatically, but enough to elicit a

moan from his mouth. Just enough to toy with him. 'Sounds like a challenge. Now, are you sure I can't entice you to call the day off?'

Simion's cheeks blushed at the comment, his eyes widening. 'Well, as steward to the King, I do believe it is your duty to guide me in decision making. So, if you convince me enough perhaps, I *will* send out the message.'

I had forgone the title of King days after our return to the past. With my... difficulties with my memories, I didn't think it was sensible accepting a crown. How could I rule a place or people when some days I woke up with no knowledge of who I was? Instead, I offered it to Simion. He would lead, and I would be the little voice on his shoulder, whispering into his ear. I could give up the crown, but the responsibility I held for the people of Aldian would never fade. This was the best option; one where I could continue working towards a better future. Not just for the North, but for the South too. A united Aldian.

'You are right, too many people deserve today's celebration.' I made a move to get off him, but Simion's warm hands grasped my thighs. The pressure of his fingers was not painful, but firm and steady. I even pulled away just a little more only for him to sink his fingers into my skin a bit deeper.

'An hour,' Simion said, his voice dipping lower as fire sparked in his eyes. 'Your King requests an extra hour from you.'

I looked over my shoulder as though contemplating the request, even though I knew I would never refuse him. 'I think I can spare an hour.'

'Not that I will need it,' Simion added, threading his fingers in mine. Our fast-marked arms connected, the silver ink of vines and leaf united as one. 'I will be done with you in... ten minutes at the most.'

'Ten minutes?' I pouted just as his spare hand traced down my back, all the way to the curve of my bare ass.

'Take it or leave it.'

Leaning down over him, I stopped when my lips brushed his. 'I'll be satisfied with five.'

The spark of pleasure awoke my dragon kin. I sensed Inyris stir across our tether and I had to force out calming emotions just to keep her at bay. Through our connection I sensed her grumble of annoyance before the connection severed, leaving me and Simion to enjoy one another.

And enjoy, we did.

I stayed sat upon him as he eased his cock within me. We were a mess of desperate touches and exploring kisses. Simion's tongue reached into my open mouth, drawing moans from the deepest part of me. We were frantic men, rushing to mark one another in ways beyond the hand-fast lines. I wanted his scent, his taste and touch. I wanted him all.

Breathless and lips swollen, I sucked and nibbled at the tender skin of his ear lobe. If my mouth was not busy, I would've exploded in moans so vicious the tavern below would have heard me.

'Dryads, Max.'

I opened my mouth to reply, but the curved tip of his length slammed into the spot deep within me, leaving me without the ability to form a coherent sentence. Instead, I rocked backwards, back aching, as pleasure erupted across every inch of me.

He held me atop him until my body grew used to his thickness swelling inside of me. 'In your own time, my love.'

That alone made me act. My thighs ached as I began to work myself atop him, encouraged by the way his face smoothed out and a song of desire broke from his mouth. His hands clasped my face as I rode him. Candles sparked to life across every surface of the room, elongating to tall pillars of warmth and light. Beneath the soft but warm brush of his palms, he shared his emotions and willed me to do the same.

It was in moments like this when we became one. It was joy and happiness. I allowed myself to be selfish, to think of nothing but him, the single passing seconds and only what occurred within the four walls of his attic room.

I was full of his skin, his love and attention. He drank me in with kind, all-seeing eyes, as I did the same. I could have closed my eyes and conjured an image of him, one imprinted in the darkness of my mind.

'I love you, always,' I said, rushed, as I desperately needed to get those words out. 'No matter what. No matter how I wake tomorrow, I will always find a way back to you.'

Simion's smile brightened his entire face. He reached out, gathered his arms around my back and pulled me down. It was his turn to thrust, long and slow deep movements that made me feel every fucking inch of him.

Like the tides of ever-changing water, our sex changed. From frantic and rushed, to slow and tender. As though time was no longer a concept either of us cared about.

'And I love you, no matter what tomorrow brings.' Simion's eyes glistened, his smile so wide it stretched from ear to ear. 'It is my life's greatest pleasure to be by your side, to help you through the maze of your unknowing. And I vow to always be here, always be at your side, always be the one to show you just how healing love can be in the face of uncertainty.'

He was speaking those words, sharing the emotion behind them with his touch and ensuring with every thrust of his cock that they were buried so deep even my mind could not forget them.

'Simion, tomorrow is always a privilege, if it is with you.'

I was taking him deeper, until my entire being was full to bursting. We were both in rhythm with one another, something that was as simple and familiar as breathing. I laid my spare hand on his heart, delighting in the curls of my fast-mark, which matched those vines that curled around the scar of his mage-mark.

He offered me another kiss, just as I knew he was close to

racing off that edge of pleasure. Sweat beaded across his fore-head, mirroring the sticky film over my bare skin.

Simion looked me deep in the eyes, studying the soul beneath, a soul that would forever be entangled with him. And he spoke his final reply, dredging it up from the most sensitive part of him. 'And there will be many tomorrows to share. I promise you that, and when you forget, I will be right here to remind you.'

* * *

Wycombe city was alight with celebration. There was not a street empty of people—eating, drinking and rejoicing. I watched them all from the podium erected before the castle, the ruined Heart Oak shadowed at my back. Dragons flew through the cloudless skies, whilst phoenixes watched from perches across the top of buildings. Even in the distance I could see the smudge of Galloway Forest, and knew the dryads too watched on. The nymphs were the only gods to retreat back into their own domain, choosing seclusion after Lilyth's downfall. I did not blame them, because I too desired to just disappear some days. But I knew, if we needed them, the nymphs would return of their own free will.

Not if, but when.

'He loves it,' Beatrice mumbled from my side, her eyes fixed on her brother's back. 'King Simion Hawthorn, suits him.'

I followed her serious stare, to find Simion stood before the crowd, arms raised out in welcome. On his head was the crown of pointed gold-cut flames and silver bands of roots, which had been crafted especially for him. The fire represented one side of his gifted magic, whilst the vines respected his magedom. Simion represented many things for those who looked on, cheering. He was a symbol of a future, one Aldian deserved.

'And what of you, Princess Beatrice. It's a long shot from

working in the smithery,' I said with a wink, nudging my friend. 'Or is it Commander you prefer? I'm forgetful, after all.'

Her hand fell to the sword she had just been gifted. It was made from the remains of the dragon's conduit. It did not hold the power to control the gods any longer, but it was a symbol of Beatrice's actions during the final battle. She had been the one to kill Lilyth, to deliver the final blow. And Simion had ensured that every soul in Aldian knew it. She had been presented the sword and offered the title of Commander of the mages. If the crowd had cheered for Simion, they had roared for Beatrice. I was certain the worlds beyond our own would have heard.

'Princess-Commander Beatrice,' she said, chin raised. 'Double-barrelled title makes it sound more exciting.'

'That is does,' I said, smiling at my oldest friend. A wave of emotion came over me, and it did her too. There was a beat of something between us, a knowing that words hardly could fathom. 'We are a long way from where we started,' I said, feeling the prick of tears in the back of my eyes. 'But I am blessed to be stood beside you, after everything.'

'As am I.' Beatrice's fingers tightened on the hilt of the sword, the other rubbed at her arm as though it bothered her. 'Who would have thought, all those years ago when we were stealing wine from the Gathrax vault, we would be stood here.'

I jumped as the crowd picked up in another collective cheer. The sound jarred through me, taking me back to a blood-soaked field miles outside of Wycombe. I pinched my eyes closed, squeezing them tight, trying to rid myself of the haunting memories.

Fingers slipped into mine. 'I am here.'

Opening my eyes, it was to find Beatrice grasping me. Just shy of the wrist of her armour, I noticed a patch of mottled, reddened skin, and my breath caught in my throat.

'How is... *Elaine*?' I asked quietly, aware of the thousands of eyes on us. I moved a hand over my mouth to prevent anyone from reading my lips.

Beatrice released me, steeling her expression as she faced the crowd. 'Better.' Her answer was simply, but the tone in her voice told me she still struggled with the secret we held. 'About tonight, I think maybe you shouldn't come. I don't want to put you in a position of conflicting relationships. It would...'

Incriminate me? Burden me with yet more secrets? It was far too late for that. 'I'm coming with you, Bea. I promised I would.'

I waited for her to refuse me, to give me another excuse to postpone the very visit that had hung over my head for days.

Instead, she whispered, 'Thank you.'

We were both distracted from our conversation as Simion asked the crowd for silence. A hush fell over all of Wycombe, so quiet there was not a single person who didn't hear the crinkle of parchment as Elder Leia handed over the roll to her nephew.

Simion cleared his throat, before lifting his chin and addressing the city. His deep voice was carried over the winds as dragons used their magic to height his speech. It filled every street, every nook and cranny of Wycombe so not a single person missed out on this. 'Before our celebrations begin, I would like to take this moment to remember those we have lost to have this very day. Without the brave mages, sorcerers, civilians and gods who stood beside us in battle, I would not be able to stand here and address you. We come together today as one united family on soil soaked with those who fell for us, those whose deaths stand as a pillar for our future.'

I held my breath, knowing what was coming before the name left his mouth.

'Leska Cyder.' Simion paused just as a ricochet of pain thundered through my chest. Even if I wished to hold my head up and watch as her name settled over the crowd, I couldn't. Her loss was still too fresh, too painful. 'Leska was our family. Her sacrifice was great, but without it Aldian would have been lost. We remember her for what she did, who she was and the effects she had personally on those dearest to me.'

I had shed many tears over the loss of my sister. Some days, even when I woke not knowing she had ever existed, my body still felt hollow from her absence. So, I would cry, without truly knowing what caused the emotion, until Simion reminded me.

Leska, my sister, the last connection to my family.

My hand went to the locket hanging from a chain on my neck, the capsule of silver that contained a portion of her ashes. Although physically she was not here, her presence echoed all throughout Aldian. She was everywhere.

Simion looked back to me, glancing from the crowd for a moment. I felt his golden-hued eyes linger over my body, and looked up to hold his stare. He saw me grasping the necklace and knew what his words meant to me. Then he faced the crowd again and continued reading from the parchment, slowly unravelling the roll until a ribbon of it stretched down the steps before him.

When he reached the name of Beatrice's partner, I held my breath and fought the urge to look at her. 'Elaine.' Simion called, just another name in a long list. But this one, like Leska, held some power over Beatrice. There were no tears to shed for this name, no loss to feel, because I knew the truth.

I knew Elaine was not dead. Well, not in the sense one would except.

The crowd held their respect, listening in complete silence until the final name was read out. The tension in the air was palpable, so thick it could be flayed with the dullest of blades. And there was no denying the collective breath everyone seemed to let out as Simion asked something of us all.

'Please, put your hands together. Show your appreciation for those who perished in the name of our future. Do so until

the souls of the departed will hear you from their perch in
Paradise.'

There was not a single soul who did not put their hands
together. I clapped through the tears, doing so with vigour until
my palms stung from the contact. Dragons roared into the
cloudless sky, phoenixes joining with a song of fire-kissed caws
and screeches. For a moment, even the far-off ocean seemed to
thrash as though joining in with our cheers. The noise we made
was so powerful, even Lilyth would have heard it in death.

It could have been hours since the cheering began, but
when it stopped the city still echoed with it. Simion looked over
to the Council stood around him, to Beatrice and me, then to
King Zendina from the North who would be our greatest ally.
He beamed, drinking the scene in before ending his speech
with one final comment.

'Everything I have ever longed for is to create a home for
those I care about. And I pledge, with every fibre of my being, to
ensure every single person stood before me is safe, healthy and
free. Enjoy the celebrations, spread joy with our new neighbours and know that in the coming months and years, we have
plans to create a united Aldian, a place we can all thrive.'
Simion offered me a hand, and I took it.

The crowd shifted as they set their eyes upon me, the man
with many names. I felt them drink in the fast-marks displayed
proudly on our arms, noticing the smiles and murmured pleas-
antries. Simion then leaned into my ear, whispering only to me.
'This is your home. We are your family. And I vow to keep it
this way.'

I swallowed hard, my chest warming at his words as the
brightest of smiles cut across my face. Although they were not
stood with me, I sensed the souls of those I had lost lingering
just beyond my shoulder. Mother, Father, Leska and so many
others.

'Ready to get out of here, my King?' I said, knowing the

coronation was finally complete and the city ready to fill their bodies with as much ale as they could.

'Does my steward require me for urgent matters?' Simion asked, his words sending a shiver across my skin.

'I do.'

Simion bristled with a laugh. 'Take us home, my love.'

Home. A place I had longed for. And a lesson I had learned the hard way. It was never something to chase, a concept on the horizon that always kept me moving. Home was made. It was people, it was those who I stood upon the dais with and also those I looked out over.

No, I was not the King, but it was in my blood to protect. And I would, by Simion's side.

A body of gold scales broke away from the roof of a distant building. Inyris cast her shadow over the city, causing a ripple of awe to spread over where she flew. By the time she landed, decorated in a saddle overspilling with splendour, Simion had already led me over to her.

'Only in death, shall we part.' Simion said, his hand tightening around mine.

I took in a deep breath, allowing those words to settle into me. I had once feared them, and now they seemed to offer nothing but comfort. Then, as I took a seat on Inyris, offering a hand for Simion to climb beside me, I answered the same thing he said to me after our handfasting. 'And in life, shall we thrive.'

CHAPTER 40

There was a violent chill in the burrows of this place, a cold that bore into the bones and refused to let go. I recognised it for what it was the moment Beatrice led me inside.

It was death.

She forged ahead into the system of caves, places of pure darkness that were barely penetrated by the burning torch she held aloft.

It had taken hours to fly to the same island we had visited the night Lilyth came under the guise of illusion to offer me a deal. Unlike then, the rain did not fall. The night was all but clear, stars watching from a blanket of darkness. I almost wished they didn't see what we did, flying from Wycombe on Glamora's back, to a place I only came to because of Beatrice.

Luckily, Simion was occupied, taking his first night as King to speak with King Zendina about the plans of creating a building similar to Saylam Academy on the old Gathrax land. It would be a place for the sorcerers to train, a place for them to learn mastery of their new abilities. There was no knowing what would become of those who had survived a phoenix-possession when they bore children. Would the powers pass on, dilute or simply fade? Whatever the outcome, they deserved a place to learn, somewhere new customs would grow.

Simion was far too occupied to notice my disappearance, but if he did wonder the Council would tell him I was with Beatrice and no further questions would be asked.

Beatrice stopped as we were fully engulfed in the cave's darkness. 'Max, I do not blame you if you wish to leave. I understand the position this puts you in and I do not wish to cause any issues between you and my brother.'

I laid my fingers on her shoulder, watching the tension ebb away from her face. 'I am here because I want to be. To help you. And, Bea, let's be honest, there is no saying I will even remember this come tomorrow.'

She winced at that. Beatrice, Simion and the Council all knew about the price I paid to journey in time. Although it was always meant to be that way. It was fate. *As has been, will be.* That was how the dryad explained it.

'And if you do forget?' Beatrice asked, almost hopefully, and I didn't blame her.

'Then do not remind me.'

She gritted her jaw, nodded and then continued into the impenetrable dark.

'My visits are becoming less frequent. I believe, in a few weeks, she will be able to return to a somewhat normal life. I have plans to find sanctuary for her in the North, somewhere far enough that no one would recognise her.'

'It is a solid plan,' I said, knowing that would mean Beatrice too would be missing for periods of time. But I understood. I knew if this happened to Simion, I would have acted the same.

It wasn't for me to tell Beatrice that she was wrong. I couldn't bring myself to do it. Instead, I asked a question, hoping she would see for herself that she was playing with something dangerous, something that should not see the light of day—even if it was physically possible.

'And her... Elaine's hunger? Is it controllable?'

Beatrice paused for a moment, her hand rubbing at her arm. It had become an unconscious action as she lost herself in thought. 'From what I understand, yes. As long as the appetite is fulfilled, she is in control.'

Somehow, I didn't believe that.

'Elaine,' Beatrice called to the dark. 'It's safe. You can come out.'

I held my breath, aware of just how the darkness around me seemed to hum. Then, out from it, parted the woman who Lilyth had killed. At least that was what everyone else believed. It was her eyes I saw first, piercing red as freshly spilled blood. Her skin had taken on a silver-hued pallor that almost looked blue in parts.

'Maximus,' she said in greeting, my name pronounced with a lisp she never had before. And I could see why, from the pointed canines that overlapped her bottom lip when she fell back into silence.

'Elaine, how are you feeling?' I gathered my magic, readying it in case it was needed. 'Better, I hope.'

Elaine pondered my question as Beatrice had already begun to roll up her sleeve. It was then I saw the true cause of her irritated skin. Twin puncture marks surrounded by a painful rash.

'I am... acclimatising,' Elaine replied, although her focus was on Beatrice's arm. 'Have you come to kill me?'

'No,' I said, even though I felt like it was the wrong answer to give. 'I am here because Beatrice means the world to me. And you mean the universe to her. Who am I to take that away from her?'

'A better person than others,' Elaine replied, almost sad at the truth of her words. 'I am a threat to everything you have fought towards.'

'That hasn't been decided yet.'

Beatrice lifted her arm to Elaine, her fist clenched until the bump of a thick vein protruded through her skin. 'You have given us no reason to think in any such way, Elaine. This... what you are... is not your fault. Lilyth did it, and Max knows that. I trust him, so trust me.'

'I do,' Elaine said, a tear slipping over her pronounced cheek bone. 'I am just frightened.'

'We all are,' I said. 'But I promise we will find a cure.'

Elaine tore her gaze from Beatrice's arm, just before her mouth lowered to it. 'How do you cure death, Max?'

I couldn't reply. I couldn't possibly form an answer. Whatever Lilyth had done to Elaine and the others she had taken was unknown, besides this physical change, and the requirement of sustenance. *Blood.* There was no knowing how many of the dead found in Voltar had come back like Elaine. Who had opened their eyes to see a world through crimson irises. I believe in time we would understand the true number. But what was important was Elaine was in control—yes, she was distracted by the offering of the flesh she gripped in her hands, but she was not evil. Not a danger, as long as Beatrice continued to feed her, to keep her unnatural desires in check.

What I did know was Lilyth had warned we were too late. That the convergence had begun. And somehow, without question, I knew I was looking at it.

'Drink, Elaine.' Beatrice took the back of her heart's head and guided it back to her arm. 'We cannot stay long, and I do not know when I can next return so you must take your fill.'

Sickness crashed in my stomach; bile burned up my throat. I tried to force my reaction down, to keep my voice void of emotion as Elaine parted her mouth and sank those two pointed teeth deep into Beatrice's vein.

Blood inked beneath her pale lips, staining them a deep pink as she settled her eyes on me. Beatrice was lost in some strange trance, her face captured an expression similar to pleasure, as a bird-like chirp slipped free of her parted mouth.

We stayed like that, the only sound my thundering heart and slurping as Beatrice's blood slipped down Elaine's throat. And it was in that moment I knew this issue was far greater than I could ever imagine.

The shadows seemed to dance around her frame as though they reached out from her. The deeper she drank, the more of Beatrice's blood transferred into her mouth, the heavier those shadows became until they grew into shapes with limbs, teeth and claws.

Soon enough the entire cave rumbled with the magic of death. Beatrice must have sensed it, because she opened her hazy eyes and held my stare. There was a silent plea of desperation in them, a look that begged me not to say a word, to stand by her and make sure Elaine was kept safe. Which I would do, but the moment Elaine posed a threat to everything I cared for, I would not hesitate to destroy her—even at the cost of the very person who stood before me, her arm in the jaws of a monster.

EPILOGUE

15 YEARS LATER

I stood upon old Gathrax soil, my husband at my side and our child skipping through the fields of wildflowers before us. My hand pressed over my heart, something I had grown used to doing since she was born. Twelve years since Aura took her first breath of life, unspoiled by the trauma of our past, and my heart still could not contain my love for her.

It was a constant pressure in my chest, as though my heart swelled so large even my ribs could hardly hold it in. Which was why my hand always found its way above, as if that could stop myself from combusting.

'Princess Aura Leska Oaken-Hawthorn, will you leave the poor creatures alone?' Simion's voice boomed from my side. In the years it has deepened, grown rougher at the edges. I put it down to a decade as King, his need to use his voice more than any bard that had sprung up across the united Aldian.

Aura's head poked up beyond a verge of blue-bells and snowdrops, her tongue poking out at us. I hid a laugh behind my fingers, catching myself as Simion rolled his eyes. Our daughter is the only subject across Aldian with the power to ignore the King.

'Leave her to expend some energy,' I said, wrapping my arm around Simion's waist. 'There will not be much time for Aura to be a child in an hour.'

'She is hardly a child, darling.' Simion gazed at Aura with the same longing. The look of someone who watched time fall away, twelve years gone within a blink. 'It is time she is given the chance to carve her own space in this world. Not one we can give her, one she finds herself.'

'I hate when you are right.'

'You couldn't possibly hate me, my darling.' Simion nudged my arm, his muscle-strained tunic practically ripping at the seams.

Simion shifted his stare across the field, to the huddle of guards that waited. Battlemages and sorcerers, both distinguishable from the armour they wore, the emblem on their breastplates. A dragon for the mages, a phoenix for the sorcerers.

Named after my mother, she bore most of her resemblances to Simion, from her brown skin to her curly hair like her Aunt Beatrice—who watched on like a sentinel guard. It was Simion's blood that filled her veins, but my essence as dryad-born. Even if she was not mine by blood, that did not take away from the endless depth of my love for her.

'Chase me, Aunty Bee,' Aura called over her shoulder, hair whipping in the light, spring breeze. I loved how, ever since Aura learned to talk, Beatrice's name had morphed into a pet-name with a new meaning. Beatrice would pretend it didn't affect her, that it didn't pierce her own love-filled heart like an arrow. But it did. Evident every time Aura referred to her as the buzzing bug when Beatrice gave chase, making the humming sound out of pursed lips.

'No fire-tricks, okay?' Beatrice called to Aura who was already giggling with mischief and plotting. 'Promise, little princess.'

Aura stopped, crossed her fingers to her heart. 'Cross my heart and hope to die, no fire-tricks.'

Somehow, Beatrice didn't believe her. None of us did. But that was what happened when children were born with fire magic in their veins. Exactly the reason we were here, South of the Galloway Forest, for an event that had been years in the making.

'Like two peas in a pod, those two are.' Simion folded his arm around my shoulder, drawing me in close. 'Don't tell my Council, but I could stand here and watch this unfold for hours on end.'

'As could I.' I leaned into Simion, inhaling his scent as though it was something I had not woken that morning forgetting. Which, I had. The confusion still clung onto the far reaches of my mind, but it was dwindling quickly. Some days were easier than others. I could go weeks with my mind intact, and then one day I would wake and forget it all.

But in the years since this ailment began, Simion was always by my side. He never left it. Even if he had morning Council meetings or late evenings with important figures in Aldian, discussing what Kings discuss, he always made time for me.

'I am worried about her,' I added, watching Beatrice trip to the ground, only to be pounced on by our Aura. Their light laughter echoed over my soul, warming me from the inside out. 'Will she thrive? Will she find it difficult? We are far from home, far from everything she has been used to.'

Simion turned me to face him, dipping his mouth close to mine. His arms ran down my upper arms, calming me. I delighted in the warmth of him, the way his fire had worn into every inch of his skin, forever instilling him with the welcoming grace of summer. 'Darling, Aura is a brave and inquisitive girl. And the Academy is a couple of days ride from home. If you miss her, you hope onto Inyris and visit.'

I exhaled through my nose, a long-suffering sigh. Simion had said these words to me over and over, but his patience never wavered. I loved him for it. And he was right. Inyris was currently chasing her own offspring a few miles away at the costal line. Years of being tethered had solidified our bond to a point that seeing through her eyes took little concentration. Inyris was always within me, her feelings a strong pulse woven into mine.

'You're right.'

Simion straightened, his grin widening. 'Of course I am right.'

I huffed out, knowing that Simion loved being told as much.

'Remember, Beatrice will be close. Any issues, she can get here quicker than us.'

Looking back to my daughter and best friend twisting around on the ground, I still had a sense of foreboding. There was a reason Beatrice was stationed in the South more often than not. A reason I knew but couldn't reach. But what mattered was she was close, and I was thankful for that.

'Come to me,' Simion sang, drawing me into the embrace of his protective arms. If anything, the years had hardened him. His shoulders had broadened, his arms thickened. I supposed that is what happened when the weight of Aldian rested on his crown. 'All is going to be fine. Aura is safe. We are all safe, we ensured as much.'

I buried my face into his chest, allowing myself a moment to close my eyes and just acknowledge the feelings rather than bury them. Years after Lilyth's fall, I could recognise where my lingering anxiety came from. The idea of loss frightened me more than anything. So many people had come into my life, only to be snatched away from me. It was as if I expected it to happen to Aura at any given moment.

A little body barrelled into us, almost knocking us both off kilter. I looked down, completely torn from my worries, to find the breathless, smiling face of my daughter looking up at me. Well, I wouldn't say looking up exactly, considering she was only a few inches shorter than me.

Sometimes, I would look to her and see the full-checked face of the little girl, and others I would see the sharper planes of a young woman. 'Daddy, Aunty Bee said that I will get to share a room at the Academy. Can I call them my sister? Am I allowed?'

Simion's belly chuckle warmed my spirit as I knelt down before my daughter. Her dress was rumpled, with grass-stains smeared over the white material. I smoothed down her hair, plucking heads of flowers out from the brown curls. 'Aura, you are still a few years away from getting a room-mate.'

'Room-mate?' she repeated, clearly confused by the title. 'What's a room-mate?'

I leaned in close, pressing the tip of my nose to hers. 'Something you will find out when you are a little older.'

Aura practically buzzed with excitement, hardly able to stand still. This was easier to see, her excitement and willingness to an adventure. But I longed for her to cry and scream, to beg me not to let her go, so I could do as she asked.

But Aura wanted this. She thirsted for it, the freedom, the knowledge. Like me, Aura was a book-worm. No, a book-dragon! She hoarded them like gold, collecting more than she read.

'Can we go? Can we go? Please, can we go!'

Simion took her hand, and mine. 'Yes. I think orientation is about to begin.'

* * *

The South was no longer split into four ruling Kingdoms. King Zendina, now Warden of the South, was glad to break down his borders and give up his crown. Aldian was simply Aldian, separated physically by a great forest, but not by spirit or soul. We were united, a world enjoying the life given after such sacrifice and change.

But there was one name that I could not completely forget.

'Calzmir Academy,' I muttered under my breath, coming to stop beneath the shadow of the grand castle.

Simion walked ahead with Aura, passing through the bustling crowd who had stopped to watch us. He didn't hear me. He didn't sense the way the name swelled in my chest. I found myself rubbing my fast-marked arm, remembering a time many years ago when another man entered my life and put me on this path.

Camron Calzmir physically left this world, but his memory lived on. In fact, it was Simion's idea to name the new Academy after him. I did not think I could ever put into words my thanks.

A place for sorcerers to hone their magic. To practice control, test the limits of this new power and thrive in all their capabilities. It only seems fitting the name is given after the first sorcerer.'

Its towering spires and thick boundary walls were made from Avarian stone carried all the way from the Northern mountain peaks. It was built upon razed Gathrax land. I could no longer tell where the old building once stood. In its centre was a courtyard so grand that first-year students could conjure flame without the concern of hurting anyone.

It was perfect. A place of education and learning.

Aura practically radiated with anticipation, pulling on Simion's hand with the strength of three bulls.

I stopped in place, in awe at everything before me. Aura noticed the lack of my presence, turned back and flashed a brief moment of sadness over her face. 'Daddy?'

Feigning a smile, I didn't wish for her to see my distress. But that was the thing about my daughter, it was not only fire magic swelling in her veins. Around her wrist, a band of Heart Oak caught my eye. Aura was a gleamer to, so acutely aware of my thoughts she could read them at any distance.

'I will miss you too.' Her arms wrapped around my middle, squeezing me tight. I closed my eyes, allowing my mind to imprint her touch on me, so that later, when she was miles away, I would still feel her hug me. And when I forgot, my body would remind me, as would the paintings, letters and journals Simion had prepared for me in case I ever forgot Aura.

The gaps in my mind could last hours and sometimes days. But I always made it through the dark when guided by the man who held my heart in his hands.

Was this how my mother felt, when we were separated? Was the ache a burning in her heart like raging wytchfire?

'Go on, my darling.' I paused, trying to repress the lump forming in my throat. 'This is the beginning for you. An adventure. Claim your future, Aura.'

'I will make you proud.' Her admission shocked me, as did the honesty in her voice.

I drew her in, pulled her close and anchored my arms around her. 'You already have, Aura. I am so proud of you. There is nothing more you can do, nothing more I expect of you. I love you.'

Her voice filled my mind, a spreading of ice across my skull like frost across glass. *And I love you, daddy.*

I watched my daughter race back to Simion. I couldn't help but feel the soul of every person I had lost beside me. My mother, my father and Leska—three guardians at my back, offering me comfort.

I had once hated magic, with every fibre of my being. Now, I thanked it for everything it had made possible. My daughter, her future and my fast-mate. Gifts given to me all because I found that bastard wand all those years ago.

There was no good to come from dwelling on the past. So, I lifted my chin, waved my hand as my daughter raced beneath the arched stone entrance into Calzmir Academy. Every price paid was for this moment.

For my future, in flesh and breath.

So, I smiled. A bright and honest smile as I watched my daughter chase after her future—a future that those who came before her ensured she could have.

A LETTER FROM BEN

Dear reader,

I want to say a huge thank you for choosing to read *Heir to Dreams and Darkness*. If you did enjoy it, and want to keep up to date with all my latest releases, just sign up at the following link. Your email address will never be shared and you can unsubscribe at any time.

www.secondskybooks.com/ben-alderson

I hope you loved the third and final book in the Court of Broken Bonds trilogy. I cannot believe the journey has come to an end. Max's story began back in 2018, and it has been one wild ride. Thank you for your ongoing support. I look forward to sharing all my future books with you, so stay tuned!

If you did enjoy reading, I would be very grateful if you could write a review. I'd love to hear what you think, and it makes such a difference helping new readers to discover one of my books for the first time.

I love hearing from my readers – you can get in touch with me on social media or through my website.

Thanks,

Ben Alderson

KEEP IN TOUCH WITH BEN

www.benalderson.com

 facebook.com/BenAldersonAuthor

x.com/BenAldersonBook

instagram.com/benaldersonauthor

ACKNOWLEDGEMENTS

Firstly, I would like to take this moment to thank each and every reader who has followed along this journey with me. It has been a joy writing Max's story, telling his tale and opening the door into his chaotic world, for you. Just know that he, although confused sometimes, is very happy. He has his family—the one he found, but also the one who found him. I could easily continue this world on and on and on... and maybe one day I will. But for now, this is it.

Second Sky Books, thank you for taking a chance on my world. It has been really eye-opening working with you for my first traditionally published series. From Jack, to Noelle and Kim, Hannah, Ewan—my incredible narrator—thank you, thank you, thank you.

Harry, I did it. My love, you have been here through it all. When I first wrote this story, you were all but a boyfriend. Then when the first book published, you were my fiancé. Now, as this final book is out, you stand at my side as my husband. You have inspired so much of this romance, I see little parts of you in so many scenes. If there was anyone I would wish to be eternally bound to, it would be you.

2023 has been the year of dragons, mages and romance. Since January, I have had my head solely in this series and I almost cannot believe I even get to write... The End. It has been a labour of love, sweat, tears and sleepless nights. But it was all worth it.

Thank YOU. If you have reached these final words, it means the world that you have taken this chance on me and my story. I do hope you stick around for all the exciting things to come... soon.

PUBLISHING TEAM

Turning a manuscript into a book requires the efforts of many people. The publishing team at Bookouture would like to acknowledge everyone who contributed to this publication.

Audio
Alba Proko
Sinead O'Connor
Melissa Tran

Commercial
Lauren Morrissette
Jil Thielen
Imogen Allport

Cover design
Maria Arteta

Data and analysis
Mark Alder
Mohamed Bussuri

Editorial
Jack Renninson
Melissa Tran

Printed in Great Britain
by Amazon